Praise for Jillian Hart and her novels

"A sweet, romantic novel, with memorable characters who will do what they must to survive during a bad economy."
—*RT Book Reviews* on *Snowflake Bride*

"Hart's tender love story has strong characters who stay true to themselves and what they believe is the right thing to do."
—*RT Book Reviews* on *Gingham Bride*

"This is a beautiful love story between two people from different stations in life, or so it appears. The characters are balanced and well thought out and the storyline flows nicely."
—*RT Book Reviews* on *Patchwork Bride*

Praise for Deborah Hale and her novels

"This is a beautiful love story readers will delight in, about a lowly governess and a captain, caught in a situation by circumstances beyond their control, who both try to make the best of it."
—*RT Book Reviews* on *The Captain's Christmas Family*

"Hale skillfully evokes the Regency period in this enjoyable installment in her Glass Slipper Brides series."
—*RT Book Reviews* on *The Baron's Governess Bride*

"A delightful addition to the Glass Slipper Brides series, this story has an intelligent, forceful, yet patient heroine."
—*RT Book Reviews* on *The Duke's Marriage Mission*

Jillian Hart grew up on her family's homestead, where she helped raise cattle, rode horses and scribbled stories in her spare time. After earning her English degree from Whitman College, she worked in travel and advertising before selling her first novel. When Jillian isn't working on her next story, she can be found puttering in her rose garden, curled up with a good book or spending quiet evenings at home with her family.

Deborah Hale spent a decade tracing her Canadian family to their origins in Georgian-era Britain. In the process, she learned a great deal about that period and uncovered enough fascinating true stories to fuel her romance plots for years to come. At the urging of a friend, Deborah completed her first historical romance novel and went on to publish over fifteen more. Deborah lives in Nova Scotia, a province steeped in history and romance. Visit her website at www.deborahhale.com.

Snowflake Bride

Jillian Hart

&

The Captain's Christmas Family

Deborah Hale

H HARLEQUIN® LOVE INSPIRED® HISTORICAL

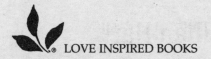 LOVE INSPIRED BOOKS

PLEASE RECYCLE
THIS PRODUCT IS RECYCLABLE

Recycling programs
for this product may
not exist in your area.

ISBN-13: 978-1-335-00544-1

Snowflake Bride and The Captain's Christmas Family

Copyright © 2018 by Harlequin Books S.A.

The publisher acknowledges the copyright holders
of the individual works as follows:

Snowflake Bride
Copyright © 2011 by Jill Strickler

The Captain's Christmas Family
Copyright © 2011 by Deborah M. Hale

www.Harlequin.com

Printed in U.S.A.

CONTENTS

SNOWFLAKE BRIDE

Jillian Hart

Therefore…put on tender mercies,
kindness, humility, meekness, longsuffering;
bearing with one another, and forgiving one
another…but above all these things put on love.
—*Colossians* 3:12–14

Chapter One

December 1884
Angel County, Montana Territory

Snowflakes hovered like airy dreams, too fragile to touch the ground. They floated on gentle winds and twirled on icy gusts. Not that she should be noticing.

"How long have you been standing here, staring?" Ruby Ballard asked herself. Her words were too small to disturb the vast, lonely silence of the high Montana prairie or to roust her from watching the beauty of white-gray sky and dainty flakes. They reminded her of the crocheted stitches of the doily she was learning to make.

"Your interview. Remember?" She blinked the snowflakes off her lashes and hiked up the skirts of her best wool dress. Time to give up admiring the loveliness and get her head in the real world. Pa often told her that was her biggest problem. Could she help it that God's world was so lovely she was mesmerized into noticing it all the time?

"Focus, Ruby. You need this job. Badly." Enough that she'd hardly prayed about anything else for days, ever since her dear friend Scarlet had told her about the opening. She quickened her pace up the Davis's long, sweeping drive because Pa hadn't been able to get any work in town so far this winter and her family was desperate.

Ping! The faint sound was at odds with the hush of the flakes plopping gently and the crunch of her shoes in the snow. A very suspicious sound. She glanced around, but there was nothing aside from fence posts and trees. The wind gusted and knifed through her shoe with the precision of a blade. Fearing the worst, she looked down.

A spot of her white stocking clearly peeked between the gaping leather tongue of her black left shoe. Her stomach dropped in an *oh-no!* way. She had lost a button. What kind of an impression was she going to make when Mrs. Davis, one of the wealthiest women in the county, noticed?

Ruby hung her head. She would look like the poor country girl she was. Not that she was ashamed of that, but she didn't think it would help her get the job.

"Don't panic. Stay calm." First things first. She needed to find the button. How hard could it be to locate in all this white snow? It would surely stand out; she could pluck it up and sew it back on her shoe. Since this wasn't the first time this sort of thing had happened, she carried thread and a needle in her reticule for emergencies. Problem solved. Job interview saved.

Except she couldn't see the button—only pure, white snow in every direction. There was no sign of a hole where it had fallen through. Nothing. Now it was time to panic. If she couldn't sew it back on, she needed to come up with another plan.

"Looking for something?" A warm baritone broke into her panic.

Ruby froze. She knew that voice. She'd heard it before when she'd overheard him talking with his family before or after church. She remembered that deep, kind timbre from the previous school year as he would answer the teacher's questions or chat with his friends during recess.

Lorenzo Davis. Her heart stopped beating. Her palms broke out in a sweat. The panic fluttering behind her ribs increased until it felt as if a hundred hummingbirds were trapped there, desperate to escape. What did she do? She straightened, realizing she must look like an idiot.

A snow-covered idiot. She swiped the damp stuff off her face and spun to him. *Try to be calm, Ruby,* she told herself. *Be dignified.*

"Ilostashoebutton," she said, the words tumbling off her tongue as if she were no more than a dummy. Honestly. The words had sounded just fine in her mind, but the instant they hit her tongue, they bunched together like overcooked oatmeal, and now she looked twice as stupid to the most handsome man in the territory.

Brilliant, Ruby. Just perfectly brilliant.

"Sorry, I missed that." Lorenzo tipped his hat cordially, disturbing a slight layer of snowflakes that had accumulated on the brim. He looked like seven kinds of dashing as he rose from his sleigh. He had a classic, square-cut face, impressively wide shoulders and enough quiet charm to send every single young lady in town to dreaming.

That was one thing she was *not* dreaming about—Lorenzo Davis. She might not be as well-schooled as her friend Meredith or as well-read as her friend Lila, but she knew a man like him would never be interested in a plain girl like her or one who could embarrass herself so easily. Not only did she have a button missing, but she had to explain it to him—again—and pray this time she regained the power of speech, or he would think she had something terribly wrong with her.

"Oh, you have a button missing." He strode toward her, a mountain of powerful male concern. She'd never realized how tall he was before, as she'd never been this close to him before or alone with him. She swallowed hard, realizing there was just the two of them and the veil of the falling snow for as far as she could see.

"Do you have any idea where you lost it?" His deep blue gaze speared hers with something that could have been friendly, but it was far too intense. "It's a long way between here and your farm."

"Ah, over here." Thankful her command of the English language had returned, she felt silly pointing in front of her, where she had been looking when he'd driven up. His horse watched them curiously, blowing air out his nose and sending snowflakes whirling. "I'm afraid it's gone for good."

"I'm afraid you're right. You may have to wait until spring to find it." A slow grin accompanied his words. There was a reason most of the young ladies in Angel Falls had a crush on the man. When he smiled, good humor warmed a face that was already perfection and gave heart to his intense, dark blue eyes, the straight, strong blade of his nose and the hard, lean line of his mouth. His cheekbones were sharp enough to cut glass, and the uncompromising angle of his square jaw spoke of strength and character. He didn't need his heart-stopping dimples, but they made him mesmerizing. Incomparable. The most handsome man ever.

"I better not wait until April for a button," she quipped. "I should be going. Thanks for stopping."

"Sure." He tilted his head slightly to one side, as if he was studying her or trying to make up his mind about her.

So far, so good, she thought. She hadn't said anything that she considered inane enough that it would haunt her for days. She tightened her grip on her reticule, nodded good day and set out like the dignified young lady she wished she could be.

Ping! Ping! Shoe buttons went flying and plunked into the snow right in front of Lorenzo.

How embarrassing. Now her stockings were really showing, plus she looked like someone who couldn't afford sturdy shoes. Mrs. Davis was never going to hire her now. If she did, the woman might worry what other part of her new maid's attire would fail next. And as for Lorenzo, he had to be thinking she was the most backward country girl he'd ever seen.

"Got one." He bent quickly and neatly plucked something out of the snow. "Let's see if I can hunt down the other."

Mortified, she watched in horror. Dreamy Lorenzo Davis dug his leather-gloved fingers through the snow in search of her battered shoe button with the patience and care he would spend looking for a fallen gold nugget.

Don't think about the patch in your shoes, she told herself. She'd carefully repaired the hole on her handed-down shoes from the church donation barrel and had oiled the leather carefully. At a distance, they could have been new, but up close, they had clearly seen better days. She feared she looked as secondhand as her shoes. Definitely not in Lorenzo's class.

"Found it." Triumphant, Lorenzo stood, all six feet of impressive male towering over her, and held out his hand. There, on his gloved palm, sat her buttons. "Are you interviewing with my mother this morning?"

"Yes. Thank you." She plucked the buttons from him quickly, because she'd made her own mittens and they were a sad sight. She was only learning to knit and the uneven gage showed more than just a tad.

He didn't seem to notice. "I know she's looking for someone dependable. Her last kitchen maid eloped with the neighbor's farmhand without giving notice, so Ma is particularly miffed about that. Mention you are as dependable as the sun, and she'll hire you."

She slipped the buttons into her coat pocket. His advice was nice, but why would he bother? "You're giving me an advantage."

"Guilty. It would be nice to see a friendly face around the house. I miss everyone from school. Don't get me wrong, I love working on the ranch, but I spend more time with cows and horses than people." Those dimples deepened and held her captive.

Surely a sign of impending doom. She could not let a handsome man's dimples draw her in like that. What was wrong with her? She tried to hide her smile and stared at the toes of her shoes. She needed to repair her shoe in time for her interview. How could she do that while he watched? Surely, as nice and kind as he was, Lorenzo couldn't help drawing conclusions.

Well, she was never going to be as stylish as her friend Scarlet, endearing like Earlee or poised like Kate.

She couldn't pretend otherwise. She could only loosen her reticule strings and fish around for the packet of needles and bobbin of thread.

"Let me drive you up to the house." His warm offer startled her.

"D-drive me?" She nearly dropped the buttons.

"It will give you time to sew everything on. My mother will never suspect." Kindly, he held out his hand, palm up, as an invitation. "You can sew while I drive."

Did his unguarded blue eyes have to be so compelling? Veiled in the snow, he could have been a western legend come to life, too dreamy to be real and too incredible to be actually speaking to her.

Don't do it, she decided. Her pa had raised her to be self-reliant. She was perfectly capable of walking the rest of the way. Besides, she was too shy to think of a thing to say to him on the drive. She should simply say no.

"C'mon. I'm not leaving without you. If you walk, I walk. Not that I mind, but Poncho might take offense."

As if on cue, the beautiful bay blew out his breath like a raspberry, making his lips vibrate disparagingly.

"See?" Lorenzo chuckled, and the sound was warm and homey, like melting butter on a stove. "If Poncho is upset, he will take it out on me all day long. You don't want that for me, do you?"

"No, as Poncho looks like a terror." The terror in question reached over to lip his master's hat brim affectionately. Even the horse adored him. "I suppose one short, little ride won't hurt. It's only so I can sew."

"Of course. That's the reason I asked." Lorenzo's assurance came quick and light.

He must offer rides to stranded young ladies all the time. He was a gentleman. It was nothing personal, which made it easier to lay her palm on his.

A current of awareness telegraphed through her with the suddenness of lightning striking. The sweet wash of sensation was like a hymn on a Sunday morning. A sweetness she had no business feeling, though it brought her a gentle peace. She didn't remember stepping forward or climbing into the sleigh. Suddenly, she was on the seat with him settled next to her and the steel of his arm pressed against hers.

How was she going to concentrate enough to sew?

"What happened to the horse you usually ride?" He snapped the reins gently. Poncho stepped forward, although the gelding swiveled his ears back, as if he wanted to hear the answer, too.

"Solomon threw a shoe, and I didn't dare ride him." She leaned forward to work on loosening her laces.

"It's a long way to walk. Three miles or more."

"I don't mind. It's a beautiful morning." Soft, platinum curls, fallen loose from her plaits, framed her heart-shaped face and fluttered in the wind.

"It's a cold morning," he corrected gently, but she didn't seem to see his point as she tugged off her shoe, shook off any melting pieces of snow and set it on her lap. He tried to think of a woman he knew who would walk three miles on a morning like this because it was better for her old horse. "You must really want the chance at the kitchen job."

"Yes. I'm sure I'm not the only one. Work is hard to find these days. Pa is always talking about the poor economy." She unwound a length of thread from a small wooden spool, her long, slender fingers graceful and careful.

Wishing swept through him as he studied her profile. Long lashes framed her light blue eyes. Her nose had a sweet little slope, and her gentle, rosebud mouth seemed to always hold the hint of a smile. The way her chin curved, so delicate and cute, made him want to run the pad of his thumb along the angle to see if her skin felt as soft as it looked. Every time he gazed upon her, tenderness wrapped around him in ever-strengthening layers. He had a fondness for Ruby Ballard, but he suspected she did not have one for him.

The sting pierced him, but he tried not to let it show. Never, not once, had he caught her glancing his way. A few times, he'd spotted her in town, but she was busily chatting with her friends or running her errands and did not notice him.

Then again, he had never been alone with her, and she was fairly new to town. She'd arrived late in the school year last year. He remembered the day. How quiet she'd been, settling onto her seat in the back of the school room. She hadn't made a sound, but he'd turned in his seat toward her, unable to stop himself. To him, she was like the first light of dawn, like the first gentle notes of a song and he'd been captivated.

"Everyone is talking about the poor economy," he agreed. The low prices of corn and wheat this last harvest had been a disappointment to his family and a hardship to many others. He didn't have to ask to know her family had been hard hit, too. "Did your father find work in town?"

"How did you know he was looking?" She glanced

up from threading her needle. Wide, honest eyes met his with surprise. "How do you know my father?"

"He came by during the harvest, looking for work. We had already filled our positions, or I would have made sure he had a job." He knew how fortunate his family was with their plentiful material blessings. He had learned a long time ago wealth did not equate to the goodness inside a person and that everyone was equal in God's eyes. Having money and privilege did not make someone better than those without. God looked at the heart of a person, and he tried hard to do the same. When Jon Ballard had come to ask for employment with hat in hand, Lorenzo had seen a decent, honest, hard-working man. "I gave him a few good recommendations around town. I had hoped it helped."

"It didn't, but that was nice of you, Lorenzo."

"It was no problem." The way she said his name tugged at his heart. He couldn't deny he was sweet on the woman, couldn't deny he cared. He liked everything about her—the way she drew her bottom lip between her teeth when she concentrated, the care she took with everything, including the way she set the button to the shoe leather and started the first, hesitant stitch.

Snow clung to her in big, fat flakes of fragility, turning the knit hat she wore into a tiara and decorating her light, gossamer curls framing her face. Snowflakes dappled her eyelashes and cheeks until he had to fight to resist the urge to brush them away for her.

"In other words, you are in serious need of employment." He kept his tone light but determination burned in his chest.

"Yes." She squinted to draw her needle through the

buttonhole a second time. "My brother has found work in Wyoming. Pa is considering moving there."

"Moving?" Alarm beat through him. "Is there work for him there?"

"No, but he has the hope for it." Her rosebud mouth downturned, she fastened all her attention on knotting her thread. "I would have to go with him."

"I see." His throat constricted making it hard to speak, harder to breathe. "You don't want to go?"

Please, say no, he thought. His pulse leaped, galloping as if he'd run a mile full out. It seemed an eternity until she answered, her voice as sweet as the morning.

"I'm happy here. I wish to stay." She bit off the thread and bent her head to re-knot it.

I wish that, too. It wasn't exactly a prayer, he did not believe in praying for himself, so it was for her happiness he prayed. *Give her the best solution, Lord,* he asked. *Please.* He had no time to add any thoughts because a shadow appeared through the gray veil of the storm, which had grown thick, blotting out all sign of the countryside and of the lamp-lit windows of the house that should have been in sight.

Poncho gave a short neigh, already anticipating the command before it happened. Lorenzo tugged briefly on the right rein anyway as the gelding guided the sleigh neatly around the figure. A woman walked up the lane, her head covered with a hood and her coat shrouded with snow. She glanced briefly at them, but he could not recognize her in the downfall. His first inclination was to stop and offer her a ride, too, but then he wouldn't be alone with Ruby. He felt Poncho hesitate, as if the horse was wondering why he hadn't been pulled to a stop.

Out of the corner of his eye, he saw Ruby, head

down, intent on sewing the final button as fast as she could go. This was his one chance, his one shot to be alone with her. He hoped that she might see something in him she liked, something that might lead her to say hello to him on the street the next time they met or to smile at him across the church sanctuary on Sunday. He gave the reins a sharp snap so Poncho would keep going. Up ahead, another shadow rose out of the ever-thickening curtain as the storm closed in.

"There. Done," Ruby said with a rush and stowed away her needle and thread. "Just in time, too. There's the house."

"It was good timing," he agreed as he slowed the gelding in front of the portico. The tall, overhead roof served as a shelter from the downfall. While she leaned forward to slip on her shoe, he drank in the sight of her until his heart ached. He didn't know why she opened a place inside of him, a deep and vulnerable room he had not known was there.

"That will have to do." She shrugged, for a glimpse of her stocking still showed between the gap in the buttons. Her eyes had darkened a shade, perhaps with worry. She didn't wait for him to offer his hand to help her from the sleigh but bounded out on her own.

That stung. He steeled his spine and straightened his shoulders, determined not to let the hurt show. She made a pretty picture circling around the back of the vehicle, her skirt snapping with her hurried gait. Snow sprinkled over her like powdered sugar. She couldn't look any sweeter. His heart tugged, still opening up to her when he knew he ought to step back and respect that she didn't feel a thing for him.

"Thank you, Lorenzo." She stared down at her toes.

Was it his imagination, or did her soft voice warm just a tad when she said his name? The wind gusted, driving snow between them, and he couldn't be sure. He cleared his throat, hoping to keep the emotion from his voice. "Glad I could help you out, Ruby."

"Help me? You saved me. This way, your mother won't see me sewing on my buttons in her entry." She bobbed a little on her feet and lifted her eyes briefly to him. "Thank Poncho for me, too."

"I will." He rocked back on his heels, shocked by the impact of her gaze. Quick, gentle and timid, but his heart opened wider.

She was shy, he realized, which was different from not being interested in him. Her chin went back down, and she swept away like a waltz without music, like a song only he could hear.

Chapter Two

Ruby stared at the marble floor beneath her, where the snow melting from her shoes had left a puddle. A stern housekeeper in a black dress and crisp apron had taken her mittens, coat and hat and left her clutching her reticule by the strings and staring in wonder at her surroundings. The columns rising up to the high ceiling were marble, too, she suspected. Ornate, golden-framed paintings marched along the walls, which were wainscoted and coved and decorated with a craftsmanship she'd never seen before. She felt very plain in her best wool dress, which was new to her, being handed down from her older cousin. Very plain, indeed.

"Lucia tells me you are quite early." A tall, lovely woman came into sight. Her sapphire-blue dress of the latest fashion rustled pleasantly as she drew near. "With this storm, I expected everyone to be a bit behind."

"My pa has a gift for judging the weather, and he thought a storm might be coming, so I left home early." Ruby grasped her reticule strings more tightly, wondering what she should do. Did she stand? Did she remain seated? What about the puddle beneath her shoes?

"Over an entire hour early." Mrs. Davis smiled, and there was a hint of Lorenzo in the friendly upturned corners. She had warm eyes, too, although they were dark as her hair, which was coiled and coiffed in a beautiful sweeping-up knot. "Why don't you come with me now, since everyone else is late? We can talk. Would you like some tea? You look as if you could use some warming up."

"Yes, ma'am." She stood, feeling the squish of her soles in the wetness. "But first, should I borrow something? The snow stuck in my shoe treads melted. I don't want to make a mess."

"Lucia will see to it. Don't worry, dear. Come along." Mrs. Davis gestured gently with one elegant hand. Diamonds sparkled and gold gleamed in the lamplight. "Come into the parlor."

"Thank you." Her interview was now? That couldn't be good. She wasn't prepared. She hadn't recovered from being with Lorenzo. Her mind remained scrambled and his handsome face was all she could think of—the strong line of his shoulders, the capable way he held the reins and his kindness to her over the button disaster.

Pay attention, Ruby. She set out after Mrs. Davis. *Squeak,* went her right shoe. *Creak,* went her left. Oh, no. She stopped in her tracks but the woman ahead of her continued on and disappeared around a corner. She had to follow. *Squeak, creak. Squeak, creak.* She hesitated at a wide archway leading into the finest room she'd ever seen.

"Come sit across from me," Mrs. Davis invited kindly, near to a hearth where a warm fire roared. "I hear you know my dear friend's daughter."

"Scarlet." *Squeak, creak.* She was thankful when she reached the fringed edges of a finely woven rug. Her wet shoes were much quieter as she padded around a beautiful sofa. *Squish, squish.* She hesitated. Mrs. Davis was busy pouring tea from an exquisite china pot. The matching cups looked too fragile to actually drink from.

"I hear you girls went to school together."

"Yes, although Scarlet graduated last May." She knew the question would come sooner or later, so she might as well speak of it up front. "I haven't graduated. I wasn't ready."

"Yes, I heard you did not have the chance for formal schooling before you moved to our town." Mrs. Davis eased onto one sofa and gestured to the one across from her. "Do you like sugar, dear?"

"Please." Her skirts were still damp from the snow, so she eased gingerly onto the edge of the cushion. She had to set her reticule down and stop her hands from shaking as she reached for the tea handed to her. *Clink, clink.* The cup rattled against the saucer. She didn't know if she was still shaky with nerves over her encounter with Lorenzo or over her interview with his mother.

A little help please, Lord. She thought of her pa, who was such a good father. She thought of her brother, who worked so hard to send money home. *For them.*

"You must know my Lorenzo." Mrs. Davis stirred sugar into the second cup. "You two are about the same age."

"Yes, although we were not in the same crowd at school." She didn't know how to say the first time she'd ever spoken to the handsome young man had been today. He'd been terribly gallant, just as she'd always known he would be. He treated everyone that way.

She knew better than to read anything into it.

"Tell me what kind of kitchen experience you have." The older woman settled against the cushions, ready to listen.

"None." Already she could see failure descending. She took a small sip of the hot tea and it strengthened her. "I've never held a job before, but I am a hard worker. I've cooked and cleaned for my pa and my brother since I was small."

"And your mother?"

"She passed away when I was born." She tried to keep the wistfulness out of her voice, the wish for a mother she'd never known.

"And your father never remarried, even with young children?" Concern, not censure, pinched in the corners of the lovely woman's dark eyes.

"No. He said his love for Ma was too great. I don't think he's ever stopped loving her." Ruby shrugged. Did she turn the conversation back to her kitchen skills? She wasn't sure exactly what a kitchen maid was required to   do.

"The same thing happened to my father when I was born." Mrs. Davis looked sad for a moment. She was striking and exotic, with her olive complexion and dark brown, almost-black eyes. Ruby thought she'd never seen anyone more beautiful. The older woman set her cup on her saucer with a tiny clink. "He raised me the best he could. In our home there were maids to do the work and a nanny to help, but nothing can replacethe hole left behind when someone is lost. You prepare meals, then?"

"Yes." Her anxiety ebbed. She'd seen the great lady in town and, of course, at church, and Mrs. Davis had always seemed so regal and distant. Ruby hadn't expected to feel welcome in her presence. Hopeful, she found herself smiling. "I'm not sure what you are looking for, but I know how to clean, I know how to do what I'm told, and I follow directions very well."

"That's exactly what Scarlet told me." Mrs. Davis smiled. "Whomever I hire will be expected to assist the cook, to help do all the cleaning of the pots and pans and the entire kitchen. Do you know how to serve?"

"No." She wilted. "I've never done anything as fancy as that."

"I see." Mrs. Davis paused a moment, studying her carefully from head to toe. It was an assessing look and not an unkind one, but Ruby felt every inch of the inspection.

What did the lady see? The gap in her shoe buttons? The made-over, handed-down dress?

"What about your schooling?" The older lady broke the silence.

Ruby hung her head. She tried not to, but her chin bobbed downward of its own accord. "I am still attending this year. I had hoped to catch up and be able to graduate in the spring, but my home circumstances have changed."

"And you need to work," Mrs. Davis said with understanding.

"Yes." She was not the best candidate for the job. She was probably not the type of young woman right for the position. It hurt, and she tried not to let it show. A blur of color caught the corner of her eye. She turned just an inch to see beyond the wide windows. Outside, a man made his way through the thick curtains of snow, a familiar man.

Lorenzo.

Don't look, Ruby. But did her eyes obey?

Not a chance.

He lifted a leather-gloved hand in a brief wave, and the snap of connection roared through her like the crackling and cozy heat from the fireplace. Hard not to remember his kind advice to her.

"I am very reliable, Mrs. Davis." She was content with who she was, and she let the fine lady see it. "I have good values, I know the importance of keeping promises, and I will do my best never to let you down. If you hire me, I will arrive early, I will stay late, and I will work harder than anyone else. I would never leave you in a lurch by not showing up when expected."

"That's nice to hear, dear." Mrs. Davis smiled fully, and it was Lorenzo's smile she saw, honest and good-hearted and kind. "Now, tell me a little more about your background."

He'd timed it perfectly, he thought, grateful as he seized Poncho's reins, thanked the horse for standing so long in his traces and gave the leather lines a snap. His heart twisted hard at the sight of Ruby slipping out of the front door and into the snow. Was he in love with her? He feared love was too small a word.

He loved a woman who hardly knew he existed. He'd pined after her whenever he'd seen her in town and long before that, during their final year of school together. Not once had she ever looked his way. Until today. She'd accepted a ride from him, she'd smiled at him, she'd given him the faintest ghost of a hope.

Time to put his heart on the line and see if the lady rejected him or if he had a chance with her.

That was one chance he wanted more than anything on this earth. The marrow of his bones ached with it, the depth of his soul longed for it. He snapped the reins, sending Poncho out of the shelter of the barn and into the fierce beat of snow and wind. But did he feel the cold? Not a bit. Not when he kept Ruby in sight, slim, petite, as sweet as those snowflakes falling.

"C'mon, Poncho," he urged. "Don't lose her."

She walked at a good clip, bent into the wind. Her blue dress flashed beneath the hem of her coat and twisted around her ankles, trying to hamper her. But she kept on going without looking back. He saw nothing more of her as the gusts shifted, stealing her from his sight. The storm couldn't stop the longing in his soul to see her again.

This was his chance to be with her. To try to get past her shyness and see if she could like him. His stomach knotted up with nerves as he snapped Poncho's reins, urging him to hurry, although he could barely see his horse's rump in the whiteout conditions. Surely Ruby couldn't have gotten far.

Poncho seemed to understand the importance of the mission, for the mighty gelding pushed into the storm, parting the thickly falling snow. He walked right up to Ruby and stopped of his own accord. Lorenzo grinned. It was nice having his horse's support.

"Poncho? Is that you?" Ruby's whimsical alto drifted to him through the storm. He could see the faint outline of her, already flocked white. "It *is* you. So that means…" She hesitated. "Lorenzo? What are you doing out in this weather again?"

Her words may be muffled from the wind and snow, but they carried a note of surprise. As if she truly had no idea what he was up to.

"I have an errand, which will take me by your place." He pulled aside the buffalo robe he'd taken from the tack room. "Would you like a ride?"

"Well..." She wavered, considering.

"It will be an awfully difficult walk with this drifting snow." He'd tried over and over to stop his feelings for Ruby. An impossible endeavor. He braced himself for her refusal and tried one more time. "You may as well let Poncho do the hard work."

She edged closer, debating, her bottom lip caught beneath her front teeth.

"I appreciate Poncho's offer." The hint of a smile tucked in the corners of her mouth deepened. "I suppose his feelings would be hurt if I turned him down?"

"Very. He's the one who insisted on stopping. Apparently he's taken a shine to you."

"Well, I think he's a very nice horse. He's as gentlemanly as my Solomon." She disappeared, perhaps believing it was the horse who cared for her and not the driver. Although he could no longer see her, the faint murmur of her voice as she spoke with the gelding carried on the wind. Just a syllable and a scrap of a sentence, and then she reappeared at his side. "Poncho talked me into accepting."

"He can be persuasive." Lorenzo held out his hand to help her settle onto the seat beside him. Her hand felt small against his own, and the bolt of awareness that rushed through him went straight to his soul. He wasn't used to feeling anything this strongly. "Besides, a storm like this can turn into a blizzard, something you don't want to be out walking in."

"It would be no less dangerous to a horse and sleigh." She settled against the cushioned seat back. "I wonder why you would venture out. Surely there isn't much ranching work this time of year?"

"I never said it was ranch work." He tucked the buffalo robe around her, leaning close enough to catch the scent of honeysuckle. The vulnerable places within him tugged, defenseless against her nearness. He didn't know why his heart moved so fast, determined to pull him along. He could not stop it as he gathered the reins, sending Poncho forward.

"In my worry over my shoe and my interview, I forgot to ask you. I heard your father was injured a while back. How is he?"

"He's still recovering." Lorenzo did his best not to let his anger take hold at the outlaws who had taken up residence west of town last summer and stolen a hundred head of cattle in a gun battle. "My father wasn't as fortunate as the others the outlaw gang shot. He was hit in the leg bone and the back. He's still struggling to walk with a cane."

"I'm so sorry." Sympathy polished her, making her inner beauty shine. Her outer beauty became breathtaking, so compelling he could not look away. Soft platinum locks breezed against the curving slope of her cheeks and the dainty cut of her jaw. "I noticed he wasn't coming to church, but I didn't know he was still struggling with his injuries. I don't get to town much."

"It's not something Pa wants everyone to know. He's a private man." He adored his father. Gerard Davis was a proud and stubborn Welshman who could have lived leisurely on his inherited wealth but chose to put his life to good use by ranching on the Montana frontier. Lorenzo hoped he took after his pa.

"I won't mention it, but I do intend to pray for him." Her hands clasped together within the rather lumpy mittens made of uneven stitches. They looked twisted somehow, as if they had not faired well through a washing. But her earnest concern shone in her voice. "I hope he has a full recovery. I know how difficult it is for a man used to providing for his family when he is too injured to work."

"It is tough on a man's pride."

"When I was little, Pa had an accident on our farm. A hay wagon overturned on him, and he was crushed. He was working alone and no one found him until my brother came with the mid-afternoon water jug. Rupert was too young to help free him. All he could do was run to the neighbors over a mile away."

"I didn't know. I'm sorry." Interesting that they had this in common. He thought of the humble, quiet man who had begged him for a job. "He obviously recovered."

"It took many years. We feared losing him at first. The doctor didn't know how he survived. A true proof of grace," she added, staring down at her misshapen mittens. "God was very good in letting us keep our pa. I don't know what Rupert and I would have done if we'd lost him, too, so I understand what you might have gone through."

"Worry, mostly. For a while we feared Pa might not walk again. Doc Frost said it was grace, too, that he's up on his feet."

"Grace is everywhere, when you look for it."

"And when you need it most." It was so easy to talk to her about what really mattered. Did she feel the same way? "How long ago was your pa injured?"

"I was five years old." The sleigh bounced in a rut as Poncho turned onto the country road. She lifted a mittened hand to swipe snow out of her eyes. She felt closer somehow. Like they were no longer strangers.

"You were five? That must have been hard on your family."

"Yes. Pa was laid up so long, we lost our crop. We couldn't pay the doctor bills. Then we lost our land and our house, and we couldn't pay any of the other bills, either. The bank took everything but Solomon. Rupert worked long days in a neighbor's field to earn the money to keep him."

"Did you have any other family to help?"

"My uncle and his wife finally took us in. It was a long spell until Pa was able to work again, and he was determined to pay back every cent of his debts still outstanding."

"Most folks would have walked away. So your family was never able to get ahead?"

"It was a hardship paying off the debts, but it was the right thing."

"Doing the right thing matters." His dark blue eyes deepened with understanding. "It's worth whatever the cost."

"Exactly." When her gaze met his, her heart beat as fast as a hummingbird's wings. It mattered that he understood honor. So many hadn't. Probably because he had honor of his own. She blushed, because it would be so easy to like him, to really like him. Just as it would be to read more into his act of kindness in offering her this ride.

"Your family owns land now, so your father must have paid off his debts." He broke his gaze away to rein Poncho to keep him on the hard-to-see road. Even speckled with snow, Lorenzo's handsomeness shone through.

Not that she should be noticing.

"Yes. Pa managed to save up enough for a mortgage, although we had to pay a lot of money down." She picked at a too-tight stitch in her right mitten to keep from looking at him again. Not looking at him was for the best. "It is good to have our own land, but it's only a hundred acres."

"A hundred acres of untilled land. Let me guess. Your first harvest wasn't as good as it could have been. A first crop on new land is always a small one."

"And on top of that, most of our crop was damaged by a summer storm." She blushed, still picking at the stitch. She could feel the tug of his gaze, the gentle insistence of his presence, and she wanted to look at him. But she was afraid of coming to care too much.

"Next harvest will be better," he promised. "As long as there isn't a drought or a twister or a flash flood."

"Or another hailstorm," she chimed in lightly. "Farming doesn't come with a guarantee, but it would be a great blessing to have a good harvest, if we manage to stay on. My pa and brother work so hard. It would be a comfort for them."

"Then I'll put it in my prayers."

His smile drew her gaze. Unable to resist, her eyes met his, and the world faded. The jarring of the sleigh ceased. The cold vanished, and there was only his sincerity, his caring and the quiet wish in her soul.

Don't give in to it, Ruby. Don't start dreaming.

"Here we are." He tugged on the reins, Poncho drew to a stop. How had three miles passed so quickly?

"Why, young Mr. Davis." Pa's voice came from far away, stupefied. He gripped a pitchfork in one gloved hand, emerging from the small barn. "Ruby, is that you?"

"Yes, Pa." Reality set in. She pushed off the buffalo robe and grabbed up her reticule. Snow slapped her cheeks as she tried to scramble out of the sleigh.

"Allow me." Lorenzo caught her hand. His warmth, his size, his presence overwhelmed her. Her breath caught. She forgot every word of the English langage. Her knees wobbled when she tried to stand on them. Little flashes of wishes filled her, but she tamped them down as he withdrew his hand.

"What are you doing on this side of the county?" Pa asked, curiously. "Looking at the property for sale down the way?"

"Not in this weather." Lorenzo released her hand."I wanted to make sure Ruby got home safe in this storm. I hear you have a horse with a shoe problem. I happen to have my tools in the back of the sleigh. If you wouldn't mind, I can take care of that problem for you."

Her jaw dropped. She stared, stunned, as Pa led the way to the barn, taking Poncho by the bridle bits. All she could see was the straight strong line of Lorenzo's wide shoulders through the storm until the thick curtain of snow closed around him, leaving her standing alone on the rickety, front doorstep of their lopsided shanty. That Lorenzo Davis. He was being charitable, that was all, but her heart would never forget.

Chapter Three

"And he went into the barn with your father?" Kate peered through dark lashes, astonished as she sorted through her embroidery floss.

"And he re-shod Solomon for you?" Newlywed Lila looked up from stitching on a new shirt for her husband. "Out of the blue, just like that?"

"Without being asked." The tea kettle rumbled, so Ruby set aside her crocheting. The wooden chair scraped against the wood floor as she rose. It was a tight squeeze to have all seven of them in the front room, but it was warm and cozy, and she loved having the chance to host their sewing circle. "You could have knocked me down with a feather, I was so shocked. I guess this proves the rumors true. Young Mr. Davis is as nice as a man can be."

"That's what we have been trying to tell you." Red-headed Scarlet set down her tatting to get up to help with the tea. "He's amazing. That's why we have all been in love with him at one time or another."

"Not all of us," Fiona corrected as she stitched on baby clothes. Her wedding ring winked in the lamplight as her needle slipped into a seam. The pleats of her dress hid the small bowl of her pregnant stomach. "I've always thought Lorenzo was nice, but I was never smitten."

"Not even a little?" Ruby set the tea to steeping in the old ironware pot. "Lorenzo is terribly handsome. Are you sure you didn't like him at all?"

"I'm positive." Fiona's smile came so easily.

"He adored you from afar. We all saw it," Scarlet added, taking a knife to the johnnycake cooling on the nearby table.

"You broke his heart when you married Ian. Don't deny it." Earlee gave her golden curls a toss as she looked up from basting an apron ruffle. When she smiled, the whole world smiled, too. "If I were penning a story about him, I would have him fall in love with one of you three. A sweet, gentle love with lots of longing and a perfect happily-ever-after."

A perfect happily-ever-after. Didn't that sound romantic? She tamped down her sigh right along with the memory of riding alongside Lorenzo in the sleigh. Her hands shook as she carried the pot and the stack of battered, mismatched tin cups to the circle of chairs in the sitting area.

"It sounds like a story I would read," Lila quipped, the voracious reader of the group. "So, Earlee, who would you match up with Lorenzo?"

"Me!" Kate spoke up before Earlee could as she separated a thin strand of embroidery floss from a green skein. "I would be perfect for him."

"True," Meredith agreed, head bent over her latest patchwork quilt block. "Except doesn't he spend a lot of time with Narcissa Bell?"

"Oh," they all sighed together. Narcissa had been their arch nemesis for as long as anyone could remember.

"I suppose it's only a matter of time before we hear of their engagement." Kate licked the end of the floss and threaded it through the eye of her needle. "It's inevitable."

"It's expected," Lila agreed. "To hear my stepmother talk, their engagement party will be any day now."

"They are both from wealthy families." Ruby couldn't explain why pain hitched through her ribs.

"And their mothers are close friends," Earlee chimed in.

"But so are Scarlet and his mother." She lowered the pot to rest on the short end table Pa had made, which now sat in the center of their circle, a coffee table of sorts. Her hands shook inexplicably. She wasn't disappointed, so no way could that be disappointment weighing like a lead brick on her heart.

"Yes, but Lorenzo and I don't keep the same friends." Scarlet bent over her work, knife in hand. "Did you see Narcissa and Lorenzo at church on Sunday?"

"Sitting side by side." Kate gave a long-suffering sigh. "Right there in the middle of their families."

Ruby hadn't noticed because she didn't have a crush on the man. She couldn't afford to have one. Romance was not in her plans. She didn't have time for it. She wasn't free to pursue her own life. Her father and brother needed her to help save the farm. And besides, if their efforts failed, she would have to leave town.

She wasn't exactly the best candidate for romance. Not for any man. As for Lorenzo, he was a dream she didn't dare have. So why did she ache down to the marrow of her bones as she crossed the room? She couldn't focus on the conversation surging around her, the laughter and friendly banter ringing like merry bells. She lifted down a stack of mismatched plates.

"How did the interview go?" Scarlet lowered her voice, so the others wouldn't hear. She cut the final slice of johnnycake.

"Good, but I'm not right for the position. Mrs. Davis is awful fancy. Nice, but fancy." She set the butter dish next to the plates on the table. She tried to tell herself it didn't matter that she wouldn't get the job. "I would be totally uncomfortable in that house. I'd worry about everything—leaving dirt from my shoes on the floor, turning around and knocking some expensive doodad to the ground, spilling something on those beautiful carpets. What a relief I'm not suitable."

"That's too bad. I thought you would be perfect. My mother said so right to Mrs. Davis. I heard her."

"Thanks, Scarlet. I appreciate it more than you know."

"So, does this mean your family will have to move?"

"I think so, since I won't be getting that job."

"I'm so sorry, Ruby."

"Me, too." She wished she felt comfortable saying more, but she wasn't good at expressing her feelings. They made her feel awkward and exposed, but she knew Scarlet understood. Best friends had that ability.

The cornmeal's sweet, warm scent and aroma of melting butter had her mouth watering. She'd been too nervous to eat all of her breakfast, fearing the interview and too unsettled to eat lunch afterwards. Leftover nerves from meeting Mrs. Davis and not because of her encounter with Lorenzo.

At least, that's what she told herself.

"So, what happened after he fixed Solomon's shoe?" Earlee asked, setting down her work to come help distribute the cake. "Did you offer him a nice, hot cup of tea?"

"And then lunch?" Lila inquired.

"And afterwards, a nice, long chat around the table?" Kate knotted the end of her thread.

"You *did* invite him in, didn't you?" Scarlet asked, two plates of cake in hand.

"Well, no. It wasn't like that. He and Pa were visiting in the barn."

"Did you even go out there?" Fiona set her sewing aside to accept a plate of cake.

All eyes turned on her.

"No. Why would I? I'm not as brazen as the bunch of you."

Laughter flourished, echoing off the walls cheerfully. She couldn't very well admit that she'd kept an eye on the window, glancing out from time to time, straining to see a glimpse of Lorenzo through the snow. She hadn't. She'd only spotted her father stomping the wet off his boots on the lean-to steps. He'd been alone.

"Next time, go out with a nice hot cup of tea for him," Meredith advised.

"And some of this cake," Earlee added. "If he takes one bite of this, he just might propose."

"Oh, I doubt that." She retrieved the last plate from the table, but her stomach had bunched in knots. She was no longer hungry. "He drove off without a word to me, but Pa was mighty pleased with the shoeing job. I'm surprised Pa accepted his charity."

"Maybe he did it for you, Ruby." Scarlet sounded

thoughtful as she brought the last plates of cake into the sitting area.

"For me? No. Don't even start thinking that." She had best forget the snap of connection when Lorenzo had taken her hand. Wishful thinking on her part, that was all it could be. "I have Pa to care for. He's the only man in my life. Besides, Lorenzo has Narcissa. Who can compete with that?"

"I wouldn't mind trying," Scarlet spoke up, making everyone laugh.

Ruby settled into a chair, laughing with her friends. How much time would they have together? She didn't know. That question haunted her as talk turned to other handsome bachelors in town. If one particular bachelor lingered in her thoughts, she didn't have to admit it.

Lorenzo leaned back against the chair cushion, grateful to be sitting in front of a warm fire at the end of a tough afternoon. Half frozen, he soaked in the fire's blazing heat, hoping to thaw. After returning from Ruby's home, he'd saddled up and resumed his afternoon shift in the fields, checking cattle, hauling feed and taking a pickax to the animals' water supply, which had frozen up solid.

Ruby. Thoughts of her could chase away the cold. He stretched his feet toward the fire. He still didn't know what his chances were, but she'd been easy to talk to. He would like to talk with her some more. But what were the chances of that if she didn't get the maid's position? She kept to herself, she lived on the other side of town, and their paths rarely crossed. He didn't want to go back to sneaking gazes at her in church because his mother or one of her friends were going to catch him at it, and then his secret love for Ruby would no longer be private.

"Hot tea for you." The upstairs maid was doubling her duties and slid a tray onto the table at his elbow with a bobbing curtsy. "Cook added some of those scones you like."

"Thank you." He didn't wait for her footsteps tapping on the polished oak floor to fade before he wrapped his hand around the scalding hot cup. He was so cold, he could barely feel the warmth. He blew on the steaming brew before he sipped it. Hot liquid slid down his throat, warming him from the inside. The first step to thawing out.

Ruby. His thoughts boomeranged right back to her. Why her? Her big, blue eyes, her rosebud smile, her sweetness had snared him the instant he'd laid eyes on her. He didn't want to feel this way, he wasn't ready to feel this way. He had a lot to learn about ranching, he had a lot to prove as his father's foreman. And responsibility? That was a huge burden on his shoulders these days. He was in charge of providing for the family and preserving the Davis legacy. No, this wasn't the time to be smitten with anyone.

But his heart kept falling in love with Ruby a little more day by day, taking him with it. He couldn't stop it. He wouldn't if he could. He wanted Ruby to be his fate, the destiny God had in store for him.

"Lorenzo." His mother swept into the room. "Look at you. You were out in that weather too long."

"I'm tough." He'd learned from his father not to let excuses stand in the way. "Work needed to be done, so I did it."

"Yes, but you've gotten frostbite." She hauled a footstool close and tried to look at his hands.

"Nothing serious." He refused to surrender his teacup. "No fussing, Ma. I'm not twelve anymore."

"You are my only son." She smiled, attempting to hide her weariness.

"How did the interviewing go?"

"So many women showed up for one opening. My heart goes out to them all. Every one of them was in sincere need of employment." She swept a strand of black hair from her eyes, troubled and worried as she always was for other people. "I can only choose one. I feel bad for all the others. What will they do?"

He thought of Ruby, of her very humble home, her unreliable shoes and her situation. Her family clearly needed the income her employment would bring. He suspected many of the others who had come during a brisk, winter storm were in as much need. "I don't have an answer. I've had the same worries ever since I took over the hiring for the ranch. Have you decided on anyone yet?"

"I've narrowed it down to a short list, but how to decide from there? I do not know." She stole a corner off one of his scones and popped it into her mouth. "One of them was a young lady about your age. You went to school with her."

"Ruby." His mother didn't miss much. He tried to hide his reaction by taking a quick swallow of tea. The scalding liquid rolled over his tongue, nearly blistering him. He coughed, sputtering.

"Oh, I see." His mother paused thoughtfully. "She seemed like a nice girl."

"Nice? I suppose." As if he was going to tell his

mother what he really thought. Fortunately, he had a burning tongue to distract him. "She would be a reliable worker."

"Yes. I thought she was very earnest, but she has no experience."

"She could learn." He hoped he sounded casual, not like a man hoping. He wanted Mother to hire her and make a difference in her life. "She takes care of her family. She does the cooking and cleaning. That's experience, right?"

"I suppose." His mother rose. "I have some pondering to do. So, have you thought about who you want to invite to our pre-Christmas ball? It's getting closer, and I have yet to get out the last of my invitations."

"And you're mentioning this to me why, exactly?" He sipped more tea, taking refuge behind the cup. Had he made a strong enough case for Ruby's sake? He couldn't tell by the look on his mother's face.

"Because I'll want to know so I can send the young lady an invitation. It's time you started thinking about a wife. I'm looking forward to the next Davis generation."

"You mean grandchildren?"

"Of course." His mother laughed, delighted. "I see that blush. It's as I thought. You have your eye on someone, and I know who."

"You do?" Tea sloshed over the rim. His heart slammed to a stop. Fine, so he'd been a little obvious. "I admit, I do have someone in mind."

"Excellent. You know the Bells are on my guest list anyway, but I wanted to send a special one to Narcissa." Poor, misguided Ma. She'd leaped to the wrong conclusion.

"I'm not escorting Narcissa." Not again. "Normally I let you do what you want, but not this time, Ma."

"Why?" Confused, his mother slipped onto the chair across from him. "I thought all that time you two spend together meant something."

"Mostly arranged by you or her mother. It's very hard to say no to either one of you."

"Yes, but she sits beside you in church every Sunday."

"Coincidence on my part. I'm thinking intentionally on hers and her mother's."

"I'm terribly disappointed."

"Of course you want me to marry your best friend's daughter, Ma, but that's not going to happen. We're just friends."

"I see. Well then, who? There's plenty of suitable young women in town. Surely her family is on my list?"

"I'll take care of inviting her myself." Just as he'd suspected. This was going to be a disappointment to his mother. He was sorry for it. He hated letting her down. He thought of Ruby. How would his parents handle it if they knew the truth?

"I think I hear your father coming. Oh, Jerry, it's you."

"Selma, there you are." Pa's cane tapped on the hardwood, and although he winced in pain with every step, he transformed when he saw his wife. "I see you are keeping our boy company. You did great work today, Renzo."

"I did my best."

"Can't ask for anything more than that. You're doing a fine job. Better than your old man can do." His father's chest puffed out, full of pride, as he slowly limped across the room. "I'm obsolete."

"Never you, Pa. I can't wait to hand you back the reins." Even as he said the words, they all knew they were only a wish. Gerard Davis had been injured far too badly to ever return to the rigors of ranching work. In deference to his father's hopes, he shrugged lightly. "I miss being bossed around by you."

"I miss doing the bossing. But I get my fill on a daily basis. What's this I overheard about your escorting a young gal to our ball? Selma, I thought we agreed you wouldn't push the boy."

"I wasn't pushing, merely suggesting." His mother sounded confused as she held out her arms and wrapped them around her husband. The pair cuddled, glad to see each other after being separated for much of the day. "I want to see Lorenzo settled."

"Yes, dear, but he has enough new responsibility to manage. This ranch is the largest in the county. Renzo ought to be concentrating on learning all there is to know about our land, crops and animals."

"He's doing a fine job. Goodness." Ma's gentle amusement rang in her chuckle as she gave her husband one final hug. She swept backward, love lighting her eyes. "Gerard, I don't see why Lorenzo needs to hold off. You managed to run a ranch and court me at the same time."

"Yes, but I wasn't barely twenty years old. Renzo's mature for his age, but I don't want him distracted. I know how distracting a pretty lady can be." Pa winked, always the charmer, and Ma blushed prettily.

Ruby was definitely distracting. She was all he could see—snowflakes sifting over her to catch in her hair, big, blueberry eyes shyly looking away, the blush on her heart-shaped face when he'd taken her hand in his to help her from the sleigh.

This wasn't the right time in his life, and his parents wouldn't like it, but his heart was set. Nothing could stop it.

"Renzo? Where did you take off to this morning?" Pa leaned heavily on his cane, tapping closer. "Was there a problem I didn't know about?"

"My trip wasn't ranch related." His pulse skipped a beat. What else had his father seen?

"He drove past the window and picked up one of the applicants. He must have taken her home." Pa's tone gentled. "She looked like a dear. That Ballard girl, I think. I know her father from church. He's a good man."

"The poor girl." Ma settled onto the sofa, compassionate as always. "My heart aches for her. Being both daughter and woman of the house. They must be as poor as church mice. I've seen her getting clothes out of the church's donation barrel. It was all I could do not to rush up and give her a big hug when she was here."

Please, he thought. *Please give her a chance.* A job would mean she could stay in town. That he would have a hope of winning her.

"Selma, I know that look." Pa chuckled as he eased painfully onto the cushion beside his wife. "Son, something tells me your mother has just made up her mind about the new maid."

"Those friends of yours are sure nice girls." Pa knocked snow off his boots on the doorstep. "You all seemed to have a good time."

"We did." She doused the last tin cup in the rinse

water, glad to see her father back safely from town. Since Solomon's shoe was fixed, there had been errands needing to be done. "We always have great fun together, and I got a lot of help with my crocheting."

"That's nice, Ruby-bug." He shouldered the door closed against the whirling flakes, and the cold followed him in as he unloaded the groceries he'd bought on the far end of the table. It wasn't much—a bag of beans, a package of tea, small sacks of cornmeal and oatmeal—but she was grateful for it. When Pa swept off his hat, he looked more tired than usual. "I'm glad you made friends here."

"Me, too." She rubbed the dishtowel over the mug, drying it carefully. With each swipe, she felt her stomach fall a notch. Had her father stopped by the post office? Was there a letter from Rupert? Her brother had been hoping to send news of a job.

Sorrow crept into Pa's eyes, and he sat down heavily on a kitchen chair. "I didn't want to say anything to you earlier, but I had chance for work in town, unloading cargo at the depot. It went to someone else. A younger man."

"Oh, Papa." She set down the towel and the cup and circled around to his side. He was a proud man, a strong man, but hardship wore on him. He fought so hard to provide for them, and had struggled for so long. Just when it looked as if life was going to get easier, the storm had hit. Without a crop, there had been no income, and they were back to desperation again.

How little of their meager savings remained? She placed a hand on his brawny shoulder. He was such a good man, and love for him filled her up. They did not have much, but they had what they needed. They had what mattered most.

"I got a letter from Rupert." Her father rubbed his face, where worry dug deep lines. "He sent money."

That explained the groceries. She hated seeing Pa like this. He'd always been invincible, always a fighter, even when he'd been injured. Every memory she had of him was one of strength and determination. He'd always been a rock, the foundation of their family, who never wavered.

Not tonight. He looked heart-worn and hopeless. Like a man who was too weary to fight. The shadows crept visibly over him as the daylight dimmed. Sunset came early this time of year, and she needed to light a candle, to save on precious kerosene, but she could not leave her father's side, not when he bowed his head, looking beaten.

Was their situation far worse than he'd told her? She bit her bottom lip, knotted up with worry. Pa did have a habit of protecting her. If only she could have gotten the job. She winced at the dismal interview she'd had, the squeaky shoes, the rattling teacup, her lack of experience and polish. "I will scour the town tomorrow, Pa. There has to be something I can do. Sweep floors, do laundry at the hotel, muck stalls at Foster's Dairy."

She would beg if she had to. Her father and brother had been carrying too much burden for way too long. She ached for them, struggling so hard against odds that turned out to be impossible. The dream of owning their own land and being farmers again was fading. At this point in Pa's life, it would likely be gone forever. She knelt before him and laid her hand on his. "I can be persuasive. I will talk someone into hiring me. Please don't worry so much."

"Oh, my Ruby." Pa cupped her face with both of his big, callused hands, making her feel safe. "You are a good girl. I'm afraid the news in Roop's letter wasn't good."

"He found you a job, and we have to leave after all." She squeezed her eyes shut for just one brief moment to hide the stab of pain ripping through her. It was selfish to want to stay when it was a burden for her family, so she firmed her chin. "This will be better for you. A job. Think what this will mean."

"No, honey, there isn't a job. Roop lost his. The mill closed down. It's gone out of business. He's coming home without his last two paychecks. The company promised but in the end couldn't pay him." Pa looked far too old for his years as he squared his shoulders, fighting to find enough internal strength to keep going. "It's a blow, but I don't want you worrying, Ruby. You must stay in school."

"I won't do it." She brushed a kiss on her father's stubbled cheek. "You know me. When I set my mind to something, nothing but God can stop me."

"And even He would give pause before trying," Pa quipped, the love in his eyes unmistakable. "We have to trust Him to see us through this. He's watching over us."

"I know, Pa." She whirled away to light a candle or two, thankful for the bountiful summer garden she'd been able to grow. Selling extra vegetables to the stores in town had given her enough pocket money to make plenty of candles and soap to see them through the winter. It was a small thing to have contributed, but she'd been proud to do it. The warmth of her friends' laughter lingered in the home, making it less bleak as she struck a match.

Encouraged, she watched the wick flare, and the light chased back the shadows. She shook out the match, shivering as the wind blew cold through the walls. Faith was like a candle dispelling the darkness, and she lit another, determined to believe they could make their upcoming mortgage payment, that they would not be homeless by Christmas.

Chapter Four

The snow whirled on a bitter night's wind as Lorenzo guided his horse and sleigh down the drift-covered driveway. Lanterns mounted on the dashboard of the sleigh cast just enough light to see the dark yard and front step of the shanty. Poncho drew to a stop before the doorway. Ruby's doorway.

Her adorable presence stayed with him like a melody, and a smile stretched the corners of his mouth as he climbed from beneath the robes. His boots crunched in the snow, icy flakes stung his face, but he kept going, untouched, seeing Ruby through a crack between the curtains.

She sat in a wooden chair, holding a crochet needle and thread up to a single candle's light to make a slow, careful stitch. Her platinum hair gleamed golden-silver. Her heart-shaped face, flushed from the heat of the fire and caressed by the candlelight could have belonged to a princess in a fairy tale. Wholesome and good, she was the most beautiful woman he'd ever seen. Captivated, he knocked snow off his hat as it continued to fall.

The muffled tap of footsteps tore his attention away from Ruby. Jon Ballard ambled into sight inside the house, reminding Lorenzo of his mission. He had a message for Ruby, one that would make her life easier. He took the few snowy steps to the front door and knocked. His pulse rattled against his rib cage. He was suddenly nervous, anxious with the anticipation of seeing her again.

The door swung open, and her father stood inside the threshold, surprise marking his lined face, proof of how hard the last few months had been for the family. "Young Mr. Davis, is that you again? What are you doing out on these roads this time of evening?"

"I'm on another errand. My father wanted to send one of the hired men, but I volunteered." His gaze arrowed straight to her. Her crochet work had fallen to her lap. She stared at him with worry crinkling her forehead. Worry. He hated it. He squared his shoulders, glad he could fix that. He pulled the folded parchment from his pocket. "I have a letter for Ruby. From my mother."

"For me?" She set aside her needle and thread, rose to her feet, and every movement she made was endearing—the pad of her stockinged feet on the floor, the rustle of her skirt, the twist of her bottom lip as she swept closer. The place she had opened within him opened more, widening his heart.

Vaguely, he was aware of Jon stepping back, disappearing from sight. Ruby remained at the center of his senses. Ruby, wringing her slender hands. Ruby, in a very old, calico work dress, the color faded from so many washings. The careful patches sewed with tiny, even stitches were too numerous to count. As she stepped into the puddle of nearby candlelight, her beauty and goodness outshone everything.

"It was nice of you to come so far in this cold." Shy,

she lowered her gaze from his. "Just to tell me I didn't get the job."

"Why would you say that?"

"Because the interview was a disaster. The missing button, my wet shoes, I dripped all over the floor, I was completely wrong for the position." Pink flushed her cheeks and her nose, making her twice as sweet. "I'm sorry you had to drive so far in this weather. Your mother could have posted the letter."

"I suppose." This was why he'd come so far in frigid temperatures. So he could see the happiness chase away the worry from her big, beautiful eyes. "Ma wants you to start working for her first thing Monday morning. Will that be a problem?"

"What?" Her jaw dropped. Disbelief pinched adorably across her sweetheart face. "I couldn't have gotten the job. I have no experience."

"My mother liked you, so she's hired you." He held out the envelope. "Here are the specifics."

"Really? Oh, Pa, did you hear?" She took the parchment. Delight chased away the worry lines, put blue sparkles into her irises and drew a beautiful smile. "I got the job. I got it."

"I'm mighty proud of you, Ruby-bug." Jon Ballard's love shone in his voice, love for his precious daughter.

Lorenzo thought she was precious, too.

"Oh, thank your mother for me. I mean, I will thank her on Monday, too, when I see her. But, oh, just *thank* you." She clutched the letter tight until it crinkled.

"I will tell her. Your interview went better than you thought."

"But how? It's a complete and total mystery."

"No mystery." His reassurance held notes of humor

and kindness. "You deserve this, Ruby. My mother wants you to start at six o'clock sharp."

"I'll be there early, just like I promised." This was too good to be true. She'd been so sure she had failed, that it was impossible, and yet here she was, an employee. She had her first job, she would be earning a wage. A real wage. Joy bubbled through her, impossible to contain. She had a job! "I hope I don't break anything. Or spill something. I don't know anything about serving."

Good going, Ruby. Point out to your employer's son exactly how much of a mistake his mother had made. She laughed. "I'm so happy and anxious and everything."

"I understand." The deep shine of his dark blue gaze met hers, sincere and powerful enough to knock the beat out of her heart. Her happiness dimmed, her soul stilled as he tipped his hat, and she could not look away. She could see the shadow of day's growth on his strong, square jaw. His masculine strength shrank the shanty and made every bit of air vanish. No man on earth could be as amazing as Lorenzo

Candlelight flickered over him, caressing the powerful angles of his face and gleaming darkly on the thick, dark fall of his hair. She lost the ability to breathe as he took a step backward into the darkness. Snow sifted over him like spun sugar.

Don't start wishing, Ruby.

"I shouldn't leave my horse standing in this cold. Good night, Ruby. I will see you on Monday."

"On Monday." The words stuttered over her tongue, her legs went weak, and she grasped the door frame before she tumbled face-first onto the snowy step. Monday. A different kind of panic clutched her, cinching tight around her middle.

She would see Lorenzo every day. She would be in his house, be in proximity with his family and washing his dishes. The warm place in her heart remembered his touch, his gallantry, his kindness. It made a girl want to dream. *Focus, Ruby.* She no longer had time for schoolgirl wishes. Pa's tired gait drummed on the floorboards behind her, coming closer. In the dying storm, Lorenzo was a shadow, then a hint of a shadow and finally nothing more. The beat of Poncho's hooves faded until there was only the whispering hush of falling snow and the winter's cold.

She closed the door firmly against the darkness. Discarded wishes followed her like snowflakes in the air as she headed toward the stove to make a cup of tea for her father. She had the chance to make a real difference for her family. Monday was what she ought to think about. Monday, when she started her new job.

In the predawn light, Ruby slid off of Solomon in the shelter of the Davis's barn. Breathing in the scents of hay and warm horse, she glanced around. Stalls were filled with animals eating out of their troughs. What did she do with Solomon? Where did she take him?

Something tugged at her hat, knocking it askew on her head. Dear old Solomon's whiskery lips nibbled the brim and the side of her face in comfortable adoration. They had been friends for a long time. She patted his neck and leaned against him, her sweet boy. "I'm sure I'm supposed to put you somewhere, but I didn't think to ask when Lorenzo delivered the letter."

Solomon's nicker rumbled low in his throat, a comforting answer of sorts. Fortunately, she did not have to wonder for long as footsteps tapped her way, echoing in the dark aisle. She couldn't see his face, but she would know those mile-wide shoulders anywhere.

"Good morning, Ruby." Lorenzo Davis ambled out of the shadows. Two huge buckets of water sloshed at his sides as he made his way to the end stall. "You are early."

"Only twenty minutes." She'd meant to be earlier, but the roads had been slow going with a thick layer of ice. It had been all Solomon could do to keep his footing. "I'm surprised to see you packing water. Isn't that the stable boy's job?"

"Sure, but I help with the barn work." His answer came lightly as he hefted one of the buckets over the wooden rail. Water splashed into a washtub. "Stay back, Sombrero, or you'll get wet again."

Inside the stall, a horse neighed his opinion. A hoof stomped as if in a protest or a demand to hurry up with the water. The man had a way with animals, she had to give him credit for that. His powerful stance, his rugged masculinity and his ease as he lifted the second ten-gallon bucket and emptied it etched a picture into her mind. That picture took on life and color, and when she blinked, it remained. Another image of the man she could not forget. Her soul sighed just a little. She couldn't help it.

Solomon nudged her a second time, gently reminding her she was doing it again—staring off into thin air when there was work to be done. She shook her head, cleared her thoughts and gently patted her gelding's shoulder. "Where can I put up my boy?"

"I'll take him." Lorenzo set down the bucket and held out a hand to Solomon. "You remember me, don't you, old fella?"

The swaybacked animal snorted in answer. His ears

pricked, he snuffled Lorenzo's palm with his muzzle, gray with age. His low-noted nicker was clearly a horsy greeting. Did every living creature adore the man?

"Are you nervous about starting your new job?" He caught Solomon's reins. If he noticed the leather straps were wearing thin, he didn't comment.

"Just a tad." That was an understatement, but she wasn't about to admit it. All she could see was doom. So much could go wrong to cause Mrs. Davis to change her mind or for the stern-looking Lucia to fire her. Anxiety clawed behind her rib cage like a trapped rodent.

Just breathe, she told herself. No need to panic.

Lorenzo's intensely dark blue eyes glowed softly as if he cared. While his gaze searched hers, she felt as if she were the only woman on earth. His slow smile spread wonderfully across his mouth. Like the sun dawning, his smile could light up her life if she let it.

"Everything will be just fine." Lorenzo's hand settled on her shoulder, a pleasantly heavy weight meant to be comforting.

It wasn't. Why was he touching her? The panic clawing inside her chest doubled. Maybe he was trying to soothe her, but it unnerved her. Air squeezed through her too-tight throat in a little hiccup.

His hand didn't move, his touch remained like out of a dream. Was she really smiling up at him, so close she could see the nearly black threads in his irises and the smooth-shaven texture of his square jaw? Good thing she was independent, because a woman less confident might be tempted to lay her cheek on the powerful plane of his chest.

Not her, but some other woman might let herself

dream what it would be like when he folded his iron-hewn arms around her and held her tightly.

It was a good thing she had her feet firmly on the ground. Because that wasn't what she wanted. Nope, not at all. What she wanted was to save her family's farm. To lessen her father's burden.

Solomon blew out his breath, drawing her out of her thoughts. Lorenzo moved away, rubbed the gelding's nose. "Go in the back door. Just follow the path around the side of the house."

"Take good care of my boy." She lifted her chin, trying to shake away the effects from being too near to the man. He was an absolute hazard.

"I'll treat him like my own. Right, Solomon?" That irresistible kindness rumbled in the low notes of his voice.

Her heart fluttered against her will as she watched both horse and man head down the dim aisle.

A little strength, Lord, please. Strength to resist the man's warmth and decency, strength to put one foot in front of the other and face the grim Lucia, strength to make it through the day without making any mistakes. It was a lot to ask for, but she thought of her father's burdens and added, *for my pa.*

Horse hooves clomped behind her, and she spun around. A roan horse flared his nostrils at her, bared his teeth and careened to a stop. On his back sat a woman she did not know, who was a few years older.

"So you are the new girl." Her tone was not friendly. Her green eyes squinted with a hint of disdain. "You must have been a pity hire."

A pity hire? Heat stained her face. Lorenzo heard that. He might have been gracious enough to disregard her patched shoes and secondhand dress, but this woman was not. Ruby lifted her chin higher. This job mattered to her. That's why she was here. Not to compete with another maid for his attention.

"Lorenzo." The newcomer brightened when she spotted the boss's son. She swung down from her horse with the air of a princess leaving her throne. Her attention riveted to the man stroking Solomon's cheek. Her smile was breathtaking. "I didn't know you would be in the barn this morning. This is my lucky day."

"Not mine, as I've been packing water." His smile had vanished, but his kindness had not. "I'll have Thacker see to your roan. Mae, this is Ruby."

The moment between them had broken. With the gelding's reins in hand, he took a step backward and tipped his hat in farewell. A tiny pain clutched behind her sternum as he withdrew into the shadows. She was *not* smitten with the man. She was utterly in charge of her heart.

"You won't last the day." Mae shook her head as if she were an experienced judge of such things. "Whatever happens, don't think I will do any of your work."

"No, of course not, I—" But the woman took off, leaving her alone in the barn. A horse stretched his neck over the top of his railing and tried to catch the hem of her scarf with his teeth.

That could have gone better, she thought as she tucked the scarf around her throat. She squared her shoulders and took a deep breath. At least there would be no shoe disasters today. Last night, she'd spent an hour and a half tightening and repairing all the threads holding her shoe buttons in place. Confidently, she launched out of the barn and into the snow.

That was the key. To be confident. To visualize a good outcome instead of disaster. This would be her new attitude. She breathed the wintry air deep into her lungs until they burned and breathed out great, white clouds of fog. Her shoes crunched on the path, her skirts rustled and swirled with her gait. She had to concentrate on her work and not on Lorenzo. Forget how handsome he'd looked. Forget how kind. Make her heart stop fluttering because he'd smiled at her.

Her family's livelihood hung in the balance.

The sky began to change to a lighter shade of gray. The beauty of the still plains, sleeping snow and amazing world buoyed her spirits. The enormous house rose up in front of her with bright windows and smoke curling from numerous chimneys. Far up ahead, Mae yanked open a door. A few moments later, Lucia appeared on the threshold, gesturing impatiently. "Let's get you in a uniform. You can't work for the mistress wearing that."

"Yes, ma'am." The panic returned, clawing her with a vengeance. She hurried up the steps and the minute her wet shoes hit the floor, *squeak. Creak.*

Great, Ruby. Just great. She slipped out of her coat and hung it on a nearby wall peg.

"Definitely a pity hire," Mae whispered from the far side of the foyer.

Not knowing what to say, Ruby dutifully followed the head housekeeper. *Squeak, creak.*

It was going to be a very long day.

A weak sun filtered through a thin blanket of quick-moving clouds. Although at its zenith, the bright disc gave no warmth. The arctic winds dominated, burning the high Montana prairie with its bitter chill. In his warmest coat, Lorenzo's teeth chattered as he trudged the snow-covered path to the house. He could tell himself he hurried along the path at a breakneck speed because he couldn't wait to unthaw in front of a fire with a cup of tea and a hot meal, but that would be a lie.

His gaze searched through the main-floor windows. His toe caught on a snow clump. His right foot skidded on a patch of ice. Did he watch where he was going? No, he didn't lift his eyes from the house. He spotted his mother in the parlor, working at her embroidery. Lucia bustled around the dining room table, checking that everything was ready for the family's meal. He spotted Mae at a window above the kitchen's water pump but saw no sign of Ruby.

He had thought of nothing else all morning. He'd finished his barn work, hauled hay and taken a pick once again to the cattle's water supply. He'd spread out bags of feed corn and stopped to doctor a cow who had a painful run-in with a coyote, but Ruby stayed front and center in his mind, a beautiful song he could not forget.

"Renzo!" Boots pounded on the path behind him. His cousin, Mateo, fell in stride beside him. Mateo was a few years older, a few inches shorter and a dedicated cattleman. "You spent a lot of time in the horse barn this morning."

"Not much more than usual." Snow scudded across the pathway ahead of him as he debated slowing down or speeding up. His cousin had a sharp eye; he didn't miss much. Not ready to have a member of his family aware that he was sweet on Ruby, he launched forward, faster. If Mateo wanted to give him a hard time, let him at least have to work for it.

"Sure, you do your fair share with the horses, but did I see you tending one of the maids' horses?" Mateo caught up, breathing hard. "Don't tell me you have an interest in that ancient, swayback horse she was riding."

"Sure I do. Solomon and I are old friends." Maybe humor would distract his cousin, because the back door loomed closer and this was not a conversation he wanted anyone in the house to overhear. "I wanted to check on his shoe. I re-shod him yesterday."

"Oh, so that was the errand you went on." Mateo didn't look fooled. "Whoever the young woman is, she's awful pretty. She's easy on the eyes."

"Maybe you should stop looking." A furious power radiated through him as strong as iron, and he heard the growl in his words. Jealousy wasn't his style, so it surprised him.

"Sorry, man. I wasn't interested, really." Mateo's smile flashed. "But you are."

Couldn't he hide it better than that? He stomped the snow off his boots on the step and grasped the doorknob. "Let's keep it quiet. Ruby doesn't know."

"Sure. But when she rejects you, I'm next in line to beau her." Mateo probably wasn't serious, but his words were like an arrow to a target.

Would Ruby reject him if she knew about his feelings? She hadn't done one thing to confirm any affection on her part. Shy smiles, gentle humor, yes. But did she feel drawn to him? A weight settled on his chest as he turned the knob. The warmth of the kitchen pulled him in, but his knees knocked as he shrugged out of his coat. What he felt for Ruby was powerfully rare. It was gentle as a December sun dawning, as everlasting as the stars in the sky and so true it came from the deepest places in his soul.

He still did not know if he had a chance with her. Would she want him for a beau? What would he do if she didn't?

He shouldered into the kitchen doorway, searching for her in the ordered chaos. Cook sliced a roast chicken, steam billowed from a potato pot while workers scurried around putting food on platters and finding a colander for the boiling potatoes. Everything faded when he spied Ruby at the farthest worktable, transferring piping hot dinner rolls into a cloth-lined basket.

Gossamer tendrils of her platinum hair curled around her face as she bent over her work. He took in the long, lean curve of her arm, the straight line of her back and the way her every movement was graceful. She plopped the last roll into the basket and covered the baked goods to keep in the heat. How dear she looked in her dove-gray maid's dress and white apron. She spun around, holding the baking sheet with a hot pad in one hand and their gazes collided.

The chaos vanished, the clatter silenced and time froze. In the stillness, he saw her unguarded, with her feelings exposed. A lasso of emotion lashed around him and roped his heart to hers. For one perfect moment, they were bound and tied together in an immeasurable way, and he could see something he hadn't before. Her heart. Tenderness washed over him like grace.

"Hey, Romeo." Mateo lightly punched him in the shoulder. "Didn't you hear your pa? He's calling you."

He heard nothing but Ruby. When she shyly broke away, hope took root in his soul for what could be.

Chapter Five

Crocheting was harder than it looked, at least for her, but it gave her something to focus on aside from the fact that she had been forced to sit at one of the worktables crammed into the corner of the kitchen for her midday meal. When she'd gone to join the others at the table near the warm stove, all the chairs had suddenly become mysteriously saved for someone else.

No matter. She suspected her knowing Lorenzo might have something to do with it. Lorenzo. She hoped a sigh hadn't escaped her as she unhooked her crochet needle from the loop of white thread and gave it a tug. Hard-won stitches disappeared before her eyes, unraveling as she counted backwards to the place where she'd made the error.

She'd decided to learn to crochet because she figured working with one crochet hook instead of two knitting needles had to be easier, but she had been sorely mistaken. She inserted the hook, checked the pattern Scarlet had copied down for her and looped the thread three times. Concentrating, the morning's troubles slipped away.

"How is it going?" A man's voice sounded close to

her ear, and she startled. The needle tumbled from her grip, more stitches unraveled and the ball of thread rolled across the floor.

"Lorenzo." She gaped up at him like a fish out of water. Dashing in a dark, blue flannel shirt and black trousers, he knelt to retrieve the ball. "What are you doing here?"

"Scaring you, apparently." He handed over the thread, kneeling before her like a knight of old, so gallant every head in the room was turned toward him. Apparently she wasn't the only young woman on the staff who couldn't keep her eyes off him. His dimples framed his perfect smile as she took the ball. Her fingers bumped his, and the shock trailed up her arm like a lightning strike.

"You were right." She dropped the skein onto her lap. "Everything has gone fine. I'm trying to learn all I can."

"Good to hear. Do you mind if I join you?" He unfolded his big frame, rising to his six-foot height. His hand rested on the back of the chair beside her. "I thought we could catch up."

"But we talked a lot on the sleigh ride, and we aren't exactly friends."

"We can change that." He pulled out the chair, turning it sideways so that when he settled on the cushion, he faced her.

Not a good thing. How could she think with his handsomeness distracting her? Worse, the women at the other table had fallen silent, openly staring.

"What are you making?" He lowered his voice, perhaps hoping to keep the conversation just between the two of them.

"It's supposed to be a snowflake. For Christmas

ornaments." She held up the poor misshapen mess of stitches. So far, her greatest aptitude in the needle arts was crocheting, but she couldn't bring herself to admit that to Lorenzo. His nearness tied her in knots, and she wondered what he really saw when he looked at her. Although she wore a uniform just like the other maids, she could still feel her patches. A world separated her and Lorenzo. So, why was he really talking to her?

"It does look like a snowflake." He tilted his head to one side, studying the rows of stitching. "You were working on this when I came by the other night."

"Yes, although I already finished that one. I'm making them for Christmas gifts and to add to my hope chest." She blushed, aware of how that must sound. "Not that I'm hopeful or anything. It's just something girls do."

"I'm aware. My sister has one, too." He relaxed comfortably against the chair back and planted his elbow on the table. A shaft of watery sunshine tumbled through the window, bronzing the copper highlights in his dark hair and worshiping the angled artistry of his face. "Bella and my mother do a lot of sewing for her hope chest. They have been at it for years now."

"That sounds nice. It must be wonderful to have a ma." She tried not to think of all the ways she missed the mother she'd never known. She fingered the half-made snowflake, trying to imagine what it would have been like to sew alongside a mother. "Yours is especially nice."

"I'll keep her. Who taught you to sew? Your aunt?"

"No, my Aunt June didn't have the time to spare." She bit her bottom lip, remembering those hard times when her father had been injured. "I'm mostly self-taught. After Pa was well and we moved out of our uncle's house, I had to figure out how to mend everyone's clothes. I wasn't that good, but when we moved here to Angel Falls, my new friends took pity on me."

"Not pity." His dark eyes grew darker with interest. "I'm sure they couldn't help adoring you on that first day you came to school."

"Me? No." Shyness gripped her, and she bowed her head, breaking away from the power of his gaze. She didn't want him to see too much or to know how sorely her feelings had been hurt on her first day of school. "I was the new girl and didn't know anyone. I think they felt sorry for me."

"I know I did."

Mortified, time flashed backward, and in memory, she was at her desk in the back row. Sunshine warmed the classroom and open windows let in the fresh smells of growing grass and the Montana wind. Shouts and shoes drummed as kids rushed toward the door for lunch break, but Narcissa Bell's voice rose above every sound. "Does it look as if I want to be friends with you? What is your name?"

"R-Ruby." She bowed her head, miserable beyond description. Her first day of school. She'd come with hopes of making friends.

"I'm going to call you Rags. Look at that dress."

Girls had laughed as they pranced by in their tailored frocks in the latest fabrics and styles, in their shining new shoes and hair ribbons and bows. She'd felt her face blaze tomato red as her dreams of making friends shattered.

She hadn't realized Lorenzo had witnessed the whole thing. What had he thought at the time? He was friends with Narcissa. They were in the same circle of friends. Had he gazed at her that first day with pity, too?

"I remember you wound up eating lunch with Meredith and her group." No sign of pity marked his chiseled, lean face. "You were hard not to notice, being the new girl and the prettiest."

"Not the prettiest, not by far." How could he say such a thing? She squirmed in her chair, uncomfortable but grateful, because his generous compliment took the sting out of the memory of Narcissa's taunting. "But I could be the most blessed. I got a new circle of friends that day. The best friends anyone could have."

"That is a great blessing," he agreed, so sincere, she found herself leaning in a little closer, drawn to him in a way she could not control.

"God was watching over me." She would never forget how it had felt when Fiona, Meredith, Lila, Kate, Scarlet and Earlee had approached her with friendly smiles and asked her to eat with them. "They asked me to join their sewing circle. We try to meet every week."

"And so they have helped you with your sewing."

"And my kitting and crocheting." She gestured to the delicate circle of stitching cradled in the folds of her apron. "They are like family to me."

"It had to be rough, thinking you might have to leave them." Understanding arced between them, and aware of the women sipping their after-lunch tea at the nearby table, he lowered his voice further. "With this job, will you be able to stay in Angel Falls?"

"I don't know, but right now I have a job, and I'm grateful for it. Thanks to you."

"Me? I didn't do a thing."

"You said something to your mother, didn't you? You were the reason she chose me."

"She did the choosing all on her own. It was my father, actually, who influenced her."

"Your father? I've never met him." Bewilderment crinkled her porcelain forehead and adorably twisted the corners of her rosebud mouth. "Why would he do that for me?"

"He's met your father and liked him." Tenderness became like an ailment that afflicted him more every time his gaze found hers. He could not forget what he'd seen her in her eyes. Encouraged, he tried not to think of all the ways she could still reject him. "Tell me about your family. Surely now your father still isn't planning to move?"

"It's hard to say." She bowed her head, and gossamer strands escaped from her braid to tumble over her china-doll face. She couldn't hide her worry, not from him. He read it in her posture, in the tight line of her fine-boned jaw and the tiny sigh that escaped her.

Something was still wrong, something he hadn't been able to fix. He wanted to. "Tell me," he urged gently.

"My brother lost his job." She shrugged one slim shoulder, as if it were nothing to worry about. "He will be home again, and that is the good news. Pa and I have missed Rupert terribly. There is always a silver lining."

He realized she hadn't answered his question. An answer of sorts. "You are an optimistic woman."

"It's new. I've made up my mind. No more visions of doom."

"That's a good philosophy. Are you able to follow

it?" He reached out, uncertain if he should touch her, if she was ready for that.

"I don't know, as today is the first day I'm using it." Her eyes widened at his touch. She took a sharp intake of breath as if she was surprised, but she didn't move away.

"How is it going so far?"

"B-better than expected."

"That's how my day has been, too." Hope was a powerful thing, and the moment his fingertips grazed her cheek, wishes came to life within him. He wanted to be the man she turned to, the man who could right all the wrongs in her life, the one man she could count on forever.

If she didn't move away with her family. If his parents accepted her. Tension knotted him up, and he willed it away. He wouldn't worry about the future, just this moment.

Her cheek was as soft as ivory silk. Her hair felt as luxurious as liquid platinum and tickled the backs of his knuckles when he brushed away those flyaway tendrils. Five kinds of tenderness roared to life within him. Please, he silently pleaded, please feel for me what I do for you.

Her gaze searched his, and in that moment of connection, he felt a click in his heart, like a lock turning. He folded those gossamer locks behind her ear, but the sensation remained, as if another room had opened within him and there was more space to fill with love for Ruby.

What would she do if she knew?

"You cook, you sew, you crochet." The words sounded strained, and there was no way to hide it. At least she couldn't tell his pulse galloped like a startled jackrabbit. "Do you sing?"

"Very badly, at least that's my fear. I hum at home while I'm doing housework, to spare my father the sound of my voice."

"Surely he hears you humming?"

"I'm very quiet, and he's been gracious enough not to complain. So far. Who knows what would happen if I were to break out in song." She picked up her needle and thread so she would have something to do besides falling into his incredible eyes. "My singing might cause Pa to go deaf, break every glass on the kitchen shelves and draw rodents in from the fields. All very good reasons for me to stick to humming."

"You're funny, Ruby." His chuckle rumbled richly, and he leaned in closer as if to consider this new side of her.

She had been serious, but if he wanted to think she was humorous she wouldn't argue. She fit the crochet needle into a stitch. She concentrated on tightening the thread around it, not too tight to ruin the gage, but her hands were trembling. Breathless, she tried to forget the lingering tingle on her cheek where Lorenzo had brushed a strand of hair from her eyes. His manly presence made her forget where she was, who she was, why she could not let herself wish.

But if she *could* wish, it would be to have the chance to lose herself in his eyes. To sit basking in the manly assurance of his presence. To listen to his laughter ring one more time.

Lorenzo was a wonderful dream. But that's all he could be. She thought of the look on her father's face when he'd told her of Rupert's letter.

"Are you joining the caroling group at church?" His velvety baritone rang as private as a whisper. "The first practice is this evening."

"Tempting, but I'm not sure if I will." She thought of her father's discouragement. The last thing she wanted was to leave him alone with his worries. "I thought maybe, but that was before Rupert's news. I should stay home, although my friends are going."

"Any chance they might persuade you?"

"Who knows? Maybe. I have to see how my father is first." She wound her needle around the thread to make a single crochet stitch. "I suppose you will be there?"

"That's my plan. It gets me out of the house."

"Why? You're obviously close to your family." She stopped midstitch. "You must like spending time with them."

"Sure, but this time of year? My mother is preoccupied with her Christmas ball planning. My sister and I barely hear about anything else."

"Sounds truly tragic. How do you survive it?"

"Exactly. She wants to know who I'm escorting this year, so the farther away I can get, the better." Humor polished his striking features. "I take refuge at the church. It's a fun time. You should think about coming."

"I should?" She nearly choked on her words. Why, it almost sounded as if he wanted her to be there, as if he had a personal interest in her. Shock rattled her, the crochet hook tumbled from her hand and clattered to the floor. Lorenzo Davis could not be interested in her. That was simply her fanciful nature carrying her away again.

"Reverend Hadly makes it enjoyable. Mostly it's the old gang from school, so it's good to see everyone and catch up. We head over to the diner during our break for dessert. It's a good time."

"Oh, I'm sure." Was she imagining the glint of hope in his eyes as he waited for an answer to his question? Authentic, patient, solid, he was gilded by the light.

Did Lorenzo Davis like her, even a little? Yes, she realized, accepting it finally. The breath rushed out of her, her lungs seized up and one hiccup squeezed out of her too-tight throat. She watched, dizzy with the possibility as Lorenzo knelt to retrieve her crochet hook.

The thick, sandy brown fall of his hair glinted in the sunlight, the muscles in his shoulders bunched as he rose from the floor, and he held out the needle on his wide palm. Why was her heart beating double time?

As she snared her crochet hook, her fingertips unavoidably bumped his hand. The emotional charge that zinged through her scared her. She cared for him more than she'd realized. She fisted her hand around the crochet hook and bowed her head.

Why now, Lord? She'd lived in Angel Falls since April. For nine months, her life had been fine, uneventful and settled. Until now.

"I imagine you have a lot of chores waiting for you at home after your shift here." Kindness was his best feature. It lit him softly, filling his soulful eyes with caring she could not deny.

"Yes. Pa is helpless in the kitchen. I'll have supper to fix and dishes to do." His caring settled within her, making her shaky, making her want to escape. "So it's not likely I'll be able to go tonight."

"That's too bad. I hope your friends can persuade you."

He rose from the chair, towering over her, and it was

his heart she saw. His regard she felt. He jammed his hands in his pockets, squared his mighty shoulders and disappointment resonated in his eyes, darkening the color to a sad, midnight blue. "You work hard, Ruby. You deserve to have a little fun."

"I'm just trying to do what's right for my family."

"I know. I admire it." The sunlight chose that moment to dim as he turned away, his boots plodding crisply on the wood floor. She squeezed her eyes shut, unable to breathe as sorrow set in.

If wishes were pennies, she would be rich. She bowed her head, wrapped the thread around her hook to double crochet but couldn't keep her hand steady.

Don't think what it would be like to be beaued by him, she told herself. Some things in life were not meant to be.

If anyone needs help, Lord, it's Ruby. Lorenzo plucked his coat from the wall peg. Saddened by her situation, he jabbed one arm into the sleeve. He understood the meaning of the word *responsibility.* Family before self. Work before play. He admired Ruby's values. He didn't know if this would ever work out. His heart kept pulling him toward her. Nothing could stop it.

"Renzo?" Pa's cane tapped in the hallway. "You got a moment? Come talk to me."

"Sure thing." With his coat unbuttoned, he left his muffler and hat on the pegs and bypassed the kitchen door. Could he help that his gaze slid into the room, searching for her? No. She sat hunched over her snowflake, carefully moving the steel needle in and out and through her crochet work, so dear his soul ached at the sight. Aware of his father watching, he tore his attention away, steeled his spine and stepped into the empty dining room. "What do you need, Pa?"

"I heard you were talking with the new kitchen maid." Pa ambled over to the tea service set up on the breakfront and chose a cup. He sounded casual, but something deeper resonated in his tone. Disapproval. "Is that right?"

"Yes." He wondered how Pa had known, and so quickly. Perhaps one of the other maids, or maybe Lucia, who had a sharp eye. "I know Ruby from school."

"So you weren't speaking to her about her work?"

"No, why would I? I didn't know I was banished from the kitchen. What's this about, Pa?"

"I know you're friendly with the girl. I have sympathy for her situation, too. But you know the rules, Renzo." Pa poured a cup of steaming tea and set down the silver pot with a clink and clatter. "No fraternizing with the hired help. It distracts them."

"Yes, but Ruby isn't just the hired help." He straightened his spine, drawing up all the inner strength he possessed. "I saw her during her lunch break so I wouldn't interfere with her work. There's nothing wrong with that."

"You can't have it both ways. She's either a maid or a friend. House rules. That's how it is." Pa dropped a sugar cube into his cup and stirred. "I thought you wanted her to get the job."

"I did. I appreciate that Ma chose her."

"Then what's the problem? It's not like she's part of your circle, anyhow. Are you heading back out to the fields?"

"I want to make sure we solve the water problem

today. I don't want to keep packing water when we could be pumping it."

"Don't blame you there." Gerard cradled his cup, unable to hide the yearning in his eyes. "Truth is, I wish I could go with you."

"I'd sure like that, but you know what Ma would say."

"She would be after my hide, that's for sure. That woman has forbidden me to lift a hand on my own land."

"For good reason. You had best keep on Ma's good side." He back trailed out of the room.

"That's the truth. I don't want to stir up that woman's ire." Pa grinned easily. "Holler if you need any supplies from the hardware store. At least I could make myself useful driving to and from town."

"Sorry, I already have what I need. If that changes, I'll let you know."

On his way to the back door, he passed by the kitchen again. Remembering Pa's warning, he didn't look into the room. No way would he cost Ruby her job. But did that stop his wish to see her?

No. Wrestling down his disappointment, he yanked on his hat and scarf and opened the door. Arctic air cocooned him as tromped down the steps. Something tugged him back, and he spun around. In the golden, lamp-lit window, Ruby was back at work pouring hot water into a wash basin. The steam rose like mist around her. It took all his strength to ignore the twist of affection in his chest. He kept on going until the cold and the storm claimed him.

Chapter Six

"Ruby, you've gotten terribly quiet." Meredith commented from the front seat of her fashionable sleigh. She gave the reins an experienced tug to turn her mare, Miss Bradshaw, off Main Street.

"Is something wrong?" Scarlet brushed red tendrils out of her eyes as she squinted at Ruby. "I couldn't believe how hard we had to argue to get you into the sleigh."

"We practically had to drag you," Lila chimed in, cuddled next to her on the backseat. "You must be tired after your first day at your new job."

"There was a lot to learn." And more she'd left undone at home, but her father had insisted. Ruby tried to bury her worry over that, glad three of her friends had driven out of their way to her home to coax her into going. And Lorenzo? Somehow she had to erase the image of him kneeling before her, holding out her crochet hook, looking so handsome her teeth ached. "Some of the other maids weren't exactly friendly to me today, so it was a little more challenging than I'd anticipated."

"How could they not love you?" Lila asked as she

tucked in the cashmere robes more snugly. "We think you are a dear."

"I am a disaster." She couldn't forget what she'd seen on Lorenzo's face. He cared about her.

"A disaster?" Meredith guided Miss Bradshaw along the snowy lane. "Did something terrible happen at work?"

"Not one thing. Multiple things." She rolled her eyes. "I burned my hand, broke a teacup and spilled beet juice down the front of my white apron. Lucia was very annoyed with me."

"You were nervous, that's all." Scarlet lifted a hand to wave at Earlee on the other side of the street as the sleigh slowed to a stop. "Tomorrow will be better, you'll see."

"Much better. You won't be nearly as nervous," Lila agreed. "Just relax. The Davis family is lucky to have you."

"Thanks. You guys are good to me." Encouraged, she sat straighter on the seat. Her friends were some of her greatest treasures. Footsteps crunched in the snow, drawing nearer as Earlee broke away from the shadowy, newly built, two-story schoolhouse, where she taught the lower grades.

"I hope you all know what you're doing, inviting me along." Happiness drew pink in her cheeks and twinkles in her blue eyes. "I'm a horrible singer."

"Then we can be horrible together." Ruby folded back the driving robe and scooted over to make room for her friend. "I can't carry a tune."

"I can't hold a note." Earlee, adorable in her fur-lined cloak, tucked her lunch pail, schoolbooks and slate onto the floorboards before settling on the cushioned seat. "You all have to be honest with me. If I'm bringing down the quality of the caroling, I will bow out joyfully."

"That goes for me, too." Ruby's head jerked as the sleigh took off. "Why am I seeing disaster?"

"You always see disaster." Lila chuckled.

"I'm trying to keep my spirits up, but it's harder than it looks." Her words made everyone in the sleigh laugh, so the atmosphere was merry as Miss Bradshaw pulled them down the road to the white, steepled church.

"Do you think Lorenzo will be there?" Scarlet asked as the sleigh bumped to a stop.

Yes. Ruby bit her lip to keep in the word. Because if she said she knew that Lorenzo would be coming, think of the questions! How on earth could she explain what had happened over her lunch break?

"He sang in the caroling group last year, remember?" Meredith was the first to climb out into the snow. "It stands to reason he will sing this year, too."

"Ruby, you work for the family." Lila took Meredith's hand and climbed carefully from the front seat. "Did you get a chance to ask him if he's coming tonight?"

"He's coming." Her heart skipped a beat. No questions, she prayed as she stumbled onto the icy ground. Her shoes skidded, and she groped for the side of the sleigh before her feet went out from under her.

"Whoopsy." Scarlet caught her elbow, helping to steady her. "Are you okay?"

"Sure, as long as I don't step on that patch of ice again." She smiled. It seemed as if no one would quiz her about Lorenzo, because her friends started calling out to Kate, who gave the final buckle of her horse's blanket a tug before trudging their way. Perfect timing.

"Guess who is walking this way? He must have left his horse at the livery." Kate swiped snowflakes out of her eyes. "Did he get extra handsome when we weren't looking?"

"I think so." Scarlet squinted through the downfall where a man's shadow skirted the side of the church. "Every time I look at him, my heart goes thump."

"Unrequited love is rough on a girl." Kate sighed as they watched him stride closer.

"Very," Scarlet agreed. "I feel so sorry for you, Kate. I'm sure he's about to fall in love with me any minute."

"No, because he's about to fall in love with me," Kate argued good-naturedly and they dissolved into muffled laughter. "What about you, Ruby? Aren't you going to pine after Lorenzo with us?"

Good question. Even from a distance, she could feel his presence. Her heart tugged, her spirit stilled. She blinked snowflakes off her lashes, staring down at the patch on her shoe. "Are you kidding? You two have been admiring him much longer than me, so you should get dibs."

"Hey, less competition for me." Scarlet gave Ruby's hand a squeeze. "Look, he's heading into the church. If we time it right, we'll be right ahead of him. He'll have to notice us."

"No, I want to help Meredith with her horse. You two go on." Shame washed over her. It was all she could do to give Scarlet a reassuring smile and a nod to go ahead. Her friends were in love with Lorenzo. How could that enormous fact slip her mind? She watched Kate and Scarlet scamper arm in arm up the walkway, Lorenzo approaching.

How would they feel if they knew about this afternoon? That Lorenzo hadn't simply been courteous to her, he'd been friendly. No, more than friendly. A horrible feeling clutched her stomach, proof she'd done something wrong. It was like going behind their backs to move in on the man both Kate and Scarlet wanted. It wasn't like that—that wasn't what had happened—but that's how she felt.

She loved her friends so dearly. She couldn't jeopardize their friendship. Ever. That was the most important reason of all for her to keep her eyes down. No more looking at Lorenzo and wishing.

She heard his boots crunch in the snow. His gait stopped. Her face heated, but she did not look up. She knew he was looking her way. Nervous, she spun around and spied the horse blanket tucked under the front seat.

"Thanks for picking me up, Meredith." She un-wedged the folded wool from beneath the springs. "But you can't go out of your way for every practice."

"Hopefully, we won't have to drag you to those. And if we do, my term is done in a few more weeks. No more teaching, so I'll have plenty of time to talk you into loving caroling practice." Meredith gave the knot she'd tied at the tether post a tug to test it and satisfied, circled around to take charge of the blanket.

"Great." Ruby rolled her eyes. It was nice being wanted. "So, do you mean done with teaching? Or done as in the term is over?"

"This will be my last term. At least for now."

"But teaching is so important to you. I thought you loved it." She hated being aware of the crackle of a man's boots in the snow. Lorenzo. Had he been standing still watching all this time? Dismay seized her stomach.

"I love my work, but I love Shane more." She shook

out the warm horse blanket. Happiness lit her up. Being engaged and in love with Shane looked good on her. "I can't wait any longer to start our life together. I can't stand being apart from him."

"Does this mean you've set a wedding date?" *Just forget Lorenzo,* she told herself. *Don't listen to him walking away.* "How soon will you get married?"

"After the new year, but don't tell anyone. I planned to announce it tonight when we took a break." Beaming, Meredith settled the blanket over the mare's broad back. "Shane has bought the Beckham place."

"That big ranch that was for sale? Oh, this means you and Fiona will be neighbors. How wonderful!" She gave Meredith a hug. She thanked God how beautifully her friend's life was coming together. Her teeth started chattering.

"It's cold out here. Go in, get out of this weather." Meredith knelt to fasten the blanket. "Don't look at me like that, I can get the buckles myself. Go on with you. Teacher's orders."

"All right, if you are sure."

"I'm sure. No reason both of us should get colder." Meredith knelt to secure the first buckle. Miss Bradshaw waited patiently, twitching her tail as the snow gathered on her mane.

Lorenzo. She hadn't taken two steps before he stopped on the path ahead of her, stopped and glanced over his wide shoulder. Their gazes collided. For one instant she forgot everything—her job, her family, her duty, her friends. The dreams buried in her soul surfaced. What would it be like to be beaued by him? To see the caring in his eyes shine only for her?

Footsteps padded behind her, fast and hurried, petticoats rustled as someone rushed up the path in a hurry. Not Meredith, she realized too late.

"What are you doing here, Rags?" Narcissa Bell circled around her as if she were avoiding a rodent in her path. "Don't tell me you're singing tonight?"

No need to answer. She held her chin steadily, refusing to let her head drop. Why Narcissa? Why now?

"Well, that's the trouble with church." She dropped her voice so only Ruby could hear. "They let in just any poor trash. Lorenzo, wait for me! Lorenzo?"

She tried to keep her chin up, she really did, but it bobbed down of its own accord. Narcissa ran away on her beautiful, perfect, brand-new shoes, racing to catch up to Lorenzo.

"Are you okay, Ruby?" Meredith took her hand. "I could bring her down a peg. In fact, maybe I will do just that."

"Please, don't. I'm fine."

"I heard what she said to you. It was just plain mean."

"I would rather forget it. Turn the other cheek." Not only was it her faith, but she could not risk Lorenzo overhearing. She was embarrassed enough. No doubt he was wondering why she hadn't spoken to him, why she hadn't smiled, when he'd expressed interest in her being here tonight. Her heart twisted with raw pain, and it wasn't because of Narcissa.

The instant she stepped into the church, the low, pleasant rumble of his voice rose above all the others. She shrugged out of her coat, hardly aware of hanging it on a peg, and followed Meredith into the sanctuary.

Maybe if she didn't meet his gaze, he would simply stop liking her. Things could go back to the way they used to be before she accepted her first ride in his sleigh.

"Gather 'round!" Reverend Hadly clapped, pitching his voice above the merry chatter of the carolers. "Grab a music book on your way up here. What a big group we have this year."

Lorenzo. She could feel the tug of his gaze, like gravity pulling her. Melted snow glistened in his thick, brown hair. Was it her imagination, or did he seem even taller, his shoulders mountain-strong, his presence more riveting?

He'd become more handsome since she'd seen him last. Kate was right.

It's better if you stopped liking him, Ruby. Just find a way to turn your feelings off. A book was shoved in her hands. She blinked against the overly bright lamplight. "Thanks, Meredith."

"Ruby? You're a soprano like Kate. Come this way." Meredith's voice came as if from miles away.

Dimly, she followed her friend, accepted a place next to Kate at the far end of the group.

The reverend's pitch pipe blared, rising above the group's chatter. Silence fell.

"Let's warm up our voices. Sopranos." The minister turned his attention to her section and held the note. "Ahhh."

"Ahhs" erupted around her. Kate's sweet soprano rang in her right ear. Scarlet, on her left, cozied up to whisper. "Sing, Ruby. You have a lovely voice."

She wanted to argue—hers was by far the worst in the group—but that wasn't the reason she didn't sing. Lorenzo's gaze found hers across the crowd of people and rising voices, silence amid the noise. Voices faded, the music dimmed until there was only the hint of his smile. Something deep within her heart leaped. How tempting to let herself sink into the feeling and into the caring in his eyes. How easy it would be to just let herself fall.

"Did you see?" Scarlet leaned in to whisper. "I think Lorenzo is looking at me."

"No, he's looking at me," Kate murmured, eyes merry. "Do you see the look on his face?"

"One of pure love." Scarlet sounded a little dreamy.

"Definitely," Kate agreed. "You know what that means? He's falling for one of us."

"Finally." Scarlet gave an endearing sigh. "Wishes really do come true."

She wanted those wishes to be for Scarlet or Kate. They deserved them. They deserved Lorenzo. She tucked away her feelings, clenched the songbook more tightly and forced her gaze from his. There could be no more moments like this, no wondering what could be. Yes, this would definitely be much easier if she didn't like him so much.

"Altos! Join in." Reverend Hadly turned to the next group and offered them a lower pitch with his pipe. "Ahhhs" broke out in a chorus, a few voices off-key so he blew the pipe again.

Father, please give Kate or Scarlet a chance with Lorenzo. They both deserve great happiness. She hoped one of them would win Lorenzo's heart. He was a good man, the very best. Absolutely good enough to marry and give one of her best friends a happily-ever-after.

"Very good!" The reverend praised. "Tenors. Here's your note."

Low-toned voices broke out in a slow, steady pitch. Why could she pick out Lorenzo's voice amid all the others? She tried to close her ears to him. Impossible. She could not close her heart, either.

Ruby wasn't making this easy for him. Lorenzo leaned forward in his chair in the busy diner. Had Pa already spoken to her, the way he'd been warned earlier? Or had Lucia done it? Anger burned in his chest. But what could he do about it? He glanced across the room where she sat at a far table talking with her friends. Not once had she glanced his way. He knew, because he'd been watching her.

"Can you believe some people?" Narcissa leaned against his arm, seated beside him at the table. The clink and clatter of the diner came back into focus and he dragged his attention away from Ruby's table. Narcissa laid her hand on his forearm. "Bringing her own food? To an eating establishment? A slice of pie is a nickel. Honestly. Who can't afford that?"

He winced and shrugged off Narcissa's hold on him. This was a side of Narcissa he didn't like. She didn't capture his attention, she wasn't the one his interest returned to. Five tables away, Ruby nibbled on a cookie she'd packed, while a cup of tea steamed on the table in front of her. He was glad his mother had hired her. He wanted her life's burdens to ease.

Which meant he couldn't risk her job. No way.

"Not everyone is as fortunate as you are, Narcissa." Margaret Roberts stirred honey into her tea. "Remember, it's important to be charitable."

"I *am* charitable." Narcissa gave her ringlets a toss with the hand that wasn't clutching his arm. "I go through my closet twice a year and contribute some very quality frocks to the church donation barrel."

"I meant to feel Christian tolerance." Margaret rolled her eyes. "That's harder to do than to simply donate stuff you no longer want. I give away my used things, too."

Ruby. He shifted in his chair to get a better view of her. Lamplight shone like pale moonlight on her long, silken hair and caressed her ivory complexion. The faint ripple of her laughter at something one of her friends said had to be the dearest sound on earth. Despite her laughter, her eyes held the same reserve he'd seen in the kitchen. Her withdrawal from him was subtle, but he felt it all the way to his soul.

He feared it was his father's doing.

"Can you imagine having to wear secondhand clothes?" Narcissa's high-pitched words sailed over the tops of the other conversations in the diner.

He bit his tongue, not wanting to be unkind to a woman, but he didn't like Narcissa's viewpoint or the fact that, tables away, Ruby stiffened. Pink crept across her endearing face. She had to have overheard.

"Clothes other people have worn? How disgusting." Narcissa continued on. "Ugh. It gives me the shivers."

"Hush." He'd had enough. He pushed away from the table, the chair scraping angrily against the floor. "Stop picking on Ruby. I mean it, Narcissa. Not one more word."

"Who, me?" Innocent eyes batted up at him. "I'm not picking on anyone. It's not against the law to have an opinion."

"Well, I don't like it." He clamped his molars together, so furious that staying silent seemed like the wisest choice. He yanked his jacket off the back of the chair and marched blindly away. And that was the woman his mother wanted him to court?

"You're just jealous because she is the most beautiful girl in the room," he heard Margaret say over the angry knell of his boots.

"Me? Jealous? Over patched rags like that?"

He tugged a fifty-cent piece out of his pocket and caught his buddy's eye, who was still crowded around the table with the rest of the gang. James arched one eyebrow in a question. Lorenzo handed the coin over to their waitress.

"The pie was especially good tonight. Thanks, Teresa. Keep the change." He buttoned up on his way out the door. The snowfall fell in whimsical, artful flakes. They sailed lightly on the wind, spiraling in fairy-tale swirls. They batted his cheek and whirled away on his breath, and when he glanced over his shoulder... Ruby. He could see her through the front window.

She chatted away with her friends, as dear as could be, sipping on her cup of tea. Her fine white-blond hair framed her face in carefree wisps and curls. Her cheeks were still flushed pink from Narcissa's insult, but her quiet inner dignity shone through as she said something that made her friends chuckle.

Ruby was a gentle soul. He cared about her. He could not stop it. He didn't even want to try. He wanted to spend time getting to know her, sharing stories and feeling the radiance of her smile, but her life was precarious. He feared his parents wouldn't understand.

As if she felt his presence, she looked up. The smile drained from her mouth, the laughter from her face, as her gaze found his. In the space of one breath and the next, it felt as if their hearts connected, beating together as one. For one unguarded moment, he felt a longing so strong it buckled his knees. Was she wishing, too? Thinking she had to choose between keeping her job or their friendship?

The diner's door swung open, and his friends spilled out onto the boardwalk.

"Lorenzo!" James rushed over, tying his scarf. Time lurched forward, and Ruby turned away, but the connection between them remained. "Did you see? Austin just drove by with his new horses. They are fine!"

"I didn't notice." He reached into his pockets for his gloves. Ruby's back was to him, standing beside her table, gathering up her things.

"...patches," Narcissa finished saying with the haughty disdain he didn't like as she tumbled out the door. Innocent eyes met his. "Hi, Lorenzo. We were just talking about your family's Christmas ball. Margaret and I have already been shopping."

He shook his head, plunged his hands into his gloves and led the way down the street. Snowflakes flitted ahead and pirouetted around him like lost dreams impossible to catch.

Chapter Seven

Lord, please help me to do the right thing and avoid Lorenzo. Ruby wasn't sure if her prayer was an appropriate one, since surely God was very busy tending to true problems in the world, but she had no one else to turn to. The frigid early morning gleamed black in every direction. Snow crunched beneath Solomon's hooves, and the wind drove in straight from the north. She shivered, clenching her teeth to keep them from chattering.

It would be easier if Lorenzo wasn't in the barn, if he didn't greet her, if she couldn't see the caring in his eyes. Caring she could never have or deserve. She could still hear Kate and Scarlet playfully arguing over him. Worse, she could still picture her father gray with exhaustion when she'd arrived home late. He'd been sick with fatigue, trying to handle the housework on top of the barn work and all day spent walking far and wide looking for work.

Please, let him not be there. She sent one more prayer heavenward for good measure, as the structure loomed overhead.

Knowing shelter from the cold was close, dear old Solomon nickered low in his throat, as if with relief, and picked up his pace. He had no desire to avoid a certain dashingly handsome man, so he was more than happy to prance into the stable and blow out his breath to get some attention.

"Hello, Miss Ruby." Mateo strode in from the shadows of the stalls. He had the same strapping strength as Lorenzo did, although his features were rougher and his black eyes full of merriment. "It's a cold one this morning. How would Solomon feel about some nice, hot oats along with his rubdown?"

"I'm sure he would like it." She swung down awkwardly, not realizing how numb she'd become. Her feet hit the ground hard enough to rattle her teeth. She couldn't feel her toes.

"You go on in and warm up before your shift starts." Mateo took the gelding's reins, gently rubbing the horse's nose as if they were fast friends.

She patted Solomon goodbye and headed out into the cold, eyes peeled for any sign of Lorenzo. So far, nothing. Maybe he was out in the fields, feeding cattle. A girl could hope. She took off at a fast pace, relieved the coast stayed clear. Her footsteps echoed in the vast, lonely morning, where deep purple clouds tried to blot out the view of the twilit sky. All alone, she skidded on the icy pathway, slid on the steps and stumbled through the door. A broad-shouldered shadow towered over her.

Lorenzo. Not out in the fields, as she'd hoped. She skidded to a stop, gasped in shock and fought the panicked urge to leap back outside.

"Good morning." His baritone rang friendly. A smile beamed across his chiseled features.

She jerked her gaze to the floor, but it was too late. She'd seen the caring in his eyes and felt it like a touch against her cheek as she unbuttoned her coat. "Good morning."

"I noticed you made it to church last night." The warmth in his voice urged her to look up. "Looked like you were having fun."

"I was. I'm not sure I should have spared the time, but Pa talked me into going." She bit her lip and shrugged out of her coat. What was she doing? Talking with him when she ought to be pushing him away. "Then Meredith came by in her sleigh with Scarlet and Lila, and they wouldn't give up until I agreed to go."

"You sound glad that you did." Gentle like a touch, that voice, impossible to ignore.

"I was." Her eyes swept up of their own accord, their gazes connected, and all the words evaporated from her brain. Gone. Vanished. Why couldn't she get her feelings for him under control? Why did they grow with each heartbeat and each breath?

"Let me hang that up for you." He took her coat, a little shabby and patched on one sleeve.

"No, I mean—" Her protest came too late. Her coat already hung from a peg. She couldn't feel more awkward, probably looking like an idiot, standing in the entryway, just standing, struggling to find the right words. Not at all sure how she could tell him what she was honestly feeling. That she would much rather just go back to not knowing him. She was uncomfortable with him liking her.

He should be liking Scarlet or Kate. They deserved him. Their lives were stable. They weren't fearing they might be homeless before month's end.

"Ruby, do you want to drink a cup of coffee together?" He jammed one iron shoulder against the wall. "I know you have some time. You arrived really early."

"Yes, but I have to change into my maid uniform. I'm sure Cook could use my help. There are some things I need to work at, to get faster." She stumbled away from him, apology in her eyes and gentleness in her voice. "I slowed her down terribly yesterday. I don't want to do that again."

"Sure, I understand." A band of tension cinched around his chest, pulling tight as he watched her scurry away with a swish of her skirts and a flip of her braids. "I know what your job means to you."

"Thanks." She offered him one tentative smile and squeaked away on her worn-out shoes. He hated that hard times had come to her family and that the Ballards had been struggling for so long. He wished there was something he could do. He would start with finding out what his father may have said to her.

"Renzo, to what do I owe this pleasure?" His mother floated into the dining room. "You are always out in the fields this time of morning."

"I finished up with the early-morning fieldwork. Pa and I have papers to go over after breakfast." He gave his coffee another stir with his spoon, pushed away from the sideboard and crossed in front of the hearth, where a cheerful fire chased away the chill from the air. "Now that the water problem is fixed and the cattle are snug in the winter pasture, Pa decided it's time for me to learn about the books."

"A word of warning. Book work vexes your father." Ma poured a cup of tea. "He would much rather be outdoors with the animals. I suppose you're likely to feel the same."

"As it's so cold out, I don't mind staying in where it's warm. For now. I imagine I'll start feeling antsy midway through the day and need to get back out there."

"You are a fine rancher, son, and a hard worker. Your father and I couldn't be more proud of you." She landed a peck of a kiss to his cheek. "Now that I have you all to myself—"

"Sugar?" He interrupted her, sure she was going to bring up the Christmas ball again. The last of the invitations were going out this morning. He plopped two sugar cubes into her cup. Best to distract her. "Are you going to town today?"

"As a matter of fact, I am." Her forehead furrowed as she studied him thoughtfully. "I'm taking your sister in for a dress fitting. Our Christmas ball is fast approaching."

"Yes, I'm aware." Seemed there was no getting around this conversation. He grabbed his cup and headed over to the fireplace to finish thawing out. "I plan to skip it this year."

"What?" His mother dropped her teaspoon. "Don't tease me like that. I almost believed you."

He grinned. As if he could disappoint his mother. "You aren't going to make me get a new suit, are you? Last year's fits just fine."

"You would be more dashing in the latest fashion."

"I don't care about fashion." He took a sip of hot, strong coffee and spotted Ruby. She carried a china teapot so carefully she seemed afraid of dropping it as she stepped into the room.

Ruby. He lowered his cup, captivated as she padded

to the table and lowered the pot. Her dove-gray maid's dress and crisp, white apron looked darling on her, but he didn't speak to her, remembering his father's rules.

"Ruby, dear." Ma set her cup on the table. "Could you please move the coffeepot to the table?"

"Of course." She gathered up the coffeepot, not looking his way once. Even when she faced him, her eyes were solely on her work. Not one glance, not one smile.

"Just put that near my husband's chair. Thank you." Anyone could tell by Ma's indulgent smile that she was fond of Ruby. Who wouldn't be? It was impossible not to like her, and he'd passed "like" a long while ago.

"Ma, can we stop at the jeweler's after school, too?" His little sister, Bella, bounded in, her petticoats rustling, looking like a page out of Godey's. Her dark hair shone in the lamplight as brightly as the hope on her face. "I need something really sparkly to go with my new gown."

"We will see." Ma's standard answer when she was likely to say no. "Breakfast, first. Then school. Besides, your fitting may take up all the time we have to spare."

"I know, but I am still going to hope." Bella dropped into her seat and poured a cup of tea.

Ruby moved the sugar and creamer to the table before silently padding from the room. Still, not a single glance his way. He hated how stilted and unnatural it felt as she slipped out of sight.

"Good morning." Pa's cane tapped on the hardwood as he limped into the room. "Renzo, looking forward to cracking the books?"

"Why not? Arithmetic was my favorite subject in school. I might even like it." He took another sip of coffee, upset over Ruby. He really needed to talk to his father, but they weren't alone. And likely Ma would side with Pa.

"For your sake, I hope you do. There's more book work with running a big ranch than anyone wants to think about. And don't you look lovely this morning, Selma." Pa held out his arms.

"The same as always, Gerard." Ma stepped into his embrace and the happy pair cuddled, their love for each other as cozy as the fire blazing in the hearth. "Will you and Renzo need all day for the books? I have hopes of stealing you away this afternoon."

"You do? I wouldn't mind being stolen as long as I'm with you."

"Careful, Pa. I was nearly roped in to try on new clothes. Sounds like she might be trying to trap you next."

"Best stay away from that." Pa laughed as he held out his wife's chair for her. "I'm busy, Selma. All day. Terrible busy. Not a thing I can do about it."

"You men. What am I going to do with you?" Ma's merriment filled the room, but he hardly heard it. His sister rolled her eyes and poured honey into her tea. He plopped down in his chair, debating what to do.

He saw how Ruby's life was. Right now, her job was the only thing supporting her family. If her family's finances didn't improve, she could be moving away. They wouldn't have a chance.

Maybe he should just let his feelings for her go. Perhaps that would be best for her.

Frustrated, he shook his head, hating the roiled-up ball of confusion lodged in his chest.

When she reappeared through the door behind Mae, carrying a tray of oatmeal bowls, tenderness surged through him. She appeared so very serious as she kept the heavy tray balanced and level and convenient for Mae, who served bowls around the table.

Ruby inched closer to him, her gaze down as if absorbed in her task. His adorable Ruby. Emotion knotted him up so tight, all he could see was the platinum-haired beauty doing her best to avoid him.

"Aren't you done with the floor yet?" Cook didn't bother to hide her irritation as she slammed a lid on the soup kettle. "I've got the noon meal to get on the table, and here you are dallying."

"Sorry, ma'am." She inched backward on the floor. She'd been cleaning all morning long. Her arms ached as she scrubbed the brush around and around on the tile. She was doing the best she could, but she'd been too slow, and she was holding up the Davis's midday meal.

"I'm not helping her." An imperial voice rose above the whistle of the tea kettle. Mae swirled around a table. "*I* got my work done on time. Lucia will not be happy to hear about this."

Just keep working, Ruby. Around and around the scrub brush went, making quick progress toward the far side of the room. She was almost there. Her knees protested as she inched backward, still scrubbing. She squeezed the brush tighter and made the last swipes.

There, done. Relieved, she relaxed back on her heels and surveyed her work, breathing hard. The kitchen was huge, far larger than her family's entire shanty.

"At least you were thorough. Very thorough." Cook padded across the wet floor, face pruned as she squinted into corners and beneath the cabinets. She gave Mae a hard stare. "Unlike some people. Ruby, you go throw out that wash water, wash your hands. We have a meal to get on the table."

"Yes, ma'am." She rose to her feet, grateful. She would do better next time. She had to. Pa was counting on her. She gathered the brush and the bucket and hurried toward the door, dodged a frowning Mae and popped outside just long enough to send the wash water sailing in a sparkling arc into the snow at the side of the house. Her breath rose in great gusts and, teeth chattering, she bounded into the hallway. Lorenzo's coat still hung on its peg. She'd been aware of his presence all morning, though she did her best not to notice.

Maybe if she stopped looking at the man, her feelings for him would stop. It was worth a try, right? She stowed the bucket and brush in the closet and hurried toward the basin. She needed to get her hands washed so she could—

Her shoe slipped on the wet tile, skating right out from under her. She went down so hard and fast, she didn't have time to grab anything. She sailed backward through the air, reached out to break her fall and heard something snap. Pain screeched up her left arm as she slammed onto the floor. The back of her head hit and bounced off the tile, only to fall back with a final thud.

Ow. She lay stunned, hardly able to breathe. Spots danced in front of her eyes as she sat up. Her head whirled, and she had to blink hard to keep the room still. Fortunately, she was on the far side of the cook's table and cabinets. Maybe no one saw. Maybe if she could get up fast enough, she could pretend this new humiliation hadn't happened.

Excellent, Ruby. Just perfectly brilliant. Everything ached, but her pride hurt most of all.

She planted the palms of her hands on the wet floor and pushed to sit up. Sharp pain lashed through her left arm, and she bit her lip to keep from crying out. It hurt terribly.

Please, Lord, don't let it be broken. It can't be. Cradling her hurt arm to her chest, she pushed off with her right hand, rose slowly to her feet and headed straight to the wash basin. Her head hurt, her arm hurt. She felt bruised where she'd landed. When she went to grab the bar of soap, it, too, was blurry. She worked the pump handle and it was blurry. Any turn of her head made her skull pound. When she glanced slowly around, the entire kitchen was fuzzy.

"Are you all right, girl?" Cook plunked the lid onto its pot and broke away from the stove. "You hit mighty hard. Sit down and get your bearings."

It was a good idea, because honestly, the spots were getting worse. They had taken to swirling a little, and she was afraid if she sat down even for a minute, she wouldn't be able to get back up. If she couldn't do her job, then she wouldn't get paid. Her family needed her wages.

"I'm fine." She rubbed the bar of soap between her hands, agony shot through her left wrist, and her vision went momentary black. Pure will kept her upright. She rinsed beneath the stream of water from the pump spout. Holding her head very still, she gingerly patted her skin dry. Any movement of her left hand and forearm made her eyesight dim.

"You don't look fine." Cook bustled over. "You hit your head."

"I have a hard head." At least, she hoped that was true.

"You're as pale as a sheet." Cook squinted carefully, assessing. "Your eyes look off. Can you see all right?"

"It's nothing to worry about, truly." She appreciated the older woman's concern, but how could she admit the truth?

"I think we should fetch a doctor." Cook pursed her lips, debating. "I wonder if Mateo can be spared from his work?"

"No. Please." A doctor cost money, and how could she pay him? She thought of the looming mortgage payment, the one her father didn't think he could make. "Bothering Doc Frost is not necessary. My shoes slipped, that's all. It's nothing to worry about."

"All right, but it's against my better judgment. If you begin to feel faint, you sit down right away. Understand, young lady?" Cook's scowl emphasized she was not a woman to be messed with. "Mae, what are you smirking at? Get out the serving tray. I'm ready to dish up the meal."

Somehow she had to help. Ruby willed the spots away and took a careful step. The dots before her eyes did not fade as she opened the cabinet with her good hand and counted out three soup bowls. Her left hand protested, but she bit her bottom lip, did her best not to wince and set the bowls gingerly on the counter for Cook to fill.

"The missus will be eating alone." Cook ladled out dipperfuls of the fragrant chicken-and-dumpling soup. "The men will take their meals in the library. Ruby, you are having trouble moving your left hand."

"I'm fine. See?" She wiggled her fingers to prove it. Okay, they didn't exactly move well, but good enough *if* she ignored the overwhelming pain radiating up her arm.

"Mae, you will serve the meal on your own." Cook appeared mightily displeased as she filled the last soup bowl and set it with a clink on the tray.

Ruby groaned. She wasn't even going to be allowed to carry the tray of food? That was her job. It felt like a disgrace not to do it. Was she being dismissed for the afternoon?

"Take this." Cook shoved a clean dish towel at her. "Fill this with snow. You need to put ice on that wrist. Now go, no arguments."

"It will be as good as new in a minute or two." She took the folded length of soft muslin and headed to the back door, feeling like a failure. Cook was unhappy with her, Mae was sure to be angry over having to do all the serving work, and what if her wrist was truly broken? How could she keep her job?

First things first. She unhooked her coat and tried to slide her left hand into her coat sleeve. More pain. She sighed. Her day *could* be going better. She gritted her teeth. Pain bolted up her arm. It's not broken, she insisted stubbornly.

"Last month, I swear I saw that same pair of shoes sitting on the top of the donation barrel," Mae commented under her breath.

Ruby tumbled out the door, breathing in the sting of bitter cold, thankful to finally be alone. She dropped onto the bottom step, unable to fight any longer. Tears burned behind her eyes but she refused to let them fall. She was stronger than this.

A little help please, Lord. Just a little help.

No answer came on the inclement wind.

Chapter Eight

Lorenzo set down his spoon, his noon meal done. He'd been trying to pay attention to his father's teaching, but his gaze kept drifting to the window where he had a perfect view of the steps off the kitchen door and of Ruby seated there. Alone, shivering in the cold, her head hung down with her left hand covered in a cloth. What had happened to her? Concern tore through him.

"Renzo, you need a break." Pa closed the ledger with a thump.

Startled out of his thoughts, he turned his attention away from the window. How long had he been ignoring his father? Guilt crept in. "Sorry. My mind drifted."

"So I see." Gerard grinned cheerfully. "I get the same way after a while. All those numbers. Then the walls start closing in."

"True." How could he admit that wasn't the reason? Now that they were taking a break might be a good time to bring up his concerns. "We need to talk about Ruby."

"I see you watching the young lady." His father turned serious. "You're unhappy with me. I'm sticking to my word. You're to treat her like any other young lady working for us, with respect and distance."

"I never intended to give Ruby anything less than respect, Pa. You know that."

"I do, but my family had the same rules when I was growing up, and they suited well. You wouldn't want to put Ruby in a difficult situation, feeling she has to be especially nice to you even if she's concerned you are taking her away from her responsibilities to Cook and Lucia."

"That isn't the issue, Pa. Did you speak to her?"

"No, as there hasn't been a need for it. You have been the culprit, not her."

"Ruby has done nothing wrong." She looked sad and despairing, with her head hung. He couldn't just sit here. He wanted to go to her. "We're friends, Pa. You can't expect me to be two-faced. To be friendly when I see her in church, but to ignore her when she's here. Look at her."

"I've never seen anyone who looks like she needs a friend more." Pa nodded once, watching her through the window.

"Don't you fire her." Lorenzo rose from his chair and circled around the desk. "I can't leave her sitting there by herself."

"The staff will help her."

"No, I will." He didn't care if his father guessed the truth. His feelings were honest ones. He adored Ruby. If Pa saw it, then fine. Maybe it was time for his parents, as much as he loved them, to understand he was a man now. He followed their rules out of respect, but he also had to make his own. "It won't cost her a job, all right?"

"Hmm." Gerard said nothing more, clutching his cane.

The shadows clung to her as she transferred the cold cloth to the back of her head. Looked like she'd had a rough morning. Sympathy filled him, sympathy he couldn't stop if a gun was pointed at him. Whether or not he ever won Ruby's heart, he would never leave her out in the cold. He would always need to help her. To do what he could to make her world right.

"I suppose this once." His father called out when Lorenzo reached the door. "And if she's on her own time, not ours."

"I'll agree to that." He hesitated on the threshold, turned back and nodded once. A curious light glinted in Pa's eyes. Maybe he was putting the pieces together.

"You'll want to spend your time with the right kind of young lady." Pa stood and leaned on his cane. "I understand the way crushes work, but you're young. You don't want to settle down before you're ready, son. Best to keep this friendly and nothing more."

Well, at least he knew for sure how his father felt. Troubled, he strode from the room, nearly ramming into one of the downstairs maids.

"Hi, Lorenzo." Mae smiled up at him, eyelashes batting. "Do you need something? I could bring you more tea."

"No. Thank you, though." He circled around her, unable to get the image of Ruby out of his head, sitting on the step, shoulders drooping, wearing that worn-thin coat of hers in such cold weather. She had to be freezing. He pulled an afghan off a chair in the parlor on his way to the back door.

Icy air drove through him, and he was glad he'd taken the time to pull on his coat. He buttoned up as his boots broke the thin sheen of ice on the porch boards.

Ruby stiffened at the crackling noise, but she didn't look up. She didn't seem surprised when he eased down on the step beside her.

"You look cold." He shook the folds from the afghan and spread it across her shoulders. The soft wool shivered around her slight form. He liked taking care of her. Very much. "Looks like you had an accident. Are you all right?"

"Oh, it's nothing to worry about." She had the cold cloth on her left hand again. "I tend to be clumsy."

"I've had my moments, too."

"I don't believe that for a second." She twisted away from him so he couldn't read her face.

Did she honestly think that would hide her feelings from him? He could feel her hurt and her embarrassment as if it were his own. Sharp and aching in his heart, where they seemed to be linked.

"It's true. I've had many clumsy moments, too."

"You're just saying that to make me feel better." A trace of a smile warmed her voice.

"You may not know it to look at me, but at one time I was such a disaster with the haying I was ordered away from all haystacks. The first wagon wheel I repaired came off ten minutes later and resulted in a broken leg." He patted his left knee. "When my pa trusted me to take care of my own horse, I forgot to tie Poncho up. When I started cleaning his stall, he took off down the road. We had to pull men out of the fields during calving season to help in the chase."

"Poncho ran away from you? I refuse to accept he could behave so badly."

"He was a barely broken two-year-old and I was ten. It was a long time ago, but it took me years to live it down. That incident was just the start of a very long list." He wasn't going anywhere. He was right where he needed to be. Committed to her, he held out his hands. "Let me take a look at your wrist."

"There is no need." Steel rang in her gentle tone, a strength that made her delicate beauty more lovely, a strength that he admired. She tugged the afghan to her with her good hand. "The swelling is going down, so I'm sure it's not broken."

"Let me be the judge of that." He leaned close enough to breathe in her warm, honeysuckle scent. The vulnerable places within him opened more. Defenseless to her, he peeled away the cloth. Snow tumbled from its folds as he peeked at her hand and arm. Bruising stained her satin, puffy skin. "It looks broken to me."

"No. Don't say that." Distress etched crinkles on her face, drew her rosebud mouth down into a frown of misery. "I have to be fine."

"You will be." He shook all the melting snow out of the cloth. Soft, fragile feelings filled him up and were revealed in his voice. "First we have to get you inside and warmed up. You look so pale. This has to really hurt."

"Not bad." She shook her head slightly and winced. "I only have a few more minutes on my lunch hour before I have to go back to work."

"Then we had better get you inside and thawed." He rolled the dish towel into one long bandage. "You can't be of any use to anyone if you're frozen solid."

"True." The distress on her face eased a notch. He leaned in closer to wind the cloth around her wrist and hand, to give it support. She needed a splint, but it would hold for now. "Does that feel better?"

"Yes, thank you. I think I can work with it like this."

How could anyone so sweet be this stubborn? He rather liked it. She was strong where it mattered most. He rose off the step and offered her his hand. "Come with me."

Her big blue eyes gazed up at him, and in them, he read her protest. "I prefer to do things for myself."

"Sure, but you're injured." He read something else in her honest heart. Encouraged, he caught her free hand with his. Ice cold, it was a wonder she wasn't frostbitten. "It's all right not to be so independent if you sprained your wrist."

"Do you really think it's a sprain?" Hope layered her words as she rose slowly, obviously struggling not to wince.

"No, but it doesn't hurt to pray that it is." He caught her elbow to give her more support as they climbed the few steps together. He knew his father was probably watching from the window, stubbornly dismissing this as a mere crush. He would be wrong.

What he felt for Ruby was amazing. Overwhelming. Peace filled his soul as he propped open the door for her. She tossed him an uncertain smile, cute and wobbling, for she was hiding so much pain. She could deny it, but he knew her. Her skirts rustled, her light step padded on the wood floor and he held on to her as long as he could. Heavenly.

Once in the vestibule, he guided her past the doorway into the kitchen where a twitter of laughter suddenly froze and turned into an uncomfortable silence. Apparently his attention to Ruby hadn't gone unnoticed. He steered her down the hallway, bypassing doorway after doorway until they reached the parlor. A warm fire crackled merrily, heating the room.

"Take my mother's chair. It's the warmest." He lifted the afghan from her shoulders and nudged her gently toward the hearth.

"I don't know what I'm going to say to my pa." She looked up at him with those eyes that could lasso his soul. Trapped, he was helpless to walk away, helpless to deny her anything.

"I'm sure he will understand."

"Understand? Of course he will. He'll be very concerned, but—" She settled into the cushions slowly, wincing, obviously fighting pain. "My job lessens his burden, whether he wants to admit it or not."

"You worry too much." He spread the afghan over her, seeing her problem. Six weeks or so for that bone to heal was a long time to be unable to work and for his mother to go without a maid. She would be forced to replace Ruby, especially with their Christmas ball in the near future. He didn't know what to say to comfort her.

"My brother lost his job and his last two weeks of pay." She lowered her voice, so it would not carry in the cavernous room and be overheard by anyone passing by. "He's coming home on Friday's train. I'm the only one with a job in my family."

"I see. I'm sorry, Ruby." He knelt before her and cradled her hand in his. "Is there anything I can do?"

"No, but thanks for listening."

"Anytime." He loosened the end and unwound the bandage. "I'm pretty sure you cracked a bone. The doctor really should take a look at this."

"Don't you dare fetch him." Her chin went up. "He will tell me not to work, and I can't do that."

"I understand." He chose two short sticks of kindling from the wood box.

The firelight gleamed bronze in his thick hair and caressed the rugged contours of his face. She couldn't help noticing the picture he made with the flames writhing in the background, tossing alternating light and shadows across the powerful plane of his back, the impressive curve of his shoulders and the strength in his muscled arms. He could have been a prince in a fairy tale come to life.

What was she doing? She had vowed to stop being fanciful, to stop wasting her time on storybook wishes that could never come true. Especially now. She squeezed her eyes shut, determined to erase from her mind the image of Lorenzo kneeling at her feet. She couldn't be carried away by her fondness for him. She didn't have the right.

"I should send for Dr. Frost. I should make you go home so you can rest and heal." He laid the kindling sticks on either side of her arm and began binding her wrist. "This is against my better judgment."

"Thank you, Lorenzo. Thank you so much." Gratitude rushed through her with such force she could hardly breathe. "I'm determined to be optimistic. I'm sure this is nothing serious."

"That is incredibly optimistic of you. And stubborn." A slow grin tugged at the corners of his chiseled mouth. "I've met donkeys less headstrong than you."

"It's my best quality." She hardly noticed the pain in her arm as he tightened the bandage. Probably because it took all her willpower not to fall for this man and his midnight blue eyes.

"You have many good qualities."

"Me?" Shy, she tried to drop her gaze but his eyes held hers captive.

The brush of his fingertip as he secured the bandage, the soothing murmur of his words and the unmistakable caring carved into his features made it hard not to fall. It was all she could do to hold herself back.

"You are incomparable, Ruby Ballard."

Her? Hardly. "Are you sure you don't mean odd?"

"Funny. You can try, but you can't use humor to distract me. You are without equal." He turned his attention to checking over her splint to make sure the knot he'd tied in the ends would hold. "That ought to get you through the afternoon if you are careful."

"I will be." The mantel clock donged one o'clock. Time to return to work. As she folded up the afghan and stood to hang it over the chair, she didn't know what to say. How to thank Lorenzo for his help. For... Oh, she didn't know how to say what she felt. It was too big and wonderful.

She cared about him much more than she wanted to admit.

"If this starts hurting worse, you have to let me know. Promise?"

"Promise." She brushed at the wrinkles in her apron with her good hand, stealing one last moment to gaze at the man. With his feet braced and hands clasped behind his back, he looked like everything she could ever want in a man. Everything she could not have. "But it won't hurt worse. I'm sure all this fuss is for nothing."

"Not for nothing." His eyes had never been so blue or mesmerizing, inviting her to fall right in.

It was time to go back to work, so she swirled away.

Heart stinging, she strolled toward the door and away from his kindness that only made her want him more.

Lorenzo sat up straight in the hard-backed chair and blinked at the scratches on the ledger page. Determining if the ranch ran at a profit or at a loss was more complicated than he'd thought; his head swam with information and his father's words ran together, making no sense at all. The ledger spread out before him began to blur. There he went, thinking of Ruby again.

How was she doing? He tried to imagine her lifting pots, packing wash water, doing whatever other tasks were required of her. Was she taking care of her wrist? Still determined to ignore her pain because her family was in danger of losing what little they had?

He shoved away from the desk, surprising his father. "I'm going for a cup of tea. Do you want one?"

"That's a dangerous question." Pa thoughtfully marked in the ledger. "Maybe you could bring back something sweet to go with that tea. I thought I smelled a cake baking in the oven."

"I'll see what I can do." He strode into the hallway. The house felt lonely without his mother in it. She had gone to town.

"Is there something I can get you, Master Lorenzo?" Lucia set down her dust cloth, her naturally stern voice echoing in the parlor.

"No, I'll get it myself, thanks." He kept going, sure he felt a hint of disapproval from the housekeeper.

A clatter of silverware echoed in the corridor, and he knew it was Ruby before she slipped into view. Her fine hair tumbled down from her up knot in fine gossamer strands to curl around her collar. Her back was to him as she stood before the table, switching around silverware on the table.

"Is that right this time, Mae?" Her question held a note of vulnerability. She must be learning to set the table.

"No. Honestly, don't you know the difference between a soup spoon, a dinner spoon and a teaspoon?" He recognized Mae's voice as she huffed, irritated. "Try it again."

"How about now?"

Poor Ruby.

"No, that's not right either. You have the forks wrong. Don't you know anything?" Mae's dislike rang in her voice. "This is a salad fork."

"Why is there more than one fork? You can only use one at a time."

"Because this isn't a hovel. The Davises can afford more than one fork for everyone."

"Oh." Ruby bent her head to rearrange the silverware. He caught sight of her left hand, still splinted. She had to be hurting as she rearranged the order of the forks.

"No, that's wrong, too." Mae apparently left Ruby to guess instead of teaching her. "Get your mind on your job. Lorenzo is not going to marry you and save you from all this."

"I'm sure he wouldn't." Ruby's answer came so small and soft, he could barely hear it.

"He isn't going to marry someone too poor to afford decent shoes."

"I already know that, Mae." Her voice was so little he didn't realize she was still talking. "Besides, I can't think of marrying anyone. I have to help support my family. There. Now, is this right?"

"No. Try again."

Ruby just filled his heart right up. His boot crossed over the threshold before he'd even realized he was moving toward her. She was perfect, absolutely flawless, everything he could ever want. He could have closed his eyes, looked into his soul and dreamed her up. He just wished her life wasn't so hard.

"Mae, please fetch a pot of tea and bring it to the library. My father would also like a slice of whatever cake Cook baked for tonight's dessert." He barely looked at the maid; he only had eyes for Ruby. His precious Ruby. "How's the wrist?"

"Better." Tiny furrows of frustration dug as she stared at the place setting. So determined to do a good job.

"Why don't I believe you?" he asked, resisting the urge to brush gossamer, platinum tendrils out of her eyes. "You're still really pale."

"That's just an illusion, I'm sure. I'm willing my arm better. I've made up my mind so my wrist will have to comply."

"You are a force to be reckoned with."

"I try."

He nudged around a few forks. "That's how it goes. I *think*. I'm no expert. Generally, I grab whatever fork is in front of me and eat with that one."

"Do you usually help the new kitchen maid?"

"Always. Lucia insists."

They laughed together. He had to believe this would work out. That the Good Lord had brought him and Ruby together for a reason.

Boots pounded in the hallway, Mateo's brash and confident gait. "Renzo, there you are. We've got trouble. Thacker spotted a cougar by the horse barn. Ray is doing a head count to make sure we haven't lost any cattle."

"I'll grab my rifle." He had more to say to Ruby, but it would have to wait.

"Be safe." Her gaze found his, and the caring he read there made him feel ten feet tall. Hopeful, he tossed her a wink before he strode away, feeling lighter than air.

Chapter Nine

The long, single note of the train whistle pierced the late afternoon's silence. Earlee Mills looked up from her desk at the head of the classroom. Behind her Charlie Bellamy was writing one hundred times on the blackboard as punishment, "I will never again pull Anna's hair."

Earlee rolled her eyes at his slow progress. *She* may well be the one punished if he didn't hurry up. Judging by the way he was going, school would be dismissed before he finished his final sentence. Unrepentant, he giggled. Two boys in the middle row chuckled in response. Apparently there was some private joke she was missing.

"Quiet, boys." She used her firmest, big-sister tone, the one that kept her eight younger siblings in line whenever necessary. The squirming stopped, and the troublemakers returned to their spelling books. She loaded her pen, tapped off the excess and set the quill tip to the sheet of parchment. She resumed writing a letter to her pen friend, Finn McKaslin.

*...so everything on our farm is going well. The
animals are snug in the barn, and now that all
the long, summer days are passed, and harvest
madness is over, I have spare time to work on my
latest story. I know, this is the first time that I'm
mentioning this—*

A commotion overhead snared her attention. It
sounded like a herd of buffalo bounding across the
ceiling and charging down the stairs. All her students
squirmed in their seats, staring at her hard, willing her
to ring her hand bell and dismiss school. Remembering what it was like to sit in those desks wishing to be
set free, she obliged. She jangled the bell, children exploded out of their seats, and chaos reigned. She turned
her chair to deal with Charlie.

"Not so fast, young man." She had to give him credit.
He almost looked guilty sneaking away. "You have
thirty more lines to write."

"But Miss Mills, I gotta go home. My ma will worry
if I'm late."

"You should have thought of that when you were dallying at the blackboard. Your brother can tell her where
you are. Right, Tommy?" She addressed the younger
Bellamy brother who was straggling up the aisle.

"I guess." Tommy sighed. "I don't like walkin'
alone."

"Then hurry and catch up with your friends. Charlie
will be staying until he is finished." She reached into
her desk drawer to hand the troublemaker a fresh piece
of chalk so there would be no more excuses.

"Yes, Miss Mills." Charlie returned to the board
while his brother dashed off. Chalk squeaked as he

wrote one line after another, remarkably faster than he'd done during class time.

Back to her letter. She reloaded her pen and continued writing.

> *...My ma says it simply isn't normal, but I can't seem to help myself from writing. Stories just bubble out of my head. I'm probably not very good at it, but it's a lot of fun—*

A knock rapped on the door frame jerking her out of her letter. A tall, broad-shouldered man with light brown hair and Ruby's smile held up one gloved hand in greeting.

"Hullo there, Earlee. Is Ruby around?" Rupert Ballard called out in his friendly, smoky baritone. "I waited for her in front of the school, but she didn't come out. I checked and she's not upstairs in her classroom. Figured maybe she was in here with you."

"Aren't you supposed to be in Wyoming?" She laid down her pen.

"Supposed to be, except for the fact I lost my job." He shrugged those dependable shoulders of his as if it was no big deal, but she knew how precarious the Ballard finances were, since her family also struggled. He straightened up to his full six-foot-plus height. "I just stepped off the train."

"Welcome back." She rose from her chair and glanced over her shoulder to check on Charlie's progress. Amazingly he had only five more lines left. She circled around her desk. "I suppose you haven't heard Ruby's news?"

"Ruby has news?" Puzzled, he crossed his arms over

his wide chest. "I can't think of what it would be. No one is courting her, so it can't be an engagement."

"She has a job working for the Davis family. She's no longer in school. I hate to be the one to tell you." She ambled down the aisle, her skirts swishing. "Does your family know you're coming?"

"Sure, but I thought I would swing by, pick up Ruby, and we could walk home together." He scooped a ruck-sack off the entry floor. "Guess I'll be walking alone. It's good to see you doing so well, Earlee. You make a good teacher."

"I try." She shrugged, aware of the plunk of a chalk stick hitting the wooden holder.

"I'm done, Miss Mills. Can I go now?" Charlie swiped his face with his hand, smearing a streak of chalk dust across his cheek.

"Go on with you." He still had to erase and clean the blackboard, but that could wait until morning. She had floors to sweep and the fire to put out and she wanted to get home. The boy, glad to be freed, dashed down the aisle, his shoes hammering the wood floor as he circled around Rupert and disappeared from sight.

"There's one in every class." He gave his hat brim a tug. "See you around, Earlee."

"Bye, Rupert." There had been a time in her life when she would have given a little, wistful sigh as the handsome man walked away. Roop could make any young lady dream of possibilities and romance. These days, another man held claim to her heart. She spun around, her skirts twirling as her thoughts returned to her letter.

Light already faded from the windows. Sunset was not far away. If she wanted to walk home before dark fell, she would have to finish her letter tomorrow. Not tonight, because she couldn't risk her sisters at home catching a glimpse of Finn's letter. Should her parents find out she was corresponding with a man currently serving time at the territorial prison in Deer Lodge, they would have an apoplexy. No doubt, they would forbid to her to continue writing him. Her heart would shatter into a million pieces if she had to say goodbye to him. Finn didn't appear to return her affections, but she loved him.

She carefully wiped her pen tip and capped the ink bottle. She folded the letter in careful thirds, letting herself dream just a little. Outside the window, snow began to fall in tiny, fragile flakes, dancing like hope on the wind.

"How is the hand, dear?"

Lost in thought, Ruby startled, dropped hold of the mop, and it landed with a smack on the floor. The sound echoed off the vestibule walls as she spun around. Mrs. Davis stood in the hallway, striking in a fashionable, yellow gown, a dress sporting beautiful ruffles, silk ribbons and pearl buttons. At least, she suspected those were pearls, since she'd never seen real ones before.

"Lucia said Cook finally admitted that you were injured." Selma Davis didn't mind the wet floor as she swept closer. "I ought to step foot inside the kitchen more often, but cooking is not my specialty. Otherwise, I would have noticed your splint sooner."

"It's nothing." She knelt to rescue the mop from the floor, using her good hand. "I'm practically fine already."

"I'm relieved to hear that, but I insist on taking a look."

"That's not necessary." She stepped back, accidentally bumping into the door handle. She knew with one look at her wrist, Mrs. Davis would send her home. "It's nothing to fuss about."

"I say differently, and I am your employer." Selma Davis knelt to set the wash-water pail against the wall, out of her path. "You will listen to me."

"Yes, ma'am." It was all over. She had spent the last few days hiding the searing agony every time she hefted a bucket of water or drained the boiling potatoes for Cook. She had improvised peeling carrots and mopping floors and carrying stacks of dirty dishes from the dining room. But no more.

"Follow me." Mrs. Davis plucked the mop out of Ruby's grip and leaned it against the wall. "I think you could use a bit of fussing over. Cook, could you fetch two cups of tea?"

"Right away, Missus." Inside the kitchen, Cook hopped to work. The tea kettle clanked onto the stove, the only sound Ruby could hear over the rushing in her ears.

She was about to lose her job. She would have to go home and explain to Pa why she could no longer help support the family. She felt like a failure. Her father had always been there for her. How could she let him down? Blindly, she tapped after Mrs. Davis.

Never had any hallway seemed so long. As she passed the dining room, she caught sight of Mae dusting. Her smug look said it all. She was probably the one who had spilled the beans to Mrs. Davis.

"Please sit, dear." Her employer gestured to the sofa, the same one Ruby had sat on for her interview.

There was one positive note—at least, her shoes weren't wet and squeaking. She eased onto the cushion, ignoring her crushing disappointment. She took a deep breath, praying for guidance. *Help me to handle this well, Lord. Any guidance would be much appreciated.*

"Let me get a good look." Mrs. Davis settled onto the cushion beside her. She deftly folded back Ruby's sleeve, took a decorative pillow from the corner of the sofa and laid the injured arm on top of it. With a motherly air, she untied the ends of the bandage and carefully unwound it. "You've splinted it carefully."

"Yes, ma'am." That was Lorenzo's doing. How she missed him. She hadn't seen him for days, not in the dining room. One of the stable hands had come for the meals. The men were putting in long days tracking the cougar. Not that she ought to be pining for him. Now it looked as if she wouldn't even be able to say good-bye to him.

"Oh, this is either the worst sprain I've ever seen, or it's broken." Mrs. Davis shook her head sympathetically. "This simply does not look right. Glad I sent out for the doctor."

"The doctor?" Oh, no. She couldn't even think about what that would cost. Misery clutched her. "I sure wish you hadn't done that, Mrs. Davis."

"Nonsense. You are my employee, Ruby. I won't have this go untreated, and the doctor is my responsibility. You slipped and fell in my kitchen." Her kindness was unexpected. It glittered like a rare gem in her dark and gentle eyes. "I suppose your father knows nothing about this?"

"Only that I told him it's a sprain." She'd taken care to hide every wince of pain as she worked in their shanty. Pa had enough to worry about.

"And he believed you? You poor dear." She leaned in to brush a strand of hair from Ruby's eyes. The softest stroke, just the way she'd always imagined a mother's touch to be. "This looks as if it's been hurting you very much."

"It's not too bad." She shrugged. What she wanted was to have not fallen in the first place.

"Lucia?" Mrs. Davis called over the back of the couch. "I hope you brought some willow bark and a good, hot poultice, but not too hot."

"Of course," came Lucia's no-nonsense answer as she breezed into the room, set down the tray and tapped briskly away with a hard look in Ruby's direction.

Mortified, she slumped in misery. This was causing far too much trouble.

"Cook told me you insisted on doing all your duties." Mrs. Davis smiled sympathetically. "Even the heavy lifting."

"I didn't want to break my promise to you." She took a shaky breath. "I just wanted to do a good job."

"That you certainly did." Mrs. Davis poured two cups of tea. One smelled particularly bitter. She left them to steep and lifted a bowl from the tray. That smelled even worse. "You will be on light duties next week and, depending on what the doctor says, maybe longer."

"Light duties?" She blinked, not understanding at first. "Does this mean you aren't going to fire me?"

"Goodness, no. Is that what you thought, child?" Mrs. Davis spooned a hot mixture of herbs and who knows what else on Ruby's swollen wrist. "Put that worry out of your mind. Cook speaks highly of you, and she is very hard to please. I'm afraid if I let you go, she would have my hide. Good kitchen maids are hard to find."

"That's not true." She thought of all the women she'd spotted on her way to the interview and the long line of them waiting in the foyer for the chance at this job. "I'm completely replaceable."

"You are indispensible, Ruby, and don't you forget it." Mrs. Davis patted her cheek with a mother's affection. "Give this a few moments to soak in, and you should begin to feel better. I'm afraid this tea is very bitter, but you must drink it. Shall I put in a lot of sugar?"

"Please." Ruby blinked hard, but her vision blurred anyway. Did Mrs. Davis know how much her kindness meant?

"This ought to help." Mrs. Davis stirred in several heaping spoonfuls of sugar before handing over the steaming china cup. "Sip as much of this as you can tolerate."

"I'll try." She didn't want to displease Mrs. Davis, but the odor emanating from that dainty floral teacup was the most horrid thing she'd ever smelled. She cradled it in her right hand and braved a sip. Her tongue curled. Her mouth puckered, her taste buds cringed, and she choked, coughing it down. It was like drinking kerosene, not that she'd ever tasted kerosene, but surely, even kerosene would taste better.

"That's a good girl, keep drinking." Ms. Davis gently tipped the cup. "At least, one more good swallow."

Sputtering, gasping, another wave of the toxic substance sluiced across her spasming tongue, assaulted her mouth and nearly blinded her as she swallowed. She lowered the cup, swallowed again but the flavor lingered, refusing to budge.

"Now this." Mrs. Davis produced the second cup and saucer of tea, smelling of sweetened chamomile and peach. "It will help wash away that nasty taste. I want you to relax here until the doctor comes."

Two sets of footsteps echoed in the hallway, one gait was as familiar to her as her heartbeat. Lorenzo. His powerful presence shrunk the room. Snow dusted his thick hair, and he brought in the scent of winter and the December wind. The blue flannel shirt he wore emphasized the multiple shades of blue in his irises. The moment his gaze found hers, her knees wobbled.

Good thing she was sitting down because she would have fallen. The cup she held rattled in its saucer, tiny nervous *clink, clinks* that betrayed her. She took a sip, and the sweet, flavorful tea rolled across her tongue, calming it, but nothing could calm her reaction to him.

He affected her. Regardless of how hard she tried to stop it, he dominated her senses, he became the only thing in her world.

"Lorenzo." Mrs. Davis welcomed her son. "I didn't expect to see you so soon. Come warm yourself by the fire. Does this mean you found the cougar?"

"We tracked him into the foothills far away from us. I'm hoping he stays there." He trailed across the room. Lorenzo smiled at her with dimples that could make a girl swoon six counties away.

Not that she should be swooning.

"The doc is on his way. I saw him riding in when I was on the doorstep knocking the snow off my boots."

The doctor. Ruby flinched, still not sure seeing a

medical man was a good idea. He would only advise her to rest her arm, and she couldn't. Not here, not at home. Maybe he will agree that it's a sprain she thought, watching as Lorenzo's gaze found hers. His mouth crooked up again, showing off those arresting dimples.

She had to stop noticing his dimples. And how handsome he was. And how her pulse stilled when he smiled.

"How prompt of Dr. Frost. He is always so busy." Mrs. Davis rose. "Ruby dear, I have an appointment at the dressmaker's, so I must leave you. Lorenzo will look after you in my stead."

Alone with Lorenzo? She set down her cup. She swallowed hard, but her throat was too tight to actually swallow. Tension rolled through her, tightening her up muscle by muscle.

"If your arm hurts too much, someone here will drive you home. I know you have your own horse, but you might not feel much like riding." Mrs. Davis gently patted the side of Ruby's face, a motherly gesture. "If he's free, maybe Lorenzo can take you home."

"Oh, I'm not sure that's a good idea. I don't trust Lorenzo. He's shifty." The quip hid the tug of emotion in her heart.

An emotion she should not be feeling.

Laughter echoed around her as Mrs. Davis swished away, leaving her and Lorenzo alone. Again.

"I wasn't the one who tattled about your wrist." Lorenzo stalked closer.

"I know that. You might be shifty, but you aren't a promise breaker."

"That's right." Chuckling, he eased onto the cushion next to her, so close the air drained from the room.

She gulped and gasped, barely able to breathe. Whatever she did, no air went into her lungs. Since she was turning red and coughing, Lorenzo was bound to notice.

"Are you all right?" He held out the cup of tea to her, the awful-tasting one.

She shook her head. That tea wasn't going to help. She pointed to the other cup, looking like an idiot. Any other young woman in town would be able to carry on a conversation with the man, but not her. The memory of the last time they were in this room together came alive again. She could feel the tender warmth of his touch and see the caring concern etched on his face as he'd knelt before her.

Her lungs squeezed harder.

"Oh, how about this tea? It smells much better." He handed her the chamomile-and-peach cup, and she slurped it gratefully.

What was wrong with her? Why did she always embarrass herself around Lorenzo? Honestly. He would think something was seriously wrong with her. Miraculously the tea slid down her throat, opened her up, and she swallowed, able to breathe again.

"Better? Good." Larger than life and so incredibly authentic that he shone with the might of it, he took her empty cup. His baritone softened with earnesty. "Even if your wrist is broken, that won't stop you from singing, right? Because tonight is our second caroling practice, and I'd hate for you to miss it."

"No, I reckon I'll be there. I'm sure Pa will insist."

"He loves you."

"That's the rumor." Whatever this emotion was that was fighting to come alive in her heart, she could not acknowledge it. It had to go away. But did it?

No. The wishes she could not hold back overwhelmed her like a blizzard's leading edge, drowning out all sense of direction, blocking out the entire world. Disoriented, she barely heard the knell of another set of boots entering the room.

"Ruby, this is Dr. Hathaway, Doc Frost's new associate."

She couldn't focus on the tall shadow at the room's entrance. Only one man held her attention as he rose from the couch, towering above her. Lorenzo's honesty, his mightiness, his integrity riveted her.

I wish, she thought, gazing up at him. *I so wish.*

Chapter Ten

"What happened to you?" Kate whispered the moment Ruby eased into place with the other sopranos. "Look at your arm."

"It's nothing. Just a little, unimportant crack." Self-conscious, she held her songbook with her good hand. Reverend Hadly shuffled up to the front of the group, everyone quieted, and across the way Lorenzo smiled at her with those dashing dimples, which could make a girl swoon six counties away.

"You mean a cracked *bone?*" Kate nearly dropped her book. "Ruby, that is a big deal. Look at the size of that splint."

"Does it hurt?" Scarlet whispered from her other side. "What about your job? Surely Dr. Frost ordered you to rest."

"I saw the new doctor." Breathless from the effect of Lorenzo's grin, she prayed she sounded normal as she desperately tried to keep her gaze on the minister. But did her eyes obey?

No. They swung to the right until a certain, stunning man filled her view. Why couldn't her eyes stop finding him against her will? Fine, maybe she could admit it. She had a crush on him, but it was just a little one. Nothing serious. Surely it would go away in time, right? All she had to do was to get back in control, keep her eyes from wandering his way and to somehow keep him out of her thoughts.

But how? That was one question she didn't have the answer to.

"Ooh, Dr. Hathaway is to die for." Kate searched through the pages of the book for the carol the reverend announced. "He's almost as handsome as Lorenzo."

"Not even close," Scarlet disagreed good-naturedly. "And I've really looked. No man can compare to Lorenzo."

"Dreamy Lorenzo," Kate whispered.

Scarlet simply sighed, and in that single wistful sound, Ruby heard shades of true caring, not the superficial fondness of a schoolgirl crush. Anguish crinkled in the corners of Scarlet's eyes as she watched Lorenzo, bowed over his songbook. His dark hair tumbled over his forehead, and a cowlick poked up at the back of his head in a thick whirl.

"Rags, what are you looking at?" Narcissa Bell crowded into place directly behind her.

Oh, no. Ruby snapped her gaze away, feeling heat scorch her face. She'd been caught red-handed, and there was no use denying it. She bit her bottom lip, miserable, hoping beyond hope Narcissa wasn't about to announce it to the entire group—and to her friends.

"He's not interested in you. Why would he be? There isn't a single man who would look twice at your patches. You aren't holding out hope, are you?"

Her tongue tied up. She tried to think up something

witty and appropriate to say, but could she? No. Not a single word came to mind. Just the flood of humiliation and shame, because any minute, Kate or Scarlet would figure out that she was seeing Lorenzo behind their backs.

"Hush up, Narcissa." Scarlet gave a withering sneer.

The minister tooted on his pitch pipe and hummed. "Sopranos." "Aahs" burst out in perfect tone all around her.

Just focus on the music, she thought, steeling her spine. Narcissa might know exactly how to hurt a person, but she was not about to do the same in return.

"Look at that dress." Narcissa pitched her voice to rise above the singing. "Our maid scrubs our kitchen with rags better than that. Of course, I hear you are a kitchen maid, so maybe it's fitting."

Faces turned toward her, and Ruby blushed. Anger built up like steam behind her ribs, but she could not give in to it. She bowed her head, she couldn't help it. Her throat closed up, so all she could do was pretend to sing along with everyone else. She prayed everyone would stop looking at her.

"Ooh, she makes me mad," Kate leaned in to whisper. "Are you all right?"

"Fine." Had Lorenzo heard? She didn't dare peek between her lashes to see if he had noticed. She cringed. How could he not? The reverend's pipe gave another pitch, and the men joined in, the crescendo of the Major C chord booming like a hallelujah in the sanctuary.

"Very good. Now scales. Ready?"

"Aahs" rippled upward, note after note, and she did her best to join in.

Throughout one Christmas carol after another, she

kept her gaze fastened on the reverend. At least, she'd finally learned her lesson. No more gazing at Lorenzo. Now she had another problem. Her ears. They seemed to search through the chorus of voices to pick out his smoky baritone. Each note he hit did funny little things to her heart. It turned tingly, as if more alive than ever before.

Not exactly the reaction she was going for. She was supposed to be ignoring him. Falling out of her crush on him. What was she going to do with herself?

"Ruby?"

She felt a tug on her sleeve. Kate, getting her attention. Her mind had wandered. Again. "Sorry." She shook her head, realizing everyone else was filing down the aisle, merry conversations bouncing off the walls and high ceiling of the sanctuary. Lamplight shone off the stained-glass windows and trailed Narcissa as she huffed away with a clear snort of disapproval.

"I couldn't believe she said that to you." Lila tumbled over with the rest of the gang in her wake. "She did it so everyone would hear, to embarrass you intentionally."

"That's nothing new." Ruby deposited the songbook on a nearby pew with the others. She didn't need to glance around to know Lorenzo had already left with his friends. Without him near, the shadows felt darker, the light less bright. That was the way she would always be without him.

"You need to stand up to her." Meredith smiled at the reverend on her way down the aisle. "She won't stop picking on you until you do."

"I don't know what to do." Ruby kept her voice low, so it wouldn't carry to the reverend behind them or anyone in the vestibule ahead of them. "What is the right thing?"

"I say give her a taste of her own medicine," Scarlet advised.

"Yes, put her in her place," Meredith agreed. "She has no right making fun of you."

"Her bullying needs to stop," Lila agreed. "I would be happy to do it for you, but what will you do when we're not around?"

"I'll help," Earlee offered. "We outnumber her and her group."

Her friends' solidarity made her feel warm all over. Snug and loved, she wanted to give each one a hug, but she was shy and held back. "Thank you for your offers, but I don't want to sink to her level. This isn't about her behavior, it's about mine."

"Hello, Ruby." A man's pleasant tenor said her name with familiar warmth, as if he knew her well, but she didn't immediately recognize it. She should have, but it wasn't until she'd stepped into the vestibule that she recognized the man hanging his coat in the closet.

"Dr. Hathaway." She had liked the new doctor. He'd been gentle when he tended her wrist and proved easy to talk to. "What are you doing here?"

"After you told me about the caroling group, I decided to come join in." Dark eyes twinkled. "I would have been on time, but I had a patient call."

"Reverend Hadly will be ecstatic you're here." She was aware of Scarlet nudging her and Kate's veiled smile. "I will see you after the break."

"See you soon, Ruby." He went to tip his hat to her, but then must have realized he wasn't wearing his hat and blushed. His square shoulders didn't waver, however, as he strode away with a confident step.

"Wow," Lila breathed. "You could have told us."

"Told you what?" She spotted her coat piled on the table pushed against the vestibule wall and reached for it.

"No need to deny it with us." Meredith unhooked her coat from the pegs in the closet. "You like him."

"I do?" That was news to her.

"I saw the look he gave you." Scarlet shrugged into her coat. "He likes you. Really likes you."

"No, that's not true." She hadn't noticed anything. She shoved one arm into her coat sleeve. "He was just being nice."

"Nice? No, I saw the sparkle in his eyes." Kate wrapped her scarf around her neck. "He's taken a shine to you. You might have a suitor and soon."

"Dr. Hathaway? You couldn't be more wrong." Regret twisted inside her chest, and she hid the wince as she fit her splinted arm into her other sleeve. Even if there was only one man she wished for, she couldn't have him. Her family came first and so did her friends.

"I saw it, too. If I were penning the story, I would—" Earlee stopped in mid-sentence as she pulled on her mittens. "Ruby, what's wrong with your coat?"

It did feel funny. She shrugged the garment over her shoulders, and it didn't sit right at all. Something pulled down the left side like weight. Her pocket bulged noticeably so she reached into it. "I don't know. Why, it's a package."

"I'll say." Earlee clasped her hands with excitement.

"What is it?" Kate whispered, moving closer.

"Open it," Scarlet urged.

"I can guess what it might be." Lila smiled in her confident way. "Go ahead, unwrap it."

She stared at the brown-wrapped parcel. What could it be? Who had put it there? With trembling fingers she folded back the paper. A beautiful, china-handled crochet hook glinted in the lamplight, and with it was a large skein of quality, heavy-weight thread perfect for making snowflakes.

"The hook is beautiful. I've never seen one like it," Meredith murmured in awe.

"Me, either." Scarlet's eyes had gone wide. "This isn't a small token. Ruby, this is a serious gift."

"I know. I'm stunned." There was only one logical explanation. Lorenzo. But could she say it out loud? Could she even think it? No. Because if she admitted it, then what would her friends think? Oh, this was so much worse than she'd thought. "Someone must have put this in the wrong coat pocket by accident."

"Oh, I don't think so. Your coat is, well, distinct," Kate kindly settled on the word. "It's not a mistake."

"Someone is fond of you." Lila beamed as if she knew a secret.

"Dr. Hathaway was in this vestibule a moment ago and all alone," Earlee surmised.

"He would have had plenty of opportunity to slip that into your coat pocket." Meredith donned her beautiful, knit hat. "I have a feeling Ruby will be the next one of us to find true love."

"Impossible, since I'm doomed to become a spinster." What would they think if they knew? *Wretched,* she ran a fingertip across the thread. Best to put this back in her pocket. "I think being an old maid will give me a certain flair."

"You, an old maid?" Scarlet laughed lovingly. "Not a chance of that. Now, are we going to the diner? We had best get moving."

"No, not me." She longed to go with them and share the sure-to-be-fun moments over tea and pie, but she had something to attend to. "You all go ahead."

"Not without you. What are you going to do?" Earlee asked so sincerely and sweetly it was impossible to deny her the truth.

"I need to sort through the church barrel. I need better shoes." She shrugged, quite as if her pride didn't sting one bit. "I can't risk slipping and sliding around the Davis's kitchen. I'm not that good of a skater."

"Then we shall come with you," Kate declared. "We are like the Musketeers. All for one and one for all."

"Yes, we are," Scarlet agreed as they linked arms. "The church basement, here we come."

The night was crisp and bitter. The raw air burned their faces and the insides of their noses as they plowed through the snow. Their laughter echoed in the empty churchyard, and several horses tied at the hitching post threw disapproving looks their way. Ruby watched Scarlet peel off from the group and duck to fill her mitten with snow.

"Don't you dare!" Meredith squealed, leaping to make a snowball of her own. Too late, an icy orb hit square on her back. "You are going to pay for that, Scarlet Eudora Fisher!"

"Oh, no!" Laughing, Scarlet dashed behind Ruby and used her for a shield. "You wouldn't risk hitting sweet, little Ruby, would you?"

"Not if she ducks." Meredith wound up and let the ball fly. Ruby, being no dummy, ducked just in time.

Scarlet did not. Snow splatted against her coat and exploded. Her laughter rang merrily. She swiped snow out of her face. "Kate, don't just stand there. Help me!"

Ruby watched the full-scale snowball tactical assault surround her. Kate joined Scarlet, Lila joined Meredith, and Earlee scooped up snow and packed it, casually watching both warring factions as if debating her battle strategy. Squeals of laughter pealed in the dark evening. Ruby laughed too, never happier.

"Ruby." Earlee smiled at her innocently, a second before she launched a snowball through the air.

"Earlee!" With a shriek she tried to duck but the ball of snow thwacked on her shoulder, spraying cold bits into her face.

"Oops, my aim was off. I was aiming higher." Earlee was rewarded by a smack of snow that came out of nowhere. She rubbed the icy chunks out of her eyes, her smile still in place. "Kate, you are going to pay for that."

"Ooh, I'm scared. C'mon, Ruby. Let's get her!"

"Time to get even." Ruby plunged her right hand into the snow, working fast to shape her own weapon. Earlee yelped as Kate launched a second ball at her, she tried to dodge it, and Ruby threw. Her snowball hurtled through the air, walloped Earlee in the back, just as Kate's hit her from the front.

"Look at Ruby, just standing there." Lila swirled around, holding a snowball in each hand. "She's hardly been hit at all."

"That isn't right," Meredith scooped up more snow. "What are we going to do about it, girls?"

"A full-scale war?" Scarlet suggested.

"Sounds good to me." Earlee smiled.

"I'm still on your side, Ruby." Kate, ever loyal, knelt to shape another snowball.

"I adore you for that, but we're outnumbered." Ruby inched her good hand toward the snowy ground, desperately wanting to make some ammunition. Her friendly adversaries were creeping closer.

"I say we can take them all and wi—" Kate's confident remark was interrupted by a pelting snowball.

The battle was on. White projectiles cannoned into the air, sailing in arcs straight toward her. Ruby squeaked, felt her shoes slip on the icy snow—she didn't dare run—so she had to stand her ground. Snowballs rained down all round her. She ignored the twinge in her left wrist, and she packed another weapon. She threw blindly, struck a target, but she was laughing too hard to see who.

The next thing she knew, Earlee was at her side, ignoring the gleeful shouts of "traitor" as she hurriedly packed and threw snow. Ruby laughed, dodging Scarlet's gentle throw and lobbed a return snowball. Joy bubbled through her while she ducked Lila's snowball and returned a volley. Snow walloped against Lila's coat, and laughter rang like bells.

"Truce!" Scarlet called out, waving both hands. "Ruby, you are deadly accurate with a snowball. Who would have guessed it?"

"It's my secret talent." Her left hand smarted, but it was worth it. She joined her friends, swiping the ice and snow residue out of their faces and off their clothes as they tromped toward the basement door. "Rupert taught me. We used to have snowball fights when we were growing up."

"Rupert." Kate said his name with the hint of a sigh. "You have a handsome brother."

"I do?" She sailed through the door Lila held and into the depths of the basement. A single lamp burned on a desk, and heat radiated from the cast-iron stove in the corner. Blessed heat. She headed toward it, realizing she was frozen clear through. "Roop is a good man. He works very hard, and he's incredibly wonderful."

"You aren't sweet on Ruby's brother, are you, Kate?" Earlee asked as she took her place around the stove. The reverend's wife's papers were on a nearby desk. She must have stepped out.

"I'm just saying he's good-looking." Kate shrugged. "A girl has to keep her options open."

"What about Lorenzo?" Scarlet held her hands toward the heat. "I could never give up on Lorenzo."

Lorenzo. Ruby winced. Could she never escape even the mention of the man?

"Let's see if we can find something for Ruby." Lila, the successful manager of the town's finest dress shop, waltzed away from the stove and plucked a very shabby, brown gingham dress from the top of the barrel. "This would be a no."

"Definitely a no." Meredith sidled up to the stove. "Keep going."

"How about this?" Lila plunged her hand inside and withdrew a fine sweater with a hole in the elbow. "It's blue, it's about the right size."

"I could fix that hole," Scarlet spoke up. "I'm a good knitter."

"Then it's a maybe." Lila set it aside and fished inside the barrel. "Ooh, I see something really good."

"I love it!" Scarlet swept up to get a better look at the dress.

A dress? It was practically a gown, in champagne-colored silk. Tiny rows of lace with scalloped edges lined the princess-cut bodice. The ruffled skirt was trimmed in matching velvet. Fine pearls sewn onto the fabric gleamed richly. A careless tear at the collar had been left unattended, so the stitching had come unraveled.

"Who would give that away instead of fixing it?" Kate breathed incredulously.

"I don't know, but it's about your size." Scarlet held up the stunning dress, eyeing Ruby. "It just needs a little taking in."

"And that collar needs to be reset." Lila examined the garment with her expert eye. "I could do it on Monday at the shop. I have the right needles and thread there to do it justice. Ruby, stand up straight."

"Me?" Shock silenced her as Lila held the dress up to her shoulders. The silk rustled luxuriously and was the finest fabric she had ever felt. The gown fell in a flowing, elegant cascade to the floor. Whoever wore this dress would feel like a princess.

"Wow," Kate breathed.

"That color on you—" Scarlet didn't finish her sentence because her jaw had dropped.

"You're beautiful, Ruby," Earlee chimed in.

"Not me." She blushed. Honestly, what was wrong with her friends? Perhaps their normally good judgment was derailed from so much exertion in the bitter cold, which had somehow frozen their brains. She wasn't sure how likely that was, but it was the only explanation she could come up with. She shrugged. "I'm just plain old me."

"You are not plain, Ruby," Meredith argued. "I suspect a certain man doesn't think you are either."

Of course her mind turned straight to Lorenzo. She prayed the soreness in her heart did not show on her face.

"It's settled, then." Lila stepped back to fold up the garment. "The dress is yours."

"But I don't need it. Where would I wear it?" She was a farm girl. It was who she was. Not a young woman who had the need for such finery.

"You never know what God has in store." Kate's words radiated comfort and love and hope. "You have a secret admirer, Ruby. I know you are worried about losing your home, but the Lord's timing is always perfect. Love can happen anytime. Don't give up hope that your life can change for the better. I haven't."

Tears bunched in her throat, making it impossible to speak.

She understood how Kate felt about Lorenzo. She felt the same way.

"Take the dress," Earlee urged. "It will be perfect to wear to the Davis's Christmas ball."

"Yes, there's no telling whose eye you will catch," Scarlet urged. "The new doctor seems taken with you."

It wasn't the doctor she thought of.

"Of course, Lorenzo will be there." Kate sighed.

"Yes, Lorenzo." Scarlet filled up with so much longing, it spilled out, impossible to miss.

You have no right to wish, Ruby Ann Ballard. Seeing the ardent hope in Scarlet's eyes and knowing it was Lorenzo she loved made Ruby bow her head. She was a terrible friend, undeserving of their unconditional love. Miserable, she turned away, pretending to warm her fingers at the stove. Inside, she was ashamed. It felt as if she had betrayed Scarlet.

The memory of her first day at the town school rushed back to her. Of the wobbly feel of her knees when she'd walked through the door, of the echoing sound of conversations and general disarray bouncing off the walls as she peered into the classroom. Her stomach had tied into knots with terror. She had never been around so many people. Where she'd lived before had always been terribly remote, so she hadn't been prepared for such a crowd.

By lunchtime she had friends. Real friends. Scarlet, Lila, Kate, Earlee, Meredith and Fiona had welcomed her with open arms and unconditional kindness, accepting her as she was. She loved them all dearly.

Do the right thing, Ruby. No more wishing for Lorenzo. Not ever again.

"I found them! A pair of good shoes." Lila's triumph echoed in the room. "Ruby, come see."

Chapter Eleven

In three-part harmony, the last note of "O Come All Ye Faithful" ended, and Reverend Hadly congratulated them. "Well done, everyone. Have a safe journey home. We will see you all next time."

Finally. Lorenzo closed his song book, squared his shoulders and searched the crowd. He heard her before he saw her.

"I can't wait to get home." Her dulcet voice somehow lifted quietly to him above all the din in the room. So dear to him, he couldn't think of a more beautiful sound. The tussle of the crowd at the front pew, where the carolers deposited their books, faded into silence as he watched her sweep down the aisle, encircled by her friends.

Did she like the gift he'd left for her? It hadn't been easy to slip it into her coat pocket unnoticed. She had to know that it was from him, but she hadn't glanced at him through the last half of practice. She didn't turn to offer him a smile now.

"I'm worried about Pa," Ruby said. "I hope he

warmed up the supper I left for him. When he's troubled, he tends to forget to eat."

Dazzled, he watched the fall of lamplight as it swept over her, danced in her light hair and worshiped the ivory splendor of her face. He had it bad for her. No use denying it. But at least he knew what stood in his way. Ruby's duty to her family came first. He understood and admired it. His heart tugged him along, taking him forward, toward her. It was as if he had no say.

Not that he minded.

"Lorenzo?" His name came from a far-off distance. He blinked, shook his head, only to see James walking beside him, looking puzzled. "Is everything all right?"

"Sure. Sorry. My mind was somewhere else."

"I can tell."

Ruby might always be at the center of his thoughts, so he would have to learn how to live with it. "What were you saying?"

"Listening to Narcissa talk, you two are going to the ball together. True or not true? I thought you weren't interested in her like that." James grinned, full of trouble. "Hey, don't scowl. I came to warn you."

"Me, too." Luken caught up to them grinning. "I heard it from Narcissa myself."

"I'm not bowing to family pressure this year." It took all his effort to keep from searching for Ruby in the dispersing crowd. Ruby, who'd stolen his heart. "I'm not taking Narcissa. End of story."

"That's what I thought, but it's good to hear." Luken blew out the breath he'd been holding. "I don't want to go after someone you're interested in—"

"I've never been interested in Narcissa."

"Well, I am." Luken grinned again.

"Who are you kidding? You're never going to beau her." James shook his head. "She is out of your reach."

"Still, it wouldn't hurt to try to win her. You never know." Luken squared his shoulders, maybe hiding the pain of unrequited love.

Lorenzo knew exactly how that felt. Needing to see her, he snatched his coat off the wall peg and shrugged into it, heading toward the door. Exceptionally icy air met him as he shouldered outside, buttoning as he went. The instant his gaze found her at one of the hitching posts, the tension coiling within him calmed. Contentment wrapped around his soul like grace.

Love was too weak of a word. He was no longer simply in love with Ruby. He was committed to her. Devoted. Captured one hundred percent.

Departing carolers plowed through the snow on the streets while others untied their horses at the hitching posts. Lanterns flared to life, swinging alongside the dashes of sleighs. But above it all, the music of her presence sang to him. As he trudged along, he noticed every dear thing she did. The brush of her mittened fingertips along her horse's nose, the knot she made worse when she tried to untie the reins with one hand and the crinkle of frustration that furrowed into her forehead.

Cute. He intended to march right over there and help her out, but someone cut in front of him. Another man appeared out of the shadows.

"Here, Miss Ruby, let me." Walt Hathaway took the knotted reins before the young lady could accept or protest. She gazed up at him in shy surprise while her friends, busy boarding sleighs and untying horses, exchanged knowing looks.

The new doc was interested in Ruby? Lorenzo's feet

froze to the ground. He stared in shock as Walt untangled the knot and presented Ruby with the reins, talking with her warmly.

Unbearable pain hammered into him, radiating heartbreak through his rib cage like a mortal blow. His knees buckled, and he blindly reached out. His fingers wrapped around something solid and icy, a hitching post, fighting just to breathe. He watched as Ruby smiled up at Hathaway, her sweetness beaming.

Something tugged at his hat brim. Poncho nibbled with his whiskery lips and gave a nicker of comfort. Chocolate-brown eyes met his, and the horse's caring was unmistakable. He rubbed the gelding's cheek, thankful for the friendliness.

"See you later," Luken called out as he headed off down the street.

"Bye." He waved to James, too, who had mounted up on his fine buckskin. The wind gusted hard, driving an arctic chill straight into his bones. It was a brutal night. Although the snow had stopped, dark clouds blanketed the sky blotting out all sign of heavenly light. He forced his attention on loosening the knot that held Poncho to the post, hands shaking. Out of the corner of his eye, he watched as Hathaway chuckled, and Ruby's soft laughter joined his.

What if she left with Walt? He swallowed hard, trying to tamp down the pain that rose in his throat. He stumbled into his sleigh, plopping on the seat. What if Ruby let the doctor see her home?

I could lose her. He shook out the driving robes, but they were as frigid as the night and offered no relief. His soul felt cold, and he glanced over his shoulder, dreading what he would see. Not that he'd ever really had Ruby. He held no claim on her heart.

It was Ruby's choice, after all, whom she would love. *If* she would love at all. The thought of losing her, of not having the hope of her in his future, crushed him.

"Good night." Ruby's soft farewell drew his attention. As she fit her shoe into Solomon's stirrup, he wanted to be the one who held her elbow to support her into the saddle. He wished to be the one who handed her the reins, to be the recipient of her bashful smile. "I will take better care of my splint. No more snowball fights."

"Not until your wrist is healed." Walt was the fortunate man who waved her off, watching as the horse plodded down the icy street with the *clink, chink* of steel shoes.

Loving Ruby was a perilous thing. He didn't know what dangers lay ahead for his heart. She rode away, a willowy slip of a thing huddled in the saddle. He wasn't the only man who didn't notice the cold, who could not tear his gaze from the woman on her horse. The fringe of her scarf caught on the rising wind, flickering behind her.

Whether or not he eventually won her hand or Walt did, or she decided she wouldn't part from her family, one thing was sure. He would always want her happiness, always fight for it, always pray for it. He would do anything he could to improve her life.

Take what You will from me, Lord, if You can give it to her. His prayer came from the most honest of places in his soul. He thought he felt heaven's hand on his shoulder as he snapped the reins. As Poncho leaped into action, he knew what he had to do.

* * *

The night prairie gleamed darkly, as luminous as a black pearl. Rich tones of ebony, onyx and charcoal glossed the miles of snow all around her. Ruby clenched her jaw tight to keep her teeth from chattering. She tipped her head to peer up at the purple-black shadows of the Rocky Mountains standing guard at the edge of the high Montana plains. Darkly velvet clouds tumbled across the sky like unrolled bolts of quilt batting.

So beautiful. She savored the wonder, cherishing the hush of the sleeping landscape, the lonely rush of the wind and the faint scent of wood smoke from some distant chimney. Concentrating on God's handiwork kept her mind off the fact that she was practically frozen solid as Solomon plodded along. The shivery ride home was worth the fun evening. The joy from being with her friends sustained her like a fire on a hearth and she didn't feel the cruel winds overly much as her mind went back over the treasured evening.

Singing alongside Kate and Scarlet, the snowball battle, her friend's cheerful help sorting through the donation barrel. Something that had always hurt her sensibilities had become bearable because of her friends. She was grateful for the nearly new shoes tucked into Solomon's saddlebags along with the winter coat she'd found for Pa—a perfect Christmas gift. Love for her friends burned like a candle in the dark, chasing away all her sorrows.

Thank You, Father, for this time with them. It would not last much longer, she feared. She fought the rending in her heart at the thought of being separated from her dear friends. And from Lorenzo, she realized, gasping at the anguish slicing through her like the frigid wind.

Even if she could no longer wish for him, her heart still wanted him.

Solomon stumbled in the thick snow, jerking her out of her thoughts. She gasped, fearful for him, but he kept going, laboring along like a trouper. What a good horse.

"I'm sorry, my friend. I hadn't thought how hard this late evening trip would be on you." She leaned forward in the saddle and wrapped her arms as far around his neck as she could. He was breathing so hard. He managed a small whicker of reassurance, as if to say he didn't mind. She did. What a good old friend he was.

Somewhere behind her, a soft chime rose above the prairie's quiet and became the ring of steeled horse hooves. Alone and in the dark, she twisted in the saddle to glance along the long, lonely stretch of road. There was nothing but a faint blur of movement, as shadowed as the landscape, nothing more substantial than a dream. Slowly the dream took on shape and substance as it loomed closer.

A big, dark horse broke out of the night. Poncho neighed a cheerful greeting as he picked up his pace. *Chink, chink!* went his hooves as he pranced closer. Nervousness kicked through her veins. Where Poncho went, his master followed.

"Hey, Ruby." Lorenzo pulled up alongside Solomon, his words rising in great clouds of fog in the frigid air. Tucked in the vehicle behind several layers of warm robes, he was nearly lost in the darkness.

"What are you doing here?" She stared at him, not quite believing. "You live in the opposite direction."

"Yes, I reined Poncho toward home, but he ignored me completely, took charge of the bit and brought me here. He tends to have a mind of his own."

"He ran away with you?" As if she believed that. "If he was a runaway, he is going awfully slow. I would expect a madcap dash at the very least."

"It's the weather. The ice slows him down." He shifted on the seat so she could see the hook of a grin at the corners of his mouth.

"Yes, I can see the danger you've been in." She eyed the gelding plodding along, a few paces ahead of Solomon, ears swiveling as if to take in every word being said. "I'm relieved you've been able to seize control again."

"Me, too. It was a near thing. I may have to punish him. Maybe a whipping."

Poncho blew out his breath, rattling his lips scornfully.

"Yes, I'm sure that will happen." She suspected there wasn't a more pampered horse in the entire territory.

"It's pretty cold to be on the back of a saddle, isn't it?"

"It *is* a bit chilly. I don't mind."

"Your teeth are chattering."

"Only because I have to unclench them to talk with you." She drew Solomon to a stop. "What are you doing here?"

"I told you. It was Poncho's idea. He must be concerned about you and Solomon and wants to offer you a ride."

"*Poncho* does?" She knew the truth, thinking of the gift she'd also tucked in a saddlebag. She couldn't help the sweet longing lifting through her. Lorenzo had come to see her safely home. She knew what it was like to sit on that cushioned seat snug beneath those warm blankets with the steel of Lorenzo's arm pressed to hers. Scarlet's face flashed before her eyes, she imagined her father alone and homeless, and those images stopped her.

She'd given up on those dreams. She straightened

her spine, determined to keep things light. It would be easier to send him on his way, easier on her heart. "So, Poncho came all this way in the harsh weather simply because of concern for me?"

"He's stubborn like that. Once you are Poncho's friend, you're a friend for life. He watches out for you."

"I suppose he doesn't like taking no for an answer."

"This terror? I try never to say no to him. There's no telling what he would do."

"Yes, I would live in fear." She laughed; she couldn't help it. Poncho arched his neck proudly, as if enjoying his reputation.

"It must be hard for Solomon to break a path through this new accumulation. Or maybe it's the cold." Lorenzo climbed out and tucked the robes back into place to hold in the heat. "He looks pretty winded."

"I know. I'm worried about him. He's not as young as he used to be." Solomon quivered in the bitter wind. Poor fella. She patted his neck, wishing she could do more. "I didn't realize it would get so cold tonight. I better keep moving. I don't want him to get chilled."

"He's shaking harder." He placed his hand on the gelding's flank. "Easy, fella. Hop down, Ruby, and let me take a look at him."

Her hand caught his and peace descended on him like grace. He helped her from the saddle, her weight light and sweet in his arms for one too-brief moment before gravity intervened. Her shoes sank in the deep snow, and he had to let her go.

Did he see a plea in her eyes? It was hard to read her in the inky darkness where secrets were easy to keep. The wind gusted meanly, growing colder by the second.

Ruby's teeth chattered, and she spun out of his hold to rub Solomon's graying face.

"My sweet boy." Her expression crinkled with concern. "I should have gone straight home tonight instead of heading to town."

"No one expected the temperature to fall like this. You couldn't know." He worked fast, untying Solomon's heavy winter blanket rolled behind the saddle, removed the saddle before covering the gelding snugly. Solomon shivered harder. Not a good sign.

"We'd best keep him moving." He stowed the saddle in back of the sleigh. "It will be easier going for him in the broken trail behind us."

Ruby nodded anxiously, taking her horse by the bits and gently turning him around. Solomon nibbled her hat with affection, his sweet gaze full of trust. That raspy breathing troubled him as he tethered the gelding to the tailgate.

"You're a good boy, Solomon." As much as he worried about the gelding, he was concerned about the woman more. "Let's get you in the sleigh, Ruby. You're shivering, too."

"Not too much."

"I call it too much."

"You're cold, too." She shook so hard, she had trouble walking the length of the sleigh. He held the robes back and handed her in.

"I'm used to the cold." He tucked the robes around her. "I'm a rancher. I burn in the summer and freeze in the winter."

"So, that's why you are here tonight. Because you don't mind the weather?"

"I told you. Poncho was worried, and so was I." He

held the reins one-handed and settled in beside her. "Friends help each other, don't they?"

"Yes, but this is a lot for you to do."

"Depends on your perspective, I guess." The soft presence of her shoulder against his arm was sweet. It was all he could do not to slip his arm around her shoulder. "Think of it this way. What if you catch cold tonight? You would miss work. I've heard you are already indispensable to Cook. We never want Cook upset, as she's responsible for the quality of our meals."

"You're not fooling me any, Lorenzo Davis."

"It was worth a try."

She said nothing more for a moment, and silence stretched between them.

He felt her gaze on his face and sensed her scrutiny. "Something troubling you?"

"I'm sure you've heard enough of my troubles."

"We're friends, remember?" And he wanted to be a good deal more. "Tell me."

"My father hasn't said for sure, but I have calculated what little we must have in savings. Even with my job, we probably won't be able to make the mortgage." She swallowed hard.

"I'm sorry to hear that, Ruby. I had hoped you would be able to keep your home."

"Me, too. When that happens, we will have to move in with relatives." She breathed in a little squeak of air. "How do I tell your mother? After I promised not to let her down?"

"Giving notice wouldn't be letting her down, Ruby."

"Yes, but she paid for the doctor for me. And now she will have to turn around and train someone in my place. It would feel as if I was breaking my promise to her."

"Maybe your brother will find another job in time." He did not want to give up hope.

"That seems like an unlikely miracle at this point." The darkness hid the sadness in her eyes, but he knew it was there, for he could read it in her heart. Against his arm, her shoulder firmed. "I have to be strong for my pa. I have to trust that God is leading us to a good place, however difficult the road may be."

"I wish your road was easier." Overhead, the thick mantle of clouds began to thin, lessening the cloying dark gripping the prairie. "Is there any chance you might stay and keep your job, even if your family loses your land? You have good friends here. And Poncho."

"Yes, however will I bear to leave Poncho? It will be a great loss, but distance cannot harm true friendship. I can write letters. Well, not necessarily to Poncho, but to my other friends with opposable thumbs so they can open the envelope."

"I have opposable thumbs." He held up his gloved hands, still maintaining command of the reins. "See?"

"Well, I wasn't planning on writing to you, but I guess I could manage a letter or two now and then." She shook her head. The man dazzled her, but at least the darkness hid some of the effect and made it easier to ignore. She couldn't let it affect her. She'd made up her mind. No more wishing. "I was talking about my good friends."

"I am, what, just a fair-weather friend?"

"What you are is yet to be determined. We will see how good of a letter writer you turn out to be."

"A faithful one." Richly spoken, the sincerity of his vow rang in meaningful, steadfast notes. "It would be a shame if you had to go. Is there any possible way your father might accept help with the mortgage?"

"Oh, Lorenzo." She turned toward him, touched by his offer. She saw the man—all he was, who he was— in that one silent moment. Could he truly care so much about her? "Pa is an independent and proud man. I don't think he would."

"I respect him for it." He turned his attention to the road, making it impossible to guess what was on his face.

She thought of the gift he'd put in her coat pocket, the one she couldn't bring herself to speak of. "I wish I could stay. Your mother is so wonderful to me, and I would love to keep working for her."

For one small instant, she let herself imagine what it would be like. She could rent a cozy room at the boarding house. Living in town, she could see her friends often. It would be a brief walk to the dress shop or to Lila's apartment. Scarlet lived on Third Street. Earlee taught at the town school. Fiona lived a short ways north of town, and soon Meredith would be married and moving into her home nearby. What fun they could all have together. Sewing circles, caroling groups and countless, happy hours of talking and shopping. It could be one, long, wonderful eternity.

But that couldn't be her future. She thought of her father, of his worries and his burdens. Of how the failure to keep his farm would affect him. She thought of her uncle's ranch so far away and the tiny shanty, originally a shed, he and Roop had fixed up after Pa's accident. Living so far to the north, with no one to visit, no church nearby, only a general store miles away—that would be her life. "I cannot leave Pa when he needs me.

He has struggled so hard all these years to provide for me. He has endured an unfair amount of hardship. I do not know how much more he can take."

"I understand." Empathetic, Lorenzo reined Poncho to a stop. "What about your brother?"

"If Roop needs to move away to find work, then Pa would be alone. I cannot do that to him." She looked up, surprised to see the faint, flickering glow behind the shanty's curtained windows. She was home already? She climbed from the sleigh before Lorenzo could circle around to help her. She could not get used to relying on him. "This place was Pa's dream, which kept him going through all those painfully hard times. It will break his heart to lose it. Honestly, I fear it will break him."

"I understand. Staying with him is the right choice." He untied Solomon. "What about you? What will it do to you?"

"Me?" She plunged through the deep snow, nearly tripping on her skirts. "This is the only real home I've had since I was five."

"It will crush you, too."

"I will recover." She reached to take the reins, but he did not let go of them, grateful for the brush of her fingertips to his. A connection roared to life within his soul, deeper than before. She jerked her hand away.

The shanty's front door blew open, and two men burst out, dressed for barn work. Jon Ballard closed the door behind him as Ruby's brother bounded into the snow.

"Roop! You made it home." Ruby beamed at her older sibling, lighting up the night.

"Good to see you, little sister. Don't even think about it. I'll get Solomon's saddle, the poor guy. Looks like he's having a hard time." Rupert ambled up, friendly and eager to help. "Lorenzo. It is mighty good of you to see Ruby home in this weather."

"She is my mother's favorite maid," he answered, making everyone laugh, easily hiding the truth. The truth behind the gift he'd left her and his offer to help her father. "Rupert, I'd like to see to Solomon."

"I'd appreciate any help." Rupert led the way, walking slow to accommodate Solomon's gait.

"Good. C'mon, Poncho." Lorenzo chirruped, taking his gelding by the bit. How perfect he seemed, glossed by the faint emerging starlight breaking through the clouds.

He was everything she ever dreamed of and everything she could never have. Nothing on earth could change it.

Chapter Twelve

Ruby dropped another log on the fire, careful of the whoosh of red ashes, which rose from the hearth like fiery bits of torn paper. They flashed and snapped as they drifted upward, fire-hot, before sailing down. One landed on her cardigan, and she brushed it off absently. The shanty echoed around her. Nearly an hour had passed since Lorenzo had disappeared into the barn with Pa and Roop. They were still there. That couldn't bode well for Solomon.

Worry gnawed at her with big, sharp teeth as she rose to rescue the tea kettle from the stove. She had no idea how long it had been whistling. She measured out fragrant tea leaves and left a pot steeping while she shivered into her coat. She grabbed the full tea kettle handle with a hot pad and slipped out the kitchen door. If the men weren't coming in, then she was going to them.

Star shine glowed along the narrow path as she pushed out the kitchen door.

"Ruby." Lorenzo's voice broke out of the dark, nearly scaring her to death. Her grip slipped, but his gloved hands caught the steaming tea kettle by the handle, covering hers. "Could you fetch some old blankets or quilts?"

For Solomon? That definitely sounded serious. "How is he?"

"We're taking precautions is all." His baritone grew tender. "He has caught a serious chill in town."

"He's never been this frail before." Her poor Solomon. "What else can I do?"

"I'll take the tea kettle and fix up a mash for him. Get something warm in his stomach."

Somehow her fingers let go. It felt awkward standing like this, alone together beneath a starry sky, when she knew how he felt for her. When he'd done so much for her already. Now this.

She could feel his caring like the silver glow on the snow, chasing the dark away. A girl dreamed of having a man like Lorenzo care for her and treat her like this. She forced her feet to carry her backward step by step. "I was going to bring tea to help warm the three of you, but I thought hot water for Solomon might be more important."

"You're right. If you want to stack the blankets on the step, I'll come back for them."

"No, I can bring them. I'll hurry." It gave her something to do, something to focus on. So she wouldn't start wanting to wish or dream. She turned the knob and stumbled into the kitchen. Her teeth chattered as she hurried through the shanty, flung open the cabinet and hauled out blankets.

You have to be practical, Ruby Ann Ballard. Keep your expectations reasonable. Even under the best circumstances—if her family wasn't facing homelessness, if her friends didn't deserve him more—wealthy Lorenzo Davis was never going to marry a kitchen maid.

He was never going to marry her.

A north wind had kicked up by the time she scurried down the steps. When she breathed in, the bitter air burned her nose and scorched her lungs. Overhead, the clouds had vanished leaving the velvety sky, which shone so darkly, she could almost see heaven. The stars glittered like millions of diamonds scattered carelessly across the sky, diamonds rich with faint lustrous colors—red, blue, yellow, white. God's great handiwork. Surely He was watching over all of them tonight.

"Ruby." Roop this time, not Lorenzo, rising out of the dark. He opened the barn door for her. "Those blankets are a welcome sight."

"I came as fast as I could." She hurried toward him, careful of her shoes on the ice. She didn't need to fall again. As if Roop was thinking the same, he caught her arm and hauled her through the door.

Lantern light chased away the dark. Clover, the milk cow, poked her nose over her stall gate, her big, bovine eyes worried. The atmosphere in the barn seemed grim as she stumbled forward. She couldn't see anything over the divider between the stalls. Only Solomon, head hung low, sides heaving.

"That's it, big boy. Lie down for me." Lorenzo circled into sight from behind Solomon. With a labored groan, the gelding's front knees sank into the extra-soft bedding, and then his rear went down, as weary as if he'd run twenty miles. Pa rose up to peer over the boards at her. Strain lined his face.

Roop took the blankets from her, but it was Lorenzo who held her attention, Lorenzo who knelt at the horse's side to straighten the blanket Rupert had given him, smoothing out the folds with soothing hands. Solomon closed his eyes, understanding they were all there to help him.

Please, Father, watch over our horse, my friend, she added. She believed God cared about His animals, too. She felt something tug on her scarf. Clover had reached over her gate to nibble on the fringe. Ruby rubbed the cow's poll, watching as Pa and Lorenzo covered the gelding with the bedding. Snug, Solomon stretched his neck out, laid his head on the downy hay and closed his eyes.

"I'll stay the night with him." Roop knelt to stroke the horse's neck. "Make sure he doesn't have any problems."

"We'll know more after he gets some rest. Maybe he'll pull out of this." Lorenzo rose, pulling on his gloves, his movements sure and strong. The lamplight found him and worshiped him, delighting in the manly angles of his face and glinting bronze in his hair.

"That's what I hope, too." Roop settled on the hay next to Solomon. "What about your horse? You don't want him getting too cold."

"I'd better head out, but I'll be back come morning."

"That would be mighty good of you." Pa laid one hand on the stall rail, shoulders up, a proud man. "Ruby is awfully in love with that horse."

"I noticed."

What was her father up to? He didn't accept help from others, but he had welcomed Lorenzo and his blacksmithing tools right from the start. Which could only mean one thing. How did she tell her hopeful father that the young Mr. Davis would never be her beau? Her pa must be hoping for a match.

"Ruby, why don't you see Lorenzo out?" Pa tried to sound nonchalant. It didn't work.

"Allkay." The nonsense word garbled out of her throat when she'd meant to say all right or okay, but neither had come out right. Tongue-tied, heat scorched across her face as she took a hurried step. Lorenzo's hand settled against the small of her back, guiding her lightly. No doubt Pa saw that.

The stars glittered, polishing the night. Worried over Solomon, tangled up inside by the hope on Pa's face, she couldn't notice the beauty surrounding her. Worse, she couldn't think of a thing to say. Maybe Lorenzo hadn't noticed how eager her father was to pair them up.

At their approach, Poncho snorted, shifting in his traces. The harness jangled softly as he blew out a breath and made a great, white cloud.

"I'll come fetch you all for church in the morning." Lorenzo folded back the robes and knocked the snow from his boots. "Even if Solomon recovers, he should rest tomorrow."

"Don't you dare come fetch me." She hiked up her chin. "I am perfectly happy to walk."

"Not in this cold. There will be no argument."

"There has to be. Lorenzo, my family is not your responsibility. We can get to the service on our own."

"I'm just being neighborly."

"You are not our neighbor."

"Not strictly speaking, but we *are* friends. I thought we established that."

"You did. I'm still deliberating."

When his gaze found hers, her pulse leaped at his

veiled affection, shining like midnight blue dreams. *Friends,* he said, but she knew he wanted more.

So did her heart.

As if he knew, his fingertips brushed her face. He stroked a few wayward tendrils scattered by the wind from her eyes, but his touch remained on her cheek, the most tender touch she had ever known.

Move, feet, she commanded. But not as much as a toe wiggled. She remained rooted to the ground, unable to escape as Lorenzo smiled into her eyes, chasing all the chill from the night. It was as if she could see into his soul. As if he could see into hers.

"Thank you for helping Solomon. For everything." Surely he could see how grateful she was.

Gratitude was all she could let herself feel.

"I'm always here for you." His gaze slid downward to land on her lips. The wish shone in his eyes, but he didn't move forward. He didn't bend closer. He didn't lean in. "Never forget that. Ever."

"As much as I would want to, that's an offer I can't accept." Think of Scarlet and Kate, she thought. Think of Pa alone in the shed on Uncle's land. Think of the Davis's manor house and the elegant daughter-in-law they would have one day. "I'm just being realistic."

"I see." Hurt crinkled in the corners of his eyes, but his understanding did not dim. Surely he could see all that divided them. "Until tomorrow." He tipped his hat, making her heart twist as he climbed into his sleigh.

Do not wish, Ruby. Not even once. She fisted her hands, trembling with the strain as he snapped Poncho's reins and the horse took off at a fast clip. The sleigh bobbed away, taking Lorenzo with it, growing distant on the beautiful prairie. The stars illuminated the entire landscape, tossing glowing lavender across the miles of radiant snow, across him.

She stood in the dark.

I'm just being realistic. Ruby's confession whispered to him over and over, all the way across the glacial prairie. He stared at the reins in his hands, not that he was really driving. Poncho had taken charge and was heading for home lickety-split. He wasted no time turning up the driveway and trotting up the lane where he'd first spotted Ruby looking for her shoe button. Soft emotions melted in his chest, warming him.

How nervous he'd been that day, and he shook his head, remembering. Wanting to badly to have a chance with her. Just one chance. The wish on her face tonight and the sweet longing for something more had been unmistakable. He'd felt the punch of hope with all the breadth of his spirit before she'd gently, sadly turned him down. That told him something. That she cared about him, but not enough. And he understood why. She couldn't let herself.

Poncho nickered, glad when the lights from the house came into sight. The sprawling, two-story home he'd been born in seemed ostentatious after seeing Ruby's humble shanty. The well-built barns and stables housing a herd of fine horses seemed far too lavish after being inside the Ballard's two-stall, sod barn. He didn't know why his family had been so materially blessed, but he did know that those blessings weren't ones he had earned, only stood to inherit. And that Ruby's circumstances were about as bad as they could get.

Solomon's symptoms troubled him as he climbed out of the sleigh, stiff from the cold. Poncho had stopped all on his own, just inside the main barn, apparently grateful for the shelter from the cold.

"You did good tonight, boy." He rubbed the gelding's nose. "Practically a hero."

Poncho nickered low, content, arching his neck with pride. He nibbled the brim of Lorenzo's hat playfully, as if to say he hadn't minded the cold. Not for Ruby.

Yes, he knew how that was. A great love shimmered within him, as pure as the starlight splashing silver across the land. He gave the reins to Thacker, glad for the boy's help, patted Poncho's neck one last time and headed for the house.

He stomped snow from his boots on the back doorstep, the great void of the night echoing around him. He couldn't feel the doorknob, his hands were so numb. He stumbled into the warmth, leaned against the door to close it. His parents and sister would still be up. He fumbled with his gloves, hat and finally got the buttons undone on his coat. He knew his mother would bring up the ball again. Best to face her and get this over with.

"There you are." Pa turned his newspaper page with a rustle, tucked in his chair near the parlor's hearth. "Your mother was starting to worry, but I told her you're a grown man. You can take care of yourself."

"I've been doing it for a long time." He resisted the urge to roll his eyes, crossing straight to the blazing fire roaring in the grate. Since his feet were a tad numb, he stumbled over the edge of the rug.

"Renzo, look at you. You're half frozen." His mother looked up from her embroidery hoop. Beside her, his sister rolled her eyes and went back to her needlework. "Jerry, what are you going to do about that boy?"

"He's a grown man. Not much I can do at this late

date," Gerard joked, eyes sparkling. No doubt his father had a good guess as to what his son had been up to. "They say you reap what you sow. If you wanted him to turn out differently, you should have done something about it long before now, Selma."

"Yes, it's all my fault how he turned out. It's a shame."

His parents' jovial laughter warmed the parlor more mightily than any hearth's flame. Bella pulled her needle through the fabric, fussing with it. He turned around to warm up his backside. If he kept rotating like a cooking spit, he might thaw completely before bedtime.

"You were gone a mighty long time. Was there another problem with the cattle?" Pa's amusement knew no end as he lowered his paper. "Is the cougar back? Or rustlers this time, maybe?"

"You know Poncho and I headed to town." He rotated again to face the fire. No sense giving his folks free reign to read his expression. What he felt for Ruby was private. Sacred.

"That's right." His father nodded. "Didn't you have a church thing?"

"The caroling group." Ma was quick to answer. Hard to mistake the happiness in her voice. "So many nice, quality young women there. It's good for you to get out and socialize, Renzo. Maybe make up your mind about who you are inviting to the ball?"

Yep, he knew that was coming. He shifted his weight from foot to foot, holding his frostbitten hands up to the fire. "I've made up my mind, but I'm not in the mood to tell you."

"Gerard, your son is torturing me." Ma's laughter rang like merry bells.

"My son? Why is he only *my* son when you're displeased with him?"

"It just seems fitting."

"Then take comfort, my dear, in the fact that he was gone long enough to escort a lady home from church and spend time talking with her and her family in their parlor."

"Which lady?" Bella's head popped up. "Is Renzo beauing someone?"

He spun around. His younger sister giggled to herself.

"I'm so pleased." His mother beamed, near to bursting with hope as she carefully threaded her needle. "Do we know this young lady?"

"I'm not inviting her to the dance." Mostly because she would be working as a maid that night. His fingertips tingled, beginning to unthaw. He stood tall, seeing his future begin to unroll before him. Somehow, he would have to convince Ruby that she wasn't alone in wanting to help her family. That she didn't need to choose between her duty and her heart.

"But, why not?" Ma's face crinkled up in dismay. "I simply don't understand this."

"I do. Think about it, my dear. There is one young lady he's been spending time with." Pa chuckled, turning his newspaper page with a rustle. "I hope you know what you're doing, Renzo."

"It really wasn't my decision, Pa." His heart had done that for him. Affection filled him, steadfast and true. He couldn't wait until morning to see her.

"You and young Mr. Davis have been spending a lot of time together." Seated in his chair near the hearth,

Pa's whittling knife flashed in the firelight. "Is there anything you want to tell your old man?"

What was she going to do about her misguided father?

"There is nothing to tell." Honestly. Ruby pulled the flatiron out of the flames with the tongs. "Young Mr. Davis, as you call him, is my employer's son. I'm bound to see him, since I work in his home."

"What about tonight?" Pa turned the slim piece of wood and set his knife's blade to carving. "That man went six miles round trip, out of his way to bring you home in his sleigh. It's freezing out there."

"I hope he's home and warm by now." She wrapped the bed iron carefully in a towel and stacked it on top of the other. Poor Pa. He had such high hopes. "Lorenzo was only being kind. Don't read too much into it."

"Kind? That's true, but he didn't have to stay and help tend Solomon. He's acting like a courting man. At least, that's my opinion." Pa's whittling knife stilled as he shifted in his chair. His hip and leg bothered him especially in cold weather. "He's sweet on you, Ruby Ann."

"He can't be anything more than a friend, and you know it."

"I know no such thing."

"You are stubborn. At least, I know where I get it." She hung the tongs on the hook on the wall. "Mrs. Davis paid me at the end of my shift today."

"What do you plan to do with your earnings?" Pa set down his knife.

"I want it to go in your savings account, for the mortgage payment." She fisted her hands, determined to ask the question she already knew the answer to. "Will it be enough of a difference?"

"No, not without Rupert's job." He hung his head, hiding his expression from her. His sadness hung in the air.

And his failure.

To hear it spoken aloud and to listen to the finality of it hit like a punch. She grasped the edge of the hearth, unsteady, the stones hot against her fingertips. How she wished there could be a different answer. Not for herself, but for Pa.

"Is there anything else I can do?" She wasn't skilled enough with a needle to take in sewing, but maybe she could find a cleaning job on Sundays—

"No, sweetheart. I know you've been hoping to keep this home, and I know this hurts you."

"Don't worry about me, Pa." She gathered the bed irons into her arms, determined to keep her chin up. "Whatever happens, we have each other. The good Lord is watching over us."

"Exactly." Pa's attempt to smile fell short. For a brief moment, devastation flashed in his dark eyes, but just for a moment. His strong jaw firmed. "You are all grown up, Ruby Ann. Your mother, God rest her, would be incredibly proud of you."

"Oh, Pa." Tears burned in her throat at his loving words and at the mention of the mother after whom she'd been named. Life was not fair, and there were so many trials, but love was the purpose. In that way she was vastly rich. "She would be proud of you, too."

"Oh, *pshaw!*" He waved her compliment off bashfully. "I'm done with this clothespin. Is that the last you need, or should I make more?"

"It's enough. Thanks." She hugged her heavy load, grateful for the steady heat seeping through the blankets when she stumbled into the night. The tears in her eyes froze on her lashes as she battled the winds to the barn.

The night came alive beneath the brilliance of the stars, casting a storybook glow across the mantled snow. The familiar land stretched out in gentle rises and falls, full of secrets waiting to be told. The wooden fence line marching along the road wore top hats of snow, slanting haphazardly. More snow flocked the bare arms of the cottonwoods, making them seem lifelike as their limbs rose and fell.

She loved this place. It held some of the best memories of her life. Walking down that road to school every morning, knowing her friends would be there to welcome her, riding up the driveway for the very first time full of hope and joy, unable to fully believe this was their own home, the laughter as she gave Solomon a bath, the fun of planting the garden and the hours she'd spent in the deliciously hot summer sun, coaxing wild jackrabbits and deer away from her growing vegetables. How happy she had been.

This home would be a lot to lose.

She shouldered into the barn where a single lantern gleamed from a support post in the aisle. Rupert crossed through the light to take the heated irons from her.

"Thanks, these will help." They clanked, muffled by the towels, as he shifted them in his arms. The night's chill tried to creep into the unheated dwelling, but the animals' heat and the insulated walls mostly kept it out. "Solomon's sleeping. He's warm and snug. I'm praying he'll be fine."

"I hope so." She followed her brother down the

aisle, where Clover drowsed and her beloved Solomon didn't stir in his slumber. Beneath the blankets, his sides heaved with each breath. "I'm to blame. I should have come straight home from work."

"No, you deserve to have a little fun with your friends. I would have done the same." He knelt to tuck both irons into the hay, one beneath Solomon's blanket and another in the bedroll he'd made next to him. "Solomon is nearing the end of his life. God is in charge of that, so don't worry. It wasn't your fault."

It was little comfort. "Do you know about the mortgage payment?"

"We've scraped and saved all we could, but it just isn't meant to be."

She bit her bottom lip to hide her grief. Leaving became real. Not some imagined fear she was desperate to stave off, but an inevitable situation. She fisted her hands, resolved to handle this sensibly, for her father's sake.

"Solomon will get better." Maybe she could will it so. She peered over the rail. All four of his hooves moved slightly beneath the blankets, lost in horsy dreams. Love for her old friend filled her. "I could take shifts with you tonight."

"Forget it. I am not letting you do that in this cold. I'm used to it." He shrugged his brawny shoulders, her big brother, able to do anything. "Now go in the house before you turn into an icicle. Or, in your case, a ruby-cicle."

"Funny." She rolled her eyes. She'd missed Rupert's humor, but she wasn't about to tell him that or the jokes would never stop coming. "I suppose we are stuck with you for a while, so I had better get used to having you back."

"Not for long." Roop leaned against the wall, arms folded across his chest, enveloped by shadow. "I've got a few possibilities. If it's God's will, I may be gone on the next train."

"Another job?" Joy leaped within her. "Oh, that would be good news indeed."

"Yes." He didn't seem happy, just coldly determined. "We must wait and see. In the meantime, get yourself out of here. I don't want you worrying, Ruby-bug."

"I'm glad you're home." Why couldn't she fight the sinking feeling that whatever kind of job Roop was seeking would not be a good situation for him?

She shut the door securely behind her, needing heaven to be closer.

Watch over my brother too, please, Father. She held her prayer close to her heart and with all the strength of her soul.

Chapter Thirteen

The thump of the cookstove's door closing startled Ruby from a sound sleep. Warm and snug in her dreams, she batted her eyes open to the arctic morning. The nail heads in the wall boards froze furry white, and the sheet serving as a curtain to separate her bed from the rest of the main room had also frozen stiff. Not the best of signs. All she wanted to do was to stay tucked in her toasty covers.

"Ruby, time to rise and shine." There was a metallic clink as Pa opened the stove's damper. The crackle of kindling and the whir of new, hungry flames filled the silent shanty. "It's the Lord's day and that means church. If Solomon is strong enough to be left alone, that is."

"I'm praying he is." Weekly church and Sunday school were pleasures she would miss. While she could love the Lord anywhere and study His teachings, irregular services from a traveling minister at the settlement near her uncle's farm simply would not be the same.

She threw back the covers, and the glacial air hit her like an avalanche. Teeth clacking, she chose her Sunday dress and her best cardigan and slipped into both. The back door clicked shut, leaving her alone. She washed up, plaited her hair in one long braid and pulled back the curtain.

"Ruby!" The back door popped open, scattering her thoughts. She grabbed the metal handle of the coffeepot and lifted it from the shelf, guilty she hadn't yet made coffee. The haggard grief on Pa's face stopped her. Devastation darkened the eyes that avoided hers. He didn't have to say a word, she could guess.

"Solomon." The coffeepot slipped from her fingers and clattered to the floor. Horror hit her like a runaway train straight to the chest. "Is he...?"

"Sick. Gravely sick." Pa scrubbed a hand over his face. His shoulders, always so straight and strong, slumped. Defeated, he blew out a ragged breath and said no more, as if he was trying to pull himself together.

"What do we do?" Her voice wobbled. Everything wobbled. She clutched the edge of the table, shaking so hard she rattled that, too.

"You sit down before you fall down, honey." Pa hefted the water bucket onto the stove top. Droplets sizzled and popped on the hot surface. "Let me brew up some coffee. I reckon Roop could use something hot. He's been up since the wee hours."

"No, I can do it." She rescued the pot from the floor and gave it a quick swipe before filling it with water. She felt wooden, no longer real as she measured out fragrant coffee grounds. Pa filled the coffeepot with water. What would they do without Solomon? He was family.

"I know this is hard, Ruby. That horse has lived a good, long life. We have all made sure he was as happy as we could make him." Pa's hand settled on her shoulder, consolation on this harsh morn. "Let's do all we can now to make him comfortable."

"Yes, Pa." Hollow inside, she knelt to grab the ring in the floor. A tug lifted the door and revealed three steps into the cellar below. She breathed in the cold scents of earth and stored vegetables as she dropped into the frigid space. Quickly, she grabbed the butter dish, last night's leftover potatoes and cut bacon strips from the slab. *Oh, Solomon.* Grief made her stagger. First she'd fix a hot breakfast for Pa and Roop, then she would go to him.

Boots plodded on the floorboards above, and a shadow fell over her.

"Ruby." Lorenzo reached down to pluck the bowl of potatoes out of her hands. "Hand up what you've got and fetch me three onions and some mustard seed, will you?"

She blinked, not quite believing her eyes. "You came."

"I promised, didn't I?" He took the bacon and butter from her and disappeared from sight.

"H-have you seen Solomon yet?" She couldn't seem to untie the onion sack. She swallowed hard, willed her fingers to shake less and tried again.

"Yes."

Nothing more. Silence settled in, and she feared what he didn't say. The string gave, and she counted out the onions. Their papery skins crackled as she handed them up.

A dark day's growth clung to Lorenzo's angled jaw, making him look like a western legend as he held out his hand. Her fingers wrapped around his, and he swept her up the steps and into the kitchen. She landed on her feet, not wanting to let go.

She shouldn't be so glad to see him. She shouldn't be wanting to lean on him. How did she stop the emotion in her heart? She didn't know. It glowed like sunlight on winter snow, lyrical and radiant with a life all its own.

"I had to come check on Solomon. I had a feeling he might not bounce back." He knelt at her feet to close the trapdoor.

"Why are you doing this? It can't be for m-me." She choked on the word, afraid to say it out loud. "It shouldn't be."

"It was Poncho's idea. He cares a great deal for you." Loving warmth gentled his deep tone. He wasn't talking about a horse's feelings.

"I care a great deal for Poncho, too." She blushed, not at all comfortable confessing her feelings. She wasn't talking about the horse, either.

"That's good to hear." He rose up to his full height, towering above her, manly and strong and good. He brushed stray tendrils out of her eyes. In his, she saw forever. A future she could not have. Being beaued by him. Being courted. Accepting a proposal and planning a wedding.

All that would happen for another girl. Someone who was free to love him in return. *Let it be Scarlet,* she prayed, as she shuttered her gaze and turned away. *If not Scarlet, then Kate.*

"Slice the onions thinly, cook them into a soft mash in the fry pan and add crushed mustard seed." His boots rang on the hardwood. He set the onion on the table with a mild thunk. "I brought this packet of herbs from home. Mix this in halfway through."

How did she thank him? The words clogged in her throat. She could only gape like a fish out of water, struggling for air. He was doing all this for Solomon. It was impossible to adore him any more than she already did, but her poor heart tumbled even farther. No way to stop it.

"I would fix the poultice myself, but I want to help Rupert. I know he's had a long night." Lorenzo's hand settled against her jaw, the warmth of his palm and the slight abrasion of his calloused fingers felt dearer than anything she'd ever known.

All her willpower was not enough to keep her from pressing into his touch just a little, just the tiniest, ittiest bit.

"Go." She put a shield around her heart, trying to resist, and wished she had the strength to step away from him. "Please help Solomon. I'll be out with the poultice when it's done."

"Bring several dish towels when you do." He moved away, as if reluctant, too. The impact of his unguarded blue gaze felt as physical as his touch had been and went deep into her soul. He broke away and strode out of the shanty, but the sweetness remained.

You are walking on dangerous ground, Ruby Ann. She plucked up the knife, the wooden handle rough against her fingers. The shield around her heart wasn't strong enough. He had gotten around it, gotten in. What was she going to do about it? How was she going to stop it? She had no clue.

She set the blade to the head of the onion and sliced through papery skin. Juice spilled over her fingertips and stung her eyes as she pried off the outside layers. She heard the faint rumble of men's voices through the walls—Pa and Lorenzo talking as they met on the path to the barn.

Lorenzo. She respected him, she adored him, she felt affection for him. But that was all. She could not go any further. She could not fall in love with Lorenzo. Her feelings were on the brink of the rocky edge of a cliff ready to plummet. She had to resist. She had to be a fortress.

Was she strong enough? She did not know.

She wasn't prepared for the sight of the man seated in the straw with the horse's head in his lap. Did he have to be so wonderful? It was Lorenzo's fault she was falling. Any woman would be defenseless again his kindness.

Poncho, tied in the aisle, moved aside for her to pass and nibbled on the edge of her hood as she squeezed by him. Clover stretched across the rails of her stall, curious to see what was in the fry pan. Pa busily forked soiled straw out of the stall, while Rupert replaced it with fresh clean hay.

"It's ready," she said simply.

"Excellent." Lorenzo gently lifted Solomon's head and slid away. He stopped to draw a handkerchief out of his coat pocket and patted dry the gelding's copiously running nose.

Touched, she drew herself up straight, gathering her willpower. *Don't fall in love him, Ruby Ann. Be completely unaffected by him.*

She uncovered the fry pan. "Is this what you meant?"

"It's just right." He smelled of winter wind and hay and horse, a manly combination as he leaned in to take the handle. Steam rolled between them, ripe with onions and the earthy scent of herbs. He took one glove off with his teeth and touched his fingertips into the mixture. "Good, not too hot. Come with me."

Solomon's heavy breathing rasped painfully. His sides heaved as if every breath of air was an impossible strain. Her poor friend. She knelt near the gelding's belly. When she placed her hand on his flesh, his short coarse coat was damp with fever. He moaned once, aware of her presence and her touch.

"You're such a good boy," she told him in her softest voice. "You are the very best horse."

Pa came to stand at Solomon's haunches. They watched as Lorenzo ladled a big scoop of the strong-smelling mash onto the gelding's side, right behind his front leg.

"Let me help." She leaned forward using her good hand to spread the mixture. Steam rose as they worked together in silence. Facing one another, she shook out a dish towel, a bit scorched from her attempt to warm it on the stove. Lorenzo caught two corners and together they lowered it over the poultice to trap in heat.

Did she dare look up? Did she dare meet his gaze? Her throat closed up. Panic popped through her bloodstream and she didn't know what to do. She didn't know how to fight what was happening to her.

"That's awful clever, young Mr. Davis." Pa broke the silence, sounding pleased and sheepish all at once. "I should have thought to do the same. It's like what my mother, God rest her, used on me when I was young."

"My grandfather said what works for us can work for horses. First we loosen up the mucus in his lungs and see if we can bring it up." Lorenzo gently patted Solomon's neck. The gelding nickered with great effort and coughed hard, a terrible hacking sound. He feared he had come too late to make a difference. For Ruby's sake, he would continue to try. He glanced toward the door, but Rupert hadn't returned yet with a bucket of boiling water.

He circled around to Solomon's nose and knelt there, so close to Ruby he could see the slight intake of her breath at his nearness. Her eyes popped wide, and the ice-blue flecks in her irises dazzled. The boom of his pulse rocked through him, and it took all his discipline to hold his hands steady as he globbed the poultice on Solomon's chest. The animal's nostrils flared in protest. He lifted his head, rocking his big body. He was too weak to get up.

"Easy, big fella," Lorenzo crooned, hand on the horse's sweaty shoulder. "Just trust me. I'll take care of you, boy."

Solomon's big, chocolate, horse eyes met his with desperation. Easy to read the fear and pain there. He knew God gave creatures a feeling heart, so he wanted to offer what care he could. He set the pan in the straw and stroked the gelding's neck with his clean hand, willing all the comfort he could into his touch. The coarse velvet coat, the feel of life beneath his fingertips, the shuddering sigh as Solomon eased his head onto his pillow of hay and closed his eyes. His sides heaved as he struggled to breathe, the ghostly rasp echoing through the small structure.

"He's hurting." Ruby sounded tortured. "What else can I do for him?"

"Comfort him." There was nothing more to do. The tinny taste of dread filled his mouth, and he wiped his hand, sticky from the poultice, on a dish towel. He couldn't look away as Ruby spread her arms wide and hugged as much of the horse, belly to back, as she could. Tears spiked her eyelashes.

"Stay with me," she whispered. "Please."

Surely heaven had to hear that plea. He cleared emotion from his throat, set aside the fry pan and studied the woman clinging to the old horse. The most vulnerable places inside him opened ever wider, leaving him without a single defense. A powerful ache he'd never known before, one of pure emotion and spirit gripped him so hard, he thought his heart failed. Love so keen it hurt roared through him with the strength of a lion and the gentleness of a lamb.

There was no going back. No changing his feelings. The iron-clad commitment binding him to her was unbreakable. Unable to resist, his hand landed on her shoulder. She was as fine-boned as a bird, as delicate as a winter's snowflake, as amazing as a miracle. That was Ruby, *his* Ruby. For the rest of his life, he would remain committed to her, bound to her.

Nothing would change that. Regardless of what happened, whether they were together or forever apart.

Across the top of Ruby's blue, knit cap, Jon Ballard nodded slowly, once. Apparently the older man understood. Heat stretched tight across Lorenzo's cheeks, but it felt good that Jon approved.

Rupert clamored in with two heavy buckets in each hand. Poncho nickered, curious as to the contents, and Lorenzo turned his efforts once again on the dying horse.

Pay attention, Ruby. She flipped a slice of bacon in the frying pan, wincing at the over-brown meat. Fat sizzled and popped in the pan as she turned the remaining pieces, fearing the worst. No, they didn't appear to be too scorched, at least Rupert and Pa would never complain. But Lorenzo would be sitting down to their breakfast table. He was not used to burned food, since she knew firsthand how exacting Cook was.

Coffee, a little over-boiled, steamed in its pot as she set it on a hot pad near Pa's place at the table. It was hard to concentrate with the knots in her stomach and the worry plaguing her. Solomon fought a high fever. Poultices and steam treatments could only do so much. She tried to imagine life without Solomon's comforting presence, his affectionate nips and snuggles and his faithful friendship. Tears burned in her throat.

The pancakes! She whirled around, realizing she'd forgotten the stove. Again. She snatched up the spatula, winced when she used her injured wrist and flipped the first cake on the griddle. She expected a black surface, but it was still golden brown.

Whew. Relief skittered through her as she flipped the rest of the cakes, one after another and watched them carefully.

"I hear you have coffee in here." Lorenzo blew in with a bracing wind.

"That rumor is true," she confirmed, every thought fleeing at his presence.

What was it about the man that affected her? Why him? Why when it was so impossible? She did not know.

The pancakes! She tightened her grip on the spatula, feeling every inch of Lorenzo's gaze as she shoveled the pancakes off the griddle and onto the platter.

"Jon insisted I come in and thaw out. I didn't want to be rude and argue with him, so I agreed." He swept off his hat, scattering tiny flakes that spiraled through the air. "Solomon seems to be improving."

"He is?" She lost hold of the spatula. It clattered to the stovetop and splashed into the bacon pan. "He's so ill. How can you be sure?"

"I can't be. He could still take a bad turn, but he's breathing easier for now. His fever is still high, but better. We've done all we can do. It is in God's hands."

"As all things are." Relief quivered through her, and she rescued the spatula. The wooden handle was slick with grease, and she rubbed it with a dishcloth.

Lorenzo's socks whispered on the plank floor behind her. "That smells good. You could give Cook competition."

"Hardly. You have to stop telling fibs."

His laughter echoed in the room, a merry note. "I'm complimenting you, Ruby. Sincerely."

"You haven't tasted my cooking yet." She flipped the bacon, fighting as hard as she could not to give in to her adoration. "Oh, the biscuits."

What was wrong with her this morning? Lorenzo, he was also the problem. The man tied up her tongue and her mind, and she grabbed the hot pad and instantly dropped it.

"Let me." He knelt, so close she could feel the cold radiating off his clothes. A dark swirl of hair formed a cowlick at the back of his head and she wanted to run her fingers through it.

Brilliant, Ruby, just perfectly brilliant. She was supposed to be resisting his charm, not doting on every little thing about the man.

Still, how could she do otherwise? He rose to his six-foot height, towering over her, ten kinds of dashing, as his solemn, midnight gaze found hers. He held her captive with a look, he captured her with his silence. She could feel the honest power of his affection as he opened the oven door and knelt to slide out the baking sheet. The connection between them cinched tighter, more binding than before.

A connection she could not allow.

She plunged a cloth into a serving bowl and spread it out, using a fork to slide the buttermilk biscuits off the baking sheet one by one. They plopped into the bowl, steaming and crumbly good, and she breathed in their sweet, doughy scent.

"Thank you." She covered the biscuits with the corners of the cloth, trapping the heat. When she looked up, Lorenzo stood before her, his gaze intent on hers.

Don't notice the light in his eyes. Don't notice his look of great caring, she told herself. *Be strong, Ruby. Don't give in. You can't fall in love with him.*

"I'm glad to help out. I'll stay as long as Solomon needs it." His gaze slid downward to focus on her mouth. More intense this time. Like he was honestly considering leaning in and kissing her.

She gulped. *Must not let him kiss you, Ruby.* Air wheezed in and out. Panic skittered through her. "I'm sure Solomon will appreciate that very much."

"I'll do everything I can to save him."

"Because you love horses?" A girl had to hope Lorenzo really did care about the horse, that Solomon was the reason he was here.

"Because I love horses." His smile and his eyes said something different.

For one precious moment, the chasm separating them closed. They were no longer divided. Firelight danced over them from the hearth, and sunshine from the window graced them like a blessing.

If only this could be. She saw the same wish in his eyes. The same longing prayer in his soul. Now how was she going to stop falling any harder for him?

Boots stamping off snow echoed in the lean-to, shattering the moment. Lorenzo stepped away as the kitchen door swung open, as Pa stumbled in, shrugging off his coat.

Chapter Fourteen

She'd worried all Sunday long, and this morning turned out to be no different. She wished she could be home, checking on Solomon's recovery. She knew he was safe in Pa's caring hands, but did that stop her from imagining the worst? Trying to think positive didn't help. Ruby balanced the serving tray in both hands, ignoring the twist of pain in her left wrist and hurried out of the kitchen.

She'd never seen such activity. The parlor was a madhouse. Both the upstairs and downstairs maids climbed ladders and handed down the yards upon yards of lace and velvet curtains to be washed, ironed and hung for the approaching ball. Others rolled up the exquisite carpets to be beaten and spot cleaned. The same activities went on in every room throughout the mansion's main floor.

"Ruby, dear." Mrs. Davis granted her a beaming smile, circling furniture and weaving among the busy workers. "You have perfect timing. Please, leave that on the coffee table. I think we could all use a mid-morning break."

"Cook thought you all might like some scones." She slid the tray onto the table, kneeling carefully, just as Cook had taught her. Not a droplet splashed over the teacup rims, and not a single scone slipped off the platter. She was making progress.

"That was very thoughtful of her. My, but you set a very nice tray." Mrs. Davis's compliment meant a lot.

"Thank you." She had worked hard at it, using the fine linen and a pretty lace runner to pretty up the silver tray. She'd folded cloth napkins like swans, and little bowls of cubed sugar, lemon slices and mint sprigs were as artful as she could make them. She took a shaky breath, preparing for what she had to do. "May I have a word with you?"

"Absolutely." The older woman clapped her hands. "You have all worked hard this morning. Take an extralong break."

Curtains were left piled and carpets unrolled as the half dozen maids broke into conversation and crowded around the tea tray.

"We can speak in the hallway." Mrs. Davis swept toward the arched doorway, her fine skirts rustling. "How is your wrist feeling?"

"Much better, thank you." Self-conscious, she shoved her left hand as far as she could manage into her skirt pocket.

"Lucia tells me you are not exactly following doctor's orders." Selma's rebuke was kindly offered. "You must not work so hard."

"I'm stubborn."

"I've noticed. So what is the trouble, my dear?"

She gulped, unable to say the words. This was even harder than she'd imagined. Shame filled her, and she had to fight hard to keep her chin up when her head wanted to bob down. "I have to give my notice. I don't want to. I like working here."

"Then what is the problem, child?" Concern softened Selma's face, and she swept to an abrupt stop in the corridor.

Ruby squared her shoulders. She'd rehearsed what to say half of last night, when she'd been too upset to sleep. "My family has to move away. We are about to lose our farm."

"Oh, that's so sad. I'm sorry. I didn't know things at home were so serious." Compassion, not blame, shone in caring, dark eyes. "Do you have someplace to go?"

"My uncle has agreed to let us move onto his land. He lives up near the Canadian border."

"That far?" Selma's distress etched into her face. Her grip tightened as she tugged Ruby into the dining room. "Come sit and tell me about this."

"Oh, there isn't much to tell." She couldn't imagine Selma Davis would want to truly hear about her family's troubles. "My brother left on this morning's train hoping to find work, but it will probably not be in time."

"I see." She drew out a chair for Ruby and motioned for her to sit. "I am sorry to lose you. You are a good employee."

"This is a terrible way to repay your kindness."

"Is there no chance you could stay behind?" The older woman settled in the neighboring chair. "You could lodge in the maids' quarters and send your wages home. I have several other employees who do the same."

That beautiful option shimmered in front of her. She wanted to reach out and grasp it. *Just think*. She could stay here and see her friends, be here when Fiona's baby was born and for Meredith's wedding, see which house Lila and her new husband settled on buying. Most of all, she would be near Lorenzo. Remembering all he had done for Solomon, affection strengthened into an emotion she could not label.

Then she thought of her father alone in that tiny, little place, how devastated he would be. Both she and Rupert feared for him. He'd had too many hopes shattered in his life, endured tough hardships and losses. No one had worked harder than Jon Ballard to rebuild his life.

How would he take this hard blow? She didn't know, but he did not deserve to be left alone, broken of spirit and void of dreams, struggling to survive.

"I wish," she said simply. "But it cannot be."

"I will be so sorry to see you go. In fact, I am heartbroken. Does Lo—" Mrs. Davis fell silent, her question left unspoken. Genuine sympathy twisted her lovely features, and she sat up straighter, as if coming to a decision. "I will not fill your position until after the new year. That will give you time to reconsider and return if you wish."

"That is incredibly generous. I can't expect you to do that."

"I am your boss, so you will simply have to endure my decisions." Selma leaned in to brush a strand of hair out of Ruby's eyes, as concerned as a mother. "Will you at least be able to stay for the ball? I need every employee I have on staff, it's such a busy evening. Your family could use the extra pay."

"It's my hope to stay here until Christmas, but I don't know for sure. It depends on the banker. My father is trying to shield me as best he can, so he isn't very forthcoming."

"You be sure and talk to me. Let me know how things are progressing. If you need anything, you can ask me." Such loving words, so honestly spoken.

"I have everything I need." It was so easy to dwell on what was missing, on what one didn't have. Her father lived a life of integrity, and she would, too. "I need to work off the doctor's bill before I go."

"I thought we agreed that was my responsibility." Mrs. Davis drew back in her chair, appraising her carefully. "I noticed you walked to work this morning. Lorenzo told me about your horse. Is he still improving?"

"Yes, thanks to your son." She tried, how hard she tried, to keep any hint of reverence from her voice. "He saved Solomon. He spent his only day off tending our horse."

"Yes, because it was your horse, my dear." Mrs. Davis patted Ruby's hand. "You be sure and take your break. Go on with you and get some tea and scones."

Her employer's words troubled her all the way to the kitchen and through her lunch break. As she crocheted at the table with Cook, who was reading her Bible, she tried not to think about Lorenzo. But did she succeed?

No. Her mind stubbornly boomeranged to the conversation in the dining room. Mrs. Davis could not have been kinder. And to suggest Lorenzo had spent a long day in their little barn for her meant she hadn't hidden her crush on Lorenzo from his mother. Heat blazed across her face, no doubt turning her nose strawberry red. She wrapped thread around her needle and triple crocheted. She was doing a very bad job of keeping control of her heart.

Her hook stilled in the middle of her next triple crochet. She couldn't seem to control her thoughts, either,

since they rolled back around to yesterday morning.
After Pa had come into the shanty that morning, Lorenzo had joined them for breakfast and pleasant conversation about farming life. He'd stayed in the barn
until suppertime, fighting to help save Solomon's life.
He'd driven away in twilight shadows, offering her
nothing more than a silent wave.

You are in big trouble, Ruby. She shook her head
to scatter her thoughts. Determined to try again, she
focused on the big window looking out into the back-
yard. The magnificent Rocky Mountains soared from
the prairie floor to the pale blue sky, the rugged peaks
wearing capes of pearled snow. No matter what, God's
handiwork always managed to soothe her.

A movement caught her eye, a blur of color against
the stretching white, shining snow, soaring purple
mountains and reaching blue sky. Lorenzo, in his black
coat, astride his bay horse, cut across a field. A trail of
cattle ambled behind him, ears pricked, noses up, obviously fond of him.

A loud clatter rocketed through the kitchen and
shook the table alongside her. She gasped, jarred from
her thoughts as Mae scowled down at her.

"You should have fetched the tray, but as you are
Mrs. Davis's favorite, I can see I will have to be doing
a lot more around here." Her gaze followed Ruby's to
the window, and a look of knowing flashed in her narrowed eyes.

Had Mae guessed? She withered. Heat flamed more
brightly across her face, making it red enough for everyone to see. Mae knew. Mrs. Davis knew. Who else
had figured it out?

"The Christmas ball is coming up." Mae's tone

turned speculative and sugary. "I'm sure he will beau someone suitable. Someone as wealthy as he is. He always takes Narcissa Bell. My guess is he will do the same this year. Wouldn't you say, Cook?"

Why did she wince at the sound of Narcissa's name? The mention of the woman made her feel two full inches shorter.

"Don't mind me." Cook didn't look up from the Good Book. "I'm simply studying my Bible, where it says a body should mind her own business and not spread malice or practice jealousy."

"Me? I'm not jealous. I'm just trying to help." Mae gave her braid a toss. "He feels pity for you, Ruby. Nothing more. About to lose your house. How embarrassing. Hey, don't look surprised. The walls have ears around here."

So, her conversation with Mrs. Davis had been overheard. Now every employee in the house would know. The thread she held went fuzzy. She blinked hard, but it didn't help. She listened to Mae's footsteps fade away.

"Don't pay Mae much heed. She's just wishin' the young master paid her such attention." Cook closed her Bible thoughtfully. "I've never seen Master Lorenzo take to any lass the way he has you. Beauty is as beauty does, and to some and to Him, that's what matters."

Across the long span of snowy yard and field, Lorenzo, tall in his saddle, faced her. Although the distance was too great, and there was no way he could see her, her spirit tugged as if he could.

There was no safe way back. She was fooling herself to think there was. That she could control her heart and stop her feelings, to save herself from heartbreak. She gave her thread a tug, thread Lorenzo had given her, and made a wobbly stitch. She had fallen too far, wanting what she could not have. It was her own fault she hurt so much. She had no one but herself to blame. At week's end, she would be packing to leave town and she would never see Lorenzo again.

Earlee Mills swept out of the post office onto the sunny, late afternoon boardwalk, heart tapping with excitement. Joy swooped through her like a sweet spring breeze as she plunked down on the nearest bench, ignored the ice and cold and ran her fingertips across the envelope.

Finn had written her name in his bold, confident script, and she took a moment to simply look at her name written in his hand. Earlee Mills. One day would she be Earlee McKaslin? Her pulse skipped a beat. It was her dearest wish.

If only Finn felt the same way about her. They had been exchanging letters since spring, regular letters, one or more every week. He'd been friendly, he'd been honest, and as time went on, he had been more and more open. But never had he given a single hint that he felt anything more for her than friendship.

Still, she dreamed.

"Hi, Miss Mills!" Tommy Bellamy skipped toward her down the boardwalk, holding his mother's hand. Beside him, his brother Charlie made a funny face.

"Hi there, Tommy and Charlie." She adored her little students, even the troublemakers. "Hello, Mrs. Bellamy."

"Good afternoon, Miss Mills." Clarice Bellamy smiled kindly. "How nice to see you. I trust my boys are behaving themselves better these days?"

"Much. Charlie had to write lines only once so far this week."

"I suppose that's an improvement." The mother shook her head slightly, in good humor, as she herded her sons down the boardwalk.

So it was with a smile on her face that she carefully tore open Finn's envelope and unfolded his letter.

Dear Earlee,
My day is always a bright one when a letter from you arrives.

Why, didn't that make a girl hope? A smile stretched across her face, and she read on.

Life is the same here, work, sleep, work, sleep. But during the long hours of moving rock in the quarry, I have a lot of time to think and reflect on what I should have done differently in my life. Lots of time to think hard on how I will make better choices when I'm out. Working for my brother on his farm sounds like heaven right now. Even in winter. I miss hearing the prairie winds howling over the plains. I can't wait to hear them again. The winds blow where I am, but it is a different sound that is lonely on the stone walls of the prison. When I'm in the quarry, the wind has a different tune in the mountains here, rustling through trees. I miss home and everyone there.

Her hopes wanted to read more into that last line. He hadn't written, I miss you, Earlee Elizabeth Mills, she told herself. So don't pretend that he did.

But she sure wished he had.

*I'm not surprised at all to learn you are a writer.
Your letters have entertained me and made me
feel connected to home, to someone, since I'm so
lonely here.*

He didn't say he felt connected to you, she reminded
herself, although the hope in her heart fluttered more.

*Have you ever thought about trying to publish
one of your stories? I think you should. I believe
in you, Earlee. You have come to be very special to me.*

Wow! She had to read that last line twice to make
sure she hadn't imagined it. He really cared about her.
She clutched the letter to her heart, unable to keep her
hopes from rising higher and taking all her wishes and
dreams with it.

Tiny flecks hovered in the air, invisible in the night-
fall. They swirled with her breath and dampened her
face and iced on the road at her feet. Ruby prayed the
buttons on her old shoes would hold for the mile walk
to town and the even longer journey home. Her newer
pair of shoes weighed down her bag, where they would
stay dry.

She picked her way along the icy ruts. While she'd
helped Cook prepare the Davis's supper, talk of rustlers'
tracks circulated through the house. Likely Lorenzo
would be too busy to go to practice tonight.

That would be a relief. She needed to start easing

her heart away from him. He'd never really been hers. She hadn't needed Mae to tell her that. She'd known it all along.

Behind her the faint squeak of approaching sleigh runners on the ice broke the stillness. The *clip* of horseshoes and the bell-like jingle of the harness grew nearer. She veered toward the edge of the road, to let whoever it was pass by. But she didn't need the horse's friendly nicker to know who was driving the sleigh. She felt the mellow glow in her soul crescendo, the way it did when Lorenzo was around.

So, he was coming, after all. She would have to see him. Have to fight the gathering heartbreak threatening to engulf her.

Poncho pulled up alongside her and stopped, his horsy eyes sparkling, glad to see her. He reached out with his whiskery lips to catch the fringe on her scarf with his teeth.

"Hello to you, handsome." She knew Lorenzo watched her as she caught her scarf before his horse could tug it off her. She rubbed that velvety nose and muzzle with her mittened hand. "You look quite dashing. Did your mane get a trim?"

"He's touched that you noticed." Lorenzo held back the robes and offered his hand. "C'mon. Accept a ride. You'll hurt Poncho's feelings if you don't."

"Poncho. What am I going to do with you?" She gave the horse one more pat, the sweet guy, before facing the man who was her real problem. The plea in his dark blue gaze was impossible to turn down. It hooked deep into her, reeling her closer like a fish on a line.

"My mother told me you gave your notice today." His

fingers closed around hers to assist her into the sleigh. "How did it go?"

"It was hard, but once I got the words out, your mother was nice about it." She gathered her skirts, settled next to him and extricated her fingers from his grip. "She offered to let me live in the maid quarters."

"Really? That's a good idea." He leaned close to tuck in the robes. "Any chance you will?"

"No." Her apology rang quietly in her words. She looked away from him, staring at the smudge of the town up ahead, dark against the endless, white prairie. "We discussed it last night after you left. This morning, Pa walked Rupert to the train and stopped by the bank on his way home."

"Then it's official." He gave the reins a snap.

"Yes. Pa told them we can't come up with the money." She shrugged her slender shoulders as if she wasn't devastated. "Oh, well." She gave a little sigh.

He wasn't fooled by it. "I really am sorry."

"The hard thing is we were planning on packing the wagon bed and driving north. But now, Solomon is too frail to make the trip north so we have leave him here." Her face crumpled. "I'm worried about what will become of him. Who would buy him in his condition? Probably someone meaning to render him."

"I'm sorry, Ruby." He wanted to reach out to her, but she sat at the far edge of the sleigh, as far away from him as she could get. "You grew up with Solomon."

"I did. He was my only friend as a child. I would make dandelion necklaces, which he would proudly wear, and I'd always share my jelly sandwiches with him."

He tried to imagine Ruby as a child. Petite and lean,

with her fine, white-blond hair and winter-sky blue eyes. He reckoned she was probably the cutest thing around. Ruby's daughter one day might look just like that.

Their little girl would have looked just like that. His throat tightened until he could barely speak.

"I have been praying for a good outcome for you and your family. For Solomon, too." He cleared his throat, but the weight of his emotions remained, making him sound gruff. "When exactly will you be leaving?"

"That's up to the banker. I'll find out from Pa when I get home tonight. This is terribly painful for him." Compassion and concern painted her eyes a deeper blue. The lantern light on the dash caressed her, finding ways to adore the curve of her cheekbone or the darling cut of her chin. Her heart-shaped face became even more stunning in the golden light. "I'm hoping I will spend Christmas here, where I have so many friends."

"I hope so, too. I hate to see you go, Ruby." He pulled back on the reins, slowing Poncho on the approach to town.

"You won't miss me one whit when I'm gone." Her Cupid's-bow mouth hooked up at the corners, an attempt at a smile. It couldn't hide the sadness in her eyes.

The sadness at leaving him? That was his hope. "I wasn't kidding. I intend to write. I might be boring, I might be dull, all I do these days is work on the ranch, but I will write."

"Then I suppose I would have to answer." Snowflakes glimmered like diamonds in her hair.

"See that you do. Poncho would be mad if I didn't keep in touch. We could always take a trip up north to visit. Just in case Poncho really gets to missing you."

"What?" She bit her bottom lip, stunned at his offer. Lorenzo wanted to come see her? Anguish swirled within her chest. *No,* she wanted to say. It was what she *had* to say.

"After all, good friends need to keep in touch." His words rumbled with intent, so intimate and respectful, his entire focus seemed to be her. His eyes were full of light, his features soft, his touch gentle as he cupped his hands to her face. Amazing tenderness filled the air, soaring from his heart to hers.

Never had she wanted anything so much. She grasped as hard as she could to her stubborn resolve, but she was not strong enough to resist. How could she be? The powerful forces of her feelings knocked down her last defenses. *I will not love him,* she thought helplessly as he leaned in kissing-close.

Escape. Quick. Now. Those were her last coherent thoughts as his lips slanted over hers, hovering, softening, only a breath could fit between them now. His eyes were as dark as a night sky and full of gently glowing affection. Her pulse galloped crazily, nerves skidded through her. His lips brushed hers as gently as a butterfly's wing for one brief moment before he hesitated and pulled away.

Pulled away. Her lips tingled with the pure sensation of his kiss, but he had ended it. Disappointment, confusion, embarrassment tore through her, and she tried to make sense of it. Had he had second thoughts, changed his mind or finally realized she was never going to be what he needed? Maybe he'd regained his senses like she had and knew they didn't belong together.

"You are the sweetest thing ever." His baritone rang softly, full of feeling.

"Proof you don't know me very well," she quipped, unable to endure the exquisite tenderness as his gaze caressed hers. She looked away at the street, at the boardwalk, anything but him. She'd done the unthinkable. She'd let him closer when she should be pushing him away.

What was wrong with her? Why had she messed up everything so badly? Her father was counting on her. Her friends—heavens, what would they think about her if they knew how weak she was? How selfish?

"I know everything I need to about you." He caught her chin in his hand and looked within her so deeply, there was no end. Only the sheen of his eyes where love lived.

This cannot be happening. She fisted her hands, trying to wrestle back to reality, but his chiseled lips captured hers again in the most wonderful, the most reverent, the most loving of kisses. Unbearable emotion stole through her as stealthy as the night, pulling at the deepest places of her spirit, cutting like a blade. Love she could not hold back tore through her like a winter's torrent, a million snowflakes blotting out the world.

No kiss had ever been so flawless. She could feel his love for her, and tears prickled behind her eyes. His love, equal to hers. She had never imagined, never dared to dream. But as his lips stroked hers one last, pure time, she caught a glimpse of what could be. A perfect life spent in his arms. A perfect love.

A vision she had to let go of.

"Look where Poncho brought us." His words rumbled against her ear.

She blinked, fighting to bring the real world into focus. A shadowed steeple speared upward as snow began to fall in earnest, airy flakes. The church, she realized as the sleigh stopped. Poncho nickered and arched his neck in pride at his cleverness.

"Ruby!" Earlee waved as she spun on the pathway. "What are you—" Her eyes popped wide in surprise as she recognized Lorenzo in the sleigh. "Oh, maybe I should just keep going."

"No, wait." The moment was over. She had to accept it. She tied up the ribbons of her heart, buried her love for him with all her might and flung back the driving robes. Lorenzo reached to help, but she stopped him with a touch of her mitten to his glove. "Thank you for the ride, but I'll be fine from here."

"Are you sure?" Furrows dug into his forehead, and his gaze searched hers again, but she had to stay closed to him.

She didn't know what to say. Her tongue tied, her thoughts tangled up in knots, making her brain completely useless. She climbed from the sleigh with all the composure she could muster. She gripped her bag tightly. She was an adult, no longer a schoolgirl, and reality could not be wished away. Within days, surely by the end of the week, she would be on a train with her father. She set her chin and walked away.

No matter how many steps she took or how hard she tried, distance did not separate them.

Chapter Fifteen

"What were you doing in Lorenzo's sleigh?" Earlee whispered, clutching Ruby's hand and drawing her up the walkway. "Tell me. Is there something I don't know? What's going on? Is he your beau?"

"No. He can never be that. He came upon me walking on the road. Earlee, I'm begging you. Please don't say anything." Disgrace washed over her. What would Earlee think, knowing how Kate and Scarlet felt about the man? The treasured memory of his kiss burdened her. She hiked her bag higher on her shoulder and blanched at the weight of her guilt.

"But why were you walking in the first place? It's a long way from the Davis ranch to town."

"Solomon is ill."

"Oh, that's why you missed church and yesterday's sewing circle. We worried." Earlee glanced over her shoulder, probably watching Lorenzo tethering Poncho at the hitching post. "Will Solomon be all right?"

"He's improving." Not fast enough. Her worries pulled her down further. Best not to dwell on what she could not change. "I'm only staying tonight for part

of the practice. I want to get home and check on him.
I shouldn't have come, except I wanted to see you all
so badly."

"I'm glad you did. You look as though you need a
friend." Earlee wrapped her in a hug. "Is there anything I can do?"

"Or me?" Kate bounded up, breathless and chapped
pink from her cold ride from her family's homestead.
"I couldn't help but overhear. We all knew it had to be
something serious for you to miss both church *and* our
meeting."

"Your prayers would sure be a help." She hugged
Kate, too. What great friends she was blessed with. The
Lord had dealt bountifully with her. She felt full up, no
longer alone. "How have you all been?"

"Don't change the subject." Scarlet sauntered up with
the rest of the girls, lovely and fashionable in a stunning, gray, tailored coat and hood. "How can you manage while Solomon is recovering?"

"I'll have Shane bring you one of ours to borrow,"
Meredith offered.

"No, I couldn't, but your offer means a lot." Ruby
swept up the steps, miserable over her kiss with Lorenzo, yet so happy to see her friends. "I don't mind
walking."

"If you change your mind, let me know." Meredith
held the door. "What are we going to do about Christmas? Will you still be here?"

"I don't know."

"Don't worry, we will just have our Christmas early,
if we have to. We can't celebrate without you, Ruby."
Scarlet leaned in to give her a hug.

She didn't deserve such good friends. Miserable, she

tumbled into the vestibule and unbuttoned her coat. Her friends talked, offering their ideas on where to meet for their Christmas party. She was too wretched to utter a single word. They were so good to her. They had no notion what she'd done. How she'd betrayed them. Even if she couldn't help it.

Lila joined the gathering, handed over a wrapped bundle—the mended dress from the church barrel—and added her opinion. Laughter surrounded her as coats were hung or laid on tables, scarves removed and mittens peeled off. For the first time since she'd met them, she didn't feel a part of them. She felt like an outsider. That was her fault, too.

"It is going to be all right." Earlee slipped her hand in hers. "You just have to believe everything will work out. Poor Solomon."

The air changed as someone opened the door and held it. She didn't have to look to know Lorenzo was nearby. He strode into sight on the steps outside, dusted with white, talking over his shoulder with some of his friends. Beside her, Scarlet gave a dreamy sigh and stumbled into the sanctuary, leading the way. Kate gazed longingly as Lorenzo, charged into the vestibule and chuckled at something James Biddle said. When he glanced up, she felt the pull from where she stood.

She let Earlee tug her away. *Squeak,* went her left shoe. *Creak,* went her right. She debated changing into her new ones but decided not to.

This is who she was.

"Do you suppose I could get Lorenzo for Christmas?" Scarlet whispered as they trounced down the aisle. "All wrapped up in a pretty red bow under the tree with a bright shining engagement ring?"

"No, he won't be under your tree, I'm sorry," Kate sympathized. "Because he's going to be under mine."

"What are we going to do about you two?" Lila asked as she scooped up a songbook. "If he walked up to us right now and asked one of you to go to his family's ball, what would you do?"

"As much as I want him, I would tell him to ask Kate." Scarlet's chin went up, her mirth fading.

"I would ask him to take you." Kate slung her arm through Scarlet's, and they leaned together, lifelong friends. "Nothing is more important than our friendship."

"Likewise."

"So neither one of you would go?" Lila asked, doling out books.

Ruby's knees buckled as a book tumbled into her hand. Losing her balance, she seized the back of the bench, bumping her knee against the edge of the wooden seat. Pain cracked through her knee cap, but she hardly noticed it for the guilt blooming through her. It ached like a bleeding wound. She was not as good of a friend—as good of a person—as Kate and Scarlet were.

Not by a long shot.

"I guess that only leaves us right where we are. Dreaming of what cannot be." Keeping her voice low, Scarlet glanced over her shoulder, pure wish telegraphing across her face as Lorenzo shouldered out of the vestibule, flanked by Luken and James.

"He is a very nice dream," Kate agreed. "Hey, I saw that, Lila. Not every girl can wind up with an amazing Range Rider for a husband."

"True, I'm very blessed. I'm sure God has great loves

in store for the rest of you." Lila squinted in her direction. "Ruby, are you all right?"

"Fine. I just banged my knee." Tearing her gaze away before Lorenzo caught her staring, she limped forward on her squeaky shoes.

"First your wrist, then Solomon, now your knee. You must need a hug." Lila wrapped her arms around Ruby. "C'mon, everyone."

"I love you, Ruby," Kate whispered as she joined the hug.

"I love you more," Earlee huddled in.

"No, *I'm* the one who loves her most," Scarlet sidled into the circle.

"No, it's me," Meredith argued, joining in.

"We're so glad you're one of us, Ruby." Lila completed the circle, her loving friends.

Tears burned behind Ruby's eyes, both of gratitude and despair. *I will have to do better,* she vowed. They accepted her just as she was, for all her foibles and faults, and she loved them all dearly. There was nothing she wouldn't do for them, nothing she would not give.

So why had she let her heart carry her away?

Lorenzo took a songbook from the pile, and she felt his gaze on her face, felt his love.

A love she could not have. Determined to be a good friend, a better person, she did not look at him again.

"Sleep in heavenly peace." The last refrain of the beloved carol rang in three-part harmony and faded into silence. The arched ceiling of the sanctuary seemed to hold the memory of the notes as Reverend Hadly smiled. "Wonderful. Just wonderful. I think we are nearly ready for the public. You all take a break. Good work."

Finally. Ruby closed the book, ran her fingertip across the frayed spine and handed it over to Kate. *Do not look over at Lorenzo,* she reminded herself as she exchanged smiles with her friend. It hadn't been easy, but she'd successfully kept her gaze from inching over in search of him.

"Poor Solomon." Kate squeezed her hand. "If he is too weak to bring you next time, I will take the other way into town and pick you up. No arguments."

"Can we talk you into staying for a cup of tea in town with us?" Scarlet took her other hand. "We're not ready to let you go."

"Oh, I wish I could." She hated turning down the chance to spend just a little more time with her friends, but she had another friend waiting for her. She wanted to spend time with him tonight, too.

"Hello, Dr. Hathaway." Meredith plucked the songbook out of Kate's hands and added it neatly to the stack. Trouble danced in her expression as she waved the handsome medical man over. "I'm so glad you've joined the group. Do you have much caroling experience?"

"None, but I'm an optimist. Off tune, but an optimist." He shouldered over, cutting politely but firmly through the departing crowd of singers. His good-natured gaze found hers. "Ruby, how is your wrist?"

"Better. It hardly hurts." Self-conscious, she tucked her left hand into her skirt pocket. In the background, Lorenzo stopped, took notice and kept on going. It was for the best, although it didn't feel that way. "Do you enjoy singing?"

"I do, but I'm not sure anyone enjoys hearing me. Reverend Hadly hasn't asked me to leave yet." Walt

Hathaway was innately likeable. Why couldn't she feel something for him? Why did it have to be for Lorenzo?

"The reverend hasn't asked me to leave yet, either." Earlee's contagious smile made everyone grin. "So there's a good chance you are completely safe. No one sings as badly as me."

"I caught you mouthing the words instead of actually singing." Lila rolled her eyes.

"That's how bad I am." Earlee laughed.

"Nice seeing you, ladies. Ruby." The doctor nodded, cast one last look in her direction. Embarrassed by the attention, she bowed her head.

"Ruby," Meredith whispered as the doctor disappeared down the aisle. "He really likes you. I think he's your secret admirer."

"I do, too." Kate's agreement rang like a merry bell. "Let's go get our coats."

"And let's see what he left for Ruby this time," Scarlet finished. "This is so exciting."

"Like a real-life love story," Earlee agreed as she led the way to the vestibule.

Every step she took felt like one of dread. Her shoes were heavy, her knees like stone. Her lips remembered the poignant brand of Lorenzo's kiss, the sweetest thing she'd ever known. The stubborn love in her heart refused to budge. What was she going to do about that?

"Ooh, Ruby's coat looks awfully bulky." Meredith's delight echoed off the close walls of the vestibule. "Her secret admirer struck again."

"Fitting, since it is the Christmas season," Earlee agreed. "Ruby, I'm dying. Hurry. I want to see what he left you."

"Me, too." Scarlet crowded close.

"Me, three." Kate sidled in.

Her hands trembled as she pulled back the placket of her coat, revealing another wrapped package. She tugged it out of her pocket. A beautiful, white, silk ribbon bound the paper. A simple pull of the bow made the ribbon fall away. As she folded the paper aside, a soul-rending crack tore through her.

"Oh," Meredith breathed.

"Beautiful," Earlee whispered in amazement.

"The best quality I've ever seen," Scarlet added.

"The yarn is perfect. It's the color of your eyes, Ruby," Kate noted.

The skeins of soft wool looked too fine to touch. On top of the fluffy skeins sat a pair of needles carved in a rosebud pattern. She'd never seen such wood, gleaming a rich red-brown that shimmered with a rare luster.

"I sold them in the dress shop," Lila smiled. "My boss, Cora, carries only the very best in her store."

"You know who sent them for sure?" Earlee asked.

"I'm not telling." Lila squeezed Ruby's shoulder. "But I will say, these are gifts of love."

Ruby closed her eyes as the cracking within her broke deeper. How could Lila not condemn her? She ran a finger over the end of one knitting needle, so smooth and lovely it brought tears to her eyes.

"Are you sure you can't join us?" Kate asked as she opened the door and waltzed out into the snow. "One cup of tea, that's all."

"I need to get going. I have to stop by the depot on my way home and pick up a telegram. Roop promised he would send one today." She took care not to slide on the icy steps. "He left on the morning train hoping to find a job in Butte."

"At the mine?" Earlee looked worried.

"He wouldn't say, but I'm afraid so. It's dangerous work." She tried not to think of it. Shafts caved in, rocks fell from overhead, gases rose up through cracks deep in the ground killing workers. Her stomach went cold. "I will see you all next time?"

"Absolutely," rang a chorus of assurances. After hugs and farewells and laughter, she watched her group of friends trudge along the beaten path toward Main Street, where the rest of the singers had gone. All but one, she noticed, as Poncho blew out a loud breath on the far side of the church. The horse was not alone. A man's silhouette broke away from the shadows pacing toward her, shoulders dependable and straight, powerful enough to carry any burden.

"Let me drive you home." Lorenzo's caring tone rang low. The wind brought his voice to her. "Poncho insists."

"I hate disappointing Poncho, but I have to this time." *You can do this, Ruby. You can be strong. You can say no this time.* She lifted her chin, unwavering, buoyed by the guilt and shame tormenting her. "I prefer to walk."

"Then I will walk with you." He closed the distance between them and held out his hand palm up in a silent offer.

One she could not accept. "No, you should go join your friends at the diner."

"Why?" Only Lorenzo, so wonderful, so perfect, could be as infinitely caring. His hand didn't waver, patiently waiting for her to accept him. "You aren't upset that I kissed you, because I saw you smile afterward. You did smile."

"Did I?" She'd been too dazed to realize it at the

time, to overwhelmed to remember it now. "I shouldn't have."

"Your moving away only means we should spend more time together before you go, while we can. Unless you don't intend to answer my letters."

His letters? She squeezed her eyes shut, wincing at the pain burrowing deep. *Lord, what should I do about him wanting to write and visit, about the connection I cannot break?* That connection lived in her like hope and fairy-tale dreams that nothing, not even her will, could diminish.

She had to do the right thing. Resolve twisted through her, stronger than any blizzard, more powerful than any avalanche. But how? How could she reject him? How could she say the words? "I'm trying not to think that far ahead."

"I don't blame you. It has to be painful. I see how close you are to your friends." His hand remained outstretched, steadfastly waiting. Nothing in the world looked more inviting. She knew how safe it would feel to lay her palm against his. To feel his fingers close over hers protectively, devotedly. "It is painful for me, too."

Her fingers crept of their own accord. Oh, she was so weak. Just one more time, she let her palm rest on his. His fingers engulfing hers felt like the most wondrous thing on earth. Caring telegraphed through his touch, through layers of leather and wool. "There can be no more kisses, Lorenzo."

"Why? I know you liked it." His forehead furrowed. "I'm embarrassing you. You're blushing."

Her face blazed warm enough to melt the snow catching on her lashes. Bashful, she dipped her chin, taking one step backward and lifted her hand from his. "It was perfection. Good night."

The dark and the storm separating them was as great as the chasm dividing them. She had duty and loyalties. He had a family ranch to run and all the choices in the world. That was the simple reality. She had to be levelheaded. Her duty and loyalty aside, only in storybooks could a penniless girl find happily-ever-after with a wealthy prince. As she headed into the brunt of the storm, snowflakes hit her cheeks like tears.

Trudging into the yard, she noticed how the shanty's windows were dark and lonely. Yet home never looked so good, iced with a fresh mantle of snow and the curtains she'd made hanging behind the paned glass. The happy memories that lived in that house warmed her as she turned toward the barn. Lantern light faintly crept beneath the door, guiding her through the storm.

"Ruby, is that you?" Pa called from Solomon's stall.

"It's me." She closed the door tight behind her to keep in the warmth.

"What are you doing home so soon?" Hay rustled, and Pa leaned over the rail. "I told you to stay and enjoy time with your friends."

"I did, but I was worried about Solomon." And worried about her father, but she didn't say so. She pulled the telegram out of her coat pocket and handed it to him with snowy mittens. "Besides, I have to get in to work early tomorrow. The Davis's ball is this week. It's a busy time for the kitchen, with so much baking and cooking to do."

"Your job is a blessing, one I don't think you should

forsake." Pa held open the gate for her, waiting while she passed into the crisp, crinkling hay.

Solomon lay upright, his hooves tucked under his warm blanket. When he spotted her, his ears went up, his eyes brightened and a weak nicker rumbled in his throat. He rocked up on his knees and rose awkwardly.

"You are my good boy." Such a relief to see him a little stronger. She set down her packages and placed her hands on either side of his long nose, treasuring the sweetness as he leaned his forehead against hers.

Lord, You are generous to spare him. Thank you. She let gratitude fill her heart along with her love for God, Who was good to them in endless ways. She listened to the rattle of paper as Pa unfolded the telegram.

"You are carrying a great deal more than you left home with." He studied her over the top of the page. "What's in those packages? Remember, I said I need no Christmas presents. We can't afford them."

"Lila mended a dress from the church barrel for me." Her tongue tied, and she didn't know how to speak of the gift of yarn and needles, so she said nothing more and stroked Solomon's nose.

"What about the other?" Pa glanced at the message, giving nothing away on his face. The news could not be good. "Did you decide to spend your wages on yourself like I told you?"

"I'm saving my money, just in case there is a chance." She knew her hopes were too high, her one foolish, illogical hope. That Roop would find immediate work in these tough times, that they could scrape together the payment with her earnings. That they could keep their home. Part of her just couldn't let that hope go.

"There will be no 'just in case.' We could sell everything we have, and we still wouldn't make it." Pa folded the telegram and slipped it into his pocket. "Roop says he will be moving on with the morning's train. Maybe he will find work farther west."

"Maybe." She battled overwhelming disappointment. There was no more optimism to have, no more positive thinking that could help. She tucked away her feelings, determined to be what her pa needed, the father who had done his best to be both a ma and a pa, who had always been kind to her. His love for her had never faltered. Hers would not now. "I'm sorry, Pa."

"We have what matters." He shrugged one brawny shoulder, as if the farm and the dream he had worked for was no great loss. His eyes told a different story. He was shattered.

There was no way she could make it better for him. No way to sweep up the pieces of those broken dreams, dust them off and sew them back together again. Solomon sensed their sadness and lifted his head, looking from one to the other, with worry quirking his horsy brows.

"I spoke to the gal who runs one of the boarding-houses in town. Just down the street from your friend Lila's place." Pa cleared his throat. He laid one hand on Solomon's flank to reassure him. "The boardinghouse gal promised to look after you. She's a motherly sort and has seen you walking to and fro with your friends. I believe she will take care of you, make sure you are eating all your meals and keep you safe for me."

"What are you saying?" She gasped, her hopes rising for one, bright moment. Could it be true? "We are going to stay in town after all?"

"You are." Pa nodded once, a man with his mind

made up. "You have a life here, Ruby. A good job. That's no small thing to throw away."

"Pa, you know I can't leave you." That one hope tumbled again and hit the ground hard. "We're a family."

"That we are, but there comes a time when a bird has to fly the coop and take to the sky with her own wings." Pa cleared his throat, but his words grew heavy with emotion and tears he did not shed. "Don't know what I will do without my Ruby-bug, but you need to stay. It isn't every day a man like young Mr. Davis comes courting."

"Lorenzo? He's not courting me." She had to agree to it before he could officially court her. Courting was not a one-sided endeavor. What he was doing was being kind, being interested, being gallant, but he could never be anything more than what-might-have-been. "You have it wrong, Pa."

"That young man is in love with you. How could he not be, my beautiful little girl?" Pa gently laid his gloved hand to her cheek, as he always used to do when she was a child. Memories of a lifetime of kindness and love snapped between them, father and daughter. "Don't let this chance for happiness get away. Chances like this come around rarely in life."

"Pa, it's not like that. I am never going to be the lady of Davis Manor." Could she imagine it? Never. She would picture Kate or Scarlet there instead and pray for it. She wanted Lorenzo's happiness and her friends' more than she wanted her own. "I appreciate the thought, but I cannot stay here. Maybe I can find work in a kitchen or caring for children somewhere up north. There's always the fields come spring."

"I want a good deal more for you, honey." Sorrow

stood in his gaze. "You remind me so much of your mother. You are just like her. Sweet and stubborn and good, the light of my life. You deserve to live in a mansion."

"Love makes a home greater than any mansion could ever be. And I'm not changing my mind. You can't make me." She smiled up at him, resolute. "How much longer do we have here?"

"Not long. I'll speak to the banker again tomorrow."

"And what about Solomon?" At his name, her old friend nibbled at her knit cap, stealing it from her head. Her heart broke more, already knowing the answer.

"He would never make the trip north. I don't know what to do, poor fellow. I do not think I can even give him away. He's too sick and old for anyone to want."

Worry choked her.

"The neighbor has offered me fifteen dollars for Clover, when the time comes." Pa's voice cracked, his only show of defeat. "That will be enough for train fare for the two of us."

It was settled. They would be leaving most everything behind. Ruby wrapped her arms around Solomon, swallowing every last tear, refusing to let even one fall. Life was not fair. God had never promised it would be so, only that they would never be alone to face it.

Tucked in the warm stable lost in heartache, heaven felt far away.

So very, very far.

Chapter Sixteen

"Son, surely you are not abandoning me now." Gerard Davis leaned on his cane, his ready grin etched into his lean face. Behind him the manor was a flurry of activity, maids scurrying to and fro with mops and dusters, ordering around stablemen carrying their ladders and who knew what else.

Lorenzo sighed. So far he hadn't been roped into helping, but that was only a matter of time. He shrugged into his coat. "Sorry, duty calls. Some of the cowboys spotted tracks. Rustlers. They came back."

"How many head of cattle are missing?" Pa's good humor vanished, replaced by ashen worry.

"None yet. We've only spotted a downed fence." Last summer's trouble with rustlers had been serious, over a hundred animals had been taken. "Looks as if the rustlers spotted one of the cowboys on his rounds and ran before they took anything. Likely a small gang, maybe an individual, judging by the prints. It was hard to tell. But we want to put an end to this before anyone gets hurt."

"You be careful." Gerard swallowed hard. "I want to go with you, but I can't sit a horse with this leg."

"Ma needs you here." He knew his father carried great guilt over not being able to pull his weight around the ranch. Lorenzo clapped him on the shoulder, son to father, and smiled encouragement into his pa's worried eyes. "Mother needs one of us to order around. It might as well be you."

"That's a fate I'm proud to suffer." A hint of his good humor returned but not strong enough to outshine his worry. "You hurry back and suffer with me, you hear?"

"I hear." He understood what Pa didn't say. He squeezed once before letting go, blessed to have such a father, and grabbed the rifle he'd leaned against the wall. "I'll be back in one piece. Promise."

Pa didn't look reassured, but perhaps that was a father's job. Lorenzo cut in front of the upstairs maid, nearly invisible beneath a mound of lace draperies, and headed toward the kitchen. He intended to drop by and see Ruby. That put a spring in his step. Things had been so busy the last few days, he'd hardly seen more than a glimpse of her. His eyes hungered for the sight of her, searching for her the moment the kitchen doorway came into sight.

She was awe-inspiring. Nothing could be finer than those gossamer, white-blond tendrils curling around her heart-shaped face. Her big, light blue eyes, the cute slope of her nose, the purse of her rosebud mouth as she patted what looked like bread dough into a mound in a big bowl and covered it carefully with a dish towel. Love strengthened within him, too powerful to contain. It spilled over the rim of his heart.

What could he do to make her see it? To make her understand?

When she'd walked away from him again in the

churchyard, it had taken every bit of his self-discipline to let her go. She'd said there could be no more kisses. Her circumstances in life must be overwhelming. With every fiber of his being, he wanted the right to fix her problems and to call her his own.

"Master Lorenzo." Cook's knowing look was full of mischief as she spooned flour into a measuring cup. "Your coffee is ready. Ruby, hand it to the young man, will you? My hands are floury."

It was nice to have Cook on his side. Ruby didn't acknowledge his presence. She swept to the counter to rescue a towel-wrapped canteen of coffee. She kept her eyes down, her chin tucked, moving like ten kinds of grace toward him. With every step she took, love arrowed more deeply into him, leaving his heart so consumed it was little good for anything else.

"Here you go." Her soft melody was his most favorite song as she thrust out the jug.

"Thank you, Ruby." What he meant was, *I love you.* What he meant was, *I don't want you to leave.* He could not say the words in front of Cook, and so he took the coffee instead. "This will help keep me warm this morning. You look busy."

"Yes, the ball is in two days, as you well know." A light dusting of flour streaked across her cheek, making her even more adorable. He resisted the urge to brush it away with the pad of his thumb.

"So I've heard." He tucked the canteen into the crook of his left arm. "I was nearly trampled by a stampede of maids on my way here."

"They are preparing the ballroom."

"I noticed." The memory of their kiss played through him, like music too gentle to endure. Something mightier than tenderness seized him, a power of love he could not describe, but it was more unbreakable than steel. Did she think distance would stop his devotion to her? Is that why she had torn away from him that evening, sure there could be no more kisses?

She swirled away from him now, her duty in bringing him coffee done, but he was not done. Separation could not stop what he felt for her. Nothing could diminish it.

Lord, I pray again for her happiness. I pray for You to show me the best way to give that to her. All that mattered was her. Whether or not God meant for him and Ruby to be together, he intended to do right by her. He opened up to the Lord's leading, not knowing where it would take him. To heartbreak or happiness? There was only one way to find out.

He squared his shoulders, passed through the door and bowed his head against the biting wind. Judging by the angry clouds sailing in from the north, a bad storm was coming.

"You've got a knack for baking." Cook sidled up to inspect the row upon row of butter cookies cooling on racks. "Not a browned one among them. I'm rarely impressed. While they cool, come help me finish the gingerbread men."

"I've never iced anything before." Nervous, she wiped her fingers on a dish towel following Cook around one work table to another one in the corner. It was lined with several different types of cookies in various stages of decoration. Elegant swirls of colorful and lacy icing, sprinkles of cocoa and sugar powder, tiny accents of homemade candies were far too artful for her inexperienced hand.

"Then I shall handle the icing. You may add the buttons." Cook gripped a pastry bag and bent to work, adding smiling, red mouths to a row of cookie men one after another. "Surely you can do that?"

"Yes, ma'am." She harbored a great fondness for the stern lady, who wasn't so intimidating once you got to know her. She would miss working here. Trying not to look ahead to a future she dreaded, she sorted through a dish of small gumdrops choosing three yellow ones and pressed them neatly into the icing placket of a gingerbread man's coat. "I've never seen these kinds of cookies before, but shouldn't they be wearing pants, too?"

"Pants?" Cook roared with laughter. "Why, that hadn't crossed my mind. Surely we cannot have barebottomed cookie men at our ball."

It was pleasant watching Cook add flourishes of pants cuffs and then marking the toes and heels of stockings, for good measure. Amused, Ruby chose gumdrop after gumdrop and after the gingerbread men were fully clothed, added peppermint disks to the top of Christmas tree cookies. It took all her discipline to keep her mind from returning to Lorenzo, but she did it.

"The wind's picking up." Cook straightened and set aside her work. "Time to get that roast in the oven. You may as well get started on the potatoes. I'm planning on baking them tonight."

"Yes ma'am." Ruby tucked the last candy into place, watching as the snow tumbled in a torrent of wind-driven ice. An angry wind struck the house and rattled the glass in the panes. The gray light of afternoon drained from the sky.

"Mercy me, we need more lamps lit. See to it, Ruby."

A roasting pot banged against the preparation table. "That is one mean storm blowing in."

She lifted the match tin off the shelf by the stove and lifted the crystal chimney of the wall sconce. One strike, the match sparked to life, and she tipped it against the wick, watching it catch.

The side of the house shook again as a harsh gust collided with it. The window turned white. She could see nothing, not one thing. Lorenzo was somewhere on the prairie in that. Was he all right? Could he find his way?

"That's one mighty blizzard." Gerard Davis ambled in, leaning heavily on his cane. Concern marked his forehead as he glanced at the closed door. Perhaps he had come to check to see if his son had made it home. "No one is coming or going in this. Ruby, looks as if you will be staying here for the night."

"Yes, sir." She replaced the chimney. She thought of Pa alone at home. "My father will worry."

"I'm sure he will miss you, but he has to know I wouldn't let you try to head home in this. You are safe, dear, that's what matters." He gazed out the back window, straining to make out any shapes in the storm, any glimpse of his son returning.

Her stomach twisted tight. What if Lorenzo hadn't made it to shelter in time? The bitter wind swirled, as if with a tornado's hand, and thunder cannoned so hard, it shook every pot and pan in the kitchen. Glasses tinkled. China rattled. Mr. Davis's shoulders sank a hint before he straightened his spine, leaned heavily on his cane and tapped away.

Worry ate at her as she lifted a second glass chimney and struck another match. Had Lorenzo felt the change in the storm and turned back from tracking the rustler?

Or was he caught in the blinding blizzard, fighting his way with every step?

"Ruby, best get to those potatoes." Cook's voice drew her back into the kitchen.

"Yes, ma'am." She set the matches down with a clank on the shelf and pulled open the knife drawer to root through it, looking for a paring blade.

The back door burst open and slammed against the wall, caught by the wind. Icy flakes blasted across the threshold, borne on the blizzard's gale. A familiar silhouette broke apart from the deluge. Lorenzo, coated in white. He stumbled stiffly, frozen, as he awkwardly wrestled the door closed.

"Quick, Ruby, help him." Cook abandoned seasoning the roast and grabbed a chair from one of the work tables. Lorenzo stood, nearly board stiff. What she could see of his face behind his muffler was bloodless and caked white.

All the warmth had fled from the kitchen in the force of the wind, and she shivered hard. Ice crackled beneath her shoes. She didn't remember crossing the kitchen, only that she was at his side. "You've looked better."

"I've been warmer." His good humor hadn't been damaged. His midnight blue eyes warmed when he saw her.

Air clogged in her throat, and she blushed at the familiarity of his gaze, oh, so dear. He was a thick layer of ice everywhere. "Where do I begin?"

"The muffler." When he unclenched his jaw, his teeth clattered. "I can't move my hands."

"Don't worry. Let me." Concern rushed through her. Her uncle had lost part of his foot to frostbite. She knew how serious winter weather could be. Hoping Lorenzo would be spared, she broke through the caked snow looking for the end of his muffler.

There it was. Ice tinkled to the floor as she seized it and unwound it in one powerful tug. Aware of Lorenzo's eyes on her, she went up on tiptoes unwrapping the wool fabric from around the back of his neck, exposing his face. White skin, pale blue lips. Panic set in, and she yanked his gloves from his hands.

White. Dangerously white. Poor Lorenzo. Misery resonated in his eyes. He shook so hard, snow tumbled off him like rain. She grabbed his arm, pulling him into the kitchen where the stove's fire seemed defenseless against the encroaching cold. She cupped her hands around his much larger ones, willing warmth into them. Stumbling, she kept walking backward until she reached the stove.

"Sit here." Cook had moved a chair into place and now grabbed a hot pad to open the stove door. "You're frozen clean through. I must be fond of you to let you track so much snow on my clean floor, young man."

"Can't be helped. I'm part snowman." He hated it when Ruby's hand left his. He couldn't feel the floor or his feet. Heat flared from the stove, heat he could barely feel. But he *could* feel it. Relief hit him hard. Something tugged at his collar. Ruby, loosening his coat buttons. The fabric was full of ice, and it had packed around the buttons, making her task harder.

She smelled like ginger cookies and candy. The radiant breeze from the fire whirled fine tendrils against her ivory cheeks. Honest fear for him drew adorable crinkles into her forehead and around her Cupid's-bow mouth. He would never forget their kiss, the sweetness of it, the awe. Like a miracle, it had transformed him. His life would never be the same.

He saw his future in the aquamarine-blue of her eyes, his children in the shape of her porcelain face as she inched so close her hair brushed his jaw and caught on his day's stubble. She eased the frozen jacket off his shoulders, and for one priceless moment, their eyes locked. His spirit brightened, his soul filled and was renewed. He could see within her clearly, see the wrinkle of her brow, the surprise, her will. She moved away to hang up his jacket, unaware of her effect on him. He listened to the pad of her shoes on the floor and the rustle of her skirt as she left his sight.

But not his heart.

"Renzo!" Mother stormed in, a perfect expression of concern, to wrap a warm blanket around his shoulders. Chilblains poked painfully on his fingertips and toes, proof he would be fine. He had been watchful of the conditions and had headed home when the storm looked to be worsening. Ruby had already left the room to sweep up the snow in the entry hall. Each rasp of that broom grated, because he hated the distance between them.

If only the wind would stop blowing. Ruby saw nothing but her reflection in the smooth, black panels of glass as she settled into the common room in the maid's quarters. A fire snapped comfortingly in the hearth, but it was no match for the extreme cold penetrating the walls and windows.

The mantle clock struck eight times.

"It's time for me to head to my room." Cook's knitting needles made a final click. One by one, the other employees had vanished to their rooms, and now Cook stood, clutching her yarn. "Can you bank the fire when you leave, or do you want me to do it?"

"I can manage." She probably should retire as well, but the room Lucia had shown her to had felt lonely. She had never spent the night by herself before, in a room of her own. "Good night."

"Good night, Ruby dear." The older woman sashayed through the doorway, her no-nonsense gait fading to silence. The fire popped, and a few sparks flew. Was Pa sitting at home watching the flames in the grate, missing her the way she missed him?

"You look lonely sitting there." A familiar baritone startled her, a beloved voice that made her tense. The crochet hook jumped out of her fingers and hit the floor with a metallic chime. Lorenzo leaned one amazingly sculpted shoulder against the door frame. "How about some company?"

Her tongue failed her. Her mind failed her. Every logical thought scattered like smoke in a wind. Apparently, Lorenzo didn't notice. His endlessly blue eyes searched hers, seeing rather than hearing her answer that was both yes and no. Yes, she wanted to see him. No, she should not.

"I'll just stay for a few minutes." He shoved off the door frame and stalked toward her with his confident, easygoing gait, friendly, not threatening at all.

Except to her heart.

"Missing your father?" He eased onto the sofa alongside her. The rustle of the cushion echoed in the vast stillness of the room.

"A little. I wish the storm wasn't so fierce. I had so

desperately wanted to go home. I've spent every evening of my life with Pa."

"He must be lonesome for you, too."

"That's what I was just wondering." It seemed as if the entire world had silenced, so that every thud of her pulse, every panicked whoosh of air into her lungs sounded shockingly loud. They were alone, just the two of them, and what was she thinking about?

His kiss. She should forget it. Forget everything. She watched as he bent to retrieve her crochet hook. Embarrassed, she felt heat stretch across her face. "I'm always dropping things."

"It's cute." He held out the hook. Firelight glinted in his dark locks and caressed the side of his lean face. Dimples bracketed a mesmerizing smile, a smile she adored.

Her shaky fingers curled around the hook he offered. *Think of something to say,* she thought desperately. But could she? No. Not one word. Seconds ticked by as his gaze stayed on hers, drawing her soul closer to his. Too close. Panicked, her mind spun. *Think, Ruby.* She bit her bottom lip. *Say something, anything.* "Your hands. How are they?"

"Much better, now I'm adequately thawed." His handsome dimples flashed more deeply. "Hazards of the job. I didn't want to quit when the snow worsened, but for all our effort, Mateo and I lost the trail."

She pictured him out on the plains riding into the teeth of a Montana storm, not knowing what lay in wait ahead of him. Worry gripped her, worry she had no right to. "Where does Mateo stay? He had to be just as frozen as you were."

"At the bunkhouse. Word is he's just fine, too."

"It was just the two of you out there? Aren't rustlers usually armed?"

"I am, too." Apparently danger was of no concern to him. A man like Lorenzo wasn't afraid of a little trouble. "I hated giving up. I wanted to catch 'em before they stole from us or our neighbors."

Don't imagine him on the back of his horse, riding like a hero through the winter snow. Don't do it, she told herself, but did it work?

No, her mind painted the picture of powerful man and undaunted horse, surrounded by snowy sky and reverent prairie. She kept seeing him through the eyes of her heart. How did she stop? Scarlet's face flashed into her mind, a friend who would put her love for a man behind that for a friend. She thought of her pa's face, haunted by worry and failure. Somehow, she had to find a way. Her fingers felt clumsy as she slipped her crochet hook into a loop and drew the thread tight.

"You are still making snowflakes?" He watched her hook slip through and around, drawing the fine length of thread into a lacy pattern.

"Yes. I'm getting much better at it."

"I'll say. That one is flawless." It was the woman he referred to, not the delicate creation that took shape in her hands, but he was too shy to say it aloud. Yet. "The thread is pretty, too."

"It was a gift." She stopped to run her fingertip across the dainty strand. It shimmered like silk in the light.

"It sounds as if the wind is lessening." His presence made the room shrink. The few feet separating them seemed like inches. "Here's hoping the storm blows itself out overnight."

"I hope so, too, so I can go home. Oh, and because of your mother's ball. After all this preparation, it would be a shame if the weather was so terrible no one could make it." Bashful, she lowered her lashes, crocheting away. Did she feel this, too? So vulnerable, his soul felt exposed, as if all he was and ever would be lay defenseless before her?

"Weather has never stopped one of my mother's balls. Folks say it is the social occasion of the season around here. Ma loves being a hostess, and everyone knows it."

"I've never seen such a fuss. The house has been cleaned from top to bottom, everything is shiny and perfect." Her slender fingers stilled. "And the food. I've never seen so much baked goods in one place. Cook promised me it's just the beginning. We start cooking food for the buffet."

"I know what I'm doing tomorrow. Helping to cut, haul and put up the Christmas tree." It was his favorite part of the holidays, the best part of his mother's party. "Have you seen a Christmas tree before?"

"My friends told me the church has one every year, but I've never seen one. It's not something my family has ever done." She turned dreamy. "I can't wait to see a tree all lit up. Cook says the decorations are from Europe."

"My mother likes imported crystal and baubles." He couldn't wait to see Ruby gazing at the tree. He wanted to experience it through her eyes. He wasn't prepared for the spaces within his heart to open wider, leaving him ever more exposed. It hurt like a wound; it healed like a prayer. He loved this woman more than he could measure. She bit her lip again as her needle came to life. She hooked another stitch, knotted it and cut the thread with a pair of tiny scissors.

"Done." She pressed it flat with her fingertips, the silk in the thread glistened and gleamed. It was lovely, what she had made. She studied it critically and shrugged, hiding secrets in her voice. "Someone gave me the thread."

"Is that right?" He tried to sound casual, but his pulse pounded through him like cannon fire. He smiled, understanding without words how much she'd liked his gift.

"Would you like this one?" She held up the snowflake, perfect with six large points and six smaller ones. Lacy and airy and whimsical, just like the maker.

"I would." Not easy to hide his heart. He didn't even try. "I would like it very much."

"It's yours." She set it on the cushion between them, so reserved she could not place it in his hand. He adored her more as he tucked it into his shirt pocket for safe-keeping.

A knock rapped on the door frame. His mother swept in, not looking surprised at finding him with Ruby. She carried a small bundle tucked in the crook of her arm.

"Renzo, your father's leg is bothering him terribly in this cold weather. Could you go help him up the stairs? Ruby, dear, I've brought you a few things of mine to make your stay overnight a little more comfortable."

"Oh. Thank you." Ruby flushed, apparently surprised at the bundle of clothing topped with a brush and comb his mother set on the sofa table behind them.

"You have a good night, dear. Renzo, hurry. You know how stubborn your father gets." A smile warmed her words as she swept out of the room.

"Good night, Mrs. Davis." Ruby twisted around, but his mother had already gone, her gait tapping away in the corridor.

"Looks like I have to go." He hated the thought of leaving her, but his pa was waiting. He'd searched her out for a reason, so he gathered his courage and whispered in her ear, "Save a dance for me."

"At the ball?" His words startled her. Her eyes widened. She gave a little gasp. Her needle rolled across her lap, and she caught it before it tumbled off her knee.

Cute. He rose, towering over her, his love for her so big, larger than the sky. "Yes, Ruby, at the ball."

He couldn't wait. There he would have the right to hold her in his arms for one dance. It took superhuman effort to break from her side. Any parting felt like a rending loss, even if it was only for the night. As he headed for the door, he told himself it wouldn't be like this forever. One day, he would win her heart, and they need never be apart again. At least, that was his hope.

He glanced over her shoulder one more time just to see her smile. Just to feel the tug on his soul.

Chapter Seventeen

"**Y**ou look beautiful, Ruby-bug." Pa stomped snow off his boots in the lean-to. "For a moment, I skipped back in time, and it was like looking at your ma when we were courting. I guess this means you might catch yourself a beau tonight."

"Oh, Pa. Really. I'm too sensible to let some man romance me." Love was putting others first above yourself. Love was not self-seeking. She twirled her bangs around her finger and hoped those fine, straight strands would keep a hint of curl. Tonight, Mrs. Davis needed everyone looking their best. What a blessing it was that this dress had been in the church barrel for her to find. "It will be a fabulous night, even if I'm there to carry serving trays."

"It was all I heard about every time I went to town." All week, he had searched newspapers and written in response to job advertisements but without success. While it was too late to save their farm, he'd hoped it might not be too late to avoid life on Uncle's ranch. A new job could change that. It was a hope they would not abandon until the very last. Pa shouldered through the door and drew it shut behind him. "Hear tell, the Davis's ball is quite an event. Maybe I'll get a peek through the windows when I come pick you up tonight."

"Pa, Solomon can't be out in this weather. He's still so terribly weak." She set down her comb, finished with her fussing. "Surely you don't plan on walking with me?"

"It will be well after midnight when your work there is done. Far too late for you to be on the roads alone." Pa cocked his head, listening. "Sounds like someone has driven up. It can't be someone from the Davis ranch come to escort you, can it?"

"No. Mateo lent me a horse from their stable to ride so I could come home and change quickly." She rolled her eyes. Honestly. The lovely velvet skirt shimmered richly as she crossed the shanty. "You have let your hopes get far too high. Lorenzo Davis isn't going to marry the likes of me."

"In that dress, he will likely consider it. Trust me." Pa probably thought he was being kind, but his words tore through her.

A dress did not make a woman. Integrity did. She checked the time—nearly five o'clock. She had best get going. Cook would be needing her soon to help with the last-minute cooking, although they had prepared most of the food ahead. She imagined all the lovely plates, dishes and platters spread across three consecutive cloth-lined tables loaded with delicious things to eat. At least it distracted her from thoughts of Lorenzo.

A knock rapped on the door, and Pa opened it. A middle-aged man in a finely tailored suit stood on the doorstep. Ruby recognized him. He was Meredith's father.

"Mr. Worthington. Good of you to drop by." Pa stepped back, opening the door wide. "Please, sir, come in."

Also the owner of the town's bank, Ruby knew. Cold fear shot like little spikes through her midsection. The important man did not smile. Tension drew lines around his kind eyes and his grim mouth. She knew why he was here. To evict them tonight. Her hands turned to ice. She went numb all over.

"I hate to bring bad news, but I have put it off as long as I can." Robert Worthington looked out of place in their humble home with his expensive clothes. "It's official. I'm foreclosing on this property. I'm sorry, Jon. But it will take some time to get the final papers, so you might as well keep living here through Christmas."

They could stay a while longer? Ruby's throat tightened. She could not believe Mr. Worthington's kindness. That would mean she could spend a little more time at her job and with her friends. They wouldn't be homeless for Christmas. They had more time for Pa and Rupert to find work.

"That's mighty generous of you." Pa looked choked up, too. "It's mighty appreciated."

"You make it easy, Jon. You have been honest with me since your crop failed. I respect that. Ruby, you must be going to Davis's ball tonight."

"Yes, sir. I'll be serving." Her skirts swished as she joined her father, standing at his side.

"Then I shall see you there." Mr. Worthington tipped his hat, offered a consoling smile and headed out into the evening's dark. "I'll be in touch, Jon."

With a single nod, Pa closed the door. The dignity with which he'd been carrying himself shattered. His strong shoulders slumped, his straight back sank, defeat stole the life from his eyes. His jaw firmed, as if he was fighting hard not to give in to sorrow completely. "Worthington is a decent man. When I saw him, I figured he was coming to evict us. That we would need to leave tonight."

"I thought so, too."

"We have a reprieve, so you go have a good time, honey."

"How can I leave you now?" Torn, she thought of Cook who would be needing help and of her promise to Mrs. Davis not to leave her in a lurch. Her father clearly needed her, too.

"What do you mean? 'Course you gotta go. It will be something to see. All the folks dressed up in their finery. A fancy ballroom. I'm hoping to catch sight of that Christmas tree tonight when I come by. Ought to be one, fine shindig." Pa chucked her chin, just as he used to do when she was young. "You go tonight. You will always regret it if you don't. Think of your responsibility to Mrs. Davis. Don't you worry about your old man."

"You aren't so old, Pa."

"I'm old enough. Now, you go on. Save up every detail so you can tell me about it on our walk home tonight." Love polished his voice and shone in his eyes, chasing away his sorrows.

For now. Ruby gave him a quick hug before pulling on her coat. It was final. It was real. This home was no longer theirs. They would be leaving this place and this life.

She blinked hard, refusing to give in to despair. It was only a farm they were losing and just a dwelling with four walls. That was all. It helped to remember this earth was not their permanent home, not the place their souls belonged.

Stars glittered overhead as she headed to the barn, gleaming so brightly, so beautifully, they had to be proof of God's word. He was watching and always present. They were not alone even when it felt like it.

There she is. Lorenzo's heart soared, his knees buckled and he had to grab the banister to keep from falling down the stairs. The house shone like a showcase, with every surface polished, wreaths and Christmas decorations and crystal-encased candles hanging everywhere. All of it paled as Ruby swept into sight down the corridor, her beauty outshining everything. He drank her in—soft, blond hair swept up, her precious face aglow, the dress skimming her frame like a princess's gown. She was his dream, everything he could ever wish for.

He could only hope she felt the same way.

He didn't know how he'd gotten so blessed, but he was grateful to the Lord above. Of all His blessings, Ruby was the most cherished. He watched captivated as she sailed out of sight, far down the hall, carrying a platter of sliced ham.

"Renzo." Pa tapped up in his best suit. Pride puffed him up, making him look once again the man he'd been before the rustlers' bullets. "I know that look on your face, since I've seen it on mine."

"What does that mean?"

"It means I looked the same way when I was courting your mother. You are a lost cause, son." Pa's grin widened. "What you feel for that young lady is no passing thing."

"It's forever."

"So I see. I've prayed the woman you fall in love with will be worthy of you."

"Pa." He grimaced, disappointed in his father. "I know you and Ma had hoped I would marry Narcissa or a woman like her, but—"

"No. You misunderstand. We were hoping you would marry *someone*." Pa shook his head, clearly amused. "All this time, you showed no signs of beauing anyone, and I was fine with that. You're young. But your ma is another matter. She thought you needed a nudge in the right direction. All this time, you had your eye on that little gal, didn't you?"

"Yes. I've loved her for a while." For so long, it felt as if he'd always adored her. As if his life hadn't started until she'd walked into it. "Then you and Ma approve of Ruby?"

"Approve of her? Why, she comes from a good family, and she's as sweet as could be. Now, about our house rules."

"I know, I know. I won't bother her while she's working."

"When I said that, I didn't know you were so serious about her. So be sure and get in a dance or two with her before the night ends, all right?" Pa clapped him on the shoulder.

Words failed him. He swallowed hard, unable to say what his father's support meant.

"There are my boys." Mother sailed into sight, resplendent in a deep green gown, radiating with the kind of happiness only hosting a party could bring her. "Don't you both look fine. Our guests are starting to arrive. One of you is going to have to come down here and help me greet them."

"That would be me." When Gerard gazed upon his wife, it was clear that true love existed and happily-ever-afters could come true. He lifted his hand from Lorenzo's shoulder. "Duty calls. And a little advice? Make sure it's a waltz."

Pa winked and tapped down the stairs.

"What are you two muttering about?" His mother planted her bejeweled hands on her hips. "Keeping secrets from me? Not for long. I will worm it out of your father."

"Worm away, darling. A kiss or two might help." Gerard slipped one arm around his wife's waist. Selma laughed as they walked away. That's the kind of happiness he wanted for his future. The kind of love that he felt for a certain kitchen maid who avoided looking his way as she swept through the ballroom doorway and into the corridor, her tray empty.

She hurried toward the kitchen and he watched her go, longing for a happily-ever-after of his own. Somehow, this had to work out between them. Because if it didn't, his heart would never recover.

He would never be whole again.

So far, so good. Lorenzo was nowhere in sight. She had managed to avoid him. No reason to think avoiding him the rest of the evening would prove any more difficult. She slid a tray of candied sweet potatoes onto the buffet table, readjusted a platter of smoked salmon and swirled on her heel. *There.* She breathed in the aromas of turkey and stuffing, of dumplings dripping with butter. The long tables of shimmering silver and glittering crystal, of ornate china and polished brass, were fit for a king.

"Do you have a moment?" A familiar voice murmured from behind.

Lorenzo. She jumped. She hadn't even heard him approach. He'd been sneaky, she realized, spinning around, glad her tray had been empty. Best to keep her eyes down and avoid the power of his gaze. He would see the sadness in her eyes and ask questions. Questions she didn't want to answer, because that would be confiding in him when she ought to be pushing him away.

You can do this, she told herself, cleared her throat and managed what she hoped was a neutral look. She had to come across as perfectly normal, completely unaffected by his presence. "Did I forget something? Is something wrong with the setting?"

"No, the feast looks wonderful. The guests think so, too. Look." He gestured toward the high, wide-arched entrance where elegant folks she didn't know swept in, sparkling with gems, replete with the finest clothes she'd ever seen. All exclaiming over the beautiful setting.

A lone pianist began to play at the grand piano in the far reaches of the room. Pure, gentle notes of great feeling lifted over the din of the crowd. Ruby fought the urge to pinch herself to be sure she was awake. Being in this grand ballroom with its two-story arched ceiling, Palladian windows and marble floor made her feel as if she'd fallen into a book, someplace far too opulent to exist.

A place where a girl's Cinderella wishes could come true.

"There is something you are needed for." He sounded serious, not that she dared to look up and see for sure. "You had better come with me."

Had she forgotten something? She had been so sure the initial spread had been laid correctly, that nothing had been forgotten. She had to follow Lorenzo through a nearby doorway, heart pounding, wondering what she'd done wrong. Why did he have to be the one to notice?

She kept her gaze trained on the alternating squares of yellow and ivory marble ahead of her toes. Whatever happened, she couldn't look at him. If she didn't see him, she could almost pretend they hadn't kissed or that he didn't care for her. If she didn't gaze into his eyes, she could deny the love staking claim in her heart.

She could never admit that love. She could not give in to storybook wishes. She would be the friend that Scarlet and Kate were. She would be the daughter her father needed. She was a homeless girl with a bleak future.

"This is the solarium." His baritone faintly echoed against the surrounding walls of bowed glass shining as dark as the night. Stars glinted in the panes overhead and cast a silvery glow to compete with the golden chandelier light tumbling in through the doorway.

"I've come to claim my dance." He held out his hand, his callused palm spread wide and waiting. The gentlest question whispered in his eyes and filled the hush in the air between them. "You promised."

"I never answered you."

"Then I heard it in your heart."

She forgot to keep her chin down. Lorenzo filled her vision, strikingly masculine in his black suit. A faint smile eased the chiseled splendor of his high cheekbones as he captured her fingers in his. She had to ignore the comfort, the *rightness* of his touch. She had to step away. Why weren't her feet moving? "I can't. My work. I'm expected to serve."

"I'm sure everyone will understand." His free hand caught her waist, as claiming as a brand. "Do you know how to waltz?"

"No. Which is another reason why you have to let me go."

"Sorry. Not my plan." His shoe nudged hers, forcing her backward in tempo to the piano music spilling into the room. "Just follow me."

His other foot guided hers one step over, one step back. She felt held captive in his arms by a force she could not break. *Dear Lord help me,* she prayed, because she could not help herself. Her heart leaped, and her hopes foolishly took flight. He guided her around the room in one slow swirling turn after another.

Pull away, she told herself. *Stop him.* But how could she? Against her will, her defenses fell, her resistance shattered and love she could not repress lifted her up by the heart. Think of Scarlet and Kate. Think of Pa. Anything but how wondrous it would be to lay her cheek against the dependable plane of his mighty chest.

It was like soaring to the music. His gentle touch at her waist, guiding her, anchored her. Otherwise, she might float away like a lost leaf in a wind. Every brush of her shoes to the marble, every lilting step taken in unison with him made her want to dream. What would it be like to be his?

Like this, she realized as his hand left her waist to settle at the nape of her neck. With infinite tenderness, he guided her cheek to rest on his chest and enfolded her in his arms. Heaven could not be this sweet or eternity this treasured. She let her eyes drift shut. Listening to his heartbeat beneath her ear brought her closer to him in spirit. Every step and every beat of their hearts were in synchrony, in perfect unity.

His chin came to lightly rest on the top of her head, so close, they shared the same breath. She was overwhelmed by the beauty of being held by him. Nothing could be finer, not in all her life to come. Her soul broke into pieces, and every shard of it was his.

I want this so much, but I know it cannot be. Give me strength to end it, she prayed. And in the same prayer, *Never let this end.* Greater love hit her hard enough to bruise, leaving a physical pain that ached in her chest like a wound. She curled her fingers into his jacket, the wool soft beneath her fingertips, wishing she did not have to let go. If only she could hold on forever. But finally, the piano music ended, the last, long note lingering like a memory.

He lifted his chin from her hair but did not move away, did not let go. Heaven could not feel as safe or secure as being in his sheltering embrace. There were no worries here, no strife, no hardship. Just the unspoken accord between two kindred spirits. Just his breath and hers, and the blue of his eyes.

"You have come to mean very much to me, Ruby." His lips brushed her temple.

She shivered with dread, knowing she should walk away right now, before there was another loving moment that had no future. But did her mouth open to protest? Did her feet carry her away from him?

No, she stood rooted and mute, lacking the will. What she felt for him was too strong, too great, too mighty. She was small by comparison, a lone swimmer drowning in a vast sea.

"I pray that I have come to mean the same to you." He took her hands in his. "I'm in love with you, Ruby."

"L-love?" Shock bolted through her. She'd dreamed of those words, but to hear them spoken aloud meant there was no going back, no pretending a romance didn't exist between them. She squeezed her eyes shut, but that didn't blot out reality. His hands cradled hers, his breath fanned her cheek, his presence filled her with a light so bright she could not deny it. Not anymore.

It was time to do the right thing. The thing she'd been unable to do. Her heart had pulled her here, although she'd known better. Scarlet wouldn't have done it. Kate wouldn't have done it. And as for her father... Self-reproach filled her. She wasn't the person she wanted to be. Now was the time to start.

"I am very flattered." She opened her eyes, struggling, still longing for the feeling of waltzing in his arms. "You know I think very highly of you."

"Just highly? That isn't exactly what I was hoping to hear." Tender, his tone. Always so caring. Hiding the disappointment that crept into his eyes, darkening them. "I was wishing for a good deal more."

"Me, too." She braced her feet, squared her shoulders and slid her hands from his. It destroyed her to do it. Pieces of her soul crumbled apart. This was it. After this, things wouldn't be the same between them. She would lose him forever.

"I know you are worried about your father. I am, too. You don't have to go through this alone, Ruby." His hands fisted, his only show of distress. "I'm here for you. You know that, right?"

"Yes, but I can't accept this." It was like dying inside to watch disappointment slip across his chiseled face.

To see his hope became bleak acceptance. Hurt filled his eyes, but it did not chase away the radiant love, his beautiful love. Oh, she so did not want to hurt him. "The banker came by today. We have to leave. Probably right after Christmas. That will give us time to pack what little we can take on the train and to figure out what to do with the rest. With Solomon."

"You've decided. I can't change your mind?"

"No."

"I could still see you. You did promise to write me."

"That was when we were friends. Before—" *you said you loved me.* Heartbreak beat through her, a fresh wound.

"I don't want to lose you, Ruby." His earnestness, his unwavering commitment undid her.

"Neither do I." The truth won. For one instant, she dreamed. Of Lorenzo driving all that way to see her at her uncle's land. Of being beaued by him. Of having the chance to see where their love could lead.

But it wasn't right, and she wasn't free. Tears stood in her eyes because she could not have those dreams. She could not have Lorenzo as her one, true love. She broke away from him, stumbling backward. Staring up into his puzzled, tender gaze, she lifted her chin and gathered her courage.

"We have to be practical, you and I." It was as simple as that. "This is where our lives part. My father's spirit is broken. It's going to take everything my brother and I can do to see him through. I'm not the right one for you. I can't love you. I just do, but I c-can't."

Hot tears blurred her vision, and overwhelmed, breaking apart, she spun around, leaving him while she still could. Everything within her screamed at her to stay with him. To accept him. To follow her heart.

She ran blindly toward the door, listening to the swish of velvet and silk of her dress. Behind her, Lorenzo did not make a sound. She'd rejected him, and she was sorry for it. Was he hurting like this, too? She was doing the right thing, but it didn't feel that way as she stumbled toward the doorway. Now he was free to find someone who belonged in his world, like Scarlet.

"Why, Rags." Narcissa stood in the threshold, her mouth pursed in a brittle smile of triumph.

Had she witnessed the whole thing? Ruby's chin bobbed downward. As if the evening couldn't get any worse. She tried to slip by, but Narcissa refused to move.

"What are you doing in my old dress?" The superior smile turned calculating. "I threw that ratty thing away. It's so last season. Here's a hint. You really ought to stop rooting around in the garbage barrel."

Narcissa's words could not hurt her. They could not humiliate her or make her feel small. But Lorenzo had overheard, and that had been the woman's intent. Maybe now he would see the real Ruby Ballard, a servant in a cast-off dress, instead of through the blinding eyes of his love.

With a laugh, Narcissa stepped aside. Fine, all she wanted to do was to escape. She felt Lorenzo watching her as she slipped into the crowd. The room felt so normal. Everyone surrounding her was having a merry time. Yet, she was shattered. How could everything around her be so festive and merry?

Ruby, you should be working, she reminded herself. Working would help. It would give her something to do, some direction. But how could she focus? Her entire soul was lost. She had never felt more devastated.

"Ruby!" Scarlet sailed over in a gown of evergreen velvet with red, silk trim. "Ooh, it's so good to see you. What's wrong? You're crying."

"No, I'm not." Denial was her only recourse. She swiped her cheek, surprised to find that her fingers came away wet. "It's been a tough night."

"I can't imagine how much work you all put into this, but it's fabulous. You look fabulous." Scarlet gave her red locks a toss and took Ruby by the hand. "You could be a princess in that dress."

"I'm no princess. I'm just me."

"A princess," Scarlet insisted, the good friend that she was. "I know you are working, but come through the buffet line with me so I won't be by myself."

Ruby managed a nod. Somehow, her feet carried her forward. Somehow, she managed to smile and chat as if nothing was wrong, as if she wasn't defeated, as if she hadn't lost the best of all dreams, her one, true love.

There was no way Lorenzo could ever be hers.

Chapter Eighteen

Lorenzo was grateful for the vicious cold, which burned away all feeling, as he headed into a brisk wind. Glad last night was over—he'd barely survived the rest of the ball for his mother's sake—and now he was on the range. Away from every reminder of Ruby. But regardless of how many miles he'd covered with Poncho and his men, his broken heart came with him.

It was a clear morning. The sky, a mild, pearled blue, stretched in all directions over the soundless prairie. Nothing moved, not a leaf in the wind or a single wild creature, as Poncho plowed through a drift, following a trail in the snow.

Right now, he was especially grateful for his work. As long as he concentrated on tracking, he wouldn't have to think. And if he didn't think and if he was too frozen to feel, then he wouldn't have to go over last night again and again, breaking his heart ever more.

Her rejection had been clear, belying the love in her eyes. The love she hadn't vowed to return. He could still see the misery on her face, how torn she was. *I can't love you. I just do, but I c-can't.* The pain he'd felt from her had burrowed into his soul. He didn't understand, so he didn't know what to do. Did he let her go, as she wished? Or did he fight harder for her?

You are doing it again, Renzo. He shook his head, trying to scatter his thoughts. He would be wise to think about the missing cow. Think about his responsibilities. He glanced over his shoulder to check on the cowboys behind him. A gust of wind sliced through his thick layers of wool and flannel, chilling him to the marrow. He welcomed it. He clenched his molars against the pain of the cold, letting it overtake all other pains.

Not even the arctic temperatures could totally stop the torment of being separated from Ruby, from knowing she would never be his to love and care for. Now, when she needed it most. What would become of her and her family? The day after Christmas, he would send Mateo to make an offer on Solomon, so the poor horse would have a comfortable place to spend his final days. That was the only thing left he could think to do for her, to make her life easier.

Poncho's head went up, his nostrils flaring to scent the air. His neck arched, and he nickered. A trained cutting horse, he knew his job and led the way, his pace quicker now. The horses and riders following struggled to catch up. Lorenzo leaned forward in the saddle. What had his horse scented? He had better concentrate on his work and forget the beauty of holding Ruby in his arms. He remembered the image of agony in her eyes as she'd turned away.

Pain threatened to shatter him, but he kept on going. But did his love for her end?

No. His devotion to her went deeper than he'd ever

guessed. It was a force that would not end. Not now. Not ever.

"Poncho was right." Mateo pulled alongside on his pinto and pointed at a small shack tucked between a stand of trees and the snowbound plains. Smoke curled from the stovepipe. A cow, tied to a post, looked over at them curiously, casually chewing her cud. "Someone is squatting in one of the ranch's line shacks. Who's gonna ride for the sheriff?"

A face peeked out from behind a patched curtain. He caught a glimpse of fear and dark curls. "Let's see what we are dealing with first."

With a press of his heels, he urged Poncho toward the shack's front stoop. He had a bad feeling, but not one of danger as the door swung slowly open. In the doorway, a stoop-shouldered man shrugged into a worn, mended wool coat. He looked beaten down, hesitating on the top step. Inside the shack came the muffled sound of a baby's cry and a woman's soothing voice.

"Yer young Mr. Davis, aren't ya?" Head down, unarmed, the rustler closed the door behind him. "I figured ya not might notice one cow missing. Guess I was wrong."

"You don't look like a seasoned criminal, mister." Lorenzo's saddle creaked as he swung down.

"Never stole nuthin' before, and that's the God's truth. My wife and my son were hungry." The man wasn't as old as he'd first appeared, maybe twenty. Maybe younger. It was despair dragging him down and drawing lines into his gaunt face. The stranger looked like he was on the brink of starvation. "Whatever yer gonna do, do it to me. Just make sure Nan and the little ones are okay."

The woman with the dark brown curls reappeared in the window. As she soothed her baby on her shoulder, the sunlight shone on her lean face. He'd never seen anyone look so scared.

"I don't appreciate you stealing my family's cow." Lorenzo trudged closer, aware that Poncho came along with him, his friend and protector.

"Sure, I get that. What I did is wrong. I knew it at the time." Fear rattled through him visibly. "All I can do is apologize. I can't pay ya for the cow. I lost my job a while back. Couldn't get another. We couldn't keep our place, so when I saw this from the road... Why, we're in a hard way, Mr. Davis. I couldn't let my little boy go hungry."

He and the stranger were not so different. They were near the same age. They both had responsibilities and loved ones to provide for. Loved ones they didn't want to disappoint.

A toddler pulled open the door and stood staring out with wide eyes. Tears streaked his face. His mother darted into sight and snatched him back. Lorenzo noticed a dwindling pile of fresh firewood slumped against the side of the shack. An axe was sunk blade first into a downed, half-cut tree.

"Mateo, why don't you take the cow back to the ranch? Have Cook wrap up leftover food from last night's buffet. The Lord above knows we have enough to spare. I'm sure Mother will have a few things of her own to contribute. Put it all on a sled and bring it back here." He didn't turn to see the expression on his cousin's face, but he knew Mateo understood as he rode off to fetch the cow. Standing there, Lorenzo felt his other hired men's curiosity. "The rest of you come help me cut and stack more wood."

"What? You mean, y-ya ain't gonna have me arrested?" The man shook his head, disbelieving.

"Today is Christmas Eve." He watched relief pass across the stranger's face, saw tears spill down the wife's. "Merry Christmas."

Hard times came to everyone. No one was immune from them. He liked to think that if his Ruby were in the same situation someone would show her mercy. The snowflake she'd crocheted felt warm in his shirt pocket, where he kept it close to his heart.

"We'll do what we can to help you," he promised.

"Thank you kindly. I intend to work on yer ranch in payment." The man swiped dampness from his eyes, embarrassed. "You don't know what this means. My family is all I've got. My wife and boys, they are just everything."

"I understand. That's the way I love my family, too." As he wrapped his fingers around the stout handle of the axe's blade, he remembered what Ruby had told him. *We have to be practical, you and I. My father's spirit is broken. It's going to take everything my brother and I can do to see him through.* The full meaning behind her words hit him.

He'd just seen a glimpse of Ruby's past and of Jon Ballard's possible future.

The agony of his broken heart faded. He knew what he had to do. *You work in strange ways, Lord, but good ones. Very, very good ones.* He positioned a chunk of pine, brought the blade down into the wood, and the split pieces fell into the snow at his feet.

* * *

Ruby rapped her knuckles on Scarlet's ornately carved front door, more nervous than she could say. How did she tell her friends she would be leaving the day after Christmas, just two days away? How could she endure saying goodbye?

Sorrow gripped her. She straightened her spine and gathered every ounce of her inner strength, but the sadness refused to let go. It held her tight in sharp claws that cut every time she breathed. There had been so many losses and many more were to come. She refused to think Lorenzo's name, because she had to hold it together. This was a celebration, her last and her only Christmas party with her beloved friends.

"Ruby!" The door swung open and Scarlet stepped back in a swish of skirts. "We were waiting for you."

"Sorry I'm so late. I'm still on foot these days."

"I've been keeping your sweet Solomon in my prayers." Scarlet grabbed her by the wrist, lovingly tugging her into a soaring foyer. "Come in, take off your wraps. Meredith was just saying she should have run out with her horse and sleigh to pick you up after work. I was all for that. Handsome men work on that ranch."

"True." Impossible to deny that. She set her bag on a nearby table, tucked her mittens and her cap into her coat pockets. "I hope I didn't miss too much. I've never been to a Christmas party before."

"No, but you've been to a Christmas ball. I was just telling everyone about the tree Mrs. Davis had decorated. Oh, give me that. I'll hang it up." Scarlet cheerfully took the old coat, treating it with care as she hung it in the closet with all the others. "Those soaring little candles and balls of colored glass. Breathtaking. Come on. We didn't want to start without you."

"You waited for me?" Clutching her bag, she stumbled around a maid carrying a tray of empty teacups and trailed Scarlet down a wood-paneled corridor. Open double doors led to a sunny parlor, where familiar faces turned to greet her.

"Ruby!" Everyone chorused, standing to hug her one at a time. First Fiona, with her skirt barely hiding her growing stomach. Then Meredith, alight with the happiness of a woman planning her wedding.

"I hear you looked amazing in that dress." Lila, still wearing a newlywed glow, held her so tight. "I wish I could have seen you in it. Scarlet says you looked like a fairy-tale princess."

"I'm no princess." She blushed. Honestly. This was why she couldn't help adoring her friends. They were good to her. If only she could be as good in return. "You were the one who repaired the dress so expertly. Besides, I think Scarlet was exaggerating. If Earlee had said it, I would have understood, but—"

"Wait! What does that mean?" Earlee wrapped her in a hug next.

"You see everything like a story," Ruby pointed out. "A wonderful, happily ending story."

"I do tend to be a little fanciful, but I can't help it. It's just the way my mind works." Earlee rolled her eyes, adorable with her blond curls and sweetness. She looked particularly cheerful these days, perhaps because her job as a schoolteacher had made such a difference for her family. But that didn't explain the sparkle of quiet joy in her blue eyes, almost as if she were in love. *Interesting.*

"She's been this way as long as we've known her." Kate stepped up next to give Ruby a hug. "I would have loved to have been at that ball so I could have given Narcissa a piece of my mind. Scarlet told us."

"Saying what she did about your dress," Scarlet explained, taking her hand and guiding her to the sofa next to her. "Come sit with me. I've been saving you a place. Narcissa said it loud enough that half the ballroom heard. I nearly lost it, but I remembered just in time that I was a lady."

"You?" Kate quipped. "I've never seen you be ladylike before. Remember when you outran the fastest boy in the fourth grade when he pulled your braids and you took off after him?"

"You tackled him right in front of the reverend who was walking by on the street, and the next Sunday's lecture was about self-control and the importance of restraining one's temper." Lila burst out laughing, joined by everyone else. The merry sound rang in the lovely room like carillon bells chiming, a melody of friendship.

"I remember." Scarlet rolled her eyes. "I had the same urge last night with Narcissa. Can you imagine Sunday's sermon if I had?"

More laughter rang. *How wonderful it is,* Ruby thought, memorizing the sound. She never wanted to forget it. She wanted to hold it close forever.

"Before we get to exchanging presents and dinner—" Earlee started.

"And then on to caroling," Lila added.

"—I copied off the first few pages of my current story." Earlee reached into her bag, pulled out a stack of parchment and handed it to Meredith to pass around.

"As you know, I've been penning stories since I was a little girl."

"No kidding. That's not news." Scarlet took two pages and passed the stack to Ruby. "Letting us read one of your stories is. This is exciting."

Ruby glanced down at the first sentence before she passed the last remaining pages to Fiona. Earlee's penmanship flowed flawlessly across the top of the paper. Unable to stop herself, Ruby began to read. *"Ma, when is Da coming back from town?" Fiona O'Rourke threw open the kitchen door, shivering beneath the lean-to's roof.*

"Hey, this is me!" Fiona nearly dropped her pages. "It's me, before I was married."

"It's the story of how you and Ian fell in love," Earlee explained. "Do you hate it?"

"No, I love it." Fiona beamed, reading on. "This is just like Ma and Da, too. Oh, you wrote about the day I met Ian."

"Well, it *is* a romance. I wanted to write about some of the people I love most—my friends. Someone I know thought I should try to publish it. What do you think?"

"Publish it? That's a fantastic idea."

"Fabulous. Does this mean we are all in the story?" Meredith asked.

"Everyone but Ruby, since we hadn't met you yet. Ruby, you make an appearance in Meredith's book."

"I get a book, too?" Meredith clapped her hands, delighted.

"Everyone will. I'm planning a series. It's so fun." Earlee ducked her chin, a little embarrassed as she pulled out carefully wrapped Christmas presents from the depths of her bag and set them one by one on the coffee table between them. "I'm hoping by the time I finish Lila's book, another one of us will be engaged, and there will be a new story to tell."

"Oh, I hope it's me," Scarlet enthused. "I need a tall, dark and handsome man to sweep me off my feet."

"What about Lorenzo?" Kate asked.

His name tore Ruby into shreds. Just when she'd been able to push the misery of losing him into the background, there it was again, stabbing through her as fresh as a new wound. Shattered, she gripped the edge of the couch cushion, holding on. She drew air in through a tight throat and tighter ribs.

"What about him?" Scarlet shrugged.

"Don't you like him anymore?" Kate asked. "What happened? I thought you were head over heels for him."

Just breathe, she told herself. *Relax. Maybe no one will notice.* She wouldn't have to confess what a bad friend she'd been, and they would never know what she'd done. Miserable, she forced herself to draw in air and breathe it out. She couldn't lose her friends, too.

"I was madly in love with him." Scarlet confessed with determined cheer, probably thinking she was hiding her heartbreak. "But I changed my mind."

"Why?" Lila wanted to know. "You've loved him forever."

"He is in love with someone else." This time Scarlet's determined words did not hold a trace of sorrow. "Someone suited to him perfectly."

"Narcissa?" Kate groaned. "Oh, no, not Narcissa. Anyone but her. Poor Lorenzo."

Ruby squeezed her eyes shut, knowing what Scarlet was about to say. It was too late. Scarlet must already know. And if she did, then she knew how Ruby had betrayed her. Grief cinched tight around her. She could not bear to open her eyes and see the disappointment on their faces, the disdain and perhaps the dislike she deserved. A good friend was loyal and true. Things she had not been. She hadn't done it intentionally, but it had happened all the same.

"It's Ruby." Scarlet's tone wasn't accusatory, but it rang with certainty.

"Ruby?" Fiona sounded confused. "Ruby and Lorenzo?"

Here it comes, she thought, bracing herself. Spine straight, shoulders square, she was ready to take the hit. They were going to be angry with her. They weren't going to like her anymore.

"I overheard Narcissa talking to Margaret at the ball," Scarlet explained to an absolutely silent audience. "She told how she saw Ruby dancing in Lorenzo's arms and that he professed his love to her."

"To Ruby?" Earlee blinked, clearly astonished.

No one said anything. She couldn't open her eyes. She couldn't face losing her friends, some of the greatest treasures of her life.

"Ruby, I want you to know how angry I am." Lila said it first, bouncing off the divan with a rustle of skirts and a groan of the cushion, her shoes striking hard against the carpet. She came closer, circling around the coffee table to loom overhead. "Judging by the way everyone looks right now, I'm not alone in my reaction. How could you?"

"It just h-happened." It felt as if the last blessing left to her was being ripped away. "I'm so sorry."

"You should be," Scarlet concurred. "A handsome man has fallen in love with you, and you didn't tell us, your best friends?"

What? Confused, she shook her head. She couldn't be hearing them right. It was her own wishful thinking changing around Scarlet's words. Surely Scarlet was hurt and angry and never wanted to see her again.

"We will forgive you, if you tell us all about it." Lila plopped down on the coffee table in front of her. "What did he say to you? Did you say you loved him, too? Is he your beau, now?"

"No. Because I ended it with him." She opened her eyes, ready to take the consequences. "I know you all h-hate me—"

"Why would we hate you?" Meredith asked.

"Because Scarlet and Kate love him. I tried not to fall for him, I honestly did. But he's so wonderful." She kept her chin up, surprised at the sympathy in Lila's eyes, at the comfort in Scarlet's understanding smile.

"We know how wonderful he is." Scarlet's heartbreak flashed on her face for one brief second before it vanished. "How could you have turned him down?"

"There's something terribly wrong with you, Ruby. Saying no to Lorenzo?" Fiona took Ruby's other hand. "Don't you love him?"

"More than anything." She may as well confess the whole truth. "But it's not right. Scarlet, you said that if Lorenzo asked to beau you, you would say no so Kate could have him. Kate, you said the same thing. I'm not that good of a friend."

"Don't you understand?" Earlee circled the table to kneel close. "You are one of us, our dear friend."

"And I said that about Lorenzo because Kate's happiness means more to me than mine, as yours does to me." Scarlet's eyes brimmed.

"We will always be the best of friends," Lila agreed.

"Which means no one wants your happiness more than we do." A single tear trailed down Scarlet's cheek as she smiled. "Accept him. No one deserves happiness more than you."

Tears blurred her eyes, making the nodding faces and encouraging smiles fuzzy. "Isn't it selfish, though, to put my happiness first?"

"Ruby, you are nothing but loving kindness. You would never hurt anyone for your own gain." Meredith squeezed in to offer a folded handkerchief. "When God gives a person one, rare chance for honest happiness and true love, only a fool would turn it down. A great, grand blessing like that comes around once in a lifetime."

"Just once," Earlee agreed.

"But I'm only me. I'm his family's kitchen maid." For the life of her, she could not imagine living in the Davis home, wearing velvet and silk and greeting fancy guests at next year's Christmas ball. Some dreams were simply too far out of reach for a girl like her. Her family was destitute.

"We are children of God, every last one of us, equal in His eyes." Fiona's fingers tightened around her own reassuringly. "We are all deserving of love, and that means you."

"Say yes to him," Kate urged.

"Accept him," Scarlet insisted. "We love you, Ruby."

"We absolutely adore you," Lila confirmed. "Now, go be happy. That would be the best gift you could give us on this Christmas Eve."

"I adore you all, too." Sobs shook her. She never imagined the friends she loved so much could love her the same way in return. She was the wealthiest person she knew, more blessed than she could say.

Chapter Nineteen

"Lorenzo just drove up." Lila reported as she un-wound her scarf in the church's vestibule.

Ruby resisted the need to peer past Scarlet and over Lila's shoulder through the doorway to see him. She thirsted for the sight of his dimpled grin, his carved features and the miraculous bond that snapped between them when their gazes locked. She shrugged out of her coat, laid it on the table, and her palms went damp. It would be hard to see him again, because she knew it was too late.

She'd said no to him. She'd turned down her one chance for real happiness.

"Don't be nervous," Meredith advised in a whisper, for there were others around.

"Nervous? Me? I'm not nervous," she confessed with knocking knees. "I shouldn't have come tonight. It's going to be too hard to see him. There are plenty of sopranos, so I won't be missed. Maybe I'll slip out the back way."

"No, stay. It will be all right," Earlee encouraged.

"Stay and sing with us," Lila urged. "Lorenzo will still want you. You'll see."

She adored her friends, but they were wrong. She thought of her father home right now sorting through their things, deciding what to take and what would become of Solomon. Her life was no fairy tale and it wasn't about to become one. No matter how much she wanted it do. "I'll stay only if I'm hidden in a crowd. You have to help me avoid him."

"I'll do whatever you need." Kate sidled up next to her in the vestibule.

"I still think you just go up to him and tell him how you feel," Scarlet advised, although she squeezed in close, too. "Come on, let's head into the sanctuary. We'll stay with you, Ruby, okay?"

"Okay." She wouldn't have many more chances to spend time with her friends. She took a ragged breath, squared her shoulders and followed Lila through the doorway. She could do this. If she didn't look at Lorenzo not even once, then she would be just fine. It would be like he wasn't even there and she could stay numb. Pretend her heart wasn't decimated.

"Ruby." A man's baritone rang with surprise.

She jumped, pulse racing, before she realized it couldn't be Lorenzo. Dr. Hathaway ambled in her direction. "How's the wrist?"

"Healing. It doesn't hurt anymore."

"Excellent. I'm glad to see you're improving." He glanced at her friends, her protectors, who didn't move from her side. "I've never been caroling before, so this ought to be a fun experience. Is there any chance you might want to walk with me tonight?"

"No, thank you, but that's kind of you to ask." She

said the words as gently as she could, realizing he really was interested in her. Bashful, she dipped her chin. "I hope you enjoy the singing, though. Merry Christmas."

"Merry Christmas." He tipped his hat, smiled briefly and ambled away.

"Look at you. Popular. In demand." Earlee squeezed her arm.

"Now we finally know he wasn't the one leaving the gifts," Meredith added as she joined them. "Who thinks Ruby is going to be the next one getting married?"

Ruby rolled her eyes at the numerous "I do's!" that rang around her. Her friends, honestly, they had romance on the brain. Or, maybe they were simply trying to make her feel less hopeless.

Reverend Hadly clapped his hands, pitching his voice over the din in the church. "Time to gather, everyone. Let's get warmed up!"

"Rags." Narcissa stepped in front of her and gave her curls a toss. In an expensive, wool dress, glittering jewelry and the finest shoes, Narcissa should have been a vision, except for the ungracious twist of her mouth and the sour look in her eyes. She said nothing more as she flounced by, but her malice and disdain spoke louder than any words.

Instead of feeling the brunt of it, the meanness bounced right off. Ruby watched her nemesis go, surprised at the pity she felt for the rich girl. Narcissa had everything a person could want—family, friends and a comfortable life full of beautiful things—but no happiness. She would spend the rest of her life putting down others because it made her feel better about herself, but it would never truly work. Unless she changed, Narcissa was doomed to a life filled with misery of her own making. She would never have what mattered most.

"Lorenzo," Scarlet whispered in her ear.

Lorenzo? Ruby fisted her hands, suddenly feeling the need to escape. She couldn't face him. Heartbreak battered her like panic. Before she could hurry out of the aisle, his presence washed over her like a sun break on a stormy day, changing everything. If she hurried, she could put enough distance between them before he came any closer and she wouldn't have to see the hurt in his eyes. She wouldn't have to feel her heartbreak. Why wouldn't her feet move an inch?

"Tell him, Ruby," Kate whispered.

"I can't."

His boots tapped a familiar rhythm up the steps, getting closer, each knelling footfall echoing in the evening's darkness. Her pulse thundered in her ears. She felt her friends leave her one by one, with a squeeze of her hand, a touch to her shoulder, a murmur of encouragement, but they were leaving her. Suddenly, she was alone with Lorenzo striding toward her.

He didn't smile. His gaze had shuttered, his face was stony. His mile-wide shoulders braced. Every shield he had went up. No caring radiated from his heart to hers. Just quiet apology as his eyes met hers.

It *was* too late. He no longer loved her. Fine. That was probably for the best but it hurt, how it hurt. Wretched, she spun on her heels, fleeing for the company of her friends.

Reverend Hadly clapped his hands. "Excellent. Great warm-up. Let's start on the corner of Main, and we won't stop until we've sung to every house on every street in our wonderful town. Now, bundle up and let's go caroling."

Cheers and comments rang out from the group as they broke apart. Somehow Lorenzo was in her peripheral vision, hands in his pockets, head down, already walking away fast, ahead of the crowd. Integrity and dignity radiated from him, unmistakable. A little sigh escaped her; she realized it too late to hide her adoration of the man. Love she could not stop cascaded through her with the force of a mountain avalanche.

Please. She thought she could feel God lean down closer just to listen. *Please take good care of him.* Lorenzo was not hers. He would never be hers to love. But she would always love him.

"Ruby?" Kate looked over her shoulder. "Are you coming?"

"What?" She glanced around, realizing she was still standing in place. Everyone else was leaving. She rushed to Kate's side, and her circle of friends closed around her.

"I couldn't believe it. He barely looked at you," Earlee said sympathetically. "Are you okay?"

She nodded. She would be.

"Maybe it will just take time," Lila agreed. "I think he's very committed to you. You just can't see it because you are afraid."

She hadn't realized how great his love for her felt, how it filled her world, until it was gone.

"We're right here with you," Meredith added.

Tears filled her eyes. Oh, what would she ever do without her friends? She set her chin, determined to handle this the right way. She did not want sadness to mar this wonderful evening of singing and joy. It was

Christmas Eve. This night would make a memory she intended to cherish forever.

"Why don't we just have fun," she said, reaching out to take Kate's hand and then Scarlet's. "We are together."

The vestibule was crowded since they were the last of the carolers to amble in. Ruby spotted her coat and snatched it from the table. An envelope stuck out of one pocket with her name on it. In Lorenzo's handwriting.

Her knees turned to jelly. Her hands shook. She stared at it in dread. What could it be? Had he written her a goodbye letter? Agony cut her like a dagger. But what if he had written asking her to stay? It would only be proof he didn't understand. Pain took root, and she couldn't move. She was a mess. Singers filed out into the starry night as she slipped shakily into her coat.

"Hurry, Ruby." Earlee gave a little waving gesture from the doorstep. "We're waiting, but everyone else is leaving without us."

"You all go on. I'll be right behind you." She waited until Earlee was out of sight before tugging the envelope out of her pocket. Her fingers felt wooden, and she had a hard time pulling out the thick piece of paper folded up inside.

It wasn't a letter. It was some official document. It looked like—no, it couldn't be. Denial snapped through her as she straightened out the heavy parchment. The words on the paper were blurry. She blinked, realizing there were tears in her eyes. Tears that streaked down her cheeks and dripped on the hem of her coat and plopped on the toes of her shoes.

It was the deed to her family's farm. Lorenzo. He had done this. She stumbled through the doorway, swiping the wetness from her cheeks with her coat sleeve. In the fading starlight, she clearly read the property number. Lorenzo had bought the land and given it to her.

"I see your secret admirer struck again." His voice broke from the shadows, where his substantial silhouette separated from the darkening night.

"Yes. This is quite a Christmas gift. It's so unbelievable. I don't know how to thank him." She carefully folded the deed into the envelope and slipped it into her pocket. What did she say to thank a man for saving her father's dream? "I'm not sure Pa will accept it. He is a proud man. He doesn't let anyone pay his way."

"Not even his son-in-law?"

"His son-in-law?" Her mind whirled, spinning in place over his words. She sputtered. She couldn't think. She couldn't speak. Did Lorenzo still love her? He couldn't mean to marry her? Could he? She shook her head. No, that simply couldn't be right.

He strode toward her, as mighty as the darkly gleaming mountains at the horizon behind him, as stalwart as the ground at her feet. No man ever had looked as committed as when Lorenzo took her hand. He tugged her gently down the steps until they were face-to-face, hand in hand, alone beneath the dark sky.

"I love you, Ruby." In his voice, in his eyes, in his touch lay the truth. The proof of an infinite love that nothing could defeat—not time, not hardship, not even death. "From the moment I first set eyes on you, I fell hard. It was as if God touched my heart. Your family is my family. Your happiness is my happiness. There isn't one thing in this life that can ever mean more than you. Be my wife, Ruby. Please. You are everything to me."

Could this really be happening to *her,* Ruby Ann

Ballard? She blinked, but the moment didn't vanish. It remained, real and true. There had never been a more beautiful night or a more amazing man. She wasn't imagining this, for Lorenzo's hands cradling hers felt real. So did the snow at her feet. Not far away, Poncho nickered, as if urging her to believe. A single snowflake swirled in the air and brushed cold against her cheek.

"You're proposing to me?" It was so hard to accept. She remembered how stony he'd looked in the church, and now she realized why. His hands trembled around her own. This moment was a great risk for him. He was offering her his world, all he was and all he would ever be.

"You are the one for me. The only one. Let me spend my life showing you. I love you so much. Every little thing about you." A muscle tensed along his jaw. His whole, vulnerable heart shone in his eyes. "Please say you love me, too. That you want to be my wife."

This was really happening. God was giving her this great chance at a once-in-a-lifetime love, and she was not going to let it pass her by. This man loved her family and had gone out of his way to show her how much he cared. She was not alone in that cherishing affection. She opened her heart fully, believing in her dreams.

"Yes." Joy lifted her up until she wasn't sure her feet touched the winter ground. All she could see was the matching joy on Lorenzo's face, lighting his eyes, filling his heart. They were connected, soul to soul, and would always be. "I love you more than I know how to say. I want to be your wife more than anything."

"Then I want you to have this." He knelt down in the snow to slip a ring on her finger. The golden band was warm from his pocket, and the gem as big as her thumbnail gleamed without a single light touching it. Snowflakes brushed the faceted surface. Never had she seen anything as stunning as his engagement ring.

"It was my grandmother's," he explained, standing again to tower over her, to shield her from the brunt of the rising wind. "The stone is a ruby."

"A r-ruby?"

"See? We were always meant to be."

Yes, that is just exactly how it felt when his lips met hers. Destined, as if God had led them every step toward each other, toward this perfect moment. In Lorenzo's flawless kiss she saw a glimpse of their future. Loving and happy, raising a family, growing old together, cherishing one another. They would be the wealthiest people she knew, rich in their priceless love for one another.

"I hear singing." Lorenzo broke the kiss, his gaze one of fathomless tenderness. In the distance rang the rise and fall of caroler's voices. "They have started without us."

"Then we had better hurry." *Think of all the happiness to come,* so easy to believe now. They walked down the street, together forever at last, in perfect harmony.

Heaven felt so close as the storm began in earnest. Snowflakes twirled like airy dreams too fragile to touch and floated on gentle breezes. They fell like Christmas Eve blessings over the happy couple as Lorenzo pulled his snowflake bride into his arms and reverently kissed her one more time.

Epilogue

Christmas Day

"Rupert! You made it." Ruby launched herself across the Davis's toasty parlor, ran past the sparkling Christmas tree and into her brother's arms. Happiness lifted her up as he swept her into a quick hug. Oh, it was good to see him. To have him back where he belonged.

"It's great to be here." He stepped back, grinning wide. "I caught a break and found a job working at a dairy near Helena. The Good Lord provides."

"He surely does." Gerard Davis gripped his cane, limping over with a welcoming smile. "So this is the brother Ruby has gone on about. I'm pleased to meet you, Rupert."

"Good to meet you, sir." He couldn't stop smiling. "I hear congratulations are in order."

"They certainly are." Selma Davis circled around the sofa, sweeping up in her lovely Christmas dress. "Welcome to the family, Rupert. I don't have to tell you how much we already love Ruby."

"That's because they don't know me yet," she spoke

up, blushing. Honestly, she wasn't exactly sure what was wrong with the Davises, but they were easy to love. Already they felt like family.

"Rupert, you look half frozen." Selma took charge, always concerned for others. "Come get warm by the fire. Bella, pour him a cup of hot tea. You're just in time for Christmas dinner."

"Glad you could make it." Lorenzo came up to shake Rupert's hand. "Did you have a chance to check on Solomon on your way here?"

"I did. He's looking stronger. We have many blessings this Christmas."

"Very many," Selma agreed, giving Ruby's hand a squeeze. It was like already having a mother. A real mother. "I'm going to check and see how Cook is coming with dinner. Oh, Lucia. There you are. Is the meal ready?"

"Yes. Please come into the dining room." With a festive smile, Lucia tapped away.

"I hope you're hungry." Lorenzo sidled up to her. "It's the Christmas ball buffet all over again."

"I know, since I helped to cook it." She laughed, feeling light and incredibly hopeful. *Happy* didn't begin to describe it. *Joy?* Even that was too small of a word. Her engagement ring sparkled on her left hand, a symbol of his love. She thought of all the Christmases to come, of family gatherings and of their life ahead. All so wonderful. "Thank you for everything. I love you so much, Lorenzo."

"Not nearly as much as I love you." He kissed her sweetly, her husband-to-be. He noticed her father hanging back. "I'll wait for you in the hall."

"Thanks." She squeezed his hand, loath to let go

of him. Her soul felt ripped apart as he left. Yes, God had been incredibly gracious to bring her here, where loved reigned.

"You look happy, Ruby-bug." Pa ambled over, looking bashful, looking proud. "That's the best Christmas present a father could want."

"Thanks for accepting Lorenzo's gift of the farm." She fussed with his collar. It was a little crooked. Then again, maybe it had more to do with her sewing. "I know it was hard on your pride."

"It was his gift for you, Ruby, and so it was easy to accept. I'd do anything for you, sweetheart. Anything at all." He brushed a kiss to her cheek. "Now, go to Lorenzo. He's waiting for you. And be happy. Grab all the happiness you can."

Bliss. That was the word. That described how she felt as she stepped into the hallway and into Lorenzo's loving arms. Some dreams were meant to come true, and this was just the beginning.

* * * * *

Dear Reader,

Welcome back to Angel Falls. *Snowflake Bride* is the fourth book in my Buttons & Bobbins Series. After reading these pages, I hope you felt as if you revisited old friends. I know I did. The Buttons & Bobbins girls are grown up and making their way in the world. Fiona is expecting a baby. Lila is a newlywed. Meredith is planning her wedding. Earlee is teaching school.

As you know, Ruby is the newest member of the Buttons & Bobbins girls. When I first met her in the schoolroom in Meredith's book, I fell in love with her meek and gentle sweetness. Ruby has a good heart, and I hope you came to love her, too, as God led her tenderly and surely toward the true happily-ever-after He intended for her. This Christmas tale reminds me of Cinderella with its Christmas ball, poverty-stricken heroine and a prince worthy of her. I hope Ruby's romance touched you the way it did me. Scarlet's story is next.

Thank you for choosing *Snowflake Bride*.

Wishing you peace, joy and love this holiday season,

Jillian Hart

THE CAPTAIN'S CHRISTMAS FAMILY

Deborah Hale

For Gloria Jackson,
and in memory of Rev. David Jackson,
who both made worship the kind of joyful,
uplifting experience it was meant to be.

Thy will be done…
—*Matthew* 6:10

Chapter One

*Nottinghamshire, England
1814*

"He's coming, Miss Murray!" A breathless housemaid burst into the nursery without even a knock of warning.

The book Marian Murray had been reading to her two young pupils slid from her slack fingers and down her skirts to land on the carpet with a soft *thud*. A tingling chill crept down her back that had nothing to do with the gray drizzle outside. The moment she'd been dreading for weeks had arrived at last…in spite of her prayers.

A new prayer formed in her thoughts now, as she strove to compose herself for the children's sake. She hoped it would do better at gaining divine attention. *Please, Lord, don't let him be as bad as I fear and don't let him send the girls away!*

Unaware of her governess's distress, Dolly Radcliffe leapt up, her plump young features alight with excitement. "Who's coming, Martha? Are we to have company?"

The housemaid shook her head. "Not company, miss. It's the new master—Captain Radcliffe. Mr. Culpepper sent me to fetch ye so we can give him a proper welcome to Knightley Park."

"Tell Mr. Culpepper the girls and I will be down directly," Marian replied in a Scottish burr that all her years in England had done little to soften.

Forcing her limbs to cooperate, she rose from the settee and scooped up the fallen book, smoothing its wrinkled pages.

"New master?" Dolly's small nose wrinkled. "I thought Mr. Culpepper was master of the house now."

"Don't be silly." Cissy Radcliffe rolled her wide blue-gray eyes at her younger sister's ignorance. "Mr. Culpepper is only a servant. Knightley Park belongs to Captain Radcliffe now by en…en… Oh, what's that word again, Miss Marian?"

"*Entail,* dear." Marian plumped the bow of Cissy's blue satin sash, wishing she had time to control Dolly's baby-fine fair hair with a liberal application of sugar water. "Come along now, we don't want to keep the captain waiting."

Likely the new master would insist on the sort of strict order and discipline he'd kept aboard his ship. It would not do for her and the girls to make a bad impression by being tardy.

"What is entail?" asked Dolly, as Marian took both girls by the hands and led them out into the east wing hallway.

Marian stifled an impatient sigh. Ordinarily, she encouraged the children's endless questions, but at the moment she did not feel equal to explaining the legalities of inheritance to a curious six-year-old.

Cissy had no such qualms. "It's when an estate must pass to the nearest male relative. If I were a boy, I would be master of Knightley Park now. Or if little Henry had lived, he would be. But since there's only us, and we're girls, the estate belongs to Papa's cousin, Captain Radcliffe."

After a brief pause to digest the information, Dolly had another question. "Do you suppose the captain will look like Papa, since they're cousins?"

"*Were* cousins," Cissy corrected her sister. The child's slender fingers felt like ice as she clung to Marian's hand.

Dolly's forehead puckered. "Do people stop being relations after they go to heaven? That doesn't seem right."

"You'll find out soon enough whether Captain Radcliffe bears any family resemblance," said Marian as they reached the bottom of the great winding staircase and joined a stream of servants pouring out the front door.

Exchanging furtive whispers, the maids smoothed down their aprons, and the footmen straightened their neck linen. They seemed curious and apprehensive about the arrival of their new master. Marian shared their qualms.

Outside, under the pillared portico, Knightley Park's aging butler struggled to marshal his staff into decent order to greet Captain Radcliffe. Shaken by the sudden death of Cissy and Dolly's father, Culpepper had let household discipline slip recently. Now he was paying the price, poor fellow.

Marian had too many worries of her own to spare him more than a passing flicker of sympathy.

"This way, girls." She tugged them along behind the shifting line of servants to stand at the far end of the colonnade, a little apart from the others.

By rights, they probably should have taken a place up beside Mr. Culpepper and Mrs. Wheaton, the cook. Cissy and Dolly were the ladies of the house, in a way. At least, they had been until today. What they would be from now on, and where they would go, depended upon the man presently driving up the long, elm-lined lane toward them. Marian wanted to delay that meeting for as long as possible.

When the carriage came to a halt in front of the house, she could not stifle a shiver.

Dolly must have felt it for she edged closer. "Are you cold, Miss Marian?"

"A little," Marian whispered back, conscious of a breathless silence that had gripped the other servants. "Drizzle like this can make midsummer seem cool, let alone October. Now, remember, bright smiles and graceful curtsies to welcome the captain."

The carriage door swung open, and a tall, rangy figure emerged, clad in black from head to toe, relieved only by a glimpse of stark white shirt cuffs and neck linen. Marian felt a mild pang of disappointment that Captain Radcliffe had not worn his naval uniform. But, of course, he wouldn't, under the circumstances. From rumors in the newspapers, Marian had gleaned that the captain was on leave from his command under a cloud of suspicion.

As Captain Radcliffe removed his hat, a breath of wind stirred his brown hair strewn with threads of gold. Tucking the hat under his arm, he strode slowly past the line of servants while Mr. Culpepper introduced each one. The movement of their bows and curtsies rippled down the line like an ominous wave rolling toward Marian and her young charges. Resisting an urge to draw the girls into a protective embrace, she took a step backward so they would have room to make their curtsies.

At that moment, Captain Radcliffe loomed in front of them, looking even taller than he had from a distance. His face was too long and angular to be called handsome. But it was quite striking, with a jutting nose, firm mouth and deep set, gray eyes beneath sharply arched brows.

Those brows slanted together at a fierce angle as he stared at Cissy and Dolly with a look of the most intense severity Marian had ever seen. Beneath his relentless scrutiny, Cissy lost her nerve. Her curtsy wobbled, and her squeaks of greeting sounded more terrified than welcoming. Dolly forgot to curtsy at all but stared boldly up at the captain.

Mr. Culpepper seemed not to notice as he continued his introductions. "Sir, these are the daughters of your late cousin, Miss Celia Radcliffe and Miss Dorothy. Behind them is their governess, Miss Murray."

A clammy knot of dread bunched in the pit of Marian's stomach as she waited for Captain Radcliffe to speak. It was the same sensation that always gripped her between a dangerous flash of lightning and the alarming crack of thunder that followed.

"Children?" His voice did sound like the rolling rumble of distant thunder, or the pounding of the sea upon a lonely, rock strewn coast. "No one said anything about children."

The man was every bit as bad as she'd feared, if not worse. Besides all the other feelings roiling inside her,

Marian felt a twinge of disappointment at the thought of another prayer unanswered. Once again, it appeared she would have to fight her own battles in defense of those she cared for. Some tiny part of her even stirred at the prospect—perhaps the blood of her warlike ancestors.

Or was it something about the captain's presence that stirred her? Surely not!

When Cissy backed away from her formidable cousin, Marian wrapped a reassuring arm around her shoulders and reached out to tug Dolly back, as well. "Perhaps we can discuss the girls and their situation this evening after I've put them to bed?"

The captain seemed to take notice of her for the first time, looking her over carefully as if to assess the strength of an adversary. His scrutiny ignited a blistering blush in Marian's cheeks. For an instant, the children and all the other servants seemed to melt away, leaving her all alone with Captain Radcliffe.

Perhaps the captain felt it, too, for he gave his head a brisk shake, collecting himself from a moment of abstraction. "Very well. Report to the bridge at eight bells of the last dog watch. That is…the Chinese drawing room at eight o'clock."

"Yes, sir." Marian dropped a curtsy, wondering if he expected her to salute. "Now I will take the children back indoors before they catch a chill…with your permission, of course."

"By all means, attend to your duties." The captain looked as if he could hardly wait for Cissy and Dolly to be out of his sight.

Marian was only too eager to obey his curt order.

"Come along, girls." She shepherded them into the house, resisting the perverse urge to glance back at him.

Neither of the children spoke until they were halfway up the broad spiral staircase.

"The captain doesn't look much like Papa." Dolly sounded disappointed.

"He isn't *anything* like Papa!" Cissy muttered fiercely.

"I don't think he likes us very much." Dolly sighed.

"I'm certain the captain doesn't dislike you, dear." Marian strove to convince herself as much as the children. "He was...surprised to find you here, that's all."

As they slipped back into the comforting familiarity of the nursery, Dolly's grip tightened with such sudden force that it made Marian wince. "The captain won't send us away, will he?"

"Of course not!" Marian stooped to gather her beloved young pupils into a comforting embrace.

They had been through so much in the two short years since she'd come to be their governess—first losing their mother and infant brother, then their father. She had done all she could to make them feel secure and loved, to protect them from the kind of harsh childhood she'd endured.

To herself she vowed, *That man won't send you away if there is anything I can do to prevent it!*

As he waited for the mantel clock to chime eight, Gideon Radcliffe paced the rounded bay end of the Chinese drawing room, peering out each of its tall, slender windows in turn.

Even in the misty dusk, they afforded a fine view down a gently sloping knoll to the lake, which wrapped around a small, green island. Gideon had pleasant memories of boating on that lake from long-ago visits to

Knightley Park when his grandfather was master. At the time, he'd enjoyed an even better view from the room directly above this one—the nursery.

That thought reminded him of his cousin's children. He would rather have been ambushed by the combined French and Spanish fleets than by those two small girls. They could not have been more alien to his experience if they'd been a pair of mermaids. He had no idea what they might need, except to sense that he was entirely unequipped to provide it.

More than ever he felt the urgent necessity to restore his reputation, regain his command and get back to sea. He was confident he possessed the skill, experience and temperament to serve his country well in that capacity. After all these years of service, it was the only life he knew. Losing it would be worse than losing a limb—it would be like losing his very identity.

"I beg your pardon, sir." The soft lilt of a woman's voice intruded upon Gideon's most private thoughts. "You told me to report here at eight. Did you not hear me knock?"

"I…didn't." Gideon withdrew into himself, like a sea creature retreating into the shelter of its tough, rigid shell. "But do come in. I wanted to talk to you about the…children."

"As did I, sir." She approached with deliberate steps, halting some distance away, behind an ornate armchair.

During their first meeting, Gideon had been so taken aback by the sight of his young cousins that he'd paid little heed to their governess, beyond her hostile glare. No doubt she had read all the scurrilous gossip about him in the papers and judged him guilty of the false accusations against him. So much for his hope of finding a sanctuary at Knightley Park to escape public condemnation!

Now he forced himself to take stock of his potential adversary. Marian Murray was small and slender, her dark brown hair pinned back with strict severity. Only a single wisp had escaped to curl in a softening tendril over her left temple. With high cheekbones and a fresh complexion, her face might have been quite pleasant to look at if she ventured to smile occasionally. At the moment, her brown eyes were narrowed and her full lips compressed in an expression of barely concealed hostility, if not outright contempt.

Though Gideon told himself her opinion was not of the slightest consequence, he could not deny the sting. "Yes. Well…about the children. I hope the entail of the estate did not leave them unprovided for."

If that were the case, he would take responsibility for their maintenance. It might ease the unreasonable guilt he felt for displacing them from their home.

"No, sir." The governess seemed surprised by his question, as if she had not expected him to care. "The girls each have a comfortable little fortune from their mother."

"I am relieved to hear it." Gideon nodded his approval. "Pray who is their guardian and why have they been left alone here?"

Surely he would have been informed if Cousin Daniel had named him in that capacity. And surely Daniel would have known better than to entrust his young daughters to the care of a distant relation who was apt to be away at sea for years on end.

"The girls have not been alone," Miss Murray corrected him. "They have had an entire household to care for them. Their mother's younger sister, Lady Villiers, is their godmother. She is to be their guardian."

"Capital!" Tension released its grip on his clenched muscles so swiftly Gideon feared he might crumple to the floor. "I mean to say…how fortunate…for the children. Will Lady Villiers be coming to fetch them soon or should they be sent to her?"

The look on Miss Murray's face grew even grimmer. A passing thought pricked Gideon's conscience. Was she too strict a person to have charge of two sensitive children? Perhaps he should suggest Lady Villiers hire a more amiable governess for his young cousins.

Captain Radcliffe didn't like her. That much was evident to Marian. Not that she minded—quite the contrary. Besides, it set them even.

She resented his obvious eagerness to palm off responsibility for Cissy and Dolly on someone else, without asking or caring whether that person might be the least bit suitable. In Marian's opinion, Lady Villiers was not.

"Her ladyship has been abroad since before Mr. Radcliffe's death. The family's solicitor has not been able to contact her. She was in Florence the last we heard, but she may have gone on to Paris."

"It does seem to be a fashionable destination since Napoleon's defeat." Captain Radcliffe sounded disappointed that Lady Villiers would not be taking the girls off his hands immediately. "I know someone in France who might be able to get a message to her."

A message to come at once and take the girls away? The prospect made Marian queasy. But would Cissy and Dolly be any better off with this glacial man about whom she'd heard disturbing rumors?

Her gaze flitted around the elegant, exotic room. At least this house was familiar to the girls. And if the new master had no fondness for them, she and the other servants did. Besides, unlike their aunt, Captain Radcliffe had no reason to harbor designs on the girls' fortunes. "Could you delay sending that message for just a bit, sir?"

"Why on earth...?"

"Knightley Park is the children's home—the only one they've ever known. If they must leave it, I would like some time to get them used to the idea, if that's all right?"

It wasn't all right. That much was clear from his taut, forbidding scowl.

"Please," she added, though she doubted any amount of begging would budge a man like him. "You've probably spent most of your life moving from one place to another. So perhaps you can't understand why a child who's lost her mother and father would want to stay in a familiar place around people she's used to."

It was not her place to speak to the new master in such a tone. Marian could imagine Mr. Culpepper's look of horror if he heard her.

"I understand better than you suppose, Miss Murray." Captain Radcliffe spoke so softly, Marian wondered if she had only imagined his words.

"You do?"

He replied with a slow nod, a distant gaze and a pensive murmur that seemed to come from some well-hidden place inside him. "I was ten years old when I was sent to sea after my mother died."

The wistful hush of his voice slid beneath Marian's bristling defenses. Her heart went out to that wee boy. A navy ship must have been an even harsher place to grow up than the Pendergast Charity School, where she had been sent. She wondered if young Gideon Radcliffe had been blessed with good friends and strong faith to help him bear it.

But she had no right to ask such questions of a man like him. Besides, the girls were her first priority.

Perhaps she could appeal to the part of him that remembered the loss and displacement he'd suffered. "Cissy is only nine and Dolly hasn't turned seven yet. I know you don't mean to send them off to sea, Captain. But *away-from-home* is all the same, no matter where, don't you think?"

His brows rose and his lower lip thrust out in a downward curve. "I see your point."

Marian sensed this was as receptive as he was likely to get. "I'm not asking anything of you, Captain, except to provide us with food and houseroom until Lady Villiers returns. This place has plenty of both to spare. I will see to the girls, entirely, just the way I have since their father died. I'll make certain they don't disturb you."

For a moment Captain Radcliffe stared down at the finely woven carpet. Then suddenly he lifted his head to fix her with a gaze that *did* see her—too clearly for her comfort. "Very well, Miss Murray. I am not such an ogre as you may suppose. I know this is *their* home and would have remained so if they'd had a brother."

"I never thought you were an—"

Before she could blurt out that bald lie, the captain raised his hand to bid her not interrupt him. "Until the New Year then."

"I beg your pardon, sir?"

"I shall delay contacting Lady Villiers until January." Captain Radcliffe sounded resigned to his decision. "That will allow the children to spend Christmas in the country. After that, the New Year is a time for new beginnings."

"Perhaps so." That sounded ungrateful. Captain Radcliffe was under no obligation to let them stay for any length of time, let alone the whole winter. "What I meant to say was…thank you, sir."

As she hurried back to the nursery, Marian thanked God, too, for granting this reprieve. Perhaps her earlier prayers had been heard after all.

Chapter Two

After his first night in his new home, Gideon woke much later than usual. He'd slept badly—the place was far too quiet. He missed the soothing lap of the waves against the hull of his ship, the flap of sails in the wind and the mournful cries of seagulls. When he had drifted off, the face of that young midshipman had appeared to trouble him. Though the charges brought against him were entirely unfounded—of causing the death of one member of his crew and threatening others—that did not mean his conscience was clear.

An iron band of pain tightened around Gideon's forehead when he crawled out of bed. He staggered when the floor stayed level and still beneath his feet. It had taken him a while to gain his sea legs when he'd joined his first crew, all those years ago. Now the roll of a deck was so familiar he wondered if he would ever feel comfortable on dry land. Nottinghamshire had some of the driest land in the kingdom, many miles from the ocean in any direction. Coming here had given Gideon a far more intimate understanding of what it meant to be "a fish out of water."

Perhaps some coffee and breakfast would help. Though he'd lived on ship's rations for more than two-thirds of his life, he could not claim they were superior to the fare available at Knightley Park.

As he washed, shaved and dressed for the day, Gideon's thoughts turned back to his unsettling interview with Miss Murray the previous evening. The woman reminded him of a terrier—small and rather appealing, yet possessed of fierce tenacity in getting what she wanted. What in blazes had possessed him to tell her about being sent to sea after his mother's death?

He seldom talked to anyone about his past and never about that unhappy time. Perhaps it was what she'd said about a bereaved child needing the comfort of familiar surroundings. It had struck a chord deep within him—far too deep for his liking. Before he could stop himself, the words had poured out. For an instant after he'd spoken, Gideon thought he sensed a thawing in her obvious aversion to him. Then she had turned and used that unintentional revelation as leverage to wring from him a concession he'd been reluctant to grant.

He counted himself fortunate that he had not come up against many enemy captains who were such formidable opponents as this simple Scottish governess.

It wasn't that he begrudged his young cousins' houseroom—quite the contrary. They had been born and lived their whole lives at Knightley Park, while he had only visited the place at Christmastime and in the summer. Though it belonged to him by law, he could not escape the conviction that they had a far stronger claim to it.

While they remained here, he would be reluctant to make many changes in the domestic arrangements they were accustomed to…no matter how sorely needed. He would always feel like an interloper in his own home, prevented from claiming the solitude and privacy he'd hoped to find at Knightley Park.

That was not his only objection to the arrangement, Gideon reminded himself as he headed off in search of breakfast. What if his young cousins needed something beyond the authority of their governess to provide? What if some harm befell them and he was held accountable? He, who had been charged with the welfare of an entire ship's crew, shrank from the responsibility for two small girls. It vexed Gideon that he had not thought to raise some of these objections with Miss Murray last night.

It was too late now, though. He had given his word. He only hoped he would not come to regret that decision as much as he regretted some others he'd made of late.

"Dolly!" That soft but urgent cry, and the light, fleet patter of approaching footsteps jarred Gideon from his thoughts; but too late to take proper evasive action.

An instant later, the child came racing around the corner and barreled straight into him. Her head struck him in the belly, like a small blond cannonball, knocking the breath out of him. Meanwhile the collision sent her tumbling backward onto her bottom. It could not have winded her as it had Gideon, for her mouth fell open to emit an earsplitting wail that made his aching head throb. Her eyes screwed up and commenced to gush tears at a most alarming rate. The sight unnerved Gideon like nothing in his eventful naval career…with one recent exception.

Before he could catch his breath or rally his shattered composure, Marian Murray charged around the corner and swooped down to enfold her young charge. "Wist ye now, Dolly!"

She looked up at Gideon, her eyes blazing with fierce protectiveness. "What did you do to her?"

"What...?" Gideon gasped. "I...?"

That was one unjust accusation too many. Somehow he managed to suck in enough air to fuel his reply. "I did...*nothing* to her! That little imp ploughed into me. A few inches taller and she'd have stove in my ribs."

Anger over a great many things that had nothing to do with the present situation came boiling out of him. "What was she doing tearing through the halls like a wild thing? Someone could have been hurt much worse."

Now he'd done it. No doubt his rebuke would make the child howl even louder, if that were possible. Less than twenty-four hours had passed, and already he'd begun to regret his hasty decision to let the children stay.

To his amazement, Gideon realized the child was not weeping harder. Indeed, she seemed to have stopped. Her sobs had somehow turned to chuckles.

"Wild thing." She repeated his words as if they were a most amusing compliment, then chuckled again.

"You needn't sound so pleased with yourself." Miss Murray helped the child to her feet and dusted her off. "Captain Radcliffe is right. You could have been hurt a good deal worse. Now tell him you're sorry and promise it won't happen again."

The little scamp broke into a broad grin that was strangely infectious. "I'm sorry I bumped into you, Captain. I hope I didn't hurt you too much. I promise I won't run so fast around corners after this."

"I'm not certain that running indoors at all is a good idea." Gideon struggled to keep the corners of his mouth from curling up, as they itched to do. "You are not a filly, after all, and this is not Newmarket racecourse."

If Miss Murray found his remark at all amusing, she certainly gave no sign. "I apologize, as well, Captain. This is all my fault. I will keep Dolly under much closer supervision from now on."

Gideon found himself torn between a strange desire to linger there in the hallway with them and an urgent need to get away. Since the latter made far more sense, he gave a stiff nod to acknowledge her assurance and strode away in search of a strong cup of coffee to restore his composure.

"Dorothy Ann Radcliffe," Marian muttered as she marched her young pupil back to the nursery, "you won't be content until you make my hair turn white, will you?"

"Could I really do that, Miss Marian?" Dolly sounded far more intrigued by the possibility than chastened.

"I don't care to find out, thank you very much." Marian pointed to a low, three-legged stool in the corner, with which Dolly's bottom was quite familiar. "Go sit for ten minutes and think about what you've done."

"Why must *I* sit in the corner?" demanded the child. "When you told the Captain it was all your fault?"

"Impudence, for a start." Marian fixed her with a stern look. "I warn you, I am not in the mood to tolerate any more of your foolishness, just now."

Though Dolly deserved her punishment, Marian could not deny her own responsibility for what had happened. Since their father's death, she had encouraged Dolly's high spirits, in the hope of lifting her sister's.

"What happened?" asked Cissy, who sat at the nursery table, an untouched bowl of porridge in front of her. "I heard shouting and bawling."

Before Marian could get a word out, Dolly announced, "I bumped into the captain and fell down."

Walking toward the corner stool, she rubbed her bottom. "He called me a wild thing and said the house isn't a racecourse. I think he's funny."

Captain Radcliffe was anything but amusing. A little shudder ran through Marian as she recalled his dark scowl, which seemed to threaten he would send the girls away if another such mishap occurred. "That's quite enough out of you, miss. I don't want to hear another word for ten minutes or I'll add ten more. Is that understood?"

Dolly opened her mouth to reply, then shut it again and nodded as she sank onto the stool.

Marian returned to her rapidly cooling breakfast but found she had no appetite for it now.

"What did he say, Miss Marian?" Cissy asked in an anxious tone.

"He wasn't happy about being rammed into on his first morning here, of course." Marian cast a reproachful look toward the corner stool. "I can't say I blame him."

Now that she thought back on it, the captain had seemed more vexed by her tactless assumption that he'd done something to hurt Dolly, rather than the other way around. She couldn't blame him for that either. No one liked to be unjustly accused, especially when *they* were the injured party. But what else was she to think, after the experiences of her past and the things she'd read about him in the newspapers? There had been reports of severe cruelty to the younger members of his crew, resulting in at least one death.

"I don't mean what the captain said just now." Cissy pushed her porridge around the bowl with her spoon. "What did he say last night when you went to talk to him…at *eight* bells?"

"Oh, that." He'd told her about being sent away to sea when he was only a little older than Cissy, though Marian sensed he hadn't intended to. "He said you and Dolly are welcome to stay at Knightley Park until your aunt comes back from abroad. That was kind of him, wasn't it?"

So it was, Marian reminded herself, though she still resented his obvious reluctance.

Cissy ignored the question. "I wish Aunt Lavinia would come tomorrow and take us away with her."

"I don't!" cried Dolly, undeterred by the prospect of ten more minutes in the corner. "I want to stay at Knightley Park as long as we can."

That was what Marian wanted for the girls, too. She feared what might become of Cissy and Dolly once Lady Villiers took charge of them. Her best hope was that she would be allowed to remain as their governess. Though she disliked the idea of having no fixed home, flitting from one fashionable destination to another, at least she would be able to shield the children from the worst excesses of their aunt's way of life.

But what if Lady Villiers decided that traveling with her two young nieces and their governess in tow would be too inconvenient? What if she dismissed Marian and placed the girls in a boarding school, while she used their money to stave off her creditors?

Worrying down a spoonful of cold porridge as an example to the girls, Marian tried to push those fears to the back of her mind. She had enough to be getting on with just now—she didn't need to borrow trouble. If she could not keep the children from disturbing Captain Radcliffe, she feared he might turn them out long before Lady Villiers arrived to collect her nieces.

Gideon had intended to catch a few days' rest before plunging into his new duties as master of Knightley Park. But after the collision with his young cousin on his way to breakfast, he decided a dignified retreat might be in order. If Miss Murray could not keep the children out of his way, then he must take care to keep out of theirs.

His belly was still a little tender where the child's sturdy head had butted it. That did not smart half as much as the memory of Miss Murray's accusation. Her tone and look made it abundantly clear her opinion had been turned against him before he ever set foot in Knightley Park. Was that the case with all the servants? He'd hoped the vile gossip about him might not have spread this far into the countryside. Apparently, that had been wishful thinking.

Such thoughts continued to plague him as he rode around the estate, investigating its operation. What he discovered provided a distraction, though not the kind he'd hoped for. Everywhere he looked, he encountered evidence of idleness, waste and mismanagement. By late that afternoon, his bones ached from the unaccustomed effort of sitting a horse for so many hours.

His patience had worn dangerously thin by the time he tracked down the steward of Knightley Park.

"Pray how long have you been employed in your present position, Mr. Dutton?" Hands clasped behind his back, Gideon fixed the steward with his sternest quarterdeck stare.

Unlike every midshipman who'd ever served under him, this landlubber seemed not to grasp the significance of that look.

The steward was a solid man of middling height with bristling ginger side-whiskers and a confident air. "Been here nigh on ten years, sir. Not long after the late master's marriage, God rest both their souls. In all that time, Mr. Radcliffe never had a fault to find with my service."

"Indeed?" Gideon's voice grew quieter, a sign his crew would have known to heed as a warning. "You must have found my late cousin a very satisfactory employer, then—easygoing, content to leave the oversight of the estate in your hands with a minimum of interference."

"Just so, sir." Dutton seemed to imply the new master would do well to follow his cousin's example. "I didn't presume to tell him how to hunt his foxes and he didn't tell me how to carry out my duties."

The man was drifting into heavy weather, yet he appeared altogether oblivious. "But there is a difference between those two circumstances, is there not? My cousin's hunting was none of your affair, while your management of this estate was very much his. Now it is mine and I have never shirked my duty."

At last the steward seemed to sense which way the wind was blowing. He stood up straighter, and his tone became a good deal more respectful. "Yes, sir. I mean... no, sir."

From his coat pocket, Gideon withdrew a folded sheet of paper on which he had penciled some notes in the tight, precise script he used for his log entries. "From what I have observed today, Mr. Dutton, you have not been over*seeing* this estate so much as over*looking* waste and sloth. I fear you have left me with no alternative but to replace you."

"You can't do that, sir!"

With a raised eyebrow, Gideon inquired what prevented him.

"What I mean to say is, I've got a wife and family and I'm not as young as I used to be." Dutton's former bluster disappeared, replaced by fear of reaping the bad harvest he had sown. "If word gets out that I've been dismissed..."

"I have no intention of broadcasting the information," replied Gideon. "Though I could not, in good conscience, provide you with a reference."

"Please, sir. Perhaps I have let things slide around here of late." The man looked a proper picture of repentance. "But if you give me another chance, I'll lick the estate into shape. So help me, I will."

Though he knew the importance of decisiveness in maintaining command, Gideon hesitated. Granting second chances had not worked well for him in the past. One might argue that it had contributed to his present predicament. Too often, offenders looked on such a reprieve as a sign of weakness to be further exploited. And yet, there was Dutton's family to consider. His wife and children had done nothing wrong, but they would suffer for his conduct, perhaps more than he.

"A fortnight." Gideon fixed the man with his sternest scowl, so Dutton would be in no doubt this was an undeserved opportunity he had better not abuse. "I will give you that long to persuade me you are worth keeping."

Ignoring the man's effusive thanks, Gideon turned on his heel and strode away. He hoped this decision would not prove as much a mistake as his last one.

Making certain Cissy and Dolly did not disturb Captain Radcliffe was proving a great deal harder than she had expected. Marian reflected on that difficulty as she put the girls to bed one evening, a week after his arrival at Knightley Park.

Part of the problem was the captain's unpredictable comings and goings. She could never tell when he might be spending time in the house, out roaming the grounds or riding off around the estate. If she knew, perhaps she could have adjusted the children's schedule of lessons to take advantage of his absences. As it was, she could not take the chance of encountering him out in the garden or on their way down to the music room.

Since their disastrous run-in, Dolly had taken an unaccountable fancy to the captain and would no doubt pester him for attention if they met again. Cissy clearly resented his presence and might offend him with a rude remark.

Neither of the girls took kindly to being confined to the nursery after enjoying the run of the house during their father's time. Just that morning, the governess had overheard Cissy muttering about being "kept prisoner."

Marian found it difficult to discourage such an attitude, since it mirrored her own far too closely. In all her time at Knightley Park, and especially after Mr.

Radcliffe's death, she'd felt at liberty to come and go as she pleased, even free to borrow books from the well stocked library. Wistfully, she recalled the master's hospitable answer when she'd first asked if she could.

"By all means, Miss Murray! Those books might as well serve some better purpose than giving the maids more things to dust."

Since Captain Radcliffe's arrival, she had not even dared return the last volume she'd borrowed for fear of meeting up with him. Considering the captain's reluctance to have his young cousins around, Marian doubted he would tolerate a servant making use of *his* library. She knew she must soon put it back, before he noticed its absence and blamed someone else.

Perhaps now would be a good time, with the girls off to bed and the captain occupied with his dinner.

"I won't be long, Martha," she informed the nursery maid, who sat by the fire darning one of Dolly's stockings. "Just a quick errand I have to run."

And run she did—first to her own room to fetch the book, then down the back stairs. She was in such a hurry that she nearly collided with the butler on the landing.

Poor Mr. Culpepper seemed more agitated than ever. "Miss Murray, have you heard? Mr. Dutton has been threatened with dismissal! I fear I shall be put on notice next."

The news about the steward did not come as a great surprise to Marian. Though she was working hard to make sure Captain Radcliffe was not conscious of the girls' presence in the house, she found herself constantly aware of his. It was as if a salty ocean breeze had blown all the way into the landlocked heart of England, bearing with it a host of unwelcome changes.

"These naval men have most exacting standards." Mr. Culpepper wrung his hands. "At my age, where should I go if I am turned out of Knightley Park?"

Marian bristled at the thought of such a good and faithful servant treated so shabbily. "Has Captain Radcliffe complained about the running of the house?"

The butler shook his head. "Not in so many words. But he is so very quiet and solemn, just the way he was as a boy. Who knows what plans he may be making? He is so little like his cousin, one would scarcely believe they could be of the same blood."

That was true enough. The girls' jovial, generous father had been a down-to-earth country squire devoted to his children, his horses and his dogs. His cousin seemed distinctly uncomfortable with all three.

"Don't fret yourself, Mr. Culpepper. I'm sure the captain would tell you soon enough if the housekeeping was not up to his standards. He seems the type that's quick to find fault. Silence is as close to praise as you can hope for from him."

The furrows of worry in the butler's forehead relaxed a trifle. "I hope you are right, Miss Murray. I will endeavor to remain calm and go about my duties."

"Good." Marian flashed him an encouraging smile, pleased that she had been able to ease his fears a little. "That's all any of us can do, I reckon."

As she continued on down the stairs, Marian strove to heed her own advice, though it wasn't easy. She would have feared the captain's disapproval less if her position was the only thing at stake. But with the children's welfare hanging in the balance, she could not afford to put a foot wrong.

As she tiptoed past the dining room, the muted clink of silverware on china assured her the captain was busy eating his dinner. A few moments later, as she hurried back from the library, a sudden crash from inside the dining room made her start violently. It sounded as if a piece of china had been hurled to the floor and smashed into a hundred pieces. The noise was immediately followed by a wail of distress from Bessie, a nervous, and often clumsy, housemaid. What had the captain done to make the poor lass take on so?

Marian marched toward the dining room, not certain how she meant to intervene but compelled to do what she could to defend the girl.

She was about to fling open the door when she heard Bessie sob, "I'm s-sorry, s-s-ir! Have I burnt ye with that tea? I told Mr. Culpepper I'm too ham-fisted to be waiting table. Now ye'll send me packing and I wouldn't blame ye!"

So it was Bessie who had fumbled a teacup. A qualm of shame gripped Marian's stomach as she realized she had once again jumped to a most uncharitable conclusion about Captain Radcliffe.

His reply to Bessie made Marian feel even worse. "Don't trouble yourself. If Mr. Culpepper asks, you must tell him it was my fault. I am not accustomed to handling such delicate china. Now dry your eyes, sweep up the mess and think no more of it."

As Marian fled back to the nursery, her conscience chided her for all the harsh things she'd thought and said about Captain Radcliffe since his arrival. She should have been grateful to him for allowing Cissy and Dolly

to stay at Knightley Park when he'd been under no obligation to keep them here. Instead, she'd compared
him unfavorably with his cousin and held those differences against him. She'd resented the loss of a few petty
privileges, as if they'd been hers by right rather than by
favor. Worst of all, she had allowed mean-spirited rumors to poison her opinion of the man without giving
him a fair opportunity to prove his worth.

Clearly she needed to pay greater heed to her Bible,
especially the part that counseled *"judge not, lest ye be
judged."* It might be that, in the eyes of God, Captain
Radcliffe had a great deal less to answer for than she.

Chapter Three

Coming to Knightley Park had clearly been a huge mistake. As Gideon returned to the house after several frustrating hours reviewing the steward's progress, he reflected on his folly.

He had come to Nottinghamshire expecting to escape his recent troubles by revisiting simpler times past. But Knightley Park was no longer the calm, well run estate it had been in his grandfather's day. And he was no longer the solitary child, made welcome by one and all.

The seeds of gossip had followed him here and found fertile soil in which to breed a crop of noxious weeds. Young footmen turned pale and fled when he approached. Tenants eyed him with wary, resentful servility. Housemaids trembled when he cast the briefest glance in their direction. His cousins' governess sprang to her young charges' defense like a tigress protecting her cubs.

Gideon had to admit he preferred Miss Murray's open antagonism to the sullen aversion and dread of the others. And he could not fault her willingness to shield the children, even if there had been no need.

Unfortunately, his flicker of grudging admiration for Miss Murray only made her suspicion and wariness of him sting all the worse.

As he entered the house quietly by a side door, Gideon could no longer ignore a vexing question. How could he possibly expect the Admiralty's board of inquiry to believe in his innocence when his own servants and tenants clearly judged him guilty?

Passing the foot of the servants' stairs, he heard the voices of two footmen drift down from the landing. He did not mean to eavesdrop, but their furtive, petulant tone left Gideon in no doubt they were talking about him.

"How long do you reckon we'll have to put up with him?" asked one.

The other snorted. "Too long to suit either of us, I can tell you that. With old Boney beaten at last, I'll wager the navy won't want him back."

Gideon told himself to keep walking and pay no heed to servants' tattle. He knew this was the sort of talk that must be going on behind his back all the time. The last thing he needed was to have their exact words echoing in his thoughts, taunting and shaming him. But his steps slowed in spite of himself, and his ears strained to catch every word.

Did part of him feel he deserved it?

One of the footmen heaved a sigh. "So he'll stay here to make our lives a misery instead of his crew's. It's not right."

"When did right ever come into it?" grumbled the other.

Gideon had almost managed to edge himself out of

earshot when a third voice joined the others—a woman's voice he recognized as belonging to Miss Murray.

"Wilbert, Frederick, have you no duties to be getting on with?" she inquired in a disapproving tone, as if they were a pair of naughty little boys in the nursery.

"We just stopped for a quick word, miss. We've been run off our feet since the new master arrived." They were obviously counting on the governess to sympathize with their disgruntled feelings.

By now Gideon had given up trying to walk away. He braced to hear the governess join in abusing him.

"Perhaps if you'd kept up with your duties during the past few months," she reminded the young footmen instead, "you might not have to work quite so hard now to get the house back in decent order."

"Why should we run ourselves ragged for a master who's done the things he has? They say he did away with a young sailor. If he wasn't the captain of the ship they'd have called it plain murder."

As he waited for Miss Murray's reply, Gideon wondered if he'd been wrong to assume her opinion of him had been tainted by the kind of gossip she was hearing now. Surely, she would not have wanted her young pupils to remain in the same house as a rumored killer. Perhaps this was the first time she'd heard the worst of the accusations being whispered against him.

Though he tried to tell himself one unfavorable judgment more or less did not matter, Gideon shrank from the prospect of Miss Murray thinking even less of him.

"I am sorely disappointed." The gentle regret in her tone troubled Gideon worse than the harsher censure he'd expected. "I thought better of you both than to condemn your master on the basis of malicious rumors."

Had he heard her correctly? Gideon shook his head.

The young footmen sputtered in protest, but Miss Murray refused to back down. "Has the captain mistreated either of you in any way since he arrived at Knightley Park?"

"No...but he is very haughty and ill-humored. You must grant that, miss."

"And did you hear he threatened to give Mr. Dutton the sack?"

"I have heard such a rumor, though that does not guarantee it is true. Besides, Wilbert, I have often heard you complain what a poor job Mr. Dutton has been doing of late. If you were in the captain's place, would you have kept him on?"

After an awkward pause, Wilbert muttered, "I reckon not, miss."

"And you, Frederick, would you be jovial and talkative in a place where you were made to feel as unwelcome as I fear we have made Captain Radcliffe?"

Gideon did not catch the young footman's muffled reply, but that scarcely mattered. What did matter was that someone had defended him against the whispered slurs he could not bring himself to acknowledge, let alone refute. What astonished him even more was to find a champion in Marian Murray, a woman he could have sworn detested him.

And not altogether without reason, he was forced to admit. None of their encounters since his arrival had been particularly cordial. And his reaction to the children's presence might have given her cause to regard him as a very hard man indeed. Yet there she was, taking his part against the prevailing opinion of the other servants. He did not know what to make of it.

To be championed in such a way when he neither expected nor deserved it stirred a flicker of welcome warmth deep within his fallow heart.

The hangdog looks of the two young footmen reproached Marian. What was she doing?

For as long as she could recall, she had felt compelled need to stand up for anyone who was the victim of mistreatment. The stronger the forces against them, the more fiercely she felt called to intervene.

It had not occurred to her that a man of strength and authority like Captain Radcliffe might need *anyone* to defend him, let alone her. But when she'd heard Wilbert and Frederick exchanging backstairs gossip about the captain, she had suddenly seen the matter in a whole new light. A sense of shame for the unfair things she'd thought about the man and her manner toward him had made her leap to his defense all the more fiercely.

Now she realized that that was not fair either. "I beg your pardon. I have no right to reproach you when I have behaved just as uncharitably toward Captain Radcliffe."

Her rueful admission seemed to have better effect on the young men than her rebuke.

"That's all right, miss." Wilbert hung his head. "I reckon we may have been too hard on the master."

Frederick nodded. "It's true enough what you said, miss. The captain hasn't done us any harm. We'll mind our tongues after this."

"We should get back to work," Wilbert added, "before Mr. Culpepper comes looking for us."

After brief bows, the pair hurried off below stairs, leaving Marian to follow as far as the ground floor. Lost in thought about her encounter with the footmen and the sudden reversal of her opinion toward Captain Radcliffe, she rounded the corner and nearly collided with him.

"I beg your pardon, sir!" She started back, frantically wondering whether he'd heard what had just passed in the stairwell. "I didn't expect to find you home at this hour."

The captain seemed every bit as rattled by their sudden meeting as she. "I...er...just got in. I'm sorry if I startled you."

Caught off guard, his whole appearance was far less severe than Marian had yet seen it. The austere contours of his face seemed somehow softened. The sweeping arch of his brow looked less forbidding. His steely gray eyes held a tentative glimmer of warmth. Had he changed so much or was it her perception that had altered?

"No, indeed," she sputtered, painfully aware that she owed him an apology for offenses she dared not confess. "I should have minded the warning I gave Dolly about charging around corners."

"Ah, yes." A half smile crinkled one corner of the captain's resolute mouth. "I hope the child has recovered from our collision."

"Entirely." Marian nodded, relieved at this turn in the conversation. Perhaps the captain had not overheard anything between her and the footmen after all. "I believe you took greater injury from it than she did."

His unexpected query about Dolly's well-being emboldened her to continue. "I believe she would be less apt to run in the house if she could use up some of that energy running and playing out of doors."

"I agree." The captain raised an eyebrow. "What prevents the children from going out? Are they ill? Do they not have warm enough clothes?"

A fresh qualm of remorse gripped Marian. Not only had she misjudged Captain Radcliffe, she had allowed her prejudice against him to make life less agreeable for her pupils. In doing so, she might have provoked Cissy's aversion to the captain.

"The girls are quite well," she replied, "and they do not lack for warm garments."

"Then what is the difficulty?"

She might as well confess and hope the captain would be as forgiving with her as he had of the clumsy serving maid. Marian inhaled a deep breath and forged ahead. "I'm afraid I thought, sir…that is… I presumed… You did tell me I should keep the girls from disturbing you. I was afraid we might disrupt one of your walks, or their noise from outdoors might bother you while you were trying to rest or read."

"I see." He flinched slightly, as if she had injured an unhealed wound but he was determined not to let her see the pain it caused. "I suppose my reputation made you fear I would have them flogged for it."

He must have overheard her talking to the footmen. Marian scrambled to recall exactly what she'd said. If the captain had heard only part of their exchange, might he think she was spreading malicious gossip about him?

"Nothing like that, sir!" she cried, though her stricken conscience forced her to confess, "Though I was worried you might send the girls away from Knightley Park."

Captain Radcliffe gave a rueful nod that seemed to excuse her suspicions. "I fear you and I have gotten off on the wrong foot, Miss Murray. For that I take full responsibility. In future, feel free to do with the children whatever you were accustomed to before I arrived. Proceed as if I am not here. All I ask is that you not seek me out. I have no experience with children and, as you have seen, no knack for getting on with them."

Perhaps not, but in spite of that he had managed to catch Dolly's fancy. In her forthright innocence, the child must have responded to something in him that had eluded Marian.

"Does that include the music room, sir?" she asked. "It can be irksome to hear a great many wrong notes struck on the pianoforte."

After only a slight hesitation the captain nodded gamely. "It is difficult to learn anything of value without making mistakes."

His assurance made Marian more conscious than ever what a grave error she had committed in her judgment of him.

"Thank you, Captain." She dropped him a curtsy that she hoped would convey an apology as well as gratitude. "I'm sure the girls will be very pleased to enjoy greater liberty."

He replied with a stiff bow. "I am only sorry they were ever deprived of it."

The captain made it sound as if that were his fault, yet Marian knew which of them was more to blame. Perhaps it was the burden of her misjudgment that made her more self-conscious than ever in Captain Radcliffe's presence. A blush seemed to hide in the flesh of her cheeks, ready to flame out at any second.

"I was just on my way to the music room to fetch a song book. If you will excuse me, I must finish my errand and get back to the nursery before the girls wonder what has become of me."

"By all means," he replied. "Do not let me detain you."

Marian made another curtsy, then hurried away, torn between eagerness to escape his presence and a strange inclination to linger.

"Miss Murray."

The sound of her name on his lips made her turn back swiftly, as if some part of her had anticipated the summons. "Sir?"

He hesitated for an instant, making her wonder if he had not intended to call out. "Thank you for speaking up on my behalf to those young men. I only hope I will have as able an advocate to defend me when the Admiralty convenes its inquiry."

The blush that had been lying in wait now flared in Marian's cheeks. "I don't deserve your gratitude. I wish I could claim I have kept an open mind about you and not let my opinion be influenced by reports I've heard...or read. But I'm afraid that would not be true."

Captain Radcliffe gave a rueful nod, as if her confession grieved him a little but did not surprise him. "If your mind was not fully open, neither was it altogether closed. May I ask what altered your opinion of me?"

His question flustered Marian even more. She could not bring herself to admit eavesdropping on his exchange with Bessie over the broken china. "I... I'm not certain, Captain. Perhaps it was hearing Frederick and Wilbert talking that made me realize I hadn't given you a fair chance. I reckon it's easier to see our own faults in others."

"Perhaps so, but it is not so easy to admit those faults

and alter our conduct accordingly." A note of approval warmed his words and went a long way toward absolving Marian's shame over her earlier actions.

She was about to thank him for understanding and head away again when Captain Radcliffe continued, "I can assure you the nonsense being written about me in the newspapers is entirely without foundation. I never laid a hand on that poor lad, nor did I drive him to do away with himself on account of my harsh treatment."

What made her believe him so immediately and completely? Marian could not be certain. Was it only guilt over her prior misjudgment of him or was it something more? Even at first, when she'd thought him a strict, uncaring tyrant, she had not been able to deny his air of integrity.

"I believe you, Captain." She strove to infuse her words with sincere faith.

She recalled how it felt to be unfairly accused and disbelieved, and how much it had helped to have even one person take her side. The image of her loyal friend, Rebecca Beaton, rose in Marian's mind, unleashing a flood of gratitude, affection and longing. Rebecca now lived in the Cotswolds, more than a hundred miles to the south. Though the two corresponded as often as they could afford, they had not seen one another since going their separate ways after they'd left school.

Captain Radcliffe's voice broke in on her wistful thoughts. "I appreciate your loyalty, Miss Murray, considering how little I have done to earn it. I hope the board of inquiry will render a decision to justify your faith in me."

"When will this board hear your case, sir?" Though duty urged her to cut their conversation short and return to the nursery at once, Marian could not quell her curiosity.

The captain replied with a shrug and a sigh of frustration. "Not soon enough to suit me, of that you can be sure. Probably not until after the New Year at this rate. In the meantime, I am forbidden to speak publicly about the matter. I must remain silent while the newspapers make me out to be some sort of heartless monster. All I want is the opportunity to prove my innocence so I can return to active duty."

"I'll pray for you, Captain." Marian wished there was more she could do. "That the inquiry be called soon and that your name will be cleared once and for all."

"Why…er…thank you, Miss Murray," he replied with the air of someone reluctantly accepting an unwelcome gift. "Though I doubt your prayers will avail much."

His reaction surprised and rather dismayed her. "Do you not believe in God then?"

How could that be? He had treated her more charitably than many people who'd claimed to be pious Christians.

Captain Radcliffe considered her question a moment, then replied with quiet solemnity. "One cannot spend as much time as I have at sea and not come to believe in a powerful force that created the universe."

Scarcely realizing what she was doing, Marian exhaled a faint breath of relief. Why in the world should it matter to her what the man believed? "But you just said…"

"It is not so much a contradiction as you suppose." The corner of his straight, firm mouth arched ever so slightly. Yet that one small alteration quite transformed his face, warming and softening its stern, rugged contours. "What I cannot imagine is that such a being knows or cares about my trivial concerns any more than the vast ocean cares for one insignificant ship that floats upon it."

No wonder the captain seemed so profoundly solitary, Marian reflected, if he did not believe anyone cared about him...not even his Maker.

"Your concerns are not trivial," she insisted. "You want to see justice done and your reputation restored so you can continue to defend this land. Even I can sympathize with them, and I could not begin to know your heart as deeply as the Lord does."

"You sound very sincere and certain, Miss Murray." He did not seem to think less of her for it, as Marian had feared he might. "Why is that, if you don't mind my asking?"

She was not in the habit of discussing her beliefs, especially with a man she scarcely knew and hadn't much liked at first. Yet there was a kind of openness in the way he regarded her that assured Marian of his honest desire to understand.

"Cannot a God who is infinitely large also be infinitely small and infinitely close?" she ventured, trying to put complex, profound ideas into words that seemed inadequate to the task. "Just as the salt water that makes up the great ocean is not so different from our sweat and tears?"

This whole conversation was becoming altogether too intimate for her comfort. And yet she felt compelled to disclose one final confidence. "Perhaps that sounds foolish to you, but I have felt the loving closeness of God in my life. Never so powerfully as when I needed His presence the most."

What had made her tell him such a thing? Marian regretted it the moment the words were out of her mouth. She had never liked talking about her past, particularly that part of it. In all the time she'd known Cissy and Dolly's father, she had hardly told him anything about herself. Yet here she was blurting out all this to Captain Radcliffe, whom she'd met only a fortnight ago.

A spark of curiosity glinted in the depths of his granite-gray eyes. If she did not cut this conversation short and make her escape, she feared the captain might ask her how she'd come to be so alone and in need of Divine comfort. If he did, she was very much afraid the whole painful story might come pouring out. That was the last thing she wanted.

"I really must go now." Lowering her gaze, she bobbed the captain a hasty curtsy. "Cissy will be worried what's become of me and Dolly will be driving poor Martha to distraction with her mischief."

Before Captain Radcliffe could say anything that might detain her a moment longer, she rushed off to seek sanctuary in the music room. Only when she was quite certain the captain had gone elsewhere did she venture out and fly back up the servants' stairs to the nursery. Yet even as she took care to avoid him, an idea concerning Captain Radcliffe began to take shape in her mind.

Though the captain denied the power of prayer, Marian wondered if he might not be the answer to hers. A man like him would make an ideal guardian for Cissy and Dolly—far better than their profligate aunt. Once that inquiry was over and he returned to his ship, she would be left to care for the girls in familiar surroundings.

All day she mulled the notion over as she and the

children relished their renewed liberty in the house and gardens. The more she considered her idea, the more certain she became that it would be an ideal solution.

That night when she knelt by her bed, Marian prayed fervently. "Lord, forgive me for misjudging Captain Radcliffe. I see now that he is a good man. Please let him be absolved of all the charges against him and permitted to return to active duty on his ship...but not before I can persuade him to challenge Lady Villiers for guardianship of Cissy and Dolly."

How exactly was she going to persuade him of that, Marian asked herself as she climbed into bed, when the captain did not want to have anything to do with the girls? Perhaps she could pray for him to come up with the idea on his own, but this was too important a task to leave up to the power of prayer alone.

Chapter Four

What had Miss Murray meant about having been alone with no one to whom she could turn to but God?

While Gideon ate his solitary dinner that Saturday evening, he reflected on his last conversation with her and the unexpected turn it had taken. How had his thanks for her defense of him led to an examination of his spiritual beliefs? Never before had he confided in another person his doubts about the value of prayer.

As captain of his ship, he had often been required to lead his crew in Sunday worship. Though he'd read many prayers aloud, and knew the *Our Father* by heart as well as any man, he had not uttered those sacred words with any particular expectation that his Creator was listening. The last time he'd truly prayed from his heart, he'd been a child imploring the Almighty to spare the life of his beloved, ailing mother. Of course his pleas had fallen on deaf ears.

Uncomforted by the words of the funeral liturgy, he'd watched them bury her poor, wasted body. Then he'd been wrenched away from everyone and everything familiar and sent to sea. The harsh conditions and the gnawing ache of loneliness had been almost more than he could bear. But somehow he had borne them, and the experience had made a man of him. Gradually he'd come to know and love the sea. In the end he'd dedicated his life to it and to the defense of his country. Those things had helped to fill the emptiness in his heart and give him a sense of purpose.

Was it possible *that* had been an answer to his unspoken prayer? Gideon dismissed the thought.

"What's for pudding, then?" he asked the young footman who collected his empty dinner plate.

"Plum duff, Captain. It's one of Mrs. Wheaton's specialties."

"And one of my favorites," Gideon replied.

Since the lecture they'd received from Miss Murray, the two footmen seemed a good deal less sullen. What she'd said must have made an impression. Could it have been gratitude for her unexpected defense of him that had made him let down his guard with her? Or had he somehow sensed a connection between them based on a common experience of loss?

As the footman set a generous serving of pudding in front of Gideon, a series of soft but determined taps sounded on the dining room door.

"Come through," he called as if he were back in the great cabin aboard HMS *Integrity*.

In response to his summons, the door swung open, and Miss Murray entered. "Pardon me for disturbing your dinner, Captain, but I wanted a word with you concerning the girls, if I might."

He did not care for the sound of that. *She* was supposed to be tending to the children's needs, not pestering him with them.

Yet Gideon found himself strangely pleased to see her all the same. "Very well, Miss Murray. I was just about to sample Mrs. Wheaton's plum duff. Would you care to join me?"

His request seemed to throw her into confusion. "I couldn't...that is, I already had some when I gave the girls their supper. It was very good. I have no doubt you'll enjoy it."

"Surely you could manage a little more." Gideon was not certain what made him so eager to have her join him. Perhaps because it would be awkward to converse with her standing there while he tried to eat.

Sensing she was about to protest more strenuously, he decided to try another tack. "I'd be grateful if you would oblige me, Miss Murray. It can be tiresome to dine night after night with only my own company."

His appeal seemed to catch her as much by surprise as his original invitation. She glanced from him to the footman and back again. "Very well then, Captain, if that is what you wish."

At a nod from Gideon, the footman pulled out a chair for Miss Murray, to the right of his place at the head of the table.

"Only a very small helping for me, please," she murmured as she slipped into the chair.

Acknowledging her request with a mute nod, the footman headed off to the kitchen.

"Now then," said Gideon. "What was this matter you wished to discuss with me?"

Miss Murray inhaled a deep breath and squared her shoulders. "Well, sir, tomorrow is Sunday, and I hoped you might accompany the girls and me to church in the village."

Gideon's eyebrows rose. "In light of what you know about my attitudes toward children and religion, that strikes me as a rather improbable hope, Miss Murray. I doubt the Creator of the Universe cares whether or not I attend services."

"That is not why I go to church!" The words burst out of her. "I go for my own sake, to…nourish…my soul."

She pushed back her chair and started to rise. "I suppose you think that is all rubbish, too."

Before Gideon had time to consider what he was doing, his hand seemed to move of its own accord and come to rest upon one of hers. "On the contrary, Miss Murray. Just because our beliefs differ does not mean I scoff at yours. I hope you will accord mine the same respect."

Her hand felt cool and delicate beneath his, calling forth feelings of warmth and protectiveness Gideon hadn't realized he possessed. But once discretion caught up with him, he knew he must not prolong such contact between them. The sound of the young footman's returning steps spurred him to withdraw his hand, leaving Miss Murray free to go or stay as she wished.

To his surprise, she stayed, dropping back into her chair and pulling her hands off the table to rest upon her lap. Gideon wondered if it was only the footman's return that had kept her from rushing away.

An awkward silence fell between them as the servant entered and placed a saucer of pudding in front of Miss Murray.

"Will there be anything else, sir?" he asked.

Gideon shook his head. "That will be all, thank you. You may go."

He didn't care to have his views on spiritual matters aired before the servants to fuel more gossip about him.

As the young footman withdrew, Miss Murray took a spoonful of custard from the dainty china bowl between them and dribbled it over her plum duff. In perfect unison, she and Gideon each took a bite.

"A sailor's pudding is that," he observed. "Though Mrs. Wheaton's is far superior to any I ever tasted while at sea."

If he'd hoped to draw Miss Murray into a conversation about food that would make her forget her original request, he was soon disappointed. "Let me assure you, Captain, I did not ask you to accompany us to church as a means of…converting you, but for the children's sake."

Gideon took another bite of pudding and chewed on it thoughtfully. What on earth did it matter to his young cousins how, or if, he observed the Sabbath?

Miss Murray seemed to sense his unasked question. "For Dolly's sake, actually. She has begun to balk at going to church. I know it can be a long while for a child her age to sit still, but I believe it is important for children to be raised in faith. Otherwise they're like ships without anchors."

The nautical comparison appealed to Gideon. "I agree. If nothing else, it is a sound foundation for their moral development. But what does that have to do with me?"

Miss Murray sighed. "Dolly says it isn't fair that she must to go to church when you do not. I didn't know what to tell her, Captain."

It was a valid point, Gideon reluctantly acknowledged. He was not certain how he would respond to the child's argument. "The matter of my beliefs aside, I cannot say I am eager to venture out in public. I know very well the sort of gossip that must be circulating about me. I have no desire to be gawked at and whispered about."

Miss Murray worried down another mouthful of pudding as if it were as tough as whale hide rather than a rich, moist confection that fairly melted on the tongue. "I understand your reluctance. But surely church is one place where you are less apt to be judged unfairly."

"It *should* be." Gideon placed skeptical emphasis on that middle word. "But can you assure me this particular church *will* be?"

She could not disguise her doubt. "I wish I could promise that, sir. But how can I expect others to behave more charitably toward you than I have? All I can say with confidence is that I believe once the local people meet you for themselves, they will be far less disposed to believe any false rumors about you."

It was hardly a ringing endorsement, but Gideon appreciated her honesty. Though accompanying his young cousins to church went against his original bargain with their governess, he found it difficult to resist her appealing gaze.

Miss Murray seemed to sense his indecision. "If people see you going about your business openly, they'll realize you have nothing to hide."

That was true, Gideon had to admit. He wondered if his reclusiveness had fostered any mistrust the local people might have had of him. He could not let that continue. Besides, he felt responsible to set a good example for the children. At least *that* was one of their needs he was capable of meeting.

Having consumed the last morsel of pudding, he set

down his spoon and carefully wiped his mouth with his napkin. "Very well, Miss Murray, I accept your invitation. You may tell Miss Dolly she will not be able to use me as an excuse to shirk attendance at church."

Gideon hoped this was not another decision he would come to regret.

"Thank you, Captain!" The governess surged out of her chair and dropped a curtsy. "I am very grateful for your assistance."

The smile that illuminated her features lent them an air of unexpected beauty. It sent a rush of happiness through Gideon unlike any he'd felt in a great while.

"There you go, Dolly." Marian smiled to herself as she tied on the child's bonnet the next morning. "Now please try not to get mussed up before church."

Since last evening, she had been more indulgent than usual with her headstrong little pupil. After all, it had been Dolly's complaints about going to church that had inspired her to invite Captain Radcliffe to join them. Stumbling upon such a fine way to bring him and the girls together had given her hope that God might endorse her plan to have the captain seek guardianship of Cissy and Dolly.

Now if only she could get her pupils to play their parts properly.

"I trust you will be polite to the captain this morning." She looked Cissy over and gave a nod of approval at her appearance. The ribbons on her straw bonnet matched the green velvet spencer she wore over her white muslin dress. The color looked well with her rich brown hair. "Remember, it is not his fault we were confined to the nursery this past while. It was mine for misunderstanding and rushing to judgment."

"I promise I will remember my manners, Miss Marian," the child replied demurely. Yet a subtle stiffness in her bearing suggested her behavior would be correct but not cordial.

Perhaps when Cissy got to know Captain Radcliffe a little better, that coolness would thaw. Marian hoped so.

"And you, Dolly." She heaved an exasperated sigh when she turned to find the younger girl kneeling on the floor to recover her sixpence offering that had somehow rolled under the bed. "Please try not to be too forward. Otherwise, Captain Radcliffe may not want to come to church with us again."

Clutching the tiny silver coin between her fingers, Dolly scrambled to her feet. "Why not?"

"Because…" Marian bent down to brush off a bit of dirt the child's skirt had picked up from the floor. "Captain Radcliffe has lived on his ship for a very long time. He isn't accustomed to the company of…young ladies."

"Why can girls not sail ships?" Dolly demanded. "I like rowing on the pond in the summertime."

Marian, too, had fond memories of their excursions to the little island in the middle of the ornamental lake. If her plan succeeded, it would mean she and the girls would still be at Knightley Park next summer to enjoy more of the same.

A glance at the mantel clock made her start with dismay. "We'll talk about that later. Now, we mustn't keep the captain waiting. Come along, girls."

Seizing them by the hands, she hurried out of the nursery and down the main staircase.

They found Captain Radcliffe waiting in the entry

hall, looking rather severe. At first Marian feared he was vexed with them for being tardy. But a second look made her wonder if he might only be nervous. Recalling what he'd said about not wanting to be stared at and whispered about, she hoped the people at church would treat the captain with more Christian charity than she'd first shown him.

"Good morning, sir." She offered him an encouraging smile and was gratified when his expression relaxed a little. "The girls and I are very pleased to have you join us this morning."

"Indeed." He glanced from solemn-faced Cissy to her grinning little sister with a flicker of mild alarm in his gray eyes. "The carriage is waiting."

Opening the great front door, he held it for Marian to usher her pupils outside.

The grounds of Knightley Park glittered with frost on this crisp, sunny November morning as the girls climbed into the carriage. When Marian followed them, her stomach sank abruptly.

She found Cissy and Dolly perched side by side in the carriage box, leaving the opposite seat empty. If Marian sat there, Captain Radcliffe would be obliged to sit beside her. The thought of being so close to him set her insides aflutter.

"Girls, budge up, please." She tried to squeeze in beside them.

"You're squashing me!" Dolly protested. "Why can't you sit over there?"

"Hush!" Marian whispered. "Cissy, will you kindly move to the other seat?"

The child's eyes widened. She shook her head.

"Then, I will," said Dolly.

Before Marian could prevent her, the child wriggled out from between her and Cissy and bounced over to the opposite seat just as Captain Radcliffe climbed into the carriage. "It's better than being squashed."

The captain settled next to Dolly, with an air of reluctance similar to the one Cissy had displayed when asked to sit beside him.

One of the footmen closed the door behind them. Then, with a rattle, a lurch and the clatter of horses' hooves, they were on their way.

Silence settled inside of the carriage box, as brittle as the thin sheet of ice on the surface of Knightley Park's ornamental lake. Marian searched for something to say that might thaw it.

Before she could think of a suitable topic of conversation, Dolly turned toward the captain. "How do you go to church when you're on your ship?"

"Dolly…" Marian addressed the child in a warning tone. Though Captain Radcliffe might not be the sort of seagoing tyrant she had mistakenly believed him, he probably expected the younger members of his crew to speak only when spoken to.

At first he appeared taken aback by the child's forthright curiosity. But after a moment's consideration he seemed to decide he might do worse than answer her question. "At sea it is not possible to go to a church building, as we are doing now. But most ships in the Royal Navy have chaplains who conduct Sunday services on deck when the weather permits or in the wardroom when it does not."

"What's a wardroom?"

A sterner warning rose to Marian's lips, but before she could utter it, the captain replied, "That is what we call the officers' mess on a ship, a sort of dining room and drawing room combined."

Dolly digested all this new information with a look of intense concentration that Marian wished she would apply to her studies. "Your ship must be a great deal bigger than the boat we row on the lake. How many rooms does it have?"

By now Marian thought better of trying to restrain the child, for Dolly had clearly discovered one subject certain to set the captain at ease. To his credit, he did not seem to mind being bombarded with questions about all matters nautical. Marian was also favorably impressed with his answers, which were couched in simple enough terms for the children to understand without insulting their intelligence.

His discourse proved so informative that Marian found herself listening with rapt attention. It was not only what he said that engaged her interest, but the mellow resonance of his voice that made it a pleasure to listen to.

Almost before she realized it, the carriage came to a halt in front of the village church.

In the middle of an intriguing explanation of sails and rigging, the captain grew suddenly quiet again. "I can tell you more about it on the ride home, if you like."

His features and bearing tensed as he gazed toward the other parishioners making their way into the church.

A qualm of doubt rippled through Marian's stomach as she speculated what sort of reception awaited them. She hoped the villagers would not be as quick to misjudge Captain Radcliffe as she'd been. Otherwise, he might refuse to accompany them to church again. That would be a great calamity because she could not conceive of any other way to bring the captain and his young cousins together without deliberately disobeying his orders.

As the footman pulled open the carriage door, Captain Radcliffe seemed to steel himself for the ordeal ahead. Once the steps had been unfolded, he climbed out. Dolly bounded after him, eagerly seizing the hand he offered to help her.

Marian nodded to Cissy, who followed her sister with a reluctant air. When Marian emerged a moment later, Captain Radcliffe assisted her with thoughtful courtesy. For the fleeting instant his gloved hand clasped hers, she could not suppress a sensation of warmth that quivered up her arm. It reminded her of the previous evening when he had grasped her hand to keep her from rushing away. For hours afterward, she could not stop thinking about that brief contact between them.

"Come, girls." Marian chided herself for succumbing to such a foolish distraction at that moment. She needed to keep her wits about her to divert the captain, if necessary, from any unpleasant reception he might receive.

She cast a swift glance around the churchyard, troubled to see a few people staring rudely in their direction. But others offered welcoming smiles.

Dolly ignored Marian's summons. Instead she seized the captain's hand and announced, "I'll show you the way to our pew."

Cissy shook her head and frowned at her governess as if to ask why she wasn't scolding Dolly for her forwardness. But Marian had no intention of doing any such thing. Instinctively, Dolly had managed to provide the captain with the diversion he required.

Perhaps he recognized it, too, for he showed no offense at the child's behavior. Indeed, her impudent grin provoked an answering flicker of a smile. "I appreciate your assistance. I have attended services at this church, but not for a very long time. I could not have been much older than you are now."

"My gracious," Dolly replied with her accustomed bluntness, "that *was* a long time ago!"

Marian was aghast. "Dorothy Ann Radcliffe, mind your manners!"

But the captain greeted the child's tactless remark with an indulgent chuckle. "Do not fret, Miss Murray. I find my young cousin's honesty refreshing. When I was her age, I remember thinking any person above five-and-twenty was hopelessly ancient."

The man had a sense of humor, Marian noted with approval, wishing she'd perceived it earlier. It was a most desirable trait in a person responsible for bringing up children.

"Please don't encourage her, Captain," she murmured as they entered the vestibule. "Or I fear she may take advantage of your good nature."

"Hush, Miss Marian." The child raised her forefinger to her lips. "You always tell me not to make noise in church."

Marian exchanged a glance with Captain Radcliffe that communicated exasperation on her part and barely suppressed amusement on his. Somehow that look made her feel as if she had accidentally wandered into a cozy room with a cheery fire blazing in the hearth.

They made their way into the sanctuary of golden-brown stone, bathed in the glow of sunshine filtered through the stained glass windows. Dolly led the captain up the aisle to the Radcliffe family pew, where he stood back to let "the ladies" enter first. Cissy scooted in at once and Marian followed. Dolly hung back, no doubt to claim her place beside the captain.

Later in the service, when it came time for prayers of thanksgiving, Marian offered a silent one to the Lord for answering her earlier plea.

His reluctant attendance at church had not turned out to be the ordeal he'd feared. Gideon reflected on it the following evening as he consumed his solitary dinner.

He'd been aware of a few hard looks, but most of the parishioners were more welcoming. That reception gave him greater hope that he might be able to get a fair hearing at the inquiry after all. During the service itself, a curious sense of peace had stolen over him as he'd listened to the familiar readings and joined in the hymns and prayers. It had scarcely seemed to matter whether or not God was listening. Surely, there was something worthwhile in a person expressing gratitude for his good fortune and identifying what he wanted in life for himself and others.

For himself, Gideon had only one wish—to have his reputation restored so he would be permitted to resume command of his ship. Had he been guilty of taking the blessings of an honorable reputation and a fulfilling career for granted in the past? If so, then his present difficulties might yield a worthwhile outcome, after all—by reminding him to appreciate all he had achieved.

When the pudding was served, Gideon cast an expectant glance toward the dining room door, half hoping Miss Murray might appear to discuss some matter about the children. He could not stifle an unaccountable pang of disappointment when she did not.

Though he had not been pleased by the governess's sudden appearance on Saturday evening, he'd soon found himself enjoying her company. At first he'd been reluctant to grant her request to accompany her and the girls to church, but now he was grateful she'd persuaded him.

He'd discovered his young cousins were not quiet the alien beings he'd dreaded, but two small people, each with her own feelings and personality. He could not help but be drawn to the younger one, any more than he could resist a frolicsome kitten that rubbed its head against his hand, hungry for attention.

The elder girl was a good deal more reserved and appeared every bit as wary of him as he was of her. Gideon could hardly fault the child for that since it showed her to be similar to him in temperament.

"Can I get you anything more, Captain?" asked the footman as he removed Gideon's plate. "Another helping of pudding? More tea?"

Gideon shook his head. "I have had my fill, thank you. More than is good for me I daresay. If I keep on at this rate, my girth may soon rival the Prince Regent's."

The young footman strove to suppress a grin but failed. "You won't be in any danger of that for quite a while, sir. When you first arrived, Mrs. Wheaton said you needed filling out. I reckon she's made that her mission."

Though he knew such an exchange between master and servant was more familiar than it should be, Gideon could not bring himself to discourage it. He had opened the door, after all, with his quip about the Regent. Besides, he preferred a little cordial familiarity to the hostile silence with which he'd been treated upon his arrival at Knightley Park.

"When I return to sea, I shall have to send my ship's cook to Knightley Park so Mrs. Wheaton can train him properly." Gideon pushed away from the table. "I have no doubt my crew would thank me for it."

In search of something to occupy him until bedtime, he headed off to the library. He had recently finished the books he'd brought with him, and he was confident he would find some suitable replacement on the well stocked shelves.

Uncertain whether he would find the room lit, Gideon took a candle from the hall table as he passed by. But when he pushed open the library door, he glimpsed the soft glow of firelight from the hearth and the flicker of another candle. It danced wildly as the person holding it gave a violent start when he entered.

Not expecting to find the room occupied, Gideon started, too. A quiver of exhilaration accompanied his surprise when he recognized his young cousins' governess.

"Forgive me for disturbing you, Miss Murray." He explained his quest for fresh reading material.

Clearly the young woman did not share his welcome of their unexpected encounter. Her eyes widened in fright and one hand flew to her chest, as if to still her racing heart.

When she answered, her voice emerged high-pitched and breathless. "It is I who should beg your pardon, Captain, for making free with your library."

She offered a halting explanation of how his late cousin had permitted her the use of it.

"Then, by all means, you must continue," Gideon assured her. It troubled him that she had feared he would be unwilling to extend her the same courtesy as Cousin

Daniel had. "Though I enjoy the pleasures of a good book more than your late master, I have never had the knack of reading more than one at a time, let alone all of the hundreds collected by my family over the years. Having so many books for one person to read strikes me as a singularly inefficient arrangement. I would appreciate your assistance in making better use of this library."

Miss Murray did not appear to grasp his attempt at levity.

"That is very kind of you, sir." She bobbed a hasty curtsy. "But I still should not have presumed without asking your permission. If you will excuse me, I shall return at another time when my presence will not disturb you."

Her eyes darted as if seeking the quickest route to the exit that would give him the widest possible berth. Did she really find him so alarming still?

"You are not disturbing me in the least, Miss Murray," Gideon insisted, though he knew it was not altogether true. Her presence *did* affect him, though not in an unpleasant way. "Besides, if one of us must withdraw, it should be me. You were here first, after all, and I believe you have far more claims upon your time than I. If you were to go away now, I doubt you would easily find another opportunity to return."

"Not very easily perhaps, but—"

"I will hear no *buts,* Miss Murray. I should feel like the worst kind of tyrant if you left this library empty-handed on my account. Surely you would not want that?"

"Of course not, Captain."

"Good. Then we are agreed you must stay long enough to choose a book at the very least."

"If you insist, sir." Miss Murray reached toward the nearest shelf and pulled out the first book she touched, without even looking at the title. It might have been in Latin, for all she knew, or a sixteenth century treatise on agriculture.

It was clear she wanted to make her escape as quickly as possible. A few days ago Gideon would have wanted the same thing. But having dined with Miss Murray and escorted her and the children to church, he'd discovered he preferred her company to his accustomed solitude.

Was there any way he might detain her there and keep her talking?

Perhaps…

"Before you go, Miss Murray, I hope you will not mind informing me how your pupils are getting on. Is Dolly still as determined to resist going to church? She seemed in fine spirits on Sunday and quite attentive to the service for a child her age."

His words had the most amazing effect on Miss Murray. All trace of diffidence fell away, and a winsome smile lit up her features. Clearly he had discovered the key to engaging her interest.

That accomplishment brought him an unexpected glimmer of satisfaction.

Chapter Five

Captain Radcliffe's inquiries about the girls banished any thought of leaving the library from Marian's mind. However uncomfortable she might feel in the captain's presence after the way she had imposed upon him, she could not neglect such a golden opportunity to further her plans. She fancied she could feel the warm hand of Providence resting on her shoulder, approving her efforts and helping to move them forward.

"The girls are quite well, thank you, Captain," she assured him, encouraged by his sudden concern for their welfare.

When he'd first entered the library to find her there, Marian had feared her presumption might cost her beloved pupils dearly. All she'd wanted was to apologize and make her escape as quickly as possible so the captain might forget she'd ever been there. To her surprise he seemed anxious for her to stay and not at all offended that she had made use of the library without his permission. Such generosity only made her more ashamed for sneaking around and assuming he would refuse her if she had asked.

"As for Dolly," Marian continued, "she has not uttered a single word of complaint about church, though she has asked a great many questions about ships and the sea. I believe you sparked her interest in those subjects. I hope to make use of that enthusiasm to engage her more fully in her studies."

The captain's brow furrowed. "And how do you propose to do that, pray?"

Did he truly want to know? It sounded as if he did.

"Today, for instance," she explained, "I had Dolly read a little verse about the sea, then choose a particular line to copy to practice her penmanship. Later we examined the atlas, and I pointed out some of the waters in which you might have sailed."

"I believe I understand your method." Was it a trick of the candlelight, or did a twinkle appear in the captain's gray eyes? "For sketching you would have her draw a ship. In music you would have her play or sing a sea shanty…one of the less bawdy variety, I hope."

His unexpected jest surprised a gush of laughter out of Marian and brought an answering quip to her lips. "Is there such a thing?"

The instant the words were out, she clapped her hand over her mouth, but it was too late. How could she have said such a thing, least of all to a man of the sea? Her years at school and later serving as a humble governess had trained Marian to guard against giving offense. Yet something in the captain's manner seemed to invite her to speak her mind.

His rumbling chuckle assured her he did not resent her thoughtless jest. "I have never heard one. Still, I approve of your manner of teaching. I wish my old tutor had used something like it."

The captain's sincere interest in her profession gratified Marian. "Thank you, sir. Far too many people regard the education of girls as nothing more than furnishing them with a few superficial accomplishments necessary to snare a suitable husband."

That was one positive thing she could say about the Pendergast School. Its pupils had received a rigorous education, training them to make their own way in the world. It had been continually impressed upon them that their lack of fortune made it highly doubtful they could ever hope to marry.

"What about you, Miss Murray?" The captain set his candle on a low table beside one of the chairs upholstered with dark leather. "How do you view the education of girls—my young cousins in particular?"

No one had ever bothered to ask her any such thing, especially in a way that suggested respect for her opinion. For that reason, the captain's question flustered her, though in a strangely pleasant way.

"I—I suppose it means cultivating the development of my pupils in all areas—not only their intellect, but artistic sense and character—to the best of which they are capable. No doubt that sounds like a lofty ambition for a simple country governess."

The captain shook his head. "It sounds like a fine aim to me, Miss Murray. My young cousins are fortunate indeed to be taught and cared for by someone so devoted to them. Your task cannot have been easy considering the losses they've suffered."

Marian raised a silent prayer of gratitude for this unexpected encounter with Captain Radcliffe. Talking to him about Cissy and Dolly was a perfect means to stir his sympathy for the girls without forcing him to spend time with them—something he was clearly reluctant to do.

"It has been difficult to witness them suffer such sad losses at so young an age. I have tried my best to fill some small part of the void left by the passing of their parents. I want them to feel secure and loved."

"It is obvious how much you care for them."

"Thank you, Captain. They are very easy children to love. There is little I would not do for them." Her greatest fear for the girls and for herself was that they might be removed from her care. Though Marian was satisfied she loved Cissy and Dolly Radcliffe more than anyone, she had no legal right to decide their future or make certain they stayed with her.

Tempted as she was to confide her worries in the captain, Marian sensed it was far too soon to raise the matter. If he suspected her hope that he might become the girls' guardian, she feared he would retreat into his earlier solitude. She needed him to learn to care for his young cousins as she did. Then he, too, might be willing to take any action necessary to protect them.

"Very commendable," he replied, though Marian sensed a slight chill of formality in his manner. Had her talk of love made him uncomfortable?

Perhaps so, for he hastened to change the subject. Gesturing toward the tall shelves crowded with books, he observed, "You must be far more familiar with this collection than I, Miss Murray. Are there any books you would recommend?"

Though part of her wished they might continue discussing the girls, Marian could not resist the chance to talk about books with someone above the age of ten or who did not live many miles away and must communicate exclusively by letter.

She swept an appreciative glance around the library, grateful to Captain Radcliffe that she would not have to give it up, as she'd feared. "I have derived many hours of entertainment and instruction from your family's books, sir. But I would hesitate to recommend any one in particular without first discovering what subjects interest you. Are you partial to poetry, biography…gothic novels?"

What had made her offer such an absurd suggestion? Could it be the hope of coaxing that twinkle back into the captain's eyes? Indeed it must have been, Marian realized when her effort succeeded, and her heart gave a sweet little flutter of triumph.

"I must confess, Miss Murray, I am not well acquainted with gothic novels. Though the two I have read proved exceedingly amusing."

She could not help but laugh. "Poor Mrs. Radcliffe read little else, rest her dear soul, and constantly urged them upon me. I must confess I found their dark melodrama and sensational subject matter all rather silly. I prefer heroic adventures or stories with intentional comedy."

The captain nodded. "Life can be quite dark and sensational enough at times without carrying those over into our reading."

Marian wondered if he could be thinking of his own situation—unjustly accused of dark deeds that would not be out of place in the pages of a gothic novel.

"What *do* you enjoy reading, Captain? What is your favorite of all the books you've read?" She did not tease him with facetious suggestions this time for she was sincerely interested in hearing his answer. His reading tastes might reveal aspects of this very private man that she might not discover any other way.

But why was she suddenly so eager to be well acquainted with Gideon Radcliffe? For the girls' sake, of course, Marian insisted to herself. The better she came to understand the captain, the better she would know how to appeal to him on Cissy and Dolly's behalf.

Captain Radcliffe stared toward the shelves with a look of intense concentration. "I like history. Gibbon's *The History of the Decline and Fall of the Roman Empire* is a work I admire. When I was younger, though, I had a thirst for adventure stories. *Robinson Crusoe* was a favorite of mine for many years. Have you read it, Miss Murray?"

Marian shook her head, almost ashamed to admit such a lapse. "I have heard of it, of course, but never actually read it. That is an oversight I must rectify at once. I know I have seen a copy in this library."

She turned toward the nearest shelf, scanning the titles. "Here it is. To think I could have passed over it so many times."

Pulling down the book, she replaced the other volume she had taken earlier. For the first time she glanced at its title. "I have no doubt I will find Robinson Crusoe's adventures more stimulating than *The History and Art of Chalcography and Engraving in Copper*."

"They could hardly be less." Captain Radcliffe tried to suppress a grin. "So tell me, Miss Murray, if you were stranded on a deserted island, like Robinson Crusoe, what is the one book you would want to have with you?"

An answer to his question sprang immediately into Marian's mind, though she hesitated to reveal it. "There are many books I would like to take with me in such a case, but only one I could not do without—my Bible."

The captain rolled his eyes. "I should have guessed. A very pious choice, indeed. I hope you will pardon me if I do not take your recommendation as eagerly as you took mine."

"I did not *recommend* you read the Bible, sir. You asked what one book I would want to have with me if I was castaway on a deserted island. I did not mean to give you a pious answer, only a true one. If I were to endure such a trial, I would need the consolation I could only find in that particular book."

"Forgive me, Miss Murray." The captain looked as if he might approach her, then changed his mind. "I did not mean to question either the sincerity or suitability of your choice."

Although she believed him, Marian felt compelled to defend her decision in a way he might understand. "Even if those writings did not hold such power for me, I still believe it would be a worthwhile book to possess if I had no others. It contains a whole library in a single compact volume. It has a great history of the Hebrew people and adventure stories of Daniel, Jonah and other such heroes. It has biography, law, romance as well as some of the most beautiful poetry ever written."

As she spoke, Captain Radcliffe nodded in earnest agreement. Then a quicksilver twinkle lit his eyes once more. "But, alas, no gothic fiction. Could you survive without that?"

"Very easily, thank you." She did not resent his good-natured teasing for it showed they could disagree without creating hard feelings. "You must admit, though, the story of Salome demanding the severed head of John the Baptist in return for her dance verges on the gothic."

"You have me there, Miss Murray. I see I may have to read the Bible again more carefully, if only so I can hold my own with you in conversation."

They continued to discuss their other favorite books until the pedestal clock beside the door chimed the hour of ten. Marian gave a start and fumbled the book she was holding. Where had the time gone? She'd only meant to stay here long enough to return one book and take another. But talking with the captain had made the evening fly by. Though she'd started out wanting only to talk about the girls, she had soon come to enjoy his company for its own sake.

But realizing how long they had been talking together also made her aware of how long they'd been alone in this room. What if one of the servants came into the library to check the fire or deliver a message to the master? Their conversation had been perfectly innocent. She trusted Captain Radcliffe would never do anything improper, even if he thought of her as anything more than a servant—which she was quite certain he did not.

Still, if they were discovered together, it might lead to gossip in the servants' hall.

The captain's recent troubles proved what a danger the *appearance* of impropriety could pose to a person's reputation. Marian could not afford the slightest blemish on her character. Her livelihood depended on it.

"If you will excuse me, Captain, I must get back to the nursery." Clasping the copy of *Robinson Crusoe* tightly to her chest, she made a hasty curtsy. "Cissy sometimes wakes with bad dreams. She would be very upset if I wasn't there to comfort her."

"Of course." Was it her imagination, or did the captain also seem surprised by the swift passage of time? "I am sorry to have kept you from your duties, though I must admit I have enjoyed this opportunity to talk to someone about books."

"As have I, Captain." Was that the only reason the evening had passed so quickly and pleasantly, because they'd been conversing about a subject she enjoyed but seldom had the opportunity to discuss?

Marian edged between the writing desk that stood against the far wall and a trio of leather upholstered arm chairs clustered in the center of the room.

Meanwhile, Captain Radcliffe moved toward one of the chairs as if he intended to sit and read awhile after she'd gone. "Do not forget, Miss Murray, you have my express permission to continue making use of this library as often as you wish. And do let me know what you think of Mr. Defoe's book. Good night."

"Good night, Captain. And thank you." Marian fled from the library as if to escape some unnameable danger. And yet, she could not deny her reluctance to part from Gideon Radcliffe.

All the way back to the nursery she cradled the book in her arms as if it were the most precious object she'd ever held.

The next evening Gideon rushed through his dinner, exchanging a few pleasantries with the young footman who served him. Afterward, he sent his compliments to the kitchen, for the chine of beef had tasted even better than usual.

The moment he finished his last bite of pudding, he rose and headed for the library. On his way, he paused for a moment to adjust his neck linen in front of a pier glass in the hallway.

The cloth was pristine white and perfectly tied, yet Gideon still scowled at his reflection. He had never noticed before that his face was so long and angular or how his sailor's tan accentuated the fine crinkled lines that fanned out from the corners of his eyes. He looked every day of his seven-and-thirty years, something that had never mattered to him before.

Nor did it now. Gideon gave his reflection a final dismissive glance, then continued on to the library. When his hand closed over the knob, he hesitated an instant, making a deliberate effort to smooth the frown from his features.

He entered the room to find a small fire glowing in the hearth, just as it had the night before. The flickering light of his candle danced over the dark, polished wood of the shelves and the rows of richly colored book spines, many with their titles embossed in gold letters. The chairs looked as inviting as ever. The portrait of his great-grandmother looked down on him with a brooding gaze that reminded him of the way Marian Murray regarded her young pupils.

Yet somehow the library felt much colder and emptier than it had the previous night. Gideon strove to ignore a vicious little stab of disappointment at finding it empty.

That was ridiculous. Until recently, he'd been quite content with his own company. Indeed, he often preferred it.

But not this evening.

His unexpected and surprisingly enjoyable encounter with Miss Murray must have spoiled him.

Slowly Gideon paced the length of the library, his gaze drifting over the book titles, hoping one might catch his interest. Yet even as he read them, the words ran through his mind in a meaningless litany while his thoughts returned to the previous evening and his conversation with Marian Murray.

He almost fancied he could hear her voice, clear and melodious with that gently rolling Scottish cadence.

It was not only the way Miss Murray spoke that appealed to him, but what she had to say. Their opinions might differ widely, particularly when it came to spiritual matters, but he could not question her sincerity or her judgment. Indeed, he respected both. The differences between them added a certain zest to their discussion that made his conversation with anyone else seem stale.

Last evening, in Miss Murray's company, time had flown by more agreeably than he'd ever experienced before. Tonight, as he paced the library, hoping she might appear again, every minute crawled as if some physical force were hindering the movement of the clock's hands. When those hands finally struggled to half-past eight, Gideon reluctantly acknowledged that he would not likely see Miss Murray that evening.

What had made him imagine he might? A sigh gusted out of him as he sank onto the nearest of the armchairs. Miss Murray had no reason to visit the library so soon again. Last evening she had procured a book that might take her many hours to finish in what little free time she had for pleasure reading. It was doubtful she would return to the library for a week at least.

To his bewilderment, Gideon found himself counting the days until Sunday when he could be certain of spending time in her company again.

"Will Captain Radcliffe be coming to church with us again this week?" asked Cissy as Marian fixed her hair the following Sunday morning. The child sounded as if she were bracing herself for something unpleasant.

"I'm not certain." Marian tried to ignore the odd little spasm that gripped her stomach when Cissy spoke the captain's name. "I suppose I ought to have asked him."

She had been strongly tempted to seek him out the previous evening for that very reason, but she'd feared she might find him at dinner again and he might feel obliged to invite her to join him. Not that she would have found it unpleasant—quite the contrary. But a repetition of such behavior might provoke comment among the servants. She did not want to risk exposing the captain to more undeserved gossip within his own household.

Now she almost wished she had consulted him, so she would know whether she and the girls could expect to see him this morning. The uncertainty made her rather anxious.

"I hope he will come." Dolly looked up from the atlas she had been examining with unaccustomed concentration. "It's much nicer driving to church in the carriage than walking. Besides, I have lots more questions I want to ask him."

"If the captain does accompany us," Marian said, brushing a lock of Cissy's lustrous dark hair around her finger to make a final ringlet, "please try not to pester him with too much chatter."

"Why not? He didn't seem to mind last week. He told me all sorts of interesting things."

So he had, Marian was obliged to admit. Just by listening to them, she had learned a few new facts. Captain Radcliffe had been remarkably patient in answering the child's endless questions about ships and the sea. In fact, he had appeared to welcome them to fill the awkward silence that might have pervaded the carriage otherwise.

"Get on your cloaks and bonnets, girls. If the captain is coming with us, we don't want to keep him waiting." And if he was not, she feared they might be late for church.

As Cissy rose from her chair in front of the dressing table, Marian stooped to glance at herself in the looking glass. She'd given in to an unaccountable whim to wear her hair differently this morning, parting it to one side rather than straight down the middle. For such a minor change, it altered her appearance considerably, softening the severe simplicity she had affected until now.

She noted other changes, as well, that the difference in parting her hair could not account for. Her lips looked fuller and her nose less prominent than usual. Her complexion had a youthful brightness that made her look less than eight-and-twenty, and her brown eyes sparkled. Marian scarcely recognized herself.

"You look very pretty today, Miss Marian." Cissy reappeared beside her, properly cloaked and bonneted.

Marian gave a guilty start. What was she doing, staring at herself in the mirror like some vain debutante when she and the girls were already running late? At school, her teachers had always impressed upon the girls the sins of pride and vanity. Humility, good character and diligence had been held up as virtues far more important than outward appearance.

Now she chided herself for forgetting those lessons. "That is kind of you to say, my dear. But remember, pretty is as pretty does. I should not have dawdled while you and your sister were busying yourselves to get ready."

Throwing her cloak over her shoulders, she snatched up her bonnet and began to tie it in place as she shepherded the girls out of the nursery. Her stomach seemed to churn harder with every step she took. Marian told herself it was only because she might have made the girls late.

Despite her earlier warnings to the contrary, Dolly hurried on ahead with a spirited skip in her step.

"What have I told you," Marian called after the child, "about bounding down the stairs two-at-a-time?"

But it was her heart that gave a bound when she heard Dolly cry, "Good morning, Captain! I've been learning all about ships and the sea. What is your ship called? How many masts does it have? Where is the farthest place you've ever sailed?"

Marian opened her mouth to remind the child not to plague the captain with questions. But just then she caught sight of him as he glanced up at her with a smile. It was unlike any expression she'd seen on his face yet. Not a wry grin at some jest. Not a cautious arch of one corner of his mouth. But an unreserved beaming smile that proclaimed his sincere pleasure at seeing them again.

The sight of it made Marian's voice catch in her throat.

Fortunately, Captain Radcliffe did not seem to notice as he turned his attention to Dolly.

"HMS *Integrity,*" he rattled off the answers to her

questions. "Three masts. And the farthest I ever sailed from England was to a place called New Zealand—a pair of islands on the other side of the world."

Before Dolly could think of more questions with which to pepper him, Cissy addressed the captain for the first time. "Have you sailed all the way around the world?"

He nodded gravely. "I have, though that was quite a few years ago, when I was not very much older than you are."

"How old are you now?" Dolly demanded. "May we call you cousin...what is your name again?"

"Dolly!" Marian gasped. "Mind your manners!"

But the captain gave an indulgent chuckle that would have astonished her if she had not previously discovered his droll sense of humor. "You are welcome to call me Cousin Gideon if you wish. As for my age, I must confess it is seven-and-thirty. Perfectly ancient, don't you agree?"

The child nodded gravely. "That is old."

"Dorothy Ann Radcliffe!"

"Don't fret, Miss Murray. When I was her age I would have said the same thing." Captain Radcliffe opened the door for them.

To Marian's surprise, Cissy spoke up. "I don't think seven-and-thirty is so very old."

Clearly she was trying to spare the captain's feelings. Marian gave the child's hand a squeeze as they made their way out of the house to the waiting carriage. "I would say it is quite the prime of life for a man—an age when his character is set in a way it is likely to continue."

Though she addressed her remark to the girls, it was intended for the captain. While he gave the appearance of not being offended by Dolly's brutal honesty, Marian sensed that perhaps their opinion did matter to him.

Chapter Six

Did Miss Murray consider him as ancient as her young pupils so obviously did? When Gideon made his self-deprecating quip to Dolly, he stole a glance at the child's governess, fearing her countenance would betray agreement.

To his relief it did not. The only reaction Miss Murray's expression communicated was concern for his feelings. Not pity, though, fortunately. His pride could not have abided that.

He appreciated the older girl's effort to relieve any sting her sister's remark might have inflicted. Until now, he'd suspected Cissy Radcliffe might resent him for taking over as master of Knightley Park. He was touched by this sign that her feelings toward him might be thawing.

Once the girls and Miss Murray had passed through the open doorway, Gideon strode out and overtook them. With a pointed look, he dismissed the footman waiting by the carriage door so that he might help the ladies in himself.

When he overheard Miss Murray telling her pupils

that she considered a man of his age to be in his prime, Gideon's chest expanded as he stood taller. At the same time, he felt vaguely disturbed by her suggestion that his character was irrevocably set.

He had little time to dwell on it, though, for no sooner had they gotten seated than Dolly demanded, "Tell us more about how you sailed around the world, Cousin Gideon. How long did it take? What places did you visit?"

"Please," Cissy added.

Although Miss Murray said nothing, the fact that she refrained from telling Dolly to stop asking questions made Gideon suspect she might also want to hear about his experiences. That made it impossible for him to refuse, even if he'd wanted to.

"Let's see." He plundered his memory for incidents that might entertain them without taking too long to tell on their short drive to church. "We set sail in 1789. The captain was an acquaintance of my uncle who had been among the crew on one of Captain Cook's famous expeditions. I was a twelve-year-old cabin boy, eager to become a midshipman."

As he told of the expedition to the west coast of North America to obtain furs for sale in China, two things surprised Gideon. The first was that young girls seemed to relish tales of adventure every bit as much as boys. The second was how flattering he found it to have a group of females hang on his every word.

Despite his best effort to keep his story brief and relate only the most interesting parts, he had just begun to describe how his ship had been captured by the Spanish when they reached the church.

"Bother!" Dolly muttered. "I wish we could keep on driving and listening to your stories."

Gideon cast a furtive glance toward Miss Murray. She had asked him to accompany her and the girls so he could be a good influence. He did not want his presence to have the opposite effect.

"Now, now," he replied. "There are plenty of fine adventure stories from the Bible, you know. I have had some interesting experiences during my career at sea, but nothing equal to being swallowed by a whale or slaying a giant with only a sling and a stone."

He climbed out of the carriage, then helped the girls and Miss Murray alight. His hand lingered on the governess's longer than he intended, but she did not seem to mind. Her eyes met his for a moment with a glow of gratitude that warmed him in spite of the November frost.

"The captain is right, girls. I should read you more of those stories. Besides being thrilling adventures, they teach important lessons about trust, faith and courage."

"It's not the same." Dolly shook her head. "I shall never meet David or that man in the whale. I can't ask them about what happened like I can with Cousin Gideon and *his* adventures."

Reluctantly, Gideon let go of Miss Murray's hand and took the child's instead. "I shall make you a bargain, then. If you can sit still in church and attend to the vicar, on the way home I'll continue my story."

"What if you're not finished by the time we get home?" Dolly was clearly a shrewd negotiator for her age. "Will you come and have tea with us in the nursery and tell us the rest?"

Gideon pretended to mull over his answer, though in truth there was no question in his mind.

"I believe I could be persuaded," he said at last. "That is if Miss Murray does not object."

"Not at all, Captain. We would be very glad to have your company." The notion sincerely pleased her. Gideon felt certain of it. She had an air of satisfaction that verged on smugness, odd as that seemed.

"Then we have a bargain," Dolly declared in a loud whisper as they moved through the church vestibule into the sanctuary.

A curious sensation spread through Gideon's chest as he looked down at the child and felt her small hand enveloped in his. There was a heaviness about it that did not burden him like too much ballast, but rather promised to anchor him when the seas of life grew rough.

But what if Dolly could not keep her part of their bargain? That tiny worry nagged at Gideon far more than it should have. She was a naturally boisterous child, after all, who reminded him of her father at that age. If she squirmed or chattered or otherwise misbehaved during the service, he would have to enforce the consequences and save the rest of his stories for another day.

Yet he feared missing out on tea in the nursery might be more of a hardship for him than for the girls.

To his relief, Dolly proved as good as her word, conducting herself with perfect restraint for every minute of the service, though it ran longer than usual. Such docility did not come easily for the child, Gideon sensed as he watched her clench her small fingers together and squeeze her eyes tightly shut during the prayers. He respected her strength of will and determination to honor their agreement. It flattered him to realize she considered his company and stories such a worthwhile inducement to put forth that kind of effort.

While they sat in the pew, his young cousin nestled up close beside him, warming his arm and his heart. During the liturgy, he held his prayer book down where she could easily see it, pointing to each word with his forefinger to help her follow along. The proportion of those words Dolly was able to read increased his respect for the skill and diligence of her governess.

As the service progressed, Gideon found himself intensely conscious of Miss Murray's presence so nearby. Twice he glanced down at Dolly, only to look up and find her governess watching them with a tender glow in the brown velvet depths of her eyes. And when she sang the hymns, the mellow sweetness of her voice lent those familiar lyrics fresh significance.

Though perhaps there was something more to it, as well. He had only come to church to oblige Miss Murray and set a good example for the children. But now that he was here, the prayers, scripture readings and sermon all engaged him in a different way than they had for many years. Somehow their message felt far more personal—as if someone was calling to him in a soft but insistent whisper.

But did he dare to heed it?

After the vicar had pronounced the benediction, Dolly looked up at Gideon with a triumphant grin. "I did it!"

He could not resist smiling back at her. That smile lingered on his lips when he looked up at Miss Murray. "It appears you may be saddled with a guest for tea. I hope it will not be too great an inconvenience."

"None at all, Captain." She leaned toward him, lowering her voice so the children would not hear. "Fond as I am of my pupils, I sometimes hanker for someone older to talk with."

"I certainly qualify." Gideon could not keep a shard of bitterness out of his quip. It wasn't that Miss Murray had any particular liking for *him*. She was so desperate for a little adult conversation that anyone would do.

He told himself he had no right to resent her motives. No doubt this bewildering fancy he'd conceived for her was only the natural attraction he might feel toward *any* woman with whom he spent time, after his long years away at sea.

Be that as it may, he made certain to spin out his story on the drive back to Knightley Park. By the time they reached the house, he had only gotten to the point where the Spaniards had finally released the ships, which then set sail for the Hawaiian Islands.

"Remember your promise," said Dolly as he helped her out of the carriage. "You must come to the nursery and tell us the rest over tea."

He nodded. "I would not think of going back on my word after you kept your part of our bargain so faithfully."

A few minutes later they entered the bright, cozy set of rooms with its bank of bowed windows overlooking the lake.

"Welcome to our nursery." Dolly ushered Gideon in with a flourish.

"Fancy that," he murmured, more to himself than to his young cousins and their governess. "This place is still exactly as I remember it. Even the old stool in the corner where Danny was made to sit when he grew too boisterous."

"You've been here before?" Dolly demanded.

"Danny?" cried Cissy. "Do you mean our papa?"

"Yes to both." Gideon made a slow circuit of the room as a host of memories came spilling out of some long locked compartment in his mind. "My family used to visit here sometimes in the summer and always at Christmastime. Your father and I were near in age and both the only children."

Only *surviving* children, but he did not want to bring that up with two young girls who had suffered more than their share of bereavement.

"Danny and I always enjoyed the holidays together," he continued. "Sometimes he and I would pretend we were brothers."

"What was Papa like as a boy?" Cissy asked in an almost pleading tone. "What did the two of you do together?"

Concerned that such reminiscences might only upset the girls, Gideon looked to their governess for guidance. She replied with a slight lift of her brows and shoulders, followed by a subtle nod.

"Let me think." He sank onto the window seat, and the two children flew to nestle on either side of him. "It has been many years, but I recall he had hair the color of yours, Cousin Celia, and a dimple in his chin like your sister. He was a year younger than me—not as tall but sturdier. He loved to be out-of-doors riding or throwing sticks for the dogs."

Gideon could picture his cousin so clearly he fancied he had only to look out the nursery windows to glimpse their boyhood selves larking about. "At Christmastime, we loved to skate on the lake and help gather boughs to deck the house. There was one special holly bush that always had the greenest leaves and the fattest, reddest berries. Afterward, we would hang about the kitchen and beg hot cider and nuggets of gingerbread from the cook."

Those memories filled his heart with wistful pleasure.

"What else?" Dolly prompted him eagerly.

But Cissy grew quiet, her head bowed. A tiny wet spot appeared on the lap of her dress, made by a fallen tear.

Suddenly Gideon felt badly out of his depth and overwhelmed by the situation into which he'd blundered. It was as if he'd waded into inviting waters only to find himself caught in a powerful current with no idea how to swim. Perhaps his first instinct upon coming to Knightley Park had been right after all. Cousin Daniel's young daughters did need things he was totally unequipped to provide.

Then Miss Murray spoke, and her words seemed to extend him a lifeline. "The captain can tell you more about all that later, girls. We invited him for tea, remember. Now we need to get ready."

Dolly leapt up at once, but Cissy hung back, swiping her forearm across her eyes. Gideon pretended not to notice, as he would have wanted if the situation had been reversed.

As he watched the girls do as their governess bid them, he recalled more of those happy Christmases when their father had so generously welcomed him to this nursery. He and his cousin had never met again after he'd been sent away to sea, something he regretted deeply.

Now another Christmas was coming—the first one

Cousin Daniel's young daughters would spend without their father and the last they would likely celebrate at Knightley Park.

Somehow that regretful thought gave birth to a much happier idea—one that brought Gideon a sweet thrill of anticipation he had not experienced in years.

He only hoped Miss Murray would approve.

Her plan to encourage Captain Radcliffe to care for his young cousins had been going so well. But as Marian headed down to the library two evenings later, she feared it might have begun to flounder.

She'd been vastly encouraged when the captain had appeared to escort them to church again without having to be reminded. Clearly when he agreed to assume a responsibility, he could be relied upon to fulfill it to the best of his ability. Knowing what she did of him, it came as no great surprise he possessed that admirable quality. His skill at storytelling, however, had come as a pleasant revelation. Hearing about his adventures on the high seas had made Cissy begin to warm to him. But listening to the accounts of his childhood visits with her late father must have been a bittersweet experience at best.

Marian had sensed Captain Radcliffe's ambivalence to relate those stories when the girls pleaded to hear them. Then, after Cissy had tried to hide her tears, the captain had grown quiet and seemed to withdraw. Marian hoped he had not been so disturbed by Cissy's reaction that he might resist her future efforts to bring him and the girls together.

At the threshold of the library, Marian paused to smooth her skirts. This dress was one she seldom wore, its rich burgundy-red a bright contrast to her usual somber browns and grays. Was she foolish to have worn it this evening? The captain might not even be in the library. And, if he was, why should he take any notice of her appearance?

Still, Marian could not keep her pulse from beating a little faster when she nudged open the library door and entered the room. Neither could she suppress an unaccountable pang of disappointment when she saw it was unoccupied.

Chiding herself for being so foolish, she strode to one of the shelves and replaced the book she'd brought. She found herself reluctant to part with it after such an enthralling read. She'd hoped to find Captain Radcliffe here so she could thank him for recommending *Robinson Crusoe* and tell him how much she'd enjoyed it. Having missed that opportunity must be the source of her disappointment. Now she wished she'd thought to mention it to him on Sunday and tell him how much his personal stories put her in mind of the book.

Carefully she scanned the shelves looking for something new to read. Twice she pulled down books and read the first page only to put them back when neither piqued her interest. Whatever she chose, she feared it would suffer in comparison to *Robinson Crusoe*.

At last the clock chimed nine. Marian told herself to choose a book and go. If one of the girls had been here in her place, she would have accused them of dawdling.

Forcing herself to take action, she pulled a copy of *The Vicar of Wakefield* off the shelf and headed for the door. Just as she reached for the knob, it turned and the door swung inward to reveal Captain Radcliffe. The sudden meeting made them both start, but the sight of him brought Marian a bewildering rush of happiness along with an almost painful self-consciousness at being so close to him with no one else around.

Marian retreated a few steps to give the captain room to enter. "Good evening, sir. I just came to return the book I borrowed and select another."

Caution warned her she should not linger alone with the captain; but now that he was here, she did not relish the prospect of leaving.

Fortunately, he gave her an excellent excuse to stay for at least a few more minutes. "I hope you enjoyed the adventures of Robinson Crusoe."

"Very much. I must admit, I pictured Mr. Crusoe looking and sounding very much like you, especially after you told the girls and me about your adventures sailing around the world."

"Did you, indeed? Well, well." The captain seemed more embarrassed than flattered.

"Ever since I first read that book, I felt a kinship with the character," he confessed.

Could that be because he'd felt so isolated and lonely, even with many people around? Marian sensed he might harbor such feelings. For his sake, as much as the children's, she longed to breach the invisible barrier around him and bring them together…if only he would let her. "Speaking of books, do I take it you have been revisiting the one I mentioned, Captain?"

He gave a rather shame-faced nod. "I suppose I gave myself away with that little lecture to the children on Sunday. Indeed I have been delving into the Bible again and finding more within its pages to engage me than I ever expected. I have gained a deep appreciation for the wisdom of your choice."

"I am pleased to hear it." Marian was more than pleased to think she might have helped Captain Radcliffe see that God was not as distant and disinterested as he had long supposed. "I respect your willingness to keep an open mind."

If only he could do the same where Cissy and Dolly were concerned. Though in their case she felt it was more important for him to keep an open *heart*.

"If there is nothing more, sir, I should be getting back."

"Actually, there is something, Miss Murray, if you would oblige me for a few minutes more. I have a proposal to make."

Proposal?

The captain must have noticed her stunned expression, for he hastened to rephrase his request. "That is…a proposition… I mean…there is a matter I wish to discuss with you…about the children."

"Of course, Captain." Marian welcomed any excuse to stay, though she still tingled from the rush of astonishment his use of the word *proposal* had provoked.

How foolish! As if a gentleman of property like him would ever think twice of someone like her…even if he wanted a wife, which Captain Radcliffe clearly did not.

She didn't want a husband either, Marian insisted to herself. Over the years, she had lost everyone she'd ever cared about. She did not want to leave herself vulnerable to that kind of hurt again. Bad enough she had allowed Cissy and Dolly deeper into her heart than she'd ever meant to. The fear of losing them reminded her how dangerous it could be to let herself care too much.

Then her befuddlement cleared and she wondered what he meant to say about the girls. Would the captain remind her of their original agreement to keep the children away from him in exchange for permitting them to stay on at Knightley Park until after Christmas? Was he going to point out that Christmastime was fast approaching, and the New Year hot on its heels? Did he want to discuss plans for tracking down the girls' aunt or what might be done with them if Lady Villiers could not be located?

That would certainly explain his sudden pensiveness in the nursery on Sunday. And his present anxious frown.

Those fears flooded Marian's mind in the instant it took for Captain Radcliffe to regain his composure and continue. "My conversation with the children about past Christmas celebrations got me thinking..."

As it had her. In previous years, Cissy and Dolly's father had made a great occasion of the season—hosting a dinner for all his tenants, the house crammed with candles and greenery and special outings and gifts for his young daughters. If Captain Radcliffe could not be persuaded to seek guardianship of the girls, then this would be their last Christmas at Knightley Park. Marian longed to make it a memorable one for them. But she had neither the resources nor the authority to recreate the kind of celebration they were accustomed to.

She feared this Christmas might only be memorable for what it lacked...beginning with a father.

"...since this will be the children's first Christmas without their father..." The captain's words echoed her anxious thoughts.

Marian's lower lip began to tremble. She wanted to beg Captain Radcliffe to reconsider whatever he was about to suggest, but she feared her voice might break or a tear might fall. After seeing how he had reacted to Cissy's furtive tears, she did not want to make things worse for the girls by blubbering in front of their cousin.

"I can see you are inclined to disapprove, Miss Murray, but pray hear me out. I would like to do something special for the children this year to provide a distraction from any mournful thoughts that might otherwise trouble them."

What was he saying? Marian wondered if she could trust her ears, or was she only hearing what she so desperately wanted the captain to say?

"I thought perhaps it might amuse them to re-create Christmastime as I remember it at Knightley Park." He spoke in a rather defensive tone, as if he expected her to interrupt at any moment with a long list of objections. "Feasting, decorating, music and gift giving. But I have never organized any such festivities before. I would not know where to begin."

Bless his kind heart! Captain Radcliffe was proposing precisely the opposite of what she'd expected. He wanted the same things for Cissy and Dolly as she did.

The curdled brew of sorrow and dread inside Marian suddenly distilled into a bubbly elixir of joyful excitement, which she found even harder to contain than her tears. Those still hovered, making her eyes tingle. Only now they were tears of happiness.

"What I am trying to say, Miss Murray, is that I will need your help if I am to realize these plans. I know it may mean extra work for you and perhaps you do not approve of any activities that might excite the girls or disrupt the orderly running of the nursery. But I would be heartily grateful if you would be so kind as to assist me."

The captain rushed through this last part as if he feared she would refuse if he stopped for breath—when instead she was fairly bursting with eagerness. By the time he paused to let her answer, her feelings had grown too volatile to contain.

"Of course I will!" Letting the book in her hands drop to the floor, she flew toward him and threw her arms around his neck as she had not done with anyone since her childhood. "I shall be delighted to help you in any way I can. Thank you, Captain! Thank you!"

It felt so natural to embrace him, soaking in his resolute strength, inhaling his brisk, briny scent. Yet Marian realized almost immediately that it was wrong.

Even with a family member or close friend, such an unrestrained gesture would be questionable. But with the master of the house in which she was employed, a man with whom she was barely acquainted, it was an act of the most grievous impropriety.

One that might cost her everything she cared about.

Chapter Seven

When Miss Murray threw herself at him with such joyous abandon, Gideon had no idea what to do.

He was not accustomed to physical contact, least of all a hearty embrace from a very attractive woman. Before he could make any conscious decision, his body reacted on instinct. His muscles tensed and he drew back.

The instant he did, part of him wished he hadn't. The soft warmth of her touch promised to restore something he'd been missing for a very long time. The scent of her hair put him in mind of a freshly washed handkerchief just taken off a clothesline on a summer's day.

Of course, it would not have been proper to wrap his arms around her and hold her close, as part of him longed to. He respected Miss Murray far too much to do anything that might frighten her or compromise her reputation. But could he not have held still and let her cling to him for as long as she would?

There was no use speculating now for the damage was done. The moment he tensed, Miss Murray jumped back like a scalded cat, refusing to meet his gaze, stammering apologies.

"Forgive me, Captain! I didn't mean... I never should have..." With every word the northern lilt of her accent grew stronger. "I was just so happy to hear what you wanted...."

She looked so distraught and mortified by her behavior that Gideon forgot all about his own feelings on the matter, anxious only to protect hers. "Please, Miss Murray, I understand. And I assure you I am not offended. You took me by...surprise, that's all."

She scarcely seemed to hear him over her own condemnation. "I don't know what came over me. I've never done anything like this before."

Could her reaction to what she'd done involve more than regret for the impropriety? Gideon wondered if she found such close contact with him repellent. Or perhaps she realized what could have happened if he'd been a less honorable man.

Stooping to the floor, she groped for the book she'd dropped. "If you will excuse me, Captain, I must be going."

Miss Murray made a rush for the door, clearly expecting he would move out of her way. This time Gideon held his ground. If he let her go before they had resolved this awkward incident, he feared his Christmas plans might fall by the wayside.

"Please stay a few minutes more. I beg you not to reproach yourself for...your actions. I assure you, I do not."

When she realized he intended to stay put, Miss Murray staggered back as if she had struck an invisible wall. "You are very understanding, sir. I promise you, nothing like that will ever happen again."

Her reassurance brought Gideon a stab of disappointment, but he did not dare let his true feelings show. "I hope this one small…lapse in self-control will not prevent us from working together to make this a merry Christmas for my young cousins."

His appeal on behalf of the children seemed to penetrate her barrier of self-recrimination. Inhaling a deep breath and squaring her shoulders, Miss Murray met his gaze. "If that is what you wish, Captain, I can assure you it will not."

"Very good." A powerful wave of relief threatened to swamp Gideon, but he took pains to conceal it from Miss Murray. "Since we have barely a fortnight to lay our plans, I believe we should arrange to meet again and discuss what needs to be done."

She gave a solemn nod. "I agree, sir. When would you like us to meet next?"

Miss Murray was more than solemn. It seemed as if she had reverted to the stern-faced governess he'd encountered when he'd first returned to Knightley Park. This woman would never think of teasing him about gothic novels. Nor would she permit herself to become so overjoyed that she would throw her arms around him. Gideon considered that a pity.

He had been inclined to suggest they sit down and start making plans immediately. Now he wasn't so sure that would be a good idea. Perhaps they both needed time to let the memory of that impulsive embrace fade a little.

"Tomorrow evening at this time?" he suggested. Then, lest Miss Murray suspect he was anxious to spend time alone with her, he added, "I would prefer to keep all this as a surprise for the children, until the time gets closer…if you don't mind."

"Not at all." She clasped the book in front of her chest like a shield. "If Dolly found out what you're planning too soon, she would get so excited I'd be up until midnight getting her to sleep. Then we would never be able to meet. So back here tomorrow night, then. At eight o'clock?"

Her gaze flitted from him to the library door and back again.

He deduced what she wanted and stepped aside to let her pass.

"I look forward to it, Miss Murray." As he spoke those words, Gideon realized he meant them far more than the usual hollow pleasantry.

The next day Marian tried to keep as busy as possible so she would not fall to brooding about the thoughtless indiscretion she'd committed. Of course, that meant keeping the girls busy, too, which did not sit well with Dolly.

"Why are you making us work so hard, Miss Marian? Is it punishment for being naughty? What did we do?"

"I haven't been naughty," Cissy protested before Marian could reply. "It's not fair if I'm being punished for something Dolly did. You should just make her sit in the corner."

Dolly stuck her tongue out at her sister. "I'd rather sit in the corner than do all this work. It would be a good rest."

"You haven't been naughty." Marian came between the children before they tried to take out their frustration on each other. "Though making faces at your sister is highly impolite and I expect you to apologize. Your lessons weren't intended as punishment. I didn't realize how hard I was making you work."

She must stop this foolish preoccupation with Captain Radcliffe. It was having an adverse affect on her dealings with the girls, and she could not permit that. Cissy and Dolly mattered more to her than anything. "I'll tell you what. Since you've managed to do a whole day's work this morning, you can spend the afternoon enjoying yourselves. We'll go out for a walk in the garden, then later we can go down to the music room and practice on the pianoforte. What do you say to that?"

"Practice?" Dolly wrinkled her nose. "That sounds like more work."

"What if I cut your practice shorter, then I play some music for you to sing and dance to? Would that be better?"

Both girls nodded eagerly.

"Let's get ready then." Marian beckoned them up from their work and supervised their dressing for outdoors.

With the help of the nursery maid, she made sure the girls put on thick wool stockings, sturdy half boots, cloaks, bonnets and gloves, for the day was clear and cold enough that the lake had frozen over.

"Can we go skating?" pleaded Dolly after they'd gotten outside.

Marian shook her head. "I'm certain the ice won't be thick enough yet. If it stays as cold as this for another fortnight, it should be safe."

Perhaps that was something she should mention to the captain at their meeting in the evening. The late Mr. Radcliffe had enjoyed every sort of outdoor activity, and skating was one in which he'd been able include his young daughters. Marian had preferred to watch from the shore, not trusting her balance on those slender metal blades.

Looking ahead to the evening, a sense of acute embarrassment overwhelmed her again. But it could not entirely stifle the sparkle of anticipation at spending time with Captain Radcliffe.

In the course of their brief acquaintance she had come to appreciate a number of fine qualities he possessed. He was hardworking, dependable and well-read. Though rather solitary and self-reliant, he could tell an entertaining story and keep up a most engaging conversation when he tried. He had a streak of ironic wit, often at his own expense, that was all the more amusing for being so unexpected.

But none of those things drew her to him as much as his kindness and willingness to forgive. After the way she'd behaved last night, the captain would have been well within his rights to demand her removal from his house. At the very least, he could have changed his mind about his Christmas plans for the girls. But he'd done neither of those things, choosing instead to excuse her outrageous conduct and seeking to ease her shame over it.

She almost wished he would do something to lessen her liking for him before it grew to threaten her happiness.

After an invigorating walk, she and the girls returned to the house for steaming cups of chocolate and currant buns warm from the oven. When Martha set down the tray she had fetched from the kitchen, Marian spied a letter propped up against the chocolate pot. She snatched it up, recognizing the handwriting at once.

"Who sent it," asked Cissy, "one of your friends from school?"

Marian nodded as she broke the seal. "I have no other correspondents, as you know."

That reminded her she must get busy writing her own Christmas letters to her friends. She was certain they would all want to know how her master's unexpected passing had affected her and her young pupils.

"Which one is it from?" Dolly said, helping herself to a bun. "Miss Beaton in the Cotswolds? Miss Fletcher in Kent? Or is it the one in Lancashire? I forget her name."

The girls had long been curious about the friends she had not seen for years, but with whom she faithfully exchanged letters. She had used that interest to foster their knowledge of geography.

"Miss Ellerby," Marian reminded Dolly. "Yes, the letter is from her."

Anxious to glance over it, she quickly filled their chocolate cups. While they all ate and drank, she skimmed Grace's letter. After her meeting with the captain this evening, she would read it over more carefully and perhaps begin her reply.

"But she is no longer in Lancashire," Marian murmured as she read. "She is looking for a new position elsewhere."

"Why?" asked Dolly, between bites of her bun. "Did she do something she oughtn't and get dismissed?"

"Of course not." Marian answered rather too emphatically, glancing up from the letter. "She is seeking a better position, that's all."

That wasn't altogether correct, but she could not possibly confide the true reason to her innocent young charges. Although Grace had been discreet in her letter, Marian gathered her friend had been the object of unwanted attentions from her master's brother. Poor Grace had been afflicted with a degree of beauty that might have been a great asset to her if she'd been born into a wealthier family. Instead, her looks had provoked charges of vanity at school, when nothing could have been further from the truth. Since they had completed their education and gone out into the world, this was the third time her friend been obliged to seek a new position because of difficulties with gentlemen in the household.

Would Captain Radcliffe have shirked her embrace if she'd had Grace Ellerby's golden hair and exquisite features? Of course he would have, Marian's reason insisted. The captain was too honorable a gentleman to take advantage of such a blunder no matter what her appearance. Reading about Grace's difficulties made Marian all the more grateful for his restraint.

"You aren't going to find a better position and leave us, are you, Miss Marian?" Cissy inquired in an anxious tone.

"Of course not!" Marian folded up Grace's letter and tucked it away to read more carefully in private. "What better position could I possibly find than here at Knightley Park with two such sweet, clever girls?"

The thought of being separated from them was like a sharp knife pressed between her ribs. But she must not worry the girls by letting on how near that danger loomed if she could not persuade Captain Radcliffe to take responsibility for them.

"Wrap your hands around your cups." Marian picked up hers to demonstrate and to divert them. "That will warm your fingers so they won't be too stiff to play."

She kept up an animated chatter until they'd finished

eating, then the three of them trooped down to the music room. There the girls faithfully practiced their scales and went over the new pieces they were learning. Finally, Marian showed them a little duet with a very easy part for Dolly. The girls managed to stumble through it without many mistakes.

"There," Dolly huffed, as if she'd just finished a very strenuous chore. "Now will you play for us, Miss Marian?"

"I don't know that it's such a great reward." She bent between the girls and wrapped an arm around each of them. "But if that's what you want…"

"It is." Cissy rose from her chair, offering it to Marian. "Play something we can dance to, but not too fast."

She held out her hand to Dolly. "Come, you be the lady and I'll be the gentleman. I'll show you what to do. First you must curtsy and I will bow. No, wait until the music starts."

Taking that as her cue, Marian began to play, all the while watching the girls out of the corner of her eye. She stifled her laughter as Cissy tried to instruct her sister in the steps while Dolly proceeded to do just as she pleased.

After the girls tired of dancing, they came and stood on either side of her while she played several favorite tunes for them to sing.

"Now will you sing for us, Miss Marian?" Dolly leaned against her, resting her head on Marian's shoulder.

How could she deny the child anything when she asked in such a way?

Marian's fingers began to move almost without conscious thought and familiar words rose to her lips. *"The water is wide, I cannot get o'er and neither have I wings to fly. Bring me a boat that will carry two and I will sail my love to you."*

It astonished her that her fingers still recalled the notes to this old song, one of the first she'd ever learned. What had made her think of it now after so many years? Marian shrank from admitting why she might have chosen to sing a love song involving ships.

"A ship there is and she sails the sea. She's loaded deep as deep can be. But not so deep as the love I'm in. And I know not how I sink or swim." As she continued on with the next verse and the next, Marian could not keep from imagining the events of the ballad played out by her and Captain Radcliffe.

"Must I be bound and he go free?" The words of the final verse sent a shiver through her. *"Must I love one that cannot love me? Why must I play such a childish part, and love a man who will break my heart?"*

No sooner had the final notes died away than a burst of energetic applause rang out behind her. Marian gave a violent start and spun around to find Captain Radcliffe standing in the doorway clapping his hands.

"Well done, indeed, Miss Murray. You have a fine voice and a most expressive manner of conveying the meaning of the piece."

His praise set her aflutter. But it alarmed her to wonder what he might make of her singing such a song the day after she had thrown her arms around him.

"Forgive me, Captain!" She leapt up and performed an awkward curtsy. "I was only obliging the girls with a song after they concentrated so well on their music lesson. I had no idea you were at home. I did not mean to disturb you."

Dolly must have taken note of her agitation for the child dashed toward Captain Radcliffe and seized his hand. "Please don't be cross at Miss Marian, Cousin Gideon! We asked her to sing for us."

A quiver ran through Marian at the sound of their first names spoken together like that.

As the child drew him into the room, Captain Radcliffe shook his head. "What makes you think I am angry? On the contrary, I wonder what feat I might perform to earn more of Miss Marian's singing as a reward."

Did he realize he'd just spoken her Christian name? It was a natural enough mistake, since it began with the same letter as her surname. No doubt he'd simply repeated what the girls called her. Still, it took Marian by surprise what a jolt of pleasure such a small error could bring her.

"I assure you, Captain, you have done it already and more with all your kindness to me and the girls." That gave her an idea for something they could do at Christmastime. She had no intention of mentioning it to him when they discussed his holiday plans that evening.

Instead, it would be a secret and a surprise for him.

Gideon could not recall a time when he'd enjoyed himself so thoroughly as in the weeks leading up to Christmas. Each morning he woke eager to experience what the day would bring. He looked ahead to the approaching holiday season with a level of anticipation that was almost childlike. He relished all the planning and the delightful secrets.

In the past he had made plans and kept secrets of an entirely different nature. Readying his crew for battle, supplying British troops on the Continent and maintaining the blockade of French imports and exports had all been vital duties, but hardly a source of pleasure. The secrets he'd kept had been a matter of life and death rather than a source of future happiness for others.

"What else needs to be prepared for our Boxing Day festivities, Miss Murray?" Gideon glanced up from the writing desk in the library, where he sat making lists of errands to run and supplies to purchase.

"I believe we've taken care of all the details for the dinner itself, sir," she replied. "Do you wish to give out hampers to the tenants, as your cousin used to?"

Gideon raised an eyebrow. "Hampers?"

She nodded. "Hampers of fruit, sugar, tea and the like. Those little comforts people cannot produce for themselves and are most likely to do without when times are hard."

The way she spoke, Gideon sensed she had known such need in her own life. Though he longed to learn more about her past, he knew it was not his place to inquire.

"An admirable tradition." He dipped his pen into the inkwell and began adding to his list. "One we must maintain. Anything else?"

Miss Murray thought for a moment. "If you're set on keeping things the same as other years, you might want to engage a few musicians to play for dancing after the dinner."

"And where would I find these musicians?"

"I can give you some names, sir."

He glanced up at her again with a grateful smile. "I don't know how I would manage all this without your assistance."

Gideon could not deny that one of the pleasures of this time was the certainty of enjoying Miss Murray's company almost every day. At first he'd told himself he would have relished any woman's society after all his years at sea. Now he was not so certain.

Marian Murray possessed a fortunate combination of the qualities he most admired. She was clever, well-read and accomplished. Ever since the day he'd overheard her singing to the girls, her clear, sweet voice had woven its way into his dreams. She was sensible and sincere, unlike some women he'd had the misfortune to encounter in various ports of call. Even that embrace, which he could not forget, had been a spontaneous mistake, not a calculated flirtation. She was open-minded and open-hearted, the first person who had been willing to believe in his innocence and trust in his honor.

But what he liked best about Miss Murray was her open affection for his cousin's orphaned daughters and her warm, nurturing spirit. From what he had observed, she was more like a mother to the girls than a governess. If he were ever to want a wife, Miss Murray would answer all his requirements and more.

His words of praise seemed to fluster her. Or was it the fact that he was staring at her like a calf-eyed schoolboy?

"I'm happy to help." She ducked her head, and her lips rippled in a self-conscious smile. "It was so kind of you to think of this."

He had no intention of taking a wife, Gideon reminded himself sternly. His heart belonged to the sea, and his first duty was to the Royal Navy. That solitary life suited him. He had been for too many years away from the company of women and children. His one recent attempt at a closer relationship had ended in failure of the worst kind. He could not bear to fail anyone else like that.

"Kindness? Tosh!" He forced his gaze away from her face and back to the safety of his list. "It is pure self-interest, I assure you. These festivities will give me an opportunity to celebrate Christmas in a way I have not had the pleasure in years."

"How did you mark the season on your ship?" Miss Murray asked.

Much as he would have liked to look up at her again, Gideon gave a shrug and continued writing. "With very little fanfare, I'm afraid. I increased rations and tried to make certain there was tolerable meat for our cook to prepare. I had plugs of tobacco and other such minor comforts distributed, when we could get them."

"It sounds like Christmas might have been nothing at all for your men if it hadn't been for you," Miss Murray suggested. "You must have been something of a father to them."

"I wouldn't go that far," Gideon muttered, though her words struck a chord. He had once considered himself a father figure to his men—a sort of Old Testament patriarch who could be depended upon. One who rewarded the good and punished the bad. "If my crew had respected me like a father, I doubt I would have found myself in my present difficulties."

With his two engaging young cousins, he saw the opportunity to experience a different kind of family relationship, however temporary.

"If you don't mind my asking, Captain, how did you come to be in your troubles? I know you could never have done what you're accused of. But I cannot understand how anyone could have accused you of such a thing in the first place. How did that poor boy come to die?"

Gideon winced, for her questions revived memories he had worked hard to suppress.

"Have you ever talked about it with anyone?" Miss Murray's voice fell to a beseeching murmur he found impossible to resist.

With a weary shake of his head Gideon laid aside his pen.

"It would do you good," she persisted. "I wouldn't repeat a word to anyone."

He knew he could trust her to keep his confidence. He had been looking forward to giving his testimony at the inquiry. But how much better would it be to unburden himself to someone he knew would sympathize and believe his side of the story? "Perhaps I was getting too soft, wanting to be a father figure to the younger members of my crew. Harry...that is, Mister Watson... reminded me of myself at that age. He'd been sent to sea as a boy after losing his family. He was a quiet lad, but diligent and dependable. I didn't mean to favor him, but perhaps I did. I reckon that was what got him killed."

When he paused to collect his thoughts and master his emotions, Gideon expected Miss Murray to jump in, firing off questions as Dolly would. But she did not. Instead, her expectant, understanding stillness invited him to continue when he was ready.

"The other midshipmen all knew one another. They came from families with more influence. They tried to curry favor with me, but when they realized their efforts were having the opposite effect, they turned their attention to my second-in-command, an ambitious young fellow itching for a ship of his own."

He should have seen the direction in which events were drifting and corrected his course, but he'd been too trusting of his men. It had never occurred to him that others might place self-interest above honor and duty.

"When Mister Watson would not countenance some of the mischief they got up to, the others started bullying him. I sensed something was wrong but when I asked, he always denied any trouble."

"Of course he would." Miss Murray's pitying whisper reminded Gideon of her presence. "He wouldn't want to worry you. He probably thought if he said anything it would only make matters worse."

"Then he was right." How did she understand the situation so well?

Gideon had been staring down at his list of Christmas preparations, not really seeing it. Now he cast a glance at Miss Murray and saw her emotions etched plainly on her irregular but appealing features. Her outrage stirred something deep within him.

"One day I overheard them threatening what they would do if he complained to me of their mistreatment."

"What did you do?" The words burst out of her as if she could not contain them.

If he had still been holding the pen, it would have snapped when his hands clenched. "I informed them in no uncertain terms that if Mister Watson so much as stubbed his toe again, I would hold them responsible no matter how strenuously he denied it. And I would punish them with the utmost severity the Royal Navy would permit."

He'd been trying to protect the lad, but he had failed.

"I thought they wouldn't dare lay a hand on him after that. But one night I returned to my cabin and found... his body. I went after those despicable bullies in a rage, vowing to make them pay for what they'd done. But my second-in-command gave them an alibi and persuaded the doctor to have me restrained. The more vigorously I protested, the more I sounded like a raving madman who had murdered one of his crew and gone after others."

Again Miss Murray could not restrain herself. "Surely anyone who knew your character..."

"My sterling record was all that saved me from immediate prosecution the moment we arrived back in port. But those allied against me have powerful friends, while I have made more than one enemy in the Admiralty with my intolerance for bungling and politics."

"What about the rest of your crew? Surely others must have known what was going on and could speak in your defense."

Gideon heaved a disillusioned sigh. "Perhaps, but I imagine they are frightened for their own safety if they testify against that wicked cabal, led by the villain who is now their commanding officer. They have seen what such men are capable of."

"I don't understand. Why did your second-in-command protect those miserable bullies? Just because they made up to him?"

"It had nothing to do with *them*. I told you he was ambitious. During the war there were more rapid promotions. Now that peace has come, it could take years for him to earn his first command. The opportunity to remove a superior officer who stood in the way of his advancement was one he could not resist."

"I'll tell you one thing…" Miss Murray's voice rang with righteous indignation. "If I'd been a member of your crew, I would have stood by you and told the truth about what happened, no matter what the consequences. If there's one thing I can't abide in this world, it's bullies. Fair makes my blood boil!"

Her fierce declaration of loyalty brought the shadow of a smile to Gideon's lips.

"I suppose you think that's no way for a woman to talk," she snapped. Clearly her blood was still up. "Or do you doubt I'd do what I said?"

"Not for a moment, my dear." Gideon leaned back in his chair, bathed in an unexpected release of tension and frustration. "I overheard you giving those two footmen a vigorous dressing down, remember? I only smiled now because I relished the thought of you making mince of those bullies aboard my ship. I know you would stand up for anyone you believe in, and I am flattered to count myself among that company."

If only he had as able an advocate as her to present his case at the inquiry, he would feel much less doubtful of its outcome.

Chapter Eight

If the Royal Navy could not appreciate what a fine officer they had in Gideon Radcliffe, then the service did not deserve him!

In the wake of his confession about all that had happened aboard HMS *Integrity,* Marian could not help reassessing her hopes and plans for the future of those she cared for at Knightley Park. That now included not only her dear young pupils but also the captain.

When she'd first come to realize what a good, honorable man he was, she had hoped to enlist him as an *absentee* guardian for the girls. Now she thought it might be better for everyone if he put the Navy behind him and stayed here in Nottinghamshire.

From all she'd seen of his interaction with the girls, she believed he could be an ideal surrogate father to them. She hadn't realized how much they needed a man in their lives until he'd begun spending time with them. Dolly responded so well to his kind firmness and his attention. Even Cissy, who had viewed Gideon as an interloper at first, was beginning to warm up to him.

Much as the girls needed him, Marian sensed he

might need them even more. When he'd spoken of his ship and the way he'd treated his crew, she could tell the man secretly yearned for a family. Surely that deep need would be better filled by two dear girls who could reciprocate his feelings for them, rather than a pack of bullies, traitors and cowards who weren't worthy of his regard.

As she and the girls headed out with Gideon to gather Christmas boughs, Marian told herself she should put aside all her planning and worries for the future and savor the joys of the season.

They made quite a numerous party, setting out from the house on Christmas Eve morning—along with the groundskeeper, a footman and a stable boy. The latter led a sturdy brown pony, which pulled a two-wheeled cart.

"This will be great fun!" Dolly skipped along at Gideon's side, clinging to his hand as they headed toward a nearby coppice to harvest all the greenery they would need to deck the halls and rooms of the house. "Other years we always had to wait back in the nursery until the boughs were brought. I'd rather go out and fetch them."

"At least the nursery was warm," Cissy grumbled under her breath.

Marian flashed the child a warning look and hoped Gideon had not overheard. She knew Cissy was only reacting to Dolly's implied criticism of how things had been done in their father's time. Still, she did not want the captain thinking the girls were as ungrateful as his former crew for everything he tried to do for them.

Dolly must not have heard her sister or she would surely have had something to say about it. Instead she asked, "Can I have a hatchet to cut some boughs myself?"

The very idea of Dolly wielding an ax brought a half stifled gasp to Marian's lips. Gideon would not agree, would he? Lately he'd become more and more indulgent of the little scamp.

"I believe it would be better to leave the actual cutting to those who know what they're doing." Gideon made it sound as if he'd actually considered the child's outrageous request. "Besides, there will be plenty of work for the rest of us, choosing what we want cut and loading it into the cart."

Dolly didn't seem too disappointed. "Maybe next year."

Marian lofted a heartfelt prayer toward the overcast heavens that they would all be together next year, gathering Christmas greenery. Even then, she doubted she or Gideon would be inclined to trust Dolly with a hatchet.

"Tell me, Cousin Celia," Gideon called over to the older girl. "How are you accustomed to decorating the house for Christmas?"

Marian caught his eye and gave a discreet nod of approval. He seemed to understand that the quickest way to Cissy's heart was to honor the traditions of the past.

Just as Marian expected, the first words out of the child's mouth referred to her late father. "Papa always liked to have evergreen boughs over the windows, with holly and ivy on the sills and over the mantelpieces."

"That sounds very festive," Gideon replied as the cart stopped before a patch of woodland. "I remember the place being decked that way in our grandparents' time. Did he still like to have the pictures hung with bay?"

"Yes, that's right." Cissy began to sound more enthusiastic.

"Don't forget the kissing bough," Dolly chimed in. "And mistletoe for over the doorways."

"No, indeed," Gideon replied. "We mustn't forget those."

Marian thought he sounded rather uneasy. Was he afraid of being accosted in doorways by a certain forward governess? She would have to make sure she gave him no such reason to want to leave Knightley Park and return to his ship.

Ah, the kissing bough. How could he have forgotten it?

As they collected boughs and other greenery for the Christmas decorating, Gideon thought back to his first and only experience with that perilous object. On his final Christmas at Knightley Park, a young lady from the neighborhood had managed to catch him beneath the kissing bough and demand the customary favor, much to his mortification.

He would have to beware of it and all the mistletoe-hung doorways throughout Knightley Park this Christmas season. Not that it would be a great hardship to kiss Marian Murray if they happened to be caught under the mistletoe—quite the contrary. The difficult part might be stopping.

Unlike her unexpected embrace in the library, a public mistletoe kiss would not pose a threat to her reputation. Still, Gideon was reluctant to risk the pleasure of it. In the unlikely event that Miss Murray did entertain any particular fancy for him, he did not want to encourage her. He thought too highly of her to toy with her affections. He did not want to risk having her feelings injured if the inquiry found in his favor and he was returned to command.

But what if that did not happen? For the first time, Gideon permitted himself to entertain the possibility with something less than dread.

For who could be low in spirits on such a day, in such good company? True, the sun was hidden behind a thick bank of gray cloud, and the ground was a damp mixture of dull greens and browns. But his young cousins scampered about in bright wool cloaks, their cheeks nipped pink and their faces alight with eager smiles. When Gideon placed an armload of fresh-cut boughs in the cart, his nose tingled with the sharp tang of evergreen.

A vigorous tug on the hem of his coat made him look down at Dolly, who immediately darted away calling, "You can't catch me, Cousin Gideon!"

She reminded him so much of her father that his years and cares seemed to fall away until he felt almost like the boy of those long-ago Christmases.

"Oh, can't I?" He lunged toward the child, but she dodged around the cart with a gleeful shriek.

"Too slow! Too slow!" She taunted him.

"We'll see who's slow." He ran after the little minx, but she picked up her skirts and tore off, leading him a merry chase.

"Be careful, Dolly," her governess warned. "The ground is muddy, and the laundress won't thank you if she has to scrub a lot of dirt out of your skirts."

Cissy laughed. "You made a rhyme, Miss Marian. Scrub the dirt from Dolly's skirt!" Perhaps wanting a share in her little sister's fun, she skipped away. "Can't catch me!"

Much running and dodging ensued to the accompaniment of more taunts, squeals and wild laughter. By the time Gideon and Miss Murray cornered the two little runners, they were all red-faced and winded. For the first time in many years, Gideon's sides ached from laughing. And he had forgotten all about the inquiry.

"Thank goodness…the others have not…shirked the job," he panted. "Or we might have…a sadly bare house…for the holidays."

"I thought we needed to get warmed up." Dolly chortled. "And it worked, didn't it?"

"I cannot deny that." He reached over and tipped down the brim of her bonnet. "But now that we are warm, hadn't we better lend a hand with the work?"

"What can I do?" The child held out her empty hands. "You wouldn't let me have a hatchet."

A hatchet, indeed—the little monkey!

Gideon tossed her a sack from the cart. "Let's go see if we can find some holly."

They located a fine bush not too far away and collected plenty of sprigs for decorating—the leaves a bright, waxy green, the clusters of berries plump and crimson.

By noon they had managed to fill the cart with everything they needed. They headed back to the house triumphant.

"My legs are tired," Dolly complained.

"No wonder," Marian Murray said, shaking her head. "After all that running around, which was your idea, don't forget."

"I know." Dolly heaved a sigh and trudged on.

"Here." Gideon picked the child up and hoisted her onto the pony's broad back. "Is that better?"

Dolly bobbed her head. "Much better, thank you, Cousin Gideon."

"It's not fair," Cissy muttered. "She gets to ride while I have to walk."

"We can't have that, can we?" replied Gideon. "If you would like to ride, I reckon this fellow can carry one more."

Cissy gave a solemn nod. She stiffened when Gideon swung her up beside her sister, but soon relaxed and seemed to enjoy the short ride home.

Once they had arrived back and removed their wraps, Gideon ushered "the ladies" into the parlor, where the Yule log crackled and glowed in the hearth, giving off fragrant, earthy warmth. Pulling chairs close around the fire, they extended cold fingers and feet to thaw. One of the maids appeared with a tray of cake and mugs of hot, spicy-sweet cider to complete their warming from the inside.

While they ate and drank, Dolly proceeded to interrogate Gideon. "Tell us all the places you've spent Christmas on your ship."

He took a long sip of cider and thought back over the years. "Out in the Channel for many of the last several. Before that, once in Mexico, which I told you about. Twice each in Malta and Jamaica. Once in Naples. Once in Nova Scotia."

"Where's that?" asked Cissy.

"Across the Atlantic, north of the American states. There is enough evergreen there in a single acre to deck a hundred-thousand halls, and a vast deal of snow."

"I wish we had some snow." Dolly took a large bite of cake. "It makes all outdoors look like it's covered in a white blanket."

Gideon glanced toward the window. "You may get your wish before the day is out."

"What makes you say that?" Cissy nibbled daintily at her cake.

"The way the clouds are massed in the northwest and the smell of the air." Gideon explained how the welfare of his ship and crew often depended on his ability to foretell the approaching weather.

Miss Murray remained quiet, yet Gideon still found himself conscious of her nearness. While he addressed his conversation to the girls, he watched out of the corner of his eye to see how she reacted. Did she lean forward to catch every word? Did her clever dark eyes sparkle with interest? Did some little quip of his coax a fleeting smile to her lips?

When all the cake and cider had been consumed, Gideon rubbed his hands together. "Now we had better get to work and deck these halls, don't you think?"

Dolly jumped from her chair. "The kissing bough first!"

The footmen fetched in boughs and bags of other greenery. Then they set up an occasional table and brought wire and trimmings for the construction. Acting on the girls' directions, Gideon bent and wrapped lengths of thick wire into several large hoops. Then he joined and fastened the hoops into the skeleton of a globe.

The procedure required additional hands to hold the hoops in place while Gideon lashed them together with finer wire. Miss Murray quietly lent her assistance. The supple strength of her long-fingered hands made her perfect for the job. As he worked, Gideon could not prevent his hands from brushing against hers. Every time it happened, his heart seemed to beat a little faster.

"Not too dismal for a first effort." He looked the thing over with a critical eye when he'd finished.

"It's fine." Miss Murray hastened to reassure him. "The frame doesn't need to be pretty. No one will see it when all the boughs and trimmings get attached. As long as it's strong and holds together, that is what matters."

She was right, Gideon acknowledged as he fastened fir and cedar boughs to the bare wire frame in overlapping rows. Gradually the kissing bough took shape. Then the girls and Miss Murray took over, adorning the plain evergreen globe with red velvet ribbons and oranges he'd purchased from the market in nearby Newark. The tart aroma of the fruit mingled with the spicy fragrance of cloves. Cissy and Dolly had studded the oranges with those in fanciful patterns.

The finishing touch was the choicest sprig of mistletoe with a rich cluster of pearly white berries. Fastened into place and trimmed with a scarlet bow, it hung down from the bottom of the kissing bough. Then the chandelier in the middle of the high parlor ceiling was lowered and the kissing bough attached to it, as had been the tradition at Knightley Park for so many years past.

When the chandelier was raised back into place and their creation hung above them in all its Yuletide glory, Dolly broke into a cheer. "You see, Cousin Gideon, it looks wonderful!"

Standing back with his arms crossed, Gideon gave a nod of satisfaction. "We can all be proud of our handiwork. I must admit, I would have had no idea how to begin without all your advice and assistance."

Though he addressed his words to all three of them, it was to Miss Murray in particular he intended to speak. He and she made a very capable partnership.

"It is a beauty." She gazed up at the kissing bough with a glow of admiration in her dark eyes.

While Marian Murray's attention was fixed elsewhere, Gideon stole the chance to admire *her* beauty. He hadn't been much impressed with her looks when they first met. But as he'd become better acquainted with her, that had changed. Now he glimpsed intelligence and humor in her eyes, courage in the tilt of her chin and tenderness and generosity in her full lips. None of her features, on its own, measured up to an accepted standard of feminine beauty. Yet, taken together, and illuminated by her indomitable spirit, they became something far more rare.

As he watched her stare up at the kissing bough, he sensed the shadow of some darker emotion beneath her initial wonder. Was she perhaps as anxious as he not to be caught beneath the mistletoe?

How had that festive symbol of Christmas come to be associated with such an amorous activity? Marian surveyed their handiwork, suspended from the chandelier in the parlor. Was it the invention of some long ago gentleman who'd wanted the opportunity to kiss a number of ladies without committing himself to only one? Or perhaps a single lady who wished to enjoy a kiss or two without ruining her reputation?

Marian could not deny she'd felt more than a trifle stirred by Gideon's nearness as they worked together to construct the kissing bough. The frequent, glancing contact of their arms and hands had made her wonder what it might be like to share a proper embrace with him.

At the same time, she knew she did not dare try to discover. Perhaps if she had not thrown herself at him that evening in the library, she could risk being caught under the mistletoe with him. But after taking such a shocking liberty, any further behavior in that vein would make it appear she was actively pursuing the master of the house. She could not afford to have him suspect any such thing, for fear it would frighten him off before he'd come to care enough about the girls.

That part of her plan was progressing too well for her to jeopardize. Watching him chase Dolly around during their morning outing, as if he were a carefree boy again, had brought her a sweet, secret pang of satisfaction. It was clear the girls' well-being and happiness had begun to matter to him. Why else would he have taken such pains to give them a merry Christmas? If anything more were needed to dispose Marian in his favor that would have been it.

"I'm certain it is the finest kissing bough in the neighborhood." She caught Cissy by the hand and gave an affectionate squeeze. "But we mustn't rest on our laurels. Or perhaps I should say, *rest on our evergreens*. There is plenty more decorating to do. The mantelpiece and windowsills are still bare and the other rooms haven't even been touched."

Realizing it might sound as if she were assuming the role of mistress of the house, she added, "Don't you agree, Captain?"

He gave a decisive nod. "Indeed. This may be our masterpiece but we do not want it to be our only decoration." He turned to Dolly. "What should we tackle next?"

"The mantelpiece." The child grabbed a fir bough from the pile they had discarded and handed it to him. "One set this way and one the other with some holly and oranges. We spent all yesterday sticking cloves in them. Don't they smell good?"

"Delectable." Gideon arranged the greenery as Dolly had bidden him. "This should look very festive indeed."

"What shall we do?" Marian asked Cissy.

The older girl glanced around the room. "Put candles in the windows with ivy and yew around them."

In far less time than it had taken to construct the kissing bough, the whole parlor was colorfully adorned for the holidays. Then they moved on to another room and then another. On the main staircase, they twined boughs through the banisters and secured them with red ribbons. Still more boughs and holly adorned the sideboard in the dining room as well as running up the middle of the long table.

When Marian glimpsed Gideon lifting Dolly up to add another orange to the mantelpiece decoration, she smiled to herself.

Later when he was trimming one of the family portraits with bay leaves, he beckoned Cissy over. "Do you know who the people in this painting are?"

"No. Who?"

"That is my grandmother." He indicated a handsome young woman who sat holding an infant. "Her name was Celia, too. The baby in her arms is my father and this little boy beside her is your grandfather."

"Who is the little girl?" asked Dolly, peering hard at the painting.

"That is their sister. Her name was Dorothy."

"Like me."

"Like you." Gideon cast her a fond look. "Now since we have all worked so hard and the dining room looks suitably festive, I hope you ladies will do me the honor of joining me for dinner."

Marian was not certain what to make of his sudden invitation. It had not been part of the Christmas plans he'd discussed with her.

But when the girls appealed to her, "Can we, please, Miss Marian?" she could not deny them. The more time they spent in the captain's company, the better, after all.

"Very well. Since it is Christmas, I suppose it will not hurt to alter our usual nursery routine."

"Excellent." The captain made it sound as if she had granted him a great favor. "It would be most unfortunate if I was obliged to dine alone on Christmas Eve."

Marian could not disagree with that.

"The invitation includes you, of course, Miss Murray," he added.

She opened her mouth to protest that it was not her place when a particular look from the captain changed her mind. It seemed to suggest he was not yet so accustomed to the girls' company that he would be comfortable dining with them on his own.

"Thank you, Captain." She curtsied to remind herself of her place in the household. Though she might care for the Radcliffe girls like a mother, she was only a hired employee. "If that is what you wish."

"It is," he replied, "and the girls', as well, I'm sure. Our celebrations would not be the same without Miss Marian, would they?"

There he went again, referring to her by her Christian name, as the girls did. Was it only a slip of the tongue or did he mean something more by it?

"Of course you must eat with us." Dolly's brow furrowed as if she was trying to puzzle out why there should be any question. "You always do."

"Then that is settled." The captain seemed well satisfied with the arrangements. "Let us retire to dress for dinner and meet back here in half an hour."

After a parting bow, he strode away before Marian could inform him that it took longer to change and groom two little girls than for him to don a fresh coat and linen.

"Come along, girls." Marian seized them each by the hand. "We'll have to hurry."

Hurry they did, racing up the stairs to the nursery where they scrubbed evergreen sap off their hands, then changed into their Sunday dresses with colorful plaid sashes and kid slippers. While Marian helped Cissy dress, Martha combed Dolly's hair and retied her ribbons. Then they switched.

The three of them made it back to the dining room with a full minute to spare, though Marian regretted having no time to do more than quickly smooth down her hair. She told herself it did not matter. She would only be there to supervise the girls and see that they minded their manners.

Yet she could not help wishing she'd been able to make a better appearance for the occasion when the captain joined them. He was freshly combed and shaved, wearing crisp snowy linen and a smart blue coat that emphasized his fine bearing. It was all she could do to stifle a sigh of admiration.

Until that moment, she had not realized how much his rugged looks had come to appeal to her. Every other man she'd ever met now suffered by comparison. The angular features and firm mouth that had appeared so severe at their first meeting now struck her as noble and courageous. Had she once thought his gray eyes cold? Now she could see the intelligence, honesty and kindness in them, as well as the occasional glimpse of wistful longing.

If he noticed her appearance for good or ill, Gideon Radcliffe gave no indication.

"I hope all our work today has given you ladies a good appetite." He held out the chair at one end of the table and beckoned Marian to be seated in what was traditionally the place reserved for the mother of the family.

Then he held chairs halfway down each side for Cissy and Dolly. "I believe the cook has prepared a fine meal for us tonight."

So she had. The soup was followed by slices of savory brawn. Then the game pie was served, its flaky golden crust encasing great lashings of meat and gravy. Though Marian felt too full to eat another bite, she could not refuse the airy lemon sponge cake and fine fruit that were served for dessert.

While they ate, Dolly interrogated the captain further about his ship and his travels while Cissy quizzed her cousin about their forebearers and times past at Knightley Park. Captain Radcliffe answered all their questions patiently and in an entertaining way. He also used the opportunity to draw the girls out, asking about their favorite colors, foods and activities.

From her place at the end of the table, Marian quietly tucked into her dinner while she listened to the others converse. Now and then, she leaned over to catch a glimpse of the captain around the pyramid of fine fruit that served as an elegant centerpiece. Whenever he glanced up to catch her watching him, she ducked back out of sight like a bashful schoolgirl.

Though the steady stream of courses brought by the footmen seemed as if it might never end, eventually their delightful meal drew to a close and their whole pleasant day with it. Marian could have stayed and listened to Gideon Radcliffe for many more hours, but it was already past the girls' bedtime. Duty won out over inclination.

"If you will excuse us, Captain." She rose from her chair when he paused to take a drink. "I believe the girls ought to get to bed soon, or they will be in danger of nodding off in church tomorrow."

The captain got to his feet. "We cannot have that, can we? Thank you, ladies, for a most enjoyable evening."

Cissy slipped out of her seat and went to join Marian, but Dolly's bottom remained firmly on her chair. "But I'm not tired!"

Her claim might have been more persuasive if she had not broken into a wide yawn.

"Come along now," Marian insisted. She knew it would be a grave mistake to put up with any nonsense so early in the Christmas season. "If you behave well, the captain may be more likely to include you in other holiday festivities."

"Will you?" the child appealed to her cousin.

"Without a doubt," he replied in a solemn tone, though Marian glimpsed a subtle twitch at one corner of his mouth.

Dolly yawned again. "All right, then."

She scrambled out of her chair and started toward her sister and governess when something outside caught her attention. She raced past them toward the window. "Look, it's snowing!"

"So it is." Marian and Cissy followed her to peer out the window that overlooked the garden.

Outside, in the frosty darkness of midwinter, large lacy flakes of shimmering white drifted lazily down from the sky. Whenever a breath of wind stirred, it set them dancing and swirling.

Behind her, Marian heard the captain's footsteps approach as he joined their huddle around the window. "I told you it would snow."

"Yes, you did." Dolly continued to stare outside. "Now everyone make a wish on the first snowflakes of the winter."

Cissy shook her head. "It's the evening star you're supposed to wish on, not snowflakes."

Dolly tilted her chin defiantly. "I think people should be able to wish on whatever they like. I'm going to wish on the first snowflakes."

Marian had no faith in Dolly's snowflake fancy. But a prayer directed heavenward on Christmas Eve—surely that would have a greater likelihood of being answered.

Intensely aware of Gideon hovering so close beside her, she repeated her often raised prayer that he might become Cissy and Dolly's guardian. But this time she neglected to ask that he be returned to his ship.

Chapter Nine

Wishing on a snowflake?

After Miss Murray took the children off to bed, Gideon lingered at the window watching the snow drift down. He shook his head and smiled to himself over Dolly's childish fancy.

Of all the things to attach one's hopes to—a tiny wisp of ice crystals that would melt away in an instant if it landed on his bare hand. At least a star, however impossibly distant, was constant and lasting.

Somehow that thought reminded him of what Miss Murray had said when they'd first talked about the power of prayer. She'd suggested that God could be infinitely small as well as infinitely great. The force that had created those massive, brilliant heavenly bodies and flung them across the universe had also wrought the transient delicacy of a single flake of snow. Who could say in which of those labors the Creator took greater satisfaction?

To humor his young cousin, Gideon made a wish, though he had no more expectation of it yielding what he desired than a prayer. What had he wished for? The thing he wanted most in the world, of course. Justice for him and for poor young Watson. A return of his life to what it had been—once again in command of the *Integrity,* serving his country and watching over his crew.

Yet when he pictured himself returning to his ship and putting this interlude at Knightley Park behind him, Gideon found it difficult to put his whole heart into that wish.

He slept well that night. Was it the belly full of hearty country fare that brought him such a peaceful rest? Or was it a daft sense of hope spawned by the wish he'd made? Gideon assured himself it must be the former. Not that it made any difference. He woke on Christmas morning with a sense that he was where he belonged on that particular day. Hard as he tried during his years at sea, he had never quite managed to quench his boyhood longing for Knightley Park at Christmastime.

On his way to breakfast a while later, he caught a whiff of spices and spied one of the maids bearing a tray to the nursery. He could not keep from following that alluring aroma.

"Pardon me," he said when Miss Murray answered his knock. The sight of her fresh-faced loveliness at this early hour felt like its own kind of Christmas present. "I thought I smelled frumenty."

"That's right, Captain." She looked surprised to see him, but not displeased. "Frumenty for Christmas breakfast in the nursery is a tradition at Knightley Park, I gather. Was it when you used to come here as a child?"

Gideon nodded and inhaled a deep breath of the rich, sweet aroma. "I have not tasted frumenty since then."

Miss Murray seemed to guess his thoughts, though

it could not have been difficult. "Would you care to join us for breakfast?"

"I would not want to deprive you or the girls of your share."

Before Miss Murray could reply, Dolly appeared at the door and practically dragged him into the nursery. "Don't fret about that. Cook always sends up more than we can eat."

He did not resist as the child drew him in and offered him a seat at the table.

"Why, thank you." He sank onto the chair after the girls and Miss Murray had taken their places.

Gideon felt rather overgrown and awkward sitting at the nursery table with three diminutive females, but he forgot all about that as soon as he consumed his first spoonful of frumenty. It was just as he remembered, the wholesome goodness of wheat boiled in milk, spiced with cinnamon and nutmeg, sweetened with sugar and dried fruit. One taste brought back all the happiness of his childhood Christmases.

"Did you see how much it snowed last night?" asked Dolly between heaping spoonfuls of frumenty. "I'm afraid the carriage might get stuck on the way to church."

Gideon exchanged a significant look with Miss Murray. Was Dolly afraid or hopeful the snow might prevent them from attending the service?

"In that case, perhaps we should travel by sleigh," Gideon suggested. "We wouldn't want to miss church on Christmas Day, after all."

"A sleigh ride!" Dolly clapped her hands, and even her more reticent sister looked pleased at the prospect.

Once he had eaten as much breakfast as he could

hold, Gideon excused himself and headed off to bid the stable men to harness the sleigh instead of the carriage.

A while later, with the girls wedged between him and their governess, they prepared for the drive to church with hot bricks at their feet and thick robes over their legs. As the sleigh skimmed over the snow-covered road, the girls squealed and giggled, and the cold air nipped their faces. Though Gideon had not had much practice handling horses, the team seemed familiar with the way and got them to church swiftly and safely.

That morning, as he sang the familiar carols and listened to readings of the Christmas story, Gideon could not help thinking what a special gift a child was. A God who could bestow such a blessing must care deeply for the people He had created, in spite of their weaknesses. A God who bestowed such a blessing might well heed and answer prayers.

Celebrating Christmas at Knightley Park with his young cousins had clearly brought the captain many happy memories.

During the Christmas service, Marian stole frequent glances at him, pleased to note how much more relaxed and at peace he appeared. Could it be that he was getting more out of his attendance at church than simply setting a good example for the girls? For his sake, she hoped so. Anyone who had been so unappreciated and badly betrayed surely needed the consolation of God's love.

After the service, she noticed him slip a large contribution into the poor box when he thought no one was watching. His actions did not surprise her. He had proven himself a charitable man who cared about those in need of his help. Yet his reserved nature clearly made him shrink from being publicly acknowledged for his generosity.

Though she admired such behavior, in contrast to some of the self-righteous but mean-spirited patrons of the Pendergast School, she wondered if the captain's reticence would make it difficult for him to present an effective defense at the inquiry. Marian reminded herself that she wanted him to stay on at Knightley Park with the girls. Yet it offended her sense of justice to think of his reputation being permanently tarnished.

As they left the church, a number of parishioners offered Captain Radcliffe the compliments of the season, including one or two who had been rather cool to him when he'd first begun attending services. It heartened Marian to realize that their neighbors appeared willing to make up their own minds about the man in spite of whatever gossip might spread from London. Even if the inquiry did not find in the captain's favor, she assured her conscience the decision would not affect local opinion of him.

When they reached the sleigh, Squire Bellamy was waiting to greet the captain. Marian liked the squire, a jovial sportsman who had been a particular friend of Cissy and Dolly's late father.

He and the captain exchanged seasonal good wishes, then the squire asked, "I wonder if you might do me the honor of attending a ball I am hosting on New Year's Eve for some of the neighbors? It would be a welcome opportunity for you to become better acquainted with the local families."

Captain Radcliffe seemed taken aback by the invitation. "I…er…that is very kind of you but—"

"No *buts*." The squire waved away any objections

with one beefy hand. "My wife is determined you shall attend. She says it will put her numbers at table out if you do not. Surely you would not wish to be the cause of ill-feeling between a man and his wife on Christmas Day."

Mrs. Bellamy had a reputation in the parish as an irrepressible matchmaker. No doubt she had a lady all picked out for the captain. As Marian got the girls settled into the sleigh, she strove to quell a stab of irritation. She had no right in the world to feel possessive of Captain Radcliffe, after all.

"Since you put it that way," the captain replied, "I most certainly would not wish to cause dissention in your house. Tell your wife I appreciate the invitation and mean to accept."

"Capital!" The squire beamed. "We shall look forward to seeing you on the thirty-first, then."

"New Year's Eve?" Dolly whispered. "But that was when we were going to—"

"Hush." Marian twitched the sleigh robes over their legs. "There will be plenty of other opportunities."

"Opportunities for what?" The captain suddenly turned back toward them.

"Opportunities…to celebrate the season with you." She recovered awkwardly. "The girls must not monopolize your company. I'm sure you would enjoy spending time with other adults."

"Not particularly." He climbed in beside Dolly and picked up the reins. "My dancing skills are almost as lamentable as my polite conversation."

"What's wrong with your conversation?" demanded Dolly. "You have heaps more interesting things to talk about than most grown-up people."

"Except Miss Marian," Cissy chimed in loyally.

Under the sleigh robe, Marian reached for the child's hand and gave it a squeeze.

Meanwhile the captain responded to Dolly's compliment with a wry chuckle as he jogged the reins, and the sleigh started back toward Knightley Park. "I'm afraid most ladies of mature years are not excessively interested in all the details of life at sea."

"I don't know why not." Dolly changed tack. "If you need to learn how to dance, Cissy can show you. She's teaching me."

"Don't be silly," her sister protested. "I don't know that much about it. I only had a few lessons with the dancing master."

"That is more instruction than I can boast." A hint of desperation tightened the captain's voice. "I would be grateful, Cousin Celia, for whatever help you can provide."

"Very well." The child looked secretly pleased with the idea, and Marian welcomed the opportunity for Cissy and the captain to become closer. At times she seemed to warm to him, then something would make her grow cool again.

"Can we play out in the snow, Miss Marian?" asked Dolly as the sleigh neared Knightley Park.

"I suppose…" It would do the girls good to have an outlet for some of their energy. "But you will have to change clothes and back before Christmas dinner."

They agreed readily and scampered off toward the nursery the moment they reached the house. Marian followed, as did the captain. She assumed he must be on his way to his rooms to change clothes or rest before dinner.

"Pardon my curiosity, Miss Murray, but are you quite well?" he asked. "You seem rather subdued on such a festive occasion. Are you missing your family in Scotland?"

His question caught her off guard. It was kind of him to notice her demeanor and care about her wellbeing. "I am not ill, Captain, nor am I pining for distant family. My parents and brother are all long dead and this day stirs no particular memories of them. Where I come from, we made more celebration of the New Year than Christmas."

"I should have known. I have served with a number of Scottish officers over the years. As for your family, forgive me for reminding you of your loss."

"You could not have known, sir."

They walked a few steps in silence before he spoke again. "May I ask what age you were?"

It had been so long since anyone cared to inquire about her background. Neither Mr. nor Mrs. Radcliffe had ever asked about her family. Though Marian was reluctant to disclose too many details about herself, she could not forget all that the captain had told her about his past. How could she refuse to return a confidence?

"I was nine when my father died. My mother passed away when I was much younger."

"Nine," he repeated, his voice suffused with a world of sympathy. "Who took care of you after that?"

She was even less inclined to talk about her years at school than about the loss of her family. Fortunately, they had reached the spot where they must part ways, he going off to his quarters and her to the nursery.

"If you will excuse me, Captain, I must go see to the girls."

"Is it such a long story?" A look of puzzlement and tender concern made his features more attractive than ever.

Marian shook her head. "I had no family but a widowed aunt who was hard-pressed to care for her own fatherless brood. So it was decided I should be sent to a charity school in England for orphaned daughters of the clergy."

Hard as she tried, she could not keep her face impassive when she spoke of that wretched institution—any more than if she'd bitten into a lemon.

The captain was too perceptive a man not to notice. "Were you ill-treated there?"

He fairly radiated fierce indignation at the mere possibility. Such sentiment proved impossible for Marian to resist. "Very ill indeed."

Bitter memories rose to torment her. If she stayed there, she feared she might lose control of her emotions. She could not afford to let that happen again. Spinning away from Gideon Radcliffe, she fled down the passage to the nursery.

No wonder the poor lady had not been able to fully embrace the joyous spirit of Christmas.

As the patter of Miss Murray's footsteps retreated into the distance, Gideon stood frozen in the grip of pity and anger far too powerful for his comfort. He had experienced something similar when Harry Watson confessed to the bullying he'd endured. But those feelings had been tempered by the belief that he had the power to remedy the situation. He'd turned out to be wrong, but he hadn't known that then. In this case, he knew very well there was no assistance he could render Marian Murray.

Whatever she'd suffered as a child at that charity school was over and done. But he sensed it had left wounds that might never fully heal, like the old injury to his hand that made it ache in certain types of weather. The scars on her spirit must trouble her more at Christmas, when the pervading happiness of the season created such a severe contrast to her childhood memories.

A potent conviction welled up in Gideon as he recalled the anguish in her eyes. He must do everything in his power to make *this* Christmas one on which she could look back fondly in future years. He must also encourage Miss Murray to confide in him about her experiences. After all, he felt much more at peace since he'd told her the truth of what had happened aboard the *Integrity.* The least he could do was offer a sympathetic shoulder on which to unburden her troubles. Knowing what she did of his past, surely she would realize he was better capable of understanding than most people.

He changed into his warmest clothes and ventured outside to join Miss Murray and the girls in the snow-covered garden. Sensing his unexpected appearance flustered her, he refrained from asking any more questions about her experiences at the charity school. Instead, he put aside his accustomed reserve and larked about with the children until he glimpsed a tentative smile on her lips.

Later, as they headed back inside to dress for Christmas dinner, he made a point of saying, "I hope it is understood that you must accompany the girls whenever they dine with me. While I have come to enjoy their company more than I ever expected, I am all too aware of my lack of experience with children. I am certain we will all be more comfortable together if you are with us."

"Thank you, Captain." She acknowledged his invitation with a curtsy. "Of course I shall supervise the girls at all times if that is what you wish."

"It is." He did not care to be reminded that Miss Murray would only join in the festivities as part of her terms of employment.

Remembering the mission he had set himself, to give Miss Murray as happy a holiday as her pupils, Gideon went out of his way to include her in table conversation while they ate Christmas dinner. To begin with, he banished the tall centerpiece of fruit to the sideboard so it would not obstruct his view of her as it had the day before.

After their play outside in the fresh, cold air, all four of them had hearty appetites to do justice to the succulent stuffed turkey and all the other holiday delicacies.

As the mince tarts were being served, Gideon addressed Cissy. "I wonder if I might begin my dancing instruction after dinner? New Year's Eve is less than a week away and there is the dinner for our tenants tomorrow. I believe I may be expected to perform a turn or two afterward. I would prefer to embarrass myself as little as possible."

The child replied with a grave nod. "Of course. We can go into the music room. Miss Marian, will you play for us?"

"I shall be happy to do whatever I can to assist your efforts. I reckon the captain will be a very apt pupil in spite of his claims to the contrary."

Her tone of friendly banter appealed to Gideon.

He could not resist replying in kind. "You think I exaggerate my ignorance, do you?"

"I believe you exaggerate all your shortcomings and minimize your accomplishments." This time he could not tell whether the lady was teasing or perfectly sincere...or perhaps a little of both. "In any case, I shall be happy to play for your dancing lesson."

Once they had eaten all they could hold, the four of them retired to the music room where Miss Murray seated herself at the pianoforte. Gideon would much rather have listened to her sing again than stumble his way through a dancing lesson, but he supposed it was necessary if he hoped to avoid humiliating himself too badly in the coming days.

Cissy took her role as instructress quite seriously. "Come stand here, please. Dolly, you stand there. Now, Miss Marian, please play that same piece as the other day."

As the music commenced at a steady, stately pace, Cissy began issuing directions. "First you must bow and curtsy to one another. Now turn to face me and join hands. Take two steps forward, then two steps back. Now face each other. Each take a step toward me, then close—that means bring your other foot over. Now bow and curtsy again...."

He and Dolly tried their best to do as they were bidden, but the dance quickly degenerated into a flat-footed muddle.

"It's no use." Cissy shook her head in disgust. "In the first place, Dolly is far too small...or you are far too tall to be proper dance partners. Besides that, the music room isn't big enough for dancing, you know."

Gideon shrugged. "Thank you for trying."

"Don't give up so soon." Dolly pressed her forefinger to her temple in thought. "We could go into the great parlor. It has plenty of space. And Miss Marian could take my place as Cousin Gideon's partner. She's much taller than me."

The child's suggestion that he dance with her pretty governess tempted Gideon far too keenly for his peace of mind. However, he feared Miss Murray might shrink from the prospect of being so near him and often taking his hand as dancing might demand.

Her response confirmed that. "But who will provide the music? There is no instrument in the great parlor and even if there were…"

But Cissy seemed quite taken with her sister's idea. "We don't really need music, just a rhythm for you to keep time. Dolly and I can clap our hands for that."

"If Miss Murray would rather not…" Gideon tried to sound as reluctant as his proposed partner, but he could not manage it. Though he did not care for idea of dancing in general, he could not deny a wish to dance once with her.

Cissy frowned. "Do you want to learn or don't you?"

For some reason, the child's response seemed to overcome Miss Murray's reluctance. "Of course he does. And I am willing to try if he is."

She cast Gideon a look of appeal that he could not resist. "I suppose it couldn't hurt…except perhaps your toes."

Her lips blossomed in a luminous smile that felt like a rich reward for his cooperation.

"Good." Dolly took Gideon by the hand. "Let's get started then."

They moved to the larger room and pushed some

pieces of furniture against the walls to create a spacious area for dancing. Then Gideon and Miss Murray took their places and Cissy resumed her instruction.

Gideon found it far easier to follow the steps and figures with a partner nearer his own height. Miss Murray claimed to have no prior experience dancing, yet she seemed to possess an instinct for graceful movement. Gideon had only to mirror her actions to feel a growing sense of confidence.

"Try that bit again," Cissy ordered, "and pretend there are other couples on either side of you. One, two, three."

As she clapped out the rhythm and Dolly joined in, Gideon fancied he could hear the melody their governess had been playing earlier.

"Very good." Cissy nodded approvingly when they had gone through the step without any mistakes. "Now one more time from the beginning. Then I think we had better stop for tonight."

She glanced toward Dolly, who was endeavoring to stifle a yawn. "It is past our bedtime again."

Miss Murray peered toward the mantel clock and gave a start. "So it is. I have been concentrating so hard I did not notice the time passing."

Gideon had not realized how late it was getting either. Could that be because he'd been so occupied with the dancing lesson? Or might it have been his enjoyment of Miss Murray's close company that made time fly? Recalling the swiftly passing evenings he'd spent with her in the library, he was inclined to credit the latter.

"Once more, then." Cissy began to clap out the time again.

Off they went, performing the steps of the dance

with greater ease than Gideon had believed possible. It occurred to him that they made excellent partners. Each seemed able to anticipate the other's movements and adjust their own accordingly, with the happy result that he did not once tread on the lady's toes.

"There," he declared when they had exchanged their closing bows. "With a patient teacher and a naturally skilled partner, it appears I am capable of improvement after all."

"Once again, you do not give yourself enough credit, Captain." Their mild exertions had brought a becoming flush of color to Miss Murray's face.

Something made her dark eyes glow. Could it have been his praise?

Then Dolly broke out in an infectious chuckle. "Look, you've ended up right under the kissing bough!"

A quick glance aloft assured Gideon it was true. He'd been so agreeably occupied he had not given the kissing bough a single thought.

"Come now, you must kiss." Cissy sounded impatient with their hesitation. "Or all our hard work making it will have been for nothing."

Swallowing the lump that suddenly formed in his throat, Gideon gave an apologetic shrug. "We wouldn't want that, would we, Miss Marian?"

For all his show of reluctance, he felt a great bubble of elation swell within his chest. With a sense of trepidation he had never felt in the heat of battle, he searched the lady's eyes for any sign of aversion. To his vast relief, he found none.

"I suppose not." She caught her full lower lip between her teeth but could not quite bite back a self-conscious grin. "It is a long-standing tradition, after all."

Clearly she had received Christmas kisses under the mistletoe before this and knew they were simple holiday pleasantries of no particular significance. Gideon wished he could view it that way.

"Go on then," Dolly urged.

The child's prompting made him realize any longer postponement could prove more embarrassing than to simply go ahead.

Inhaling a deep breath, he bent toward Miss Murray and aimed his lips to meet hers. It was a more delicate procedure than he had reckoned and one with which he was not especially familiar. Yet, as with their dance, he seemed able to anticipate her, tilting his head slightly so their noses did not collide.

There! His lips pressed against hers with what he hoped was the proper amount of pressure. The smooth warmth of hers was the single most delightful sensation he had ever encountered. It brought him a feeling of connection...belonging...homecoming. The only thing he could imagine better would be if she wrapped her arms around his neck and pulled him close, as she'd tried to do that evening in the library.

Just as he had feared the first time his young cousins mentioned the kissing bough, Gideon discovered how difficult it was to take leave of Marian Murray's soft, sweet lips.

Chapter Ten

She was actually receiving her first kiss from a man—and such a man!

When Gideon Radcliffe's lips sought hers in a tender, restrained connection, Marian's breath stuck in her throat and her knees threatened to give way.

The harsh, sensible voice of reason chided her not to be such a sentimental fool. This was not a proper kiss, bestowed out of affection for her. It was only a token gesture to satisfy Christmas tradition and two insistent little girls.

Yet it felt the way she'd imagined a proper kiss might, those few times she had permitted her thoughts to stray in that improbable direction. His lips pressed against hers, warm and gentle, kindling fancies of a chivalrous knight pledging his chosen lady his loyalty, his protection…and his heart.

But that was preposterous.

Captain Radcliffe had commanded great ships in defense of King and Country. Now he was also the master of a fine estate and a gentleman of fortune. What could he want with a plain, orphaned governess of no particular distinction, who had scarcely a penny to her name? He had treated her with courtesy because of his kind nature…and perhaps out of loneliness. She must not mistake his feelings for anything more.

If she hung on to his kiss an instant longer, she risked humiliating herself with a yearning sigh or worse yet, swooning to the floor. Mustering every scrap of restraint she had cultivated during those miserable years at school, Marian pulled away from the captain.

"There, are you satisfied, girls?" She strove to curb her ragged breath, lest it betray feelings she had no business entertaining.

"Oh, yes." Dolly sounded rather smug about something. "That was a fine, long kiss. Not the quick peck I saw Wilbert give Bessie in the dining room doorway. Of course that sprig of mistletoe is much smaller than the bough. Perhaps that's why."

Had she permitted their kiss to go on for too long? Marian fled from under the kissing bough, fussing around the girls like a ruffled mother hen with a pair of chicks. "I'm glad you approve. Now you must get to bed or you'll be out of sorts tomorrow."

She refused to let her gaze stray toward the captain for fear of detecting signs that her behavior had shocked him. "Say good-night, then we'll be off."

"Good night, Captain." Cissy dropped him a curtsy. "Perhaps I can give you another dancing lesson before New Year's Eve."

Dolly followed her sister's example. "Good night, Cousin Gideon."

"Good night," he replied in a subdued tone that made Marian certain he must be displeased with her.

She never should have agreed to take part in the

dancing lesson, especially in the face of Captain Radcliffe's obvious reluctance. But Cissy had been so set on it, and Marian was committed to encouraging any possible connection between the girls and their cousin. Their entire future might depend upon it. Bitter memories of school that the captain's earlier questions had revived made her more determined than ever to spare her dear pupils a similar fate. A place even half as bad would crush Cissy's sensitive nature, while Dolly's high spirits and strong will would be harshly repressed at every turn.

And yet her concern for the girls did not account for how sincerely she had enjoyed the opportunity to be near Gideon Radcliffe, with his hand often holding hers. All the years she'd sat quietly in the corner at assemblies or glimpsed a ball from the top of the stairs had stood her in good stead as she'd executed the steps she had often seen performed by others. Just as she had suspected, the captain was far more agile than he claimed. Marian found a sweet sense of satisfaction working with him to accomplish something worthwhile, be it making Christmas plans or learning the steps of a dance.

Then that ridiculous kissing bough had spoiled everything.

Although she cherished the opportunity to receive a kiss from a man like Gideon Radcliffe, she wished it had not brought her so close to losing control of her secret feelings.

As she ushered the girls off to bed, a sweet sound drifted toward them from the entry hall.

"Carol singers!" Dolly dug in her heels and refused to budge another inch toward the staircase. "Can we go listen to them? Please, Miss Marian!"

"Please!" Cissy echoed. "Just for a little while. Then we'll go straight to bed."

"It is Christmas," Dolly reminded her, as if she could forget after that tender, terrifying kiss under the bough.

Marian could only resist their combined coaxing for so long. "Oh, very well, but only for a little while. When I say you must come away, do you promise you will, without any arguing?"

The girls nodded vigorously. Then Dolly sped to the doorway of the great parlor and called in, "Carol singers, Cousin Gideon! Can you hear them? Miss Marian says we may go listen. Will you come, too?"

A quiver went through Marian as she tried to decide whether she wanted the captain to join them. Her sense of duty urged her to seize every opportunity to bring the girls together with him. But could she bear to be near Gideon Radcliffe again until the memory of their kiss had dimmed a little? It might not take long for him to forget, but she doubted the same could be said for her.

Whether she wanted his company or not, it appeared they would have it. Just as she and Cissy caught up with Dolly, he emerged from the great parlor and took the child's hand. "Carolers is it? Of course we must listen to them. I believe it is an offense against the spirit of Christmas to do otherwise."

A soft sigh of relief escaped Marian's lips as the four of them headed to the entry hall. Whatever the captain's reaction to their kiss, he sounded as if he had put it out of his mind already. She should have known better than to suppose it would matter to him one way or another.

When they reached the front door, Captain Radcliffe pulled it open, and they filed out under the portico. Marian wrapped her arms around the girls and pulled them close to keep them from getting too cold. The night was clear and crisp, the winter moon a slender sickle in the black, star strewn sky.

A little ways away, a group of men and boys clustered, well-muffled against the cold. In the flickering light cast by several lanterns they bore, their breaths frosted the air as they sang. *"Whilst shepherds watched their flocks by night all seated on the ground, the angel of the Lord came down and Glory shone around."*

Marian could picture local shepherds guarding flocks in the surrounding fields of Knightley Park, when angels robed in glittering starlight appeared with glorious news.

When the final notes of the carol died away, Captain Radcliffe led Marian and the girls in a round of applause.

"Come sing some more for us inside." He beckoned the group.

As Marian drew the girls back into the entry hall, the captain called to her over his shoulder, "Kindly summon any of the servants who might wish to hear, Miss Murray. And ask Mr. Culpepper to fetch mulled cider and pies for everyone."

She acknowledged his order with a nod. "Right away, sir."

Though he had phrased it as a request, she wondered if he meant to remind her, or himself, of her position in his household.

Kissing Miss Murray under the mistletoe had been a mistake. Gideon knew it the instant she'd pulled away from him so abruptly. Now, as she headed off to the servants' hall, he sensed a chill in her manner as cool as the winter night outside.

Why had his self-control chosen the worst possible moment to desert him? He had faced many a moment of crisis in his career, including some in which life and death had hung in the balance. Yet he had always managed to keep a cool head and act as reason and honor demanded. Unfortunately, he had no experience in how to curtail a kiss with an attractive woman—one he liked too much for his own good…and hers.

The last thing he wanted was for her to think he would use his position to impose himself upon her. By the nature of their work, men of sea had a reputation for seeking female companionship where they could find it, without regard for morality. He could not bear to have Marian Murray think he would stoop to such behavior.

Until that moment, he'd been celebrating his best Christmas in years, and he congratulated himself that Cousin Daniel's young daughters seemed to enjoy the day, too. Having threatened his very agreeable friendship with their governess, Gideon decided he must make an even greater effort to ensure the children a happy Christmas.

Once all the carol singers had filed in, he asked the girls, "Is there a particular favorite you would like to hear?"

Dolly only shrugged, but Cissy answered readily. "Could they sing 'The Holly and the Ivy'? Miss Marian has been teaching me to play it on the pianoforte."

Gideon turned toward the leader of the group. "Do you know that one?"

"Indeed we do, sir. Come, lads. For the little lady. *The holly and the ivy when they are both full grown, of all the trees that are in the woods, the holly bears the crown."*

The others joined in, singing lustily on the chorus. *"Oh the rising of the sun and the running of the deer, the playing of the merry organ, sweet singing in the choir."*

By the time they had sung through all the verses, the servants had begun to slip into the entry hall to swell the audience. This continued while the carolers sang two more pieces. The group had just finished "The Boar's Head Carol" when Miss Murray, the cook and the scullery maid appeared bearing trays of cups. Mr. Culpepper followed with a large crock borne upon a wheeled serving table. An enormous covered platter rested on its lower tier. The mellow, spicy aroma of mulled cider seeped into the room along with a hearty, savory smell. Several of the younger singers broke into broad grins at the prospect of refreshment.

"Singing is thirsty work," said Gideon. "Since you have done such a fine job of entertaining us, I hope you will accept our hospitality."

The carolers did not hesitate to accept. Soon the maids, assisted by Miss Murray, set about serving hot cider and small pork pies. As they all ate and drank together, the servants from Knightley Park mingled with the carol singers, some of whom appeared to be friends or relations. A satisfying sense of community stirred in Gideon, which he had never expected to feel for any folk other than the crew of his ship.

After they had partaken of refreshment, the carolers sang a few more pieces. The whole company joined in on a spirited rendition of "Joy to the World." Finally, the performers wished them all a Merry Christmas in song before going on their way. Gideon thanked them and made certain they were well-rewarded for their efforts.

He turned back into the entry hall to find Miss Murray trying to coax Dolly up from a low stool where she had fallen asleep, resting against Cissy's shoulder. "I should have known this would happen. Come now, Dolly, you can't spend the whole night here."

Gideon approached them, still rather uneasy in Miss Murray's presence. "May I be of assistance?"

She started at the sound of his voice but quickly regained her composure. "Perhaps you might have more success trying to wake her than I've had, sir. Imagine falling sound asleep in the midst of all that hubbub. It's my fault, of course. I should never have let the girls stay up for the whole thing."

Perhaps if he hadn't sent her away to fetch the servants, she might have been able to keep her mind on her duties.

"I have a better idea." He bent down and hoisted Dolly up until her small golden head lolled against his shoulder and her body hung limp in his arms.

He had never thought it could feel so natural and pleasant to clasp a sleeping child to his chest. Yet, at the same time, it provoked a mild ache in his heart, rather like hunger pangs in his stomach.

Forcing himself to ignore it, Gideon strode off toward the staircase with Cissy and her governess trailing behind him. When they reached the nursery, Miss Murray scurried ahead to open the door for him.

"Thank you for your help, Captain. Dolly's bed is this way." She led him through the dimly lit nursery, then turned down the child's bedcovers.

With a gentleness of which he'd never suspected himself capable, Gideon eased his small burden down. In spite of his best effort not to wake her, Dolly stirred and blinked her eyes.

"Where are the carol singers?" she asked in a drowsy, puzzled voice. "Please let us listen to one more, Miss Marian."

Her governess perched on the edge of the bed, removing Dolly's slippers and stockings. "The carol singers have gone. You fell asleep listening to them. If the Captain hadn't carried you up to bed, you might have had to sleep in that drafty entrance hall. Now what do you say to him?"

Dolly yawned. "Thank you, Cousin Gideon."

He was certain she'd be back to sleep in no time. She might not even recall this brief half-waking. "You're quite welcome, my dear. Good night and Merry Christmas."

He turned to leave when the child's reply stopped him in his tracks. "When Papa came to the nursery he would always kiss us good-night. Will you, Cousin Gideon?"

The request rather unnerved him. One kiss this evening had already gone badly. Still, that empty ache in his heart urged him to reply. "I…suppose I could, if you wish?"

He looked from Dolly to Cissy. The older girl shook her head. "Not tonight, thank you."

"Well, I do!" Dolly sounded wider awake than she had a moment before.

Approaching gingerly, as if putting his head in a lion's mouth, Gideon brushed a feather light kiss on her plump cheek. But when he tried to draw back, the child threw her sturdy arms around his neck and planted a hearty smack on his cheek, much to his disquiet and secret pleasure.

At least he could offer Dolly some of the affection he dared not show her pretty governess.

On New Year's Eve, in her small, spartan chamber adjoining the nursery, Marian rolled over in her bed and sought to find her way into the elusive state of sleep. But all the paths she tried only circled back on themselves. The Land of Dreams seemed to have closed its borders to her.

She must get some rest soon or she would be perfectly useless tomorrow. Keeping up with two young girls, one a high-spirited bundle of energy, could present a challenge under the best of conditions. Besides, she was not certain what sort of festivities Captain Radcliffe had planned for tomorrow. Since Christmas Day, there had been all manner of special activities and outings, beginning with a feast for Knightley Park's tenants on Boxing Day. Dolly had enjoyed mixing with the tenants' children while Cissy had been pleased to help dispense the hampers, in keeping with family tradition.

This evening had been unusually quiet with the captain going off to Squire Bellamy's ball. But that had *nothing* to do with her present sleeplessness, Marian told herself.

She wondered how he was managing on the dance floor. They'd had two more lessons in the past week, neither of which had been as successful as the first. Could that be because she and the captain were constantly aware of the kissing bough and taking more care to avoid it than to perform the proper steps?

She also wondered with which lady the Squire's

matchmaking wife hoped to pair him. Part of her questioned whether it might benefit the girls if Gideon Radcliffe took a wife. Marriage would give him a reason to stay at Knightley Park, even if the inquiry decided in his favor. And if it came down to a legal battle between him and Lady Villiers for guardianship of the girls, surely it would look better before a court if he were a married man.

In spite of all that, when she considered the possible matches Mrs. Bellamy might have in mind for the captain, none met with her approval. The Squire's widowed sister was as incurably silly as a green girl half her age. Miss Hitchens was notorious in the parish for her temper and sharp tongue. Miss Piper spent money like water. Unfortunately, all three were quite handsome and much more suitable wives for Captain Radcliffe than...

Marian rolled over and pounded her pillow to relieve her feelings. It did not help nearly as much as she'd hoped. She needed some diversion to occupy and calm her thoughts. Reading would be the perfect activity, if only she had a book on hand. But she had returned *Evelina* to the library three days before Christmas, then neglected to borrow another book to replace it.

After another hour taunted by thoughts of which she wanted no part, Marian rose and fumbled her candle alight. Shivering, she pulled on her dressing gown, shawl and slippers. Then she crept out of the nursery and headed down to the library. A glance at the pedestal clock surprised her with the information that it was not much past eleven. She could have sworn she'd been lying awake for hours.

It did not take her long to select a book, for she only wanted something capable of holding her attention without being too stimulating. Once she found a promising volume, she hurried back toward the nursery as quickly as she'd come. Yet she was not quick enough.

Marian had only gone a few steps when she heard the main door open and shut, and Captain Radcliffe came striding in. "Miss Murray, what on earth are you doing up at this hour? Is one of the girls unwell?"

Her unease at being seen by the captain in her night-clothes was tempered by the evidence of his concern for Cissy and Dolly.

"Don't fret, sir. They are both quite well and sleeping soundly. I only wish I could say the same for myself." She held up the book. "I hoped having something to read might help me sleep."

"A good idea." The captain seemed to be making an effort to ignore her state of dress. "I have read myself to sleep on a number of occasions. Warm milk is another useful remedy. Perhaps you should investigate whether there is any to be had in the kitchen."

"Thank you for the suggestion, sir. I may try that another time. I wouldn't want to disturb anyone tonight."

"Of course you wouldn't." He spoke in a low murmur, as if musing to himself. "May I ask if there is some particular difficulty that keeps you from sleeping? No problems with the children, I hope?"

"None at all, Captain." The last thing Marian wanted was for him to guess what sort of thoughts had kept her awake. She had a guilty feeling he would unless she offered him some other reason. "I must admit I have been rather worried about a friend of mine. We met at school and have kept in contact ever since. This is the first Christmas I have not received a letter from her."

Everything she'd said was true—Marian could not

bring herself to tell him a falsehood. She *did* wonder what could have happened to prevent Rebecca from writing. A stab of guilt pierced her for having lain awake thinking about something other than her dear friend.

"You met at *that* school?" Gideon Radcliffe's tone grew harsh. "The place you told me about? Was your friend also the orphaned daughter of a clergyman?"

She should not stand there conversing with the master of the house at this hour, in her nightclothes, Marian's sense of propriety warned. But after imagining him dancing, dining and talking with a bevy of marriageable ladies, it felt so pleasant to have him all to herself for a few stolen moments.

"We all were. The only thing that made my years at the Pendergast School remotely bearable was the support and affection of the friends I made there. Several of us became especially close—almost like sisters. Though we have not seen each other since we left that institution, we have tried to remain in contact, scattered about as we are."

He nodded gravely. His palpable concern enveloped Marian like a thick wool blanket on a cold winter night. "Is there any way I can assist you? Where was your friend when you last heard from her? Perhaps I could dispatch someone to make inquiries on your behalf?"

Send someone over a hundred miles to the Cotswolds, paying for food, inns and stabling for no other purpose than to set her mind at ease? His generosity touched her. Yet his caring gesture made her feel even more ashamed for making him believe her concern for Rebecca had prevented her from sleeping.

"You are too kind, Captain. I would not want to put

you to so much trouble on my account. It may be that my friend's letter is only delayed by bad roads. If I have not received word from her by Twelfth Night, I will write to one of our other friends to inquire whether they have had news of her."

"I would consider the effort well worthwhile if it set your mind at rest."

His assurance made Marian's pulse quicken. But it was only a measure of his thoughtfulness…wasn't it?

"Speaking of rest, I should retire for the night and let you do the same for the hour is late. It will soon be eighteen-hundred and fifteen." In spite of that, part of her searched for an excuse to linger. "I am surprised to see you home so soon from the Bellamys'. I thought you would stay at least until they rang in the New Year. Did you not enjoy yourself at the ball?"

He gave an indifferent shrug. "Squire Bellamy neglected to inform me that tonight's entertainment would be a *hunt ball* and that I would be the principle prey."

"I beg your pardon, Captain?"

He rolled his eyes. "I was the only bachelor in a company that included several marriageable ladies. Not merely marriageable, but rather desperately intent on securing a husband. It is not a pleasant experience to be stalked that way."

So he had not taken a fancy to any of the ladies Mrs. Bellamy threw in his path? Marian struggled to keep from smiling.

But with her self-control concentrated on that task, she had none left over to govern her tongue. "Perhaps you ought to consider taking a wife, now that you have a good income and a settled abode."

"*Et tu,* Miss Murray?" His upper lip curled. "Do

you reckon it is my social obligation to wed, simply to furnish some spinster with a home and generous pin money?"

"Of course not!" She turned defensive, stung by his question and what it implied. "Surely you don't suppose every woman who shows an interest in you is only after the comfortable life you can afford to give her?"

"What else?" he demanded. "That was clearly the object of those ladies at the ball tonight."

Marian struggled to frame a reply that would not betray the kind of feelings he did not seem inclined to trust.

"Who would want a husband like me otherwise?" he continued. "I am hardly the answer to a maiden's prayer."

He'd been the answer to her prayer...as a responsible, caring guardian for her young pupils. As for the other, Marian had never bothered to pray for a husband. It had seemed so futile. "Not every woman is looking for Romeo or Sir Galahad. You have a great many qualities a sensible woman would look for in a husband."

She meant that as high praise, but the captain flinched at her words. "A sensible woman—you mean the kind with bluestockings, a plain countenance and rapidly advancing years, who knows enough to settle for what she can get by way of a husband?"

Now it was her turn to flinch from his brutally accurate assessment of her. His lip had curled into a full sneer. It proclaimed his distaste for such a woman and his certainty that she would only want to wed him for mercenary reasons.

Marian's throat tightened until she wondered how she could draw any air down into her lungs, much less force words up. What a perfect fool she'd been to worry herself sleepless about potential rivals for Gideon Radcliffe's affections when it was clear he would never think of her in that way.

"All that aside," he continued in a gruff tone. "Even if I were capable of making a lady attached to me, I am not cut out for marriage. I had better stick with my mistress."

"Mistress?" The word burst from Marian's lips like a stopper from a jug of fermented cider.

"It does sound ridiculously unlikely, doesn't it?"

Not to her. In fact, it explained a great deal. And yet it puzzled her, too. He was such a fine, honorable man. That was why she'd never been afraid to be alone with him, apart from her concern for appearances and propriety. She'd never entertained a moment's worry that he might take advantage of her. Even if she'd been as beautiful as her friend Grace Ellerby, Marian believed she would still be safe in Gideon Radcliffe's company.

"I didn't mean I was surprised you could attract a… mistress, if you wanted one. Only you seem too respectable a man to—"

"I am the one who should explain, Miss Murray. I meant, of course, that the sea is my mistress—a demanding one but not all that discriminating."

Marian scavenged up a wan smile at his self-deprecating jest. But all the while her heart was sinking. Even if she were more attractive and eligible, even if she could persuade the captain that she cared for *him,* not his fortune and position, the sea was a rival with whom no woman could hope to compete. She must take care to remember that.

As she strove to master her voice so she could make

her excuses and escape to the nursery, several clocks in the house began to chime the hour of midnight. From off in the distance came the muted sounds of church bells ringing.

"There we are," said Captain Radcliffe after the noise had died away. "The New Year has arrived. I wonder what it will bring us?"

His use of the word *us* made Marian's heart give a broken-winged flutter, even though she knew he only meant it in a general way to include everyone at Knightley Park. Perhaps the whole of Great Britain.

"I hope it will be a quiet one with no great events to make it memorable in the future. After so many years of war, I pray for one of peace. As for you, Captain, I wish a year of health, happiness and justice."

"Why, thank you, Miss Murray." He extended his hand almost gingerly, tensed to pull away if she tried to surprise him with a kiss or embrace. "A happy New Year to you. I hope God will answer all your prayers."

She took his hand and shook it, savoring the contact between them while trying to maintain all possible restraint. "I thought you didn't believe in prayer."

"I'm not certain I do. But since coming to Knightley Park, I am less certain that I don't." Like that kiss under the mistletoe, their handshake went on longer than it should have. "Perhaps I should have said I hope all your wishes for this New Year come to pass."

"Thank you, Captain." Slowly, reluctantly, she disengaged her hand from his.

Would he still extend her such a hope if he knew what secret wishes she kept locked in her heart?

Chapter Eleven

Would God answer his prayers for the New Year? It might help if he was certain what he wanted to ask for. Those thoughts lurked in the back of Gideon's mind the next day and the next, along with an unsettling realization he'd come to on New Year's Eve.

Attending the Bellamys' ball had been one sour note in an otherwise happy, harmonious Christmas season. When he'd been besieged by those ladies at dinner, he'd felt like a stag set upon by a pack of she-hounds! The whole ordeal had made him see he was quite mistaken about his liking for Marian Murray.

Until then, he had tried to dismiss his feelings as the natural reaction of a man enjoying the company of *any* woman after many years at sea. Now he could not deny there was more to it than that. If anything, his lack of experience had prevented him from recognizing just how rare and fine a woman she was. A few hours spent with those friends of Mrs. Bellamy's had made him properly value Miss Murray's good sense, compassion and loyalty.

Like the Christmas season itself, his acquaintance

with her had transformed what could easily have been a period of barren darkness into something festive... perhaps even blessed.

But that did not change their situation, he sternly reminded himself as he stared out the great bay windows of the Chinese drawing room toward the frozen lake. Like Christmas, this surprisingly agreeable interlude must soon come to an end one way or another. The girls' aunt would return from her travels to whisk them and their governess away. Gideon hoped with all his heart that he would be acquitted of any wrongdoing by the Admiralty and returned to active duty before then. He could not bear to contemplate staying on at Knightley Park without them.

As if drawn by his thoughts, the swift patter of footsteps approached, and Dolly raced in, warmly dressed in her scarlet pelisse and matching bonnet. "Where are you taking us, Cousin Gideon? Miss Marian won't tell me."

"That's because I swore her to secrecy." The moment the child appeared, his lips relaxed into a broad smile and a sense of well-being engulfed him. "I am happy to hear she has kept her word."

Miss Murray appeared then with Cissy. "I'm not certain you ought to take that wee scamp anywhere, Captain, after the way she ran ahead and wouldn't come back when I called her."

Gideon tucked his arms behind his back and strove to force his countenance into the stern stare that used to come so easily to him. It no longer did—at least not when Cissy and Dolly were around. He could scarcely believe how much he had come to care for them in such a short time. It was as if his young cousins had woken and befriended the lonely boy he'd once been.

"I am disappointed to hear of you running in the house and failing to heed Miss Marian. Do you remember what I told you about that?"

Dolly gave a chastened nod. "You said I'm not a filly and the house is not a racecourse. You won't leave me at home, will you, Cousin Gideon? I'm sorry I ran, but I was so excited to find out where we're going."

He could understand that. Perhaps her behavior was partly his fault for keeping the children in suspense. "I reckon we can still take her this time, don't you, Miss Murray? But if she makes a habit of this sort of conduct, I fear she will miss out on future excursions."

"I suppose," Marian Murray said, pretending to be persuaded against her will, "provided she stays on her best behavior while we're away from home."

"What's an *excursion?*"

"It's another way of saying an *outing,*" Gideon explained. "Going somewhere a bit different and doing something rather special."

"Going where?" Cissy piped up. "Doing what?"

"Well, since Twelfth Night is approaching—" Gideon watched the girls' faces for their reaction to his announcement "—I thought you might like to go shopping for gifts…in Newark."

"In town?" Dolly bounced up and down on her toes, clapping. "Oh, yes! We haven't been there in ever so long."

"After we've made our purchases," he continued. "I wondered if you might care to see a pantomime at the theater."

"I would." A subdued sparkle in Cissy's wide blue eyes betrayed her excitement.

"What's a pantomime?" demanded Dolly.

"Something you will enjoy, I believe," Gideon replied. "I can tell you more about it on our drive into town. But we must be on our way soon if we want to get our shopping done and have something to eat before the curtain rises."

The weather had turned milder, so their drive to Newark was a pleasant one. Dolly chattered away, scarcely able to contain her excitement. Even Cissy seemed more talkative than usual. Now perfectly at ease in their company, Gideon sometimes joined in the conversation and other times simply basked in the enjoyment of it. Miss Murray said little but watched him and the children with a brooding air that lent her features a glow beyond mere beauty.

Now and then their gazes met, and they exchanged brief smiles of shared affection for the girls. That's all it was, Gideon insisted to himself. That was all it could ever be.

By and by they reached Newark, a prosperous, bustling town that straddled the Great North Road where it crossed the River Trent. They drove into the market stead, a large open square surrounded by shops, inns and public houses. The magnificent spire of the parish church loomed behind the southeastern side of the square, dwarfing all the buildings in its shadow.

"I suggest we go separate ways to make our purchases," said Gideon as their carriage drew to a stop in front of an inn called The Kingston Arms. "Each of us can take one of the girls. That way the presents may be a surprise when they are opened on Twelfth Night."

"That's a very good idea." Dolly latched onto the sleeve of his coat.

"I'm glad you think so." He fought back a grin. "Though it was Miss Murray's approval I was seeking."

"I agree with Dolly." She took Cissy by the hand. "It is a good idea."

When they alighted from the carriage, he drew Miss Murray aside and slipped her a sum of money. He pitched his voice low and leaned in close so the girls would not hear. "Help the child pick out a gift for her sister. And if you should see anything the girls need or might enjoy, I would be grateful if you make the purchase on my behalf. If the sum I have given you is not sufficient, kindly take note of the item and the shop so I can return for it later."

"I shall be happy to help, Captain." She slipped the money into her reticule. "Where and when should we meet up again?"

He nodded toward the inn. "I shall order us dinner and a private parlor where we can eat. Let us meet back here in two hours, if that will give you enough time?"

"I believe it should." As she and Cissy headed toward a nearby shop, Miss Murray called back. "We will see you in two hours, then."

With Dolly dancing along at his side, Gideon entered The Kingston Arms and made arrangements for their dinner. Then he and the child began walking around the cobblestoned square in the opposite direction from Cissy and their governess.

A year ago, if anyone had told him he would take pleasure in shopping with a high-spirited little girl, he would have dismissed such claims as the ramblings of a lunatic. Yet here he was, going from shop to shop, seeing everything with fresh, wondering eyes, evaluating every possible purchase in terms of the enjoyment it might bring his young cousins.

Then his gaze lit upon an item he felt certain their governess could use. Never in his life had he wanted so badly to give someone a particular gift. If only that harsh taskmaster, propriety, did not make it impossible.

Suddenly he became aware of a persistent tugging on his coat sleeve. How long had Dolly been trying to get his attention? "Forgive me, my dear. What do you want?"

"I was thinking," Dolly pressed her forefinger to her temple. "We should buy a present for Miss Marian."

The child's idea was like the answer to a prayer, only better, for he had not even formed his wordless longing into a petition. Instead, it felt as if someone knew him well enough to anticipate his need and supply it.

"That is a fine idea!" He wrapped his arm around Dolly's shoulders and pulled her close. "What's more, I believe I know just what she might like."

"I'm glad the Captain suggested we go our separate ways to do our shopping," said Marian as she and Cissy skirted the perimeter of the cobbled market square, peering into shop windows. "It isn't often you and I have a chance to be by ourselves."

Perhaps, in future, she could persuade the captain to take Dolly now and then so she could spend more time with Cissy. It couldn't be easy for the child, always having to share attention with her boisterous little sister.

"Yes." Cissy tugged her toward the confectioner's shop, which had a mouthwatering display of Twelfth Night cakes in the window. "If Dolly came with us, she would try to peek all the time at what I was buying for her."

Marian chuckled. "And I don't suppose you would ever think of doing that?"

"Of course not." Cissy seemed mildly offended. "That would spoil the surprise."

"So it would," Marian agreed. "See that cake decorated with all the marzipan fruit? The tiny grapes and cherries look so real."

"I like that one best." Cissy pointed to a cake with seven swans swimming around the edge. "Mrs. Wheaton's Twelfth Night Cake may not look as fancy as these, but I'm sure it will taste every bit as good."

"I have no doubt of that." Marian nodded toward the milliner's shop next door. "These cakes are lovely to look at, but this isn't getting Dolly's Christmas present bought."

"What do you think I should get her?" asked Cissy as they entered the milliner's and began to look over the colorful array of bonnets and hats on display. "I'm not certain she'd want any sort of clothes."

"I suppose not." Marian gazed with longing at a blue hat trimmed with lace and white silk flowers. She had never owned anything so pretty in her life and probably never would. But she should not be ungrateful. Her present circumstances were a vast improvement over her wretched years at school.

With Cissy's hand firmly in hers, they emerged back onto the market square. "If you don't want to give her clothing, that narrows down our search. We needn't bother looking in any of the drapers' shops."

They passed by two of those.

"Or the shoemakers."

"What about that place?" Cissy pointed toward a shop that sold china, glassware and cutlery.

"It looks worth a try." Marian doubted Dolly would care for a piece of decorative china either. But she might find something for Cissy from her cousin. "It was very kind of the captain to bring us shopping in Newark, wasn't it?"

"Yes." Cissy did not elaborate.

"Do you like him better now than when he first came to Knightley Park?"

The child nodded, though not with the degree of enthusiasm Marian had hoped for. "He isn't very much like Papa, but he is rather nice in his way. You seem to like him a great deal more than you used to."

Were her feelings for Gideon Radcliffe so transparent? Marian tried not to let on how much Cissy's remark flustered her.

Fortunately, they had reached the china shop which provided plenty of distractions. It turned out the place also sold toys. Away from the fragile china and glassware were several shelves containing jacks, marbles, toy soldiers and the like.

"I should be able to find something here for Dolly." Cissy looked carefully over the items for sale.

Marian did, too, taking note of one or two that Captain Radcliffe might wish to purchase for the girls. Though she wanted to carry out his commission, she felt uncomfortable spending his money without consulting him.

She hoped the girls would like the beaded coin purses she had made for them. How she wished she could afford to give them special shop-bought presents. But her salary was not large and she needed to save every penny to support herself when she got too old to work.

After careful deliberation, Cissy made her choices. Marian counted out from her reticule the sum they would cost so the child could pay for her purchases.

As they headed back out to the market square, Cissy clutched her parcel as if she feared someone might try to take it from her. Without any warning she asked, "When is Aunt Lavinia coming? Has there been any word from her? I hoped she would be here to spend Christmas with us."

Marian hoped Lady Villiers would stay away from Knightley Park for at least ten years. "Your father's solicitor has tried to contact her but no one is quite certain where she might be... Paris... Vienna... Naples."

Cissy's questions dismayed her even more than the too-perceptive remark about her feelings for the captain. She had been trying so hard to make him care for his young cousins. Now it seemed she should have done more to foster Cissy's liking for him.

"The bookseller's." Marian headed toward a handsome stone building that occupied the south corner of the square. "Let's see what they have, shall we? I could happily browse there for hours."

The shop was quite crowded with prosperous-looking people in search of gifts for friends and family. Marian inhaled the mellow pungency of ink, paper and leather as avidly as the children might sniff sweet smells coming from a bakery.

No sooner had they arrived than a friend of Cissy's came to greet her. "Merry Christmas! Have you had a pleasant holiday? We've come to town to see the pantomime."

"So have we," Cissy announced proudly. "And to shop for Christmas presents."

The girls wandered off, chatting together, while Marian perused the shelves that reached all the way to the high ceiling.

"May I help you find a particular title, ma'am?" A young shop assistant approached her. "*Mansfield Park,* perhaps? It is the newest work by the authoress of *Sense and Sensibility* and *Pride and Prejudice.* All the ladies are clamoring for it."

Marian would have liked very much to purchase all three books by that lady. Her friend Rebecca had read the first two and praised them highly in her letters. Ah, well, she had the Radcliffes' whole library at her disposal. Those books might not be the newest, but there were many good ones among the collection. "Thank you, but I am not looking to make a purchase for myself."

"For a gift. Of course." The young man held up a book he was holding. "I highly recommend this for a father, brother or husband. *Waverley,* a historical novel set in Scotland."

That sounded good, too, though Marian feared it might make her homesick to read about the land she had been forced to leave so long ago. Even if she could afford to buy the novel, she had no male relative to whom she could give it. She would have liked to give a copy to Gideon Radcliffe, but that was impossible for so many reasons.

"I'm sure it's excellent," she replied, "but I am looking for gifts for two young girls."

The assistant beckoned her over to the counter. "We have a fine selection of books for children, printed on

Dutch paper with tinted engravings, as well as some new items that have proven very popular."

As he brought out several of these for her inspection, Marian kept casting glances over her shoulder to make certain Cissy's friend was keeping her well occupied.

She was just about to check again when she heard the captain's voice behind her. "I thought we might meet up here, since it is halfway around the square from where we started."

A sharp gasp burst from her lips as she spun around. "Captain, you startled me! Where is Dolly? I don't want her to see what I've been looking at."

He nodded toward Cissy and her friend, whom Dolly had joined. The three girls seemed to be discussing the pantomime and their Christmas celebrations. "She appears to be diverted for the moment. Do I take it you have found some suitable gifts?"

"I believe so." Only now did Marian notice his arms were filled with a number of parcels, one quite bulky. "Though perhaps you have already found what you would like to give them."

"These, you mean?" He rested his parcels on the edge of the counter, shielding the items she'd been looking over from Cissy and Dolly's view. "No, indeed. So tell me what we have here?"

He stood close beside her, their arms touching. Was that also to prevent the girls from spying?

Whatever the reason, Marian savored his nearness, happy to see him again after even such a brief absence. "I am certain the girls will find these things both amusing and instructive. What is even better, I doubt they are aware such playthings exist. That should make their surprise all the greater."

As the shop assistant showed them to him, Captain Radcliffe nodded. "Well done, Miss Murray. These will do very nicely."

"Which do you wish to purchase, sir?" asked the young man.

"Why, all of them, of course." The captain turned slightly toward Marian. "Could I trouble you to fetch the girls back to the inn so I can pay for these without fear of discovery?"

"Of course, sir." She hastened to do his bidding, though she would rather have lingered there at his side.

The girls reluctantly bid Cissy's friend goodbye and headed back to the inn with Marian. On the way, they traded accounts of what they had seen on their shopping excursions. When Dolly heard about the cakes in the confectioner's window, she insisted on stopping so she could see them for herself.

They were still lingering there when the captain caught up with them. Though he was laden with even more parcels, he whisked the girls into the shop and proceeded to buy a bag of barley sweets and toffees for them to eat during the pantomime.

Marian could not imagine they would have much appetite for those treats after the excellent dinner they tucked away back at The Kingston Arms—cold meats, salads, pies and delicious cheese.

"There." The Captain leaned back in his chair with a contented sigh. "That should give us the strength to walk to the theater. It is only a little way past the other side of the square. The carriage can wait here to drive us home."

Dolly jumped up at once. "Let's go, then. Nell told us we want to be there early to get good seats."

"Never fear," he assured the child. "I have sent Wilbert ahead to reserve us a box."

He had spared no effort or expense to make certain the girls enjoyed their excursion to Newark. Marian savored that thought like a sweet, creamy toffee that melted slowly in the mouth. Whether he realized it or not, Gideon Radcliffe had clearly become attached to his young cousins.

Later, as they watched the rollicking, riotous pantomime, Marian noted how his acquaintance with the children had done him so much good. Gone was the fiercely solitary man who had stalked into Knightley Park two months ago. In his place was one capable of laughter, thoughtful generosity and an ability to enjoy the small pleasures of life.

Newark's playhouse was not a large one, or so Marian guessed, having never attended the theater before. The compact box she shared with the Radcliffes had an excellent view of the stage, where the company performed *The Misadventures of Robin Hood,* a very popular production in Nottinghamshire. As Robin and his band of clownish outlaws cavorted about, playing tricks upon the foppish sheriff and his buffoon of a henchman, the crowded little theater throbbed with laughter.

Dolly fell about in fits of giggles whenever Robin stole up behind the sheriff and gave him a resounding smack on the bottom with his slapping stick.

Later, when the henchman stalked Robin and Maid Marian, Cissy got so caught up in the action she cried, "Look out behind you!"

The poor child hid her face in shame when she realized what she'd done, but the rest of the audience roared with mirth and the actors incorporated her warning into their performance.

Though Marian laughed as much as anyone at the exaggerated falls, blows, tumbling and comical songs, a tiny part of her remained detached, observing Captain Radcliffe and the girls, taking added pleasure in *their* enjoyment. The captain's plan to give Cissy and Dolly a merry Christmas had worked better than she could have hoped. It was quite clear that her prayers for him to care about the girls had been answered.

Now all that remained to crown her efforts was an opportunity to broach the subject of guardianship with Captain Radcliffe. Surely, when he learned what kind of woman Lady Villiers was, he would not wish to see his young cousins fall into her clutches any more than Marian did.

Glancing around at the other families who occupied surrounding boxes, she reckoned a chance observer might suppose she and the Radcliffes were also a close-knit, happy family. Spending so much time together over Christmas, they had come to feel like a family, too.

Knowing how unlikely it was that she would ever have a family of her own, Marian had never permitted herself to think too much about wanting one. But now that she had tasted the joy of family unity, she was not certain she could repress that longing.

After the curtain fell to thunderous applause and the performers took their final bows, Marian and the captain helped the girls bundle up for their return to Knightley Park.

"That was the funniest thing I ever saw," Dolly crowed. "My tummy hurts from laughing so hard."

"I wish we could see it all over again." Cissy pulled

on her gloves. "Wasn't it lovely how Robin and Maid Marian were able to get married at last in spite of that awful sheriff?"

"Robin Hood had a *Maid* Marian," Dolly said, her eyes twinkling with mischief, "and we have a *Miss* Marian. I think after this, I will call you Maid Marian."

"Call me what you will." Marian playfully batted Dolly's nose. "But I will choose what name I answer to."

Over the child's head her gaze met the captain's, and they exchanged a comradely smile.

"May I have a barley sweet, now?" Cissy asked him.

"What do you say, Miss Marian?" He pulled the bag from his pocket.

"Go ahead." She plumped the bow of Dolly's bonnet. "Now that the pantomime is over, I won't be afraid of them choking when they laugh."

Having secured her approval, Captain Radcliffe fished out sweets for the girls. "And you, Miss Marian?"

"Yes, please." She held out her hand.

As he slipped her one of the hard-boiled sweets, she gave silent thanks for all the joys, great and small, that Gideon Radcliffe had brought into her life.

Once out on the street, they walked briskly toward The Kingston Arms and their waiting carriage. Marian wondered if the girls might fall asleep on the drive home, leaving her and the captain a chance to talk. If they did, it might be the right time to raise her doubts about Lady Villiers as a suitable guardian for the girls. But part of her shrank from spoiling this lovely outing by bringing up such an unpleasant subject.

They had nearly reached the inn when they met an elderly gentleman who doffed his hat and wished them a Happy New Year. Captain Radcliffe returned his cordial greeting.

"Have you seen the pantomime?" Dolly asked the man. "It's very funny, especially Robin Hood's slapping stick. I laughed and laughed!"

The old gentleman stopped in a pool of light cast by one of several street lamps scattered around the square. "Bless my soul, child, I have not seen a pantomime in years. But now that you mention it, I believe I shall go. I could do with a good laugh."

He beamed at the girls, then smiled up at Marian and the captain. "A very handsome family you have been blessed with, sir. I trust you appreciate your good fortune."

Marian sensed a sudden tension in the captain's posture, but he replied with only the slightest hesitation. "Thank you, sir. I do, indeed. Good evening to you."

As they hurried on, Cissy piped up in an accusing tone, "Why did you not tell that man we aren't your family?"

"Because you are…in a way."

Cissy was not satisfied with that excuse. "But you know he thought Miss Marian must be your wife and Dolly and me your daughters. You should have told him the truth."

"Perhaps," replied the captain. "But his praise was kindly meant. It would have been more awkward to explain. Besides, I cannot deny you are handsome."

"We *aren't* your family," Cissy repeated. "Not in the way he meant."

"I sometimes wish we were," announced Dolly, who had been unusually quiet during their exchange.

"I sometimes wish Cousin Gideon was our papa and Miss Marian our mama."

Those words brought Cissy to an abrupt halt. She let go of Marian's hand as if it had suddenly caught fire. "Dolly Radcliffe, how could you wish such a wicked thing?"

"It isn't wicked!" Dolly cried.

"Please, Cissy." Marian had been afraid the late hour and all the treats and excitement might catch up with the children. "Your sister didn't mean—"

"Yes, she did!" Cissy backed away, glaring at all three of them. "And she had no business wishing any such thing. She should wish Mama and Papa had not died!"

With that, the child spun away and ran off across the square.

"Cissy!" Marian started after her only to feel Gideon's restraining hand on her arm.

"Stay with Dolly," he ordered in a tone of command the brooked no refusal. "Take her into the inn to keep warm until I fetch her sister back."

He spoke those words as he hurried past in pursuit of the fleeing child.

Marian wanted to protest. Cissy was much more likely to listen to her. But for that to happen, she would first have to catch the child. Gideon was better suited to that task for he had longer legs which were not hampered by skirts. Besides, it might not be prudent for a woman and young girl to be out at night on their own, even in a respectable town like Newark.

As she turned back toward Dolly, Marian raised a wordless prayer that Gideon would be able to catch Cissy quickly and somehow find the words to reach her heart.

Chapter Twelve

Dread clawed at Gideon as he raced across Newark's market square, trying to keep from losing sight of the fleeing child. If he did not catch up with her soon, he feared she might duck into one of the narrow lanes around the church and lose him.

What might become of her then? It was a cold night, and he doubted Cissy knew anyone in Newark with whom she might seek shelter. Even if she repented running away and wanted to return, would she be able to find her way back through unfamiliar streets in the winter darkness? The thought of her lost, alone and perishing with cold terrified Gideon as no peril to his own life ever had. Almost as acute as his fear for her safety was the alarming realization of how much his cousin's young daughters had come to mean to him.

Cissy had almost reached the other side of the square! How could such a slender little creature run so fast? She was like a frightened fawn fleeing for her life.

Out of his desperation, a plea rose in his thoughts. "Dear God, help me catch her before it's too late!"

A prayer? Part of him scoffed at the futility of it.

Even if the Creator of the Universe did heed the pleas of insignificant human beings, why should God deign to answer his first prayer in nearly twenty-five years? If anyone was going to reach Cissy, it would have to be him alone, by his own efforts.

That thought spurred him to a final burst of speed.

Was the child slowing down a bit? Perhaps he might catch her yet.

Then in a confused instant, his foot landed on a patch of ice and flew out from under him. Gideon flailed his arms in a futile effort to regain his balance. A cry burst from his lips as he crashed down hard on the cold cobblestones.

Stunned and in pain, he struggled to drag himself back to his feet and continue the chase. A groan collided in his throat with a sob of despair, for he knew it was too late. Cissy would have disappeared from sight, and his chances of finding her would be far too slim.

But as he tried to pull himself up, ignoring a stab of pain in his ankle, Gideon heard footsteps. They could not be the child's, though, for the sound was coming closer rather than fading into the distance.

"Cousin Gideon?" That was Cissy's voice. Or had the fall addled his wits enough to make him hear things?

"Are you much hurt?" She gasped for breath. "I heard you fall. It's all my fault…if you are injured."

Hearing him cry out, she had stopped and come back? That mishap had accomplished his goal when his own best efforts might have failed. What strange irony. Or could it be the unlikely answer to a prayer?

"Don't fret yourself, child." Much as pride urged him to get back on his feet as quickly as possible and pretend nothing was wrong, he sensed that might make Cissy run off again.

A soft whisper from deep in his heart suggested that perhaps an admission of weakness might serve him better that a show of strength. "You came back. That counts for a great deal more. Can I trouble you to help me up? I fear my leg may be injured and my balance is none too steady."

Cissy hesitated for a moment, then Gideon felt her hand on his. Leaning upon her, he struggled to his feet. "Could you assist me back across the square? I believe your Miss Marian will be worried about us, don't you?"

"Yes," came the forlorn answer. "Do you think she will be very angry with me for running off like that?"

"More relieved to get you back than angry, I should think." His arm slung over the child's shoulders, Gideon took one halting step forward, then another.

After a few more steps, he spoke again. He hoped—prayed—that what he was about to say would not make the child take flight again. "I understand why you were upset with me and with your sister."

"You do?" Cissy sounded skeptical yet mildly curious.

"Yes, indeed." Much as it went against his nature to speak of his past, Gideon sensed the child needed to hear about it. Besides, he now had some practice confiding in Marian Murray—enough to know that while the experience might be painful, it often brought a sense of relief. "I was around Dolly's age when my father died. My mother lingered after him for nearly two years, but she had never been strong...."

"Did you miss them very much?" Cissy asked in a plaintive murmur. "Did you pray they would come back again? Did you think if you were very, very good, they might?"

The anguish in her voice revived Gideon's deeply buried feelings of loss. Old wounds reopened, stinging and bleeding afresh. "During my mother's final weeks, I made all manner of bargains with God for good behavior if He would spare her life."

A long overdue realization gashed his heart. "When she died at last, I wondered if it was my fault for not behaving well enough."

Was that why he had blamed God—because it was easier than carrying that burden of irrational guilt?

Cissy sniffled. It might be just the cold air making her nose run, but Gideon did not think so.

"Now I understand," he continued, "that my mother's death was not my fault...nor was it God's."

He wasn't certain Cissy would be able to grasp that yet. It had taken him twenty-five years. Perhaps it would not have taken so long if he hadn't spent so much of that time trying to bury his memories and feelings about that part of his life.

In spite of their slow progress across the square, he and Cissy were drawing near The Kingston Arms. Since it was doubtful he would have another opportunity to talk privately with the child, there was one more thing he needed to say.

"I hope you know I have no desire to take your father's place in your life. Any kindness or affection you show me would not be disloyal to his memory. Indeed, from what I remember of him, I believe he would approve. Even in death, he would not want to cause you any guilt or sorrow. More than anything, I believe he would wish for you to be happy."

Beneath his arm, Gideon could feel the child's slender shoulders tremble and heave.

Oh, no. His effort to comfort her had only made her weep.

His first day back at Knightley Park, when he'd seen those two beautiful children, he had been beset by the conviction that he was not equipped to provide what they might need, though he'd only had a vague suspicion of what those needs might be. In the weeks since, he had gradually gained more confidence in dealing with the girls. False confidence apparently.

Now that he understood what they needed, the knowledge made him feel more inadequate than ever. That self-doubt urged him to hurry those last few steps to the inn and shift responsibility onto the capable shoulders of Marian Murray. But some other feeling he scarcely recognized pleaded with him to try at least. He was the child's flesh and blood after all, the closest living relative to the father she mourned so deeply.

Did he dare turn to the Lord for help again so soon, when he was not entirely convinced his first prayer had been answered? Perhaps he did not deserve the help he sought, but surely it could do no harm to ask. "Please, Lord, tell me what to say. Let me know what she needs to hear."

But no words leapt instinctively to mind. He could not summon any powerful phrases certain to reach her. Gideon tamped down a foolish sense of disappointment. How could he have been so daft as to expect an answer?

Or could his loss for words be part of the inspiration he sought? Was it a sign that no words could provide what a confused, guilty, grieving young girl needed now?

What *did* she need then? He was in no mood to puzzle out riddles from a Higher Power…or some forgotten corner of his own mind.

Then, without conscious effort on his part, the arm he had slung over Cissy's shoulders subtly increased its pressure, encouraging her to turn toward him. He expected her to resist, perhaps even take flight again. Instead, to his amazement, she surrendered to the gentle urging. As her weeping gained momentum, she slowly turned until her face rested against the breast of his coat.

There was only one thing to do at that point. In spite of how self-conscious it made him feel, Gideon raised his other arm to wrap the child in a comforting, protective embrace.

Perhaps he didn't know the right things to say, but at least he had a sense of what *not* to say. He would not try to shush her and tell her not to weep. It might make *him* feel better, but that was not the point.

"Go ahead," he murmured. "Cry as long as you like. I'm here."

Cissy accepted his invitation, letting her tears flow freely for several minutes, gulping in air to fuel her sobs. When she began to quiet at last, he rummaged in his pocket for a handkerchief and pressed it into her hand in silent sympathy.

The child wiped her eyes and blew her nose.

"We should get inside," she murmured. "It's cold out here and Miss Marian will be worried."

"An excellent suggestion." Gideon loosened his hold on her, only to discover how reluctant he was to let her go.

But that was nothing to his astonishment when instead of taking the opportunity to disengage from his embrace, Cissy pressed tight against him. "Thank you,

Cousin Gideon. I still don't wish you were my papa, but I am glad you came to Knightley Park."

His throat tightened as he bent to drop a kiss on the crown of her bonnet. "Then we are in complete agreement, my dear."

"Cissy!" Marian swooped down on the child the moment she peeped into the waiting room at The Kingston Arms. "Thank God you are back!"

Noting Cissy's red, swollen eyes and nose, she asked, "Are you all right? You weren't hurt, were you?"

The child gnawed her lower lip as she shook her head. "Cousin Gideon was, though. He fell on some ice in the square and hurt his leg."

Cousin Gideon? This was the first time Marian had heard Cissy refer to him that way. An intense impulse of concern for him pushed that trifling thought out of her mind.

"Captain!" She was barely able to keep from throwing her arms around him. "Come in and sit down. Should I send for a physician?"

"Don't fret, Miss Marian," he bid her rather gruffly. "I'm certain nothing is broken. Only bumps and bruises. Fortunately, Cissy was kind enough to come to my assistance."

Seeing how he had one arm draped over Cissy's shoulders, Marian slid in under his other arm. She chided herself for welcoming this excuse to be close to him.

As she and Cissy helped the captain to a nearby bench, a loud yawn reminded everyone of Dolly, curled up half asleep at the far end of the bench. "Aren't you going to punish Cissy, Miss Marian? She shouted at me and ran away. It's her fault Cousin Gideon got hurt chasing after her."

"Not now, Dolly." Marian fixed her younger pupil with a firm stare. "We'll talk about all that later."

"We'd better." Dolly eyed her sister with a scowl. "You never wait 'til later to punish me when I've been naughty."

Marian was about to scold the child for her impudence, but the captain only chuckled. "Ah, Dolly, you are practically a pantomime all on your own."

The corners of her fierce little frown arched upward. "I wish I had a slapping stick. That would be great fun."

"Great *havoc* you mean." Marian gave an exaggerated shudder. "None of us would be safe."

After the captain had taken a few minutes to rest and get warm, he refused any suggestion of seeking medical attention but said they should head back home at once. To Marian's surprise, Cissy quietly insisted on sitting beside him in the carriage. It took some persuasion for Dolly to surrender her accustomed spot, but at last she gave in with rather ill grace and they were on their way.

"What on earth did you say to Cissy to bring about such a change in her?" Marian asked when the drone of the girls' breathing assured her they were both asleep.

"Not a great deal," Gideon replied. "I only told her a little about losing my parents when I was her age and how it affected me. Then I assured her I have no intention of trying to take her father's place in her life."

He didn't? Not ever, under any circumstances? His words made Marian rethink her intention to raise the subject of the girls' guardianship.

What had gone wrong? Until an hour ago, she'd been

certain God was smiling upon her efforts. Could this be a test of her resolve?

"Strange that saying a thing like that should make her take such liking to you."

"Believe me, I am quite as surprised as you. Perhaps it helped her to know I understand her feelings because I have shared them."

Should she have told Dolly and Cissy about her experiences being orphaned at an early age? Marian wondered. She had held her tongue on the subject, fearing it might prompt prying questions about her experiences at the Pendergast School. She did not want to make them afraid of being sent to such a place. It was bad enough that she must live with that worry on their behalf.

A sudden thought drove every other from Marian's mind.

"Dear me. How could I have forgotten?" She groped for her reticule while trying not to disturb Dolly, who had fallen asleep with her head on Marian's lap. "That money you gave me, I only spent a wee bit of it on Cissy's gift to Dolly."

She fished out what was left—heavy gold guineas, silver shillings, halfpennies. "Here is the rest. I would have returned it to you sooner but with dinner and the pantomime and everything else, it slipped my mind until now."

She hoped he wouldn't suspect her of trying to keep his money.

"Oh, that?" Gideon sounded as if he had never given it a thought. Or was he only trying to be polite? "Do not trouble yourself over it, I beg you, Miss Murray. Please keep it, with my compliments."

"I couldn't do that, Captain." The very idea made her

feel ill. "It is a great deal of money…at least to someone like me."

"Nonsense," he replied gruffly. "You deserve every farthing and more for the way you have looked after the girls since their father died. Consider it a Christmas box."

Though it pleased her to know he valued her efforts so highly, the notion of taking money from Gideon Radcliffe only emphasized the gulf between her position and his.

"Please, Captain, I cannot accept this." She held out the money to him, but she could not reach any farther without the risk of waking Dolly—something she was loath to do. "It would not be fair for me to take this when the other servants work so much harder than I do at far less congenial tasks."

"Servants?" Gideon Radcliffe sat stubbornly back in his seat, refusing to extend his hand and take the money she sought to return. "Surely you know I do not think of you as a servant!"

The fierce tone of his insistence rocked Marian back. How did he think of her then? She longed to know, but dared not ask for fear his answer might crush her foolish illusion that some degree of friendship existed between them.

"In that case," she edged a little closer and opened her palm. "Please do not insult me by insisting I keep this money."

"Fine." He snatched the coins out of her hand in a swift, almost violent movement. "If that is what you wish."

He'd told Marian Murray he did not think of her as a servant. Why had she refused to ask how he did think of her? In the final few days of Christmas leading up to Twelfth Night, Gideon could not decide whether he was sorry or grateful he'd been denied the opportunity to tell her.

Would he have been able to explain if she had asked? The privacy and darkness of the carriage box might have tempted him, but at what cost?

He admired the woman, liked her…even fancied her, heaven help him. But entertaining such feelings for her did not give him any right to reveal them or, worse yet, act upon them. He might not think of her as a servant, but she was employed in the house of which he was master. Any declaration would shatter the precious illusion of a family that he treasured more and more.

This time with Cissy and Dolly…and Marian…was only temporary. Gideon knew and accepted that. But for a short while he'd been able to experience the small domestic joys of family life. For that gift, he would be forever grateful.

What made it all the sweeter was knowing he had been able to do something for his young cousins. He'd given them the opportunity to remain in their home and grow accustomed to the changes that would soon take place in their lives. With Marian's help, he'd turned a Christmas that might have been shadowed with sad memories into a festive celebration of light and hope. On the most personal level, he had helped a grieving young girl understand that she was not alone.

Those accomplishments brought him a deeper sense of satisfaction than any of the battles in which he'd fought or voyages of exploration on which he'd sailed. Yet, as the last few days of the Christmas season passed, a hint of wistfulness colored the pleasure of his celebration.

On the day before Twelfth Night, they invited a number of children from the parish to a skating party. Round and round the youngsters glided on the frozen lake, laughing and calling to one another. Cissy and Dolly even persuaded Gideon to strap on skates for the first time in twenty-five years to help push a small sleigh full of younger children around the ice. Later, they gathered in the pavilion that stood on the little island in the middle of the lake. There, Marian and the kitchen staff dispensed cups of steaming cider and chocolate, baked potatoes, hot meat pies and buns, followed by gingerbread.

"I wish Christmas never had to end." Dolly took Gideon's hand as he and the girls stood in front of the house waving farewell to the last of their guests. "I'd like it to go on and on."

Her childish wish echoed his own recent thoughts so closely, it took Gideon aback.

"Now, now." He squeezed her hand, not looking forward to the day he would bid Dolly and her sister goodbye. "Don't let the thought of happy times coming to an end spoil your enjoyment of them. If every day were Christmas you'd soon grow tired of it. I reckon we enjoy special times all the more because they don't last forever."

"You sound just like Miss Marian," the child grumbled.

Once again, Gideon could not help but laugh at the things she came out with. They were a tiny pinch of yeast that leavened his day. "Why, thank you! That is one of the nicest compliments anyone has ever paid me."

"It wasn't meant to be a compliment," Dolly muttered, making him laugh again.

"Don't look so sour." He scooped her up and jiggled her until she began to chortle. "The best of Christmas is yet to come, remember? A fine dinner and presents and Twelfth Night cake. I have it on good authority that Mrs. Wheaton has quite outdone herself this year."

"Presents!" Dolly threw her arms around his neck, a gesture he had grown accustomed to and come to enjoy. "What did you get me?"

"He mustn't tell," piped up Cissy, who'd been standing quietly beside them. "It's meant to be a secret."

"So it is." Something in the look she cast him made Gideon set Dolly on her feet and pick up her sister. "And speaking of secrets, I've noticed a bit of whispering going on and conversations that mysteriously stop when I enter the room. You wouldn't be planning some sort of trick to spring on me by any chance?"

"Not a trick," Dolly insisted.

"Hush!" Cissy bid her sister. "You mustn't tell."

"Now I am intrigued," said Gideon. "Come, don't keep me in suspense. Surely you can tell me something."

Cissy grinned and her eyes sparkled. "Wait and see."

The next morning Knightley Park was abuzz with preparations. Succulent aromas of roasting meat, fresh baked bread and cooking spices wafted up from the kitchen. Eager for every opportunity to spend time with the girls, Gideon joined them for their last breakfast of frumenty.

While they were eating and talking over plans for the day, Mr. Culpepper appeared with the post. "A letter for you, Captain Radcliffe, and one for Miss Murray."

Gideon's stomach sank at the sight of the Admiralty seal on his letter. Stuffing it in his pocket to read later, he hoped the ever curious Dolly would not quiz him about it. Fortunately for him, Marian's post diverted attention from his entirely.

"Oh, thank goodness." She pressed it to her heart with a look of relief.

"Who is your letter from, Miss Marian?" demanded Dolly.

Gideon found himself quite as eager as Dolly to learn the answer to her question. Everything about Marian Murray had become of particular interest to him.

Perhaps she sensed his curiosity, for when she replied, she looked toward him. "It is a Christmas letter from my friend Rebecca Beaton. I was beginning to worry some trouble might have befallen to prevent her from writing."

"What does she say?" asked Dolly. "Why did her letter come late?"

"I won't know that until I read it, will I?" Marian turned the thick packet of paper over and over in her hands. It was clear she was as curious as her young pupil to learn those things.

"Go on then," Dolly coaxed her. Bolting her last spoonful of frumenty, the child leaned back in her chair, waiting to be informed.

"Don't be rude," Cissy chided her. "Letters are private, you know."

For all that, she eyed her governess's letter with ill-disguised interest.

"True." Marian stared at the letter longingly. "Besides, it would not be polite to read it at breakfast in front of everyone."

Would she have hesitated if he were not there, Gideon wondered. He did not want to stand between her and whatever news the letter might contain.

"Pray do not suppose I would object to you looking over your friend's message," he assured her. "At least enough to rest your mind that she is not in any difficulty."

"Thank you, Captain. That is most considerate of you." The gratitude in her voice made him feel a trifle guilty, for his suggestion had not been entirely free of self-interest.

Without further ado, she broke the seal on the letter with eager, jerky movements, as if she had been itching to do that from the moment it arrived. Pulling it open, she hurriedly scanned the page.

"Oh, my." Her eyes widened in wonder. From her tone it appeared the letter did not bear any bad news.

"Well, what does it say?" Dolly prompted Marian, ignoring a sharp look from her sister. "Why did Miss Rebecca take so long to write you?"

"She has been very busy." Marian continued to read the letter with a look of dreamy abstraction that Gideon found far too appealing. "Rebecca is engaged to be married. To a viscount, no less. Lord Benedict."

"What's a viscount?" asked Dolly.

"Lord Benedict?" Gideon repeated. "During the war, he once sailed aboard the *Integrity* to Portugal to see for himself how British troops were being supplied. He struck me as a fine man."

Clever, hardworking and passionately committed to his mission, but not necessarily cut out for marriage. Now that the war was over, perhaps Lord Benedict had decided to allow himself the luxury of a family life. Gideon wished him well. If Marian's friend was anything like her, then his lordship was a fortunate man to have secured her affection.

Chapter Thirteen

Rebecca was going to be married. Her friend's wonderful news hovered in Marian's thoughts as she got the girls ready for their Twelfth Night celebrations.

It appeared their teachers' stern admonitions were wrong after all—and how very wrong. Marian could not help gloating a little over that. She wondered what they would think if they knew one of their former pupils was betrothed to a peer of the realm.

She should not let any foolish ideas get into *her* head on that account. Marian fancied she could hear the voice of their strictest teacher reproaching her. Rebecca Beaton might have been the orphaned daughter of a clergyman, like all the other girls at the Pendergast School. But on her late mother's side, she had noble blood and aristocratic connections. Some of their teachers had treated her a little better because of her background. Others had been even harder on her, claiming a virtuous desire to help her conquer her pride.

Perhaps Viscount Benedict valued Rebecca's good breeding in spite of her humble position as a governess. Marian had no such advantages. She came from a respectable, educated Scottish family, but nothing compared to the Radcliffes in wealth or social standing.

Still, Gideon had said he did not think of her as a servant. And Rebecca Beaton had proved it was possible for a pupil from the Pendergast School to secure a fine husband.

Encouraged by those thoughts, in spite of her doubts, Marian took special care with her appearance for the festivities. When the time came, she ushered the girls down to the Chinese drawing room, where Gideon was waiting to give them their presents.

Outside, tiny flakes of snow swirled in a cold breeze. Gideon beckoned them from the wide seat of the great bow window. A pile of packages rested on top of a small table beside him. Marian thought it was a nice informal spot for them to gather to give the girls their gifts. Anyone looking in the window at that moment might easily mistake them for an affectionate family group— like that kind old gentleman in Newark had thought.

"May I go first?" Marian asked in a rush the moment she and the girls were seated. Her gifts were certain to be the most modest. She would rather see the girls' pleasure mount after that humble beginning than face their disappointment if they opened her presents later.

"Certainly, if you wish," Gideon agreed. Perhaps he guessed her reason for the request.

"There you are, Cissy, and for you Dolly." She handed them each a small parcel, wrapped in colored paper and tied with pretty ribbons.

"Thank you, Miss Marian!" The girls opened their gifts each in their accustomed manner. Cissy carefully untied the ribbon and pealed open the wrapping while Dolly ripped the paper off without ceremony.

"What is it?" She jiggled the small beaded bag in her hand.

"It's a coin purse, of course." Cissy gave the younger girl a pointed nudge with her elbow. "They're lovely, Miss Marian. The beadwork is beautiful. Isn't it, Dolly?"

"Oh, yes." Dolly took the unsubtle hint. "Very beautiful. They will come in handy if we go shopping in Newark again. And if we get any money to put in them."

"Since you mention it—" Gideon dug in his pocket and came out with several coins he divided between the girls "—I meant to give you these the other day, but since you had no purses, I was afraid they might get lost."

Dolly looked much more pleased with her purse now that it was no longer empty. She shook it to make the coins jingle.

After a few moments of that, she thrust a rather clumsily wrapped parcel into her sister's hands. "Now open mine."

Cissy returned the favor with a package upon which greater pains had been taken. She winced when Dolly proceeded to rip it open, then decided to do the same with the one she'd been given.

"A muff—how pretty!" She rubbed the handsome fur hand-warmer against her cheek. "How soft it feels. Thank you, Dolly."

Meanwhile Dolly gasped with delight when she unwrapped the toy sailboat from her sister. "I hope the lake will thaw soon so I can sail it!"

When the girls opened their presents from Gideon a few moments later, they were equally pleased, though a little baffled at first.

"It's a dissected puzzle," Marian explained when Dolly's brow furrowed. "When you put each of the countries of Europe in their proper place, the edges will fit together to make the whole map. It will be a great help to you learning geography."

"Look at mine!" cried Cissy. "I thought it was a pretty book, but see it has a cut out figure of a girl with paper costumes to change how she is dressed through the story. Her name is Little Fanny. Isn't that clever? Thank you, Cousin Gideon!"

"Yes, thank you!" Dolly bounded up to give him a hearty kiss on the cheek.

The child's impulsive gesture seemed to please him. "I'm delighted you approve."

His obvious pleasure in the girls' happiness touched Marian. He might not intend to take their late father's place, but surely he would want what was best for Cissy and Dolly. He would never allow Lady Villiers to help herself to their inheritance or pack them off to school.

"While I was happy to make the actual purchases," he continued, "I would never have guessed what you might like without Miss Marian to advise me. I hope you will think of these gifts as coming from both of us."

Having said that, he leaned down and whispered something in Dolly's ear. She nudged her sister and pointed to the one remaining parcel on the table.

Scrambling up from the window seat, the girls retrieved the package and presented it to Marian. "Merry Christmas!"

"Cousin Gideon paid for it," Dolly confessed. "But he says it's from us."

"My goodness. This is quite a surprise." Like Cissy,

Marian untied the string with great care and folded back the paper. "I cannot imagine what it might…oh, my!"

It was a writing box made of fine dark wood with a sloped lid, which folded open to reveal all the supplies she would need for letter writing—paper, ink, quills, a pen knife, sealing wax and a jar of pounce for drying the ink.

"Do you like it?" asked Cissy anxiously as a fine mist rose in Marian's eyes.

"Like it?" She swallowed the lump in her throat and sought to reassure the child with a wide smile. "I cannot imagine any gift I would like better. Thank you so much!"

She raised her gaze to meet Gideon's, eager for him to know how much she appreciated his thoughtfulness. Not only had he shown how well he knew her by choosing such an ideal gift, he'd also found a way to give it that would not violate propriety.

More than ever, she wished she could have afforded one of those new books for him. But she would have to be content with a different kind of offering—one she hoped would please him even half as much as his gift delighted her.

"We have something for you, too, Cousin Gideon." Cissy took the rolled paper tied with red ribbon that Marian handed her. Turning toward the captain, she presented it to him with great ceremony.

"Really, this is not necessary." He seemed torn between self-consciousness and curiosity as he unrolled the little scroll. "What have we here? A program of festive music and recitations in my honor? What an excellent gift and a fine way to conclude the Christmas season!"

The silvery radiance of his eyes left no doubt of his sincere gratitude and desire to hear the girls perform.

After an excellent dinner, the four of them headed to the music room where the girls took turns playing simple renditions of Christmas melodies on the pianoforte. Their duet of "The First Noel" made the captain applaud so vigorously Marian feared he might hurt his hands.

Then it was her turn to take the keyboard and accompany the girls while they sang. Again Gideon proved a very appreciative audience. His attention did not flag for the recitations either—some little rhymes about Christmas the girls had practiced every day in the nursery. They concluded their concert by taking turns reading verses from St. Matthew's account of the wise men visiting Baby Jesus, followed by a spirited duet of "I Saw Three Ships."

"Bravo!" cried Gideon as the girls proudly made their curtsies. "That was a splendid evening's entertainment and without a doubt the best Christmas present I have ever received."

By now they had digested their dinner sufficiently to do justice to Mrs. Wheaton's Twelfth Night cake. Retiring to the dining room, they watched in amazement as it was brought out, swathed in snow-white icing and topped with a tiny sailing ship cleverly fashioned out of marzipan.

The girls clapped excitedly when they saw the marvelous confection. "It is fancier than any in the shop-window in Newark!"

Gideon sent for the cook to receive their praise and congratulations in person. Despite their frequent insistence that the cake looked too beautiful to cut, they could not resist the temptation indefinitely. When they finally began to eat, they were delighted to discover the cake tasted as good as it looked. They ate, drank and made merry until Marian reluctantly announced that it was long past the girls' bedtime.

Cissy and Dolly protested, but not as much as she feared they might.

As they gathered up their gifts from the drawing room, the captain picked up Marian's writing box. "Let me carry this for you. It is not heavy, but rather cumbersome."

Though Marian had no doubt she could have managed it on her own, she did not protest, but thanked him for his assistance. He probably wanted an excuse to be on hand in case Dolly requested another kiss good-night.

As they headed upstairs, Marian noticed dry evergreen needles on the floor from the decorative boughs. On closer inspection, the holly, mistletoe and ivy all looked badly wilted. It reminded her that while Twelfth Night was the culmination of the Christmas season, it was also the end of the festivities. Tomorrow, all the dried out, wilted greenery would be taken down, the kissing bough would be dismantled, and life at Knightley Park would return to its usual safe, dull routine.

"I meant to mention," Gideon's resonant voice interrupted her wistful musing. "While I was purchasing the girls' gifts at Ridges, that young clerk persuaded me to acquire a few new books for the library. One is a novel set in Scotland, which I am enjoying immensely and believe you will, too. The others are by an anonymous authoress whose work is said to be very popular."

Words of thanks rose to her lips, but Marian suppressed them firmly. Thanking the captain would imply that he had purchased those books for her benefit—another covert gift.

"An excellent idea," she said instead. "It is a fine collection, but it has not been added to in quite some time."

Searching for a way to change the subject, she recalled his presence at breakfast in the nursery. "I am anxious to use my new writing box to compose a message of congratulations to my friend on her betrothal. You received a letter in the morning post, as well, Captain. I hope the news it contained was equally good."

He hesitated a moment before replying. "It was. I am summoned to London to appear before the board of inquiry. At last I shall have the opportunity to present my case and defend my actions."

"That *is* good news," she replied in spite of her sinking spirits.

If the inquiry absolved him of any wrongdoing, would Gideon Radcliffe come back to Nottinghamshire, or would he return to his ship immediately?

The prospect of never seeing him again cast Marian down lower than she had been for many years. She tried to tell herself it was on account of the girls. If he did not return to Knightley Park, there would be nothing to prevent their aunt from taking them.

Yet, deep down, she knew her feelings were more personal than that.

He was eager to get to London and face the inquiry.

Gideon told himself so repeatedly during the following week as he prepared for his journey south. He had enjoyed his Christmas interlude playing happy family with the girls and their governess. But the time had come to stop pretending and remember his obligations.

As much as he longed to redeem his reputation for his own sake, he also had a duty to the crew of the *Integrity*. What a time they must have had of it, poor devils, serving under his ruthlessly ambitious second-in-command with his pet pack of bullies to intimidate any opposition. Though it troubled him that none of his crew had come forward in his defense, Gideon understood what was at stake for them. The worst that had befallen him was exile to a quiet corner of the country to enjoy a good rest, better food and the best possible company. His crewmen had far more to lose if they fell afoul of his enemies.

Now, as he prepared to leave Knightley Park, one of Gideon's most important tasks was deciding whether he dared leave Mr. Dutton in charge as steward during his absence. From what he could tell, the man appeared to have mended his ways. But could he be trusted to continue in that vein once his master left for London and perhaps even returned to sea?

Though Gideon was tempted to give him the benefit of the doubt, he recalled how dearly a decision like that had cost him before. And not him alone. His crew had paid a far higher price. In this case it was the tenants of Knightley Park who would suffer if the steward returned to his lax ways.

If only there was someone he could trust to oversee the overseer and report any problems directly to him. Gideon believed that was all it would take to keep Dutton from shirking his responsibilities in future. Unfortunately, the only person at Knightley Park he trusted that much would soon be leaving, too.

With that thought in mind, Gideon tried to keep busy to distract himself from the hollow ache that nagged at him. With the Christmas season over, the girls had returned to their usual nursery routine, meaning he saw much less of them…and their governess. Perhaps that was for the best, though. It would give him a chance to grow accustomed to their absence gradually before he must depart for London.

Yet he could not keep from straining his ears to catch the faintest cadence of their voices in the distance. On his way to breakfast in the mornings, he found all manner of ridiculous excuses to linger in the hallway, hoping a small human cannonball might come hurtling around the corner toward him. In the evenings he retired to the library, hoping those new books might lure Marian Murray to join him.

He had nearly given up hope when, on the fourth evening, the library door opened tentatively and she peeped in. "I hope I am not disturbing you, Captain."

"Not in the least," he assured her, though it was not altogether true.

During Christmas they had been so often together that his awareness of her had mellowed. But now that feeling had intensified again to the point where it was rather disturbing…in a pleasant way.

As she entered the room, Miss Murray seemed more self-conscious around him, too, without the girls present. Did she recall that meeting of their lips under the kissing bough and wonder whether she would be safe alone with him?

"I thought I might borrow one of those new books you acquired." She scanned the shelves. "If you don't mind."

"Not at all." Did she not realize he had purchased them for her benefit? "I have finished *Waverley* and just started *Pride and Prejudice.* The latter may be intended for ladies, but I am enjoying it very much."

He gestured toward the table beside him where the new books lay.

Miss Murray approached with an air of hesitation. She picked up one of the books and read a little from the first page, then laid it back down and tried another. In the end she chose the one titled *Sense and Sensibility.*

Once she'd made her selection, Gideon feared she would go away again. But she lingered, though her glance often flickered toward the door. "I must confess, Captain, I had more in mind than seeking a book when I came here. May I sit?"

"Please, do." Had their time together at Christmas made her realize she enjoyed his company?

When she sank onto the armchair opposite his, Gideon sat back down. "May I inquire as to your other reason?"

He wasn't entirely certain he wanted to know. Flattering as it would be to think that such an admirable young woman might have some slight fancy for him, their respective duties made it impossible for anything to come of it. He must return to the *Integrity,* and she must accompany her young pupils to their new home with their aunt. He knew better than to suppose she would ever desert them.

"It's about Cissy and Dolly, sir."

He should have guessed. Gideon strove to ignore a sting of disappointment. The girls were her top priority. He doubted there was anything in the world she would not do for them.

"They are well, I hope." That sting swelled to a stab of fear he could not ignore. For the past few days, he had missed the girls but never taken the trouble to inquire about them. "All the rich food, late hours and time out in the cold have not made them ill?"

A soft smile lit Marian Murray's features as she shook her head. It seemed to hold a warm glow of gratitude and a faint flicker of…triumph? "They are very well, Captain, though Dolly is having a little trouble settling back down to her lessons after all the excitement of Christmas. It is kind of you to inquire after them. I believe you have come to care for the girls."

He could not deny it. "I must admit, it is a great surprise how much they have come to mean to me in such a short time. They are so different from one another, yet each so dear in her way."

"That is exactly how I feel." Her warm brown eyes shone with a depth of love that Gideon might have envied if he did not share it. "Which is why I would like you to seek guardianship of Cissy and Dolly."

Her suggestion stunned him as badly as if she'd hurled the book at his head.

"Guardianship?" he stammered. "You must be joking!"

His reply ripped the smile from her lips and the glow from her eyes. "I would never joke about the girls' welfare. If you do not become their guardian, their future will be no laughing matter, I assure you. You would make an excellent guardian. It is obvious by the way you treated them at Christmas."

Now that the shock of Miss Murray's proposition was wearing off, Gideon could not deny a traitorous flicker of temptation, which alarmed him. "Nonsense! Playing father for a few days at Christmas hardly qualifies me to take permanent responsibility for the girls. I am simply not cut out for that sort of role."

"I reckon you could be if you wanted to. If you were willing to try." Gone was his congenial companion of the past few weeks. In her place sat the steely creature he'd had the misfortune to encounter when he first arrived at Knightley Park.

"It has nothing to do with wanting or trying." Gideon sprang from his chair and stalked around to stand behind it. This felt like a stronger position from which to repel her challenge. "I have responsibilities to my crew and my country. They are the most important things in the world to me. Besides, it is not as if the girls are without anyone to care for them. They will have you and their aunt. She is a much more suitable person to have charge of two young girls."

"You might not say that if you knew her." Miss Murray surged up from her chair, the better to confront him. "It has been months since the girls' father died, yet there has not been a word from Lady Villiers. Who knows when, or if, she will return?"

"She must have a man of affairs who can get in contact with her," replied Gideon. "I will look into it while I am in London. If you are concerned about the girls having to leave Knightley Park in the meantime, you may put your fears to rest. They are welcome to stay here until their aunt comes to collect them."

If he became the children's guardian, they would never have to leave until they were old enough to marry and have homes of their own. That would mean Marian Murray would stay, too, for many years. If by chance the inquiry went against him, guardianship of the girls would give him an alternative sense of purpose.

No! Duty and conscience protested. He must fight for his reputation and his command with every ounce of determination he possessed. Not just against the Admiralty and the powerful influence of those who had disgraced him, but against the siren song of home and family at Knightley Park.

Miss Murray drew a deep breath and squared her shoulders. It was clear she did not intend to make this easy for him. "It is kind of you not to turn the girls out, Captain, but there is far more to it. Lady Villiers is a woman of very different character from Cissy and Dolly's mother. She values her independence. She likes to travel and keep herself amused. The children need continuity and stability in their lives, especially after the upheaval they have suffered in the past few years. Please believe me when I say you would make a far better guardian for the girls than their aunt."

Marian Murray did not consider him capable of regaining his command. She could not propose such a scheme otherwise. After all he had confided in her, that felt like a betrayal.

"If you had such grave reservations about Lady Villiers, why am I only hearing them now?" he demanded in a tone as chill as the winter air that frosted the library windows.

His question rocked her back, putting her on the defensive. Her gaze shifted, guiltily. "Be-cause, I did not think it would do any good. I assumed there was no alternative to her ladyship. But when I saw how much you have come to care about the children, it gave me hope that you might be willing to intervene on their behalf."

An appalling suspicion took hold of Gideon. "You planned this from the very beginning, didn't you? Coaxing me to spend time with the girls, to become close to them so I could be persuaded to seek guardianship?"

Had their accidental meetings in the library also been in furtherance of her scheme? What about that impulsive embrace? Had she used her charms on a lonely man to lure him into spending time with her and her young pupils? Gideon cursed himself for a fool, being so quick to trust again after being betrayed. Worse yet, he had let the pretty Scottish governess far deeper into his heart and confidence than any of his officers aboard the *Integrity*.

The answer to his accusation was written plain on her pale features. "I... I...not from the very beginning. When you first came here, I didn't think you would make any better guardian for the girls than their aunt. But as I got to know you, it seemed you were the answer to my prayers."

"Your prayers?" Gideon infused the word with all the scorn he felt for his own foolish weakness. How could he have imagined a woman like her might take a fancy to a charmless old sea dog? To think he had fretted about injuring her reputation and her feelings, when her only interest in him had been to further her plans.

"So you believe the Lord and Master of the Universe dances to your tune, Miss Murray? I suppose you think He had a young man killed and my reputation dragged through the mud all for your convenience!" As if it wasn't daft enough of him to believe she might care for him, he had even begun to swallow all her moonshine about the power of prayer and God's personal interest in him.

"I think no such thing!" Her eyes blazed with violent indignation. "I do not believe God makes ill-fortune befall us. What happened on your ship was the doing of men who put their desire to dominate others ahead of anything else. But I *do* believe the Lord can bring good out of evil in answer to our prayers."

There was something dangerously appealing about that notion, but Gideon refused to surrender to it. Marian Murray had never cared for him except as a means to provide the sort of future she deemed best for his young cousins. "I fail to see how even God can answer both your prayers and mine when the things we want are so vastly opposed."

The hostile tension that had gripped Marian Murray seemed to let her go all at once. "I thought you would want to help Cissy and Dolly."

Those plaintive words posed a greater threat to Gideon's resolve than her earlier hostility. "I do, but I fail to see how my seeking guardianship would accomplish that."

"Why?" she challenged him again, but with less vigor, as if she knew it was hopeless. "Because you hold yourself partly to blame for what happened to that young midshipman? Because he was your responsibility and you feel you failed him?"

Hearing his deepest regrets laid bare that way shook Gideon to the core.

"Yes, if you must know." He turned and stalked toward the door. "Now I see nothing to be gained by discussing this matter any further. Your duty is to your pupils. Mine is to my ship and my crew."

"God forgives you," she called after him, her voice shrill with desperation. "Please do not punish the girls because you cannot forgive yourself!"

When he refused to rise to the bait, Miss Murray

hurled one final accusation after him. "I thought you cared about Cissy and Dolly. Clearly you are capable of pretending greater feelings than you possess!"

Pretend *greater* feelings that he possessed? Absurd! When he recalled how it had taxed his self-possession to conceal the extent of his feelings for her, Gideon longed to turn back and set Miss Murray straight. But he knew he did not dare.

Chapter Fourteen

She'd had no right to accuse Gideon Radcliffe of pretending more affection than he felt.

In the week following his departure for London, Marian often recalled their final conversation with regret. It was not *his* fault she had come to care more for him than she had any right to. He had done nothing deliberate to encourage her. The fault was hers for reading more into his kind actions than he'd ever intended.

"I wish Cousin Gideon took us to London with him." The words burst out of Dolly one morning in the middle of their history lesson. "I miss him."

Marian stifled an almost overwhelming urge to agree. Finding she could not keep silent altogether, she offered a tepid reply. "Knightley Park does not seem quite the same without him."

Not the same at all. Indeed, it felt as if he had taken all the air and warmth and light away with him. Since his departure, Marian often caught herself listening for his footsteps or gazing out the window, hoping to glimpse him riding in the distance. More often than ever, she visited the library in the evenings. Not to borrow more books, but because it was there she felt a lingering echo of his presence most strongly.

"Perhaps Aunt Lavinia will take us to London when she comes," suggested Cissy, her nose buried in her book. Though she did not ask about Captain Radcliffe as incessantly as her sister, his going seemed to have left the child more subdued than ever.

The thought of Lady Villiers taking the girls anywhere sent a chill down Marian's back and loaded her with a crushing burden of guilt. God had presented her with an ideal means of delivering Cissy and Dolly from their aunt, but she had destroyed any hope of it. She should have persuaded Gideon gently rather than allowing his resistance to make her angry and spout hurtful words.

How could she blame him for his reluctance to take charge of his young cousins after his last effort to play a fatherly role had ended so disastrously? She'd mouthed glib platitudes about God's forgiveness, but would she ever be able to forgive herself for failing the girls in this most important task?

"I don't want to go with Aunt Lavinia." Dolly wriggled out of her seat and ran over to admire her toy boat. "She wouldn't take us anywhere interesting in London. I want to see all the ships on the River Thames."

With a sigh of impatience and regret, Marian went after the child. "You may play with your boat later. Now come back to the table and we'll have a geography lesson with your dissected puzzle."

"But this is the time for history," Cissy complained. "Besides, we've put that silly old puzzle together so many times we could do it with our eyes closed."

"Well, I like it." Dolly stuck out her tongue at her sister.

Cissy glared back at her.

"Enough," Marian warned them both in a stern tone. "We'll do something different this time. I shall tell you a clue about the country and if you guess its name, I will give you the piece to add to the puzzle."

"That sounds like fun." Dolly skipped back to the table.

Cissy slammed her book shut.

Marian was about to speak sharply to her when she spied a film of unshed tears in the child's eyes. "Here's your first clue. It is a country on the North Sea and its capital city is Copenhagen."

As they proceeded with the game, using the Christmas gift Gideon had bought for Dolly, Marian knew she was right that the girls needed him far more than the Royal Navy did. She also believed they enriched his life beyond the measure of his naval duties. If only she had not allowed her secret feelings for him to interfere with the girls' interests, perhaps she could have made him see that, too.

She managed to get through the day by focusing her attention strictly on the children, trying to make up for how she had failed them. Once they were in bed she slipped down to the library for a half hour where she allowed herself to indulge in missing him, reliving the evenings they'd spent there discussing books and getting to know one another. But she did not choose a new book to read. Having read *Sense and Sensibility* through once, she'd already started on it again. Both the characters of Edward Ferrars and Colonel Brandon reminded her of Gideon. Reading about them made her feel a little closer to him.

As she slipped through the darkened nursery to her bedchamber, the sound of a sniffle stopped her. She held her breath, listening closely. Dolly's breath was coming in deep, slow gusts. Groping her way toward Cissy's bed, Marian perched on the edge.

"Are you feeling ill?" she whispered, reaching to lay her palm on the child's forehead. "Or did you have a bad dream?"

Cissy's face was a bit warm but not feverish. In answer to Marian's question, she shook her head.

"What's the matter, then?" Marian's hand trailed down to wipe a tear from the child's cheek. "Is it because of the captain going away? You don't talk about him all the time as Dolly does, but I believe you still miss him."

Cissy gulped for air as her small frame trembled with sobs. "It's m-my fault...he went away. Dolly said so. Be-because I wasn't...nice to him."

"Shh!" Marian gathered the child into her arms. "That isn't true at all. The captain had important business in London. I'm certain he misses you and Dolly as much as you miss him."

"Will he come ba-back?" The child's weeping quieted a little. "When he's taken care of that bus-business?"

Marian wished she could reassure Cissy that Gideon would return to Knightley Park. But she could not lie to the child. That would only make matters worse in the long run. "I'm not certain. We will have to hope and pray that he does. But if by chance he is not able to return soon, you must not think it is because of you."

If anyone was to blame, Marian knew it was her.

She sat with Cissy and rubbed her head until the child finally fell asleep. All the while, a silent prayer ran through her mind. *"Please, Heavenly Father, let Gideon Radcliffe have a change of heart. Bring him back to Knightley Park to seek guardianship of the girls. They need him and he needs them. Please, please make him see that."*

Could Marian Murray seriously believe he would make a good guardian for Cissy and Dolly? That question and many others plagued Gideon on his long, cold journey to London. He knew he should be planning his defense for the upcoming inquiry, but somehow the future of those two dear girls seemed at least as important as his future in the Royal Navy.

As vigorously as he'd tried to deny the things Miss Murray had said, some of them rang uncomfortably true. He *did* feel responsible for Harry Watson's death, almost as much as if he'd committed the vile deed with his own hands. He hadn't protected the boy as he should. He'd placed too much trust in the wrong people and in his own authority. A distant, disinterested God might be able to forgive him, but his own conscience was a harsher tribunal.

As for showing more affection than he felt, that was patently absurd. Over the past weeks, he had fought against his reticent nature to demonstrate even a little of the feelings in his heart. He had not even admitted to himself how much the children…and their governess… had come to mean to him. Only when he reached London, with a hundred and twenty miles of frozen countryside between them, did he truly plumb the depths of his feelings.

An aching emptiness gnawed at him as if he had not eaten in days. Except that the void afflicted his chest rather than his stomach. The only remedy he could find was to reflect upon his memories of the time he'd spent with them—the evening at the pantomime, the concert they'd performed for him on Twelfth Night, even their Sunday morning attendance at church. Savoring such sweet memories helped fill the void, yet it made the ache of longing more acute.

As the days passed, he strove to distract himself by consulting with his counsel, reviewing his testimony for the inquiry, making contact with any retired naval officers who might testify to his character. Such activities helped to occupy his thoughts; but whenever his concentration lapsed, he found himself wondering if there had been more snow in Nottinghamshire. Had Dolly caught the cold? Had Marian read all the new books he'd purchased for the library?

With each day that passed, he grew sorrier for having reacted so angrily to her well-intended suggestion that he become the girls' guardian. He still felt like a fool that he'd misinterpreted her efforts to bring that about. But he no longer suspected she had deliberately sought to engage his affections to further her cause.

He knew he should be flattered that she considered him worthy to have charge of the children she loved so dearly. He wondered why she was so set against Lady Villiers having the girls. The reasons she'd given him hardly sounded sufficient. Could it be that, having assumed a motherly role in the children's lives, she could not bear to step aside for another woman?

Gideon could understand such feelings. How would he take it, if Lady Villiers remarried and her new husband became a father figure to Cissy and Dolly? Though that man was nothing more than a shadowy abstraction who might not ever exist, he still roused Gideon's suspicion and hostility. How much more might the very real Lady Villiers loom as a threat to Marian Murray, who had no claim upon her young pupils except love?

At last the board of inquiry convened, and Gideon duly presented himself at the Admiralty to give evidence. As he entered the imposing Board Room, his gaze was drawn to an elaborate bay at the far end of the chamber. He could not help wondering what Dolly would think of the immense globe it held. No doubt Marian would be more interested in the tall, narrow bookcases that flanked the bay. Would Cissy ask why the big clock above it had only one hand rather than two? When he revealed that it was not a clock but a wind dial, Dolly would surely demand to know all about the workings of such an instrument.

One of the members of the inquiry board cleared his throat, reminding Gideon of his purpose there. "Now, Captain Radcliffe, if you would please give us an account of the events aboard HMS *Integrity* that led to your being suspended from command."

"Certainly." Gideon inhaled a deep breath and began to speak. To his relief, his earlier thoughts of Marian and the girls gave him confidence. He knew they had faith in him and would never believe the false accusations against him. "It began when the late Mister Watson was assigned to my crew as a midshipman...."

The officers and gentleman of the board listened gravely, a few nodding in agreement with some point he made. But others scowled as he spoke, their brows raised in dubious expressions. Gideon recalled how Marian had offered to pray that justice would be done in his case.

It appeared he would need all the prayers he could get.

Over a month had passed since Gideon Radcliffe left Knightley Park. Dolly no longer asked about him quite so often. Cissy never mentioned him at all. If Marian hadn't known better, she might have thought his visit was only a pleasant dream. Yet she found it hard to let go of that dream and the dwindling hope that Gideon might return before Lady Villiers arrived to collect the girls.

The clock in the library struck ten, jarring Marian from her concentration upon the newspaper. Every day she could get a copy of the paper, she brought it here to scan the pages, searching for any mention of Gideon's inquiry. Again today, she'd found nothing.

Folding up the newspaper with a sigh, Marian wished she had asked Gideon to write her with his news. Not that he would have been disposed to agree after the way they'd quarreled. But he might have sent a note to the girls at least.

Perhaps she had been right to claim that he pretended to care for Cissy and Dolly more than he truly did. At the time, however, she'd been thinking more about his feelings for her.

Was it futile for her to keep searching the newspapers? For all she knew, the inquiry might have concluded days ago. If the press failed to report the fact, it could only be because Captain Radcliffe had been exonerated of all wrongdoing. Having been avid to publish every vile rumor against him, they would surely be embarrassed to be proven wrong.

Pausing behind the chair in which Gideon had sat so many evenings, Marian ran her hand over the upholstery where his head had once rested. If the men on that board of inquiry had any sense at all, they would have known at once that Captain Radcliffe was incapable of dishonorable conduct. As soon as they heard his testimony, they had likely found him *innocent* and dispatched him back to his ship. If he ever returned to Knightley Park in the future, she and the girls would be long gone.

Marian wrenched her hand away from the chair and marched out of the room. She must stop coming here so often to scrutinize the newspapers. Above all, she must stop pestering God with her incessant prayers to fetch Gideon back to Knightley Park. Either He was ignoring her prayers or He had given her an answer and that answer was no. All she could do now was ask for the strength to bear His will and pray that Lady Villiers would not separate her from the girls.

When she heard the front door open and shut, Marian thought it must be Mr. Culpepper checking that the house was well secured for the night. After an uncertain beginning, he and Captain Radcliffe had reached a point of mutual respect. With the captain gone, Mr. Culpepper seemed to have found fresh purpose in keeping Knightley Park running smoothly for his absent master.

The sound of footsteps behind her made Marian pause on the staircase and turn to bid the butler goodnight. So sure was her expectation of seeing Mr. Culpepper that for a moment she scarcely recognized the tall, tired-looking man standing there in his greatcoat.

When recognition finally dawned, it took her breath away. The newspaper she'd been holding fluttered to the floor as her hand flew to her chest.

"Gid—er... Captain, you're home!" Elation bubbled up within her until it felt as if she floated toward him. "Thank heaven you're back. I prayed you would change your mind!"

Somehow she managed to keep from throwing her arms around him. But she could not prevent her gaze from sinking deep into his. The shadow of anguish in his eyes shattered her fragile delight.

"What's wrong?" More than ever she yearned to take him in her arms. But that would only cause more trouble. "Are you ill?"

Gideon shook his head wearily and nodded toward the library door. "Only sick at heart."

Those words tore at her as if she had inflicted this suffering upon him. Had she? She'd prayed so fervently for his return, had she bullied God into granting her request, no matter what it cost Gideon?

"Did the board of inquiry hold you to blame for what happened on your ship?" Taking his arm, she led him into the library where they could talk without fear of interruption. "Then they must be a pack of fools!"

"They haven't...yet." Gideon followed her with ponderous steps. "But they will. I have no doubt. It will make no difference who else testifies or what other evidence is presented. Three members of the panel are related to the ones truly responsible. They will not want the taint of any wrongdoing to besmirch their family names."

"Are you certain?" She helped him out of his greatcoat and laid it over a nearby chair. "Perhaps it is not as bad as you think. If the board has not announced its findings yet, there may still be hope."

When she turned back toward him, she found that Gideon had sunk onto the chair he usually occupied— the one she had caressed only a few minutes ago, longing for his return. It went against his courteous nature to sit while she stood. That told Marian more about his state of despair than any words could.

Fearing he might try to rise, she knelt beside his chair. If only there was something she could do to relieve the sense of defeat she glimpsed in his eyes and in the bowing of his broad shoulders.

"I have seldom been more certain of anything in my life." He heaved an arid sigh. "My naval career is over, my reputation blackened beyond any hope of rehabilitation. I could tell by the tone of their questions, by the way they looked at me and each other. I am to be made a scapegoat for this whole unfortunate affair because I have no influence with those in power."

It was difficult to imagine a man of his integrity and strength being bullied, but that was how it sounded. The notion roused Marian's indignation. "If that's the way the Royal Navy is run, then perhaps you're better out of it."

His hands rested on the arms of the chair. Forgetting propriety, she covered one with hers, aching to offer him whatever comfort she could. "The people around here know what kind of man you really are. They won't take any notice of what some corrupt politicians in London have to say. Instead of being in command of a single ship, you'll have a whole estate. Just think what you can make of it. Perhaps this will turn out to be all the best for you."

If she'd hoped he might take consolation from her words, she was badly mistaken.

"It does not signify what is best for *me!*" He wrenched his hand out from beneath hers. "What about poor Watson? How is he to rest in peace when those responsible for his death are not brought to justice? What about the men and boys of my crew, serving under that ambitious villain and his pack of scoundrels? My return to command was their only hope of rescue!"

Conditions aboard that ship would be worse than the school of her youth with the strict, embittered teachers, the corrupt matron and the *great girls* who used their size and seniority to claim more than their share of what little food and warmth there was to be had. Only the solidarity of her circle of friends and the intervention of a kind headmistress had made existence bearable. What if someone had taken Miss Chapel away, for her own good and the benefit of a few others?

"I failed them." Gideon hunched forward, burying his face in his hands. "First Harry Watson and now my whole crew."

Marian could almost feel the waves of misery rolling off him. This was not his fault. It was hers for misusing the power of prayer. Who was she to decide what was best for everyone? Had she used Cissy and Dolly's welfare as an excuse to keep Gideon around where she could pretend they were a happy family?

"You did not fail anyone." Instinctively she strove to comfort him as she would one of the children, wrapping her arms around him, drawing his head to rest against her shoulder, stroking his hair. "You tried your best to do what was right and protect those who needed it. I didn't understand. I am so sorry. I promised to pray you would get justice but…"

The whisper of his hair against her cheek and the lure of his fresh, briny scent overwhelmed her, making her forget what she meant to say. She turned her face toward his, grazing his cheek with her lips.

At the same instant, he tilted his head toward her. Their lips met.

At first, Marian could only think of her need to comfort him and to atone for what she'd done. Her lips moved against his, softly and slowly, offering a respite from his bitter regrets and feelings of failure. At the same time, her kiss implored his forgiveness. Though she had believed she cared for him, she had still been willing to disregard his needs and wishes to get what she wanted.

She cherished a flicker of satisfaction when Gideon stirred from his breathless stillness and began to return her kiss. His firm, daunting mouth relaxed, and his lips brushed against hers in a tender rhythm, accepting her consolation and granting forgiveness.

He brought his hands up to cradle her face. With a blissful sigh, Marian sank into the welcome warmth of their kiss. Her original motives of comfort and atonement melted away, exposing more vulnerable feelings beneath. She cared for Gideon Radcliffe in a way she had never expected to feel for any man, a way she'd never dared hope could be returned. She wanted nothing from him but the opportunity to share his company and provide him with whatever support and companionship he was willing to accept from her. As their kiss intensified, she opened her heart, laying it bare for him to claim.

A sudden, insistent rap on the library door made them spring apart with sharp gasps. Like a barrage of cannon fire, that sound heralded an invasion of the small, defenseless island of intimacy they'd created. The world crashed in on them with all its roles and expectations. Suddenly they were no longer simply two people sharing a tender moment. She was a hired servant who had no business embracing the master of the house.

"I'm sorry, Captain!" She pulled away and surged to her feet. "I did not mean to presume. I was only trying to make you feel better."

Her desperate apology collided with his. "Forgive me, Miss Murray. I should never have taken advantage of your kind gesture!"

Adding to the confusion, the butler called in, "Are you there, Captain? Is there anything you require, sir?"

Unable to bear the raw, inflamed feelings their kiss had provoked, Marian flew to the door and flung it open. "The captain is here, Mr. Culpepper. He seemed quite exhausted when he arrived, so I helped him in. Now I must leave him to your capable ministrations and get back to the nursery."

She scarcely recognized her own voice, so shrill and breathless. The Scottish accent for which she'd often been ridiculed at school sounded more pronounced than ever.

"Thank you for your assistance, Miss Murray." Gideon Radcliffe's voice rang out behind her. Cold and sharp as the icicles hanging from the eaves of the house, each word pierced her.

It was clear he wanted to pretend their kiss had never taken place. No doubt he wished it hadn't. She had hurled herself upon him in a moment of weakness, tempting him to forget himself.

"Think nothing of it, Captain." She sought to assure him that she would not divulge their secret embrace. "I hope you are soon recovered from your journey. Good night."

With that, she slipped past the bewildered butler and fled.

How could he have exploited Marian Murray's kind attempt to console him?

For the next few days, as she made a determined effort to avoid him, Gideon rebuked himself repeatedly. It was clear he had upset her, perhaps frightened her with his show of unwelcome ardor. Was she also afraid that being discovered alone with him in the library might damage her reputation?

He longed to reassure her that he would do the honorable thing and make her an offer of marriage...if that was what she wanted. Under the circumstances, that course of action appealed to him intensely. Now that it appeared certain he would not be returning to command, the prospect of settling down at Knightley Park and taking a wife offered him a renewed sense of purpose.

As Marian had tried to tell him, it seemed the Lord might have provided an opportunity for something good to come out of the ruin of his naval career. He still regretted the circumstances in which he'd left his crew. But perhaps if he prayed upon the matter, he might receive some divine guidance on how to assist his men. In the meantime, it was quite possible his cousin's young daughters did need him more than the crew of the *Integrity*. Perhaps almost as much as he needed them.

He longed to see the girls again, yet he shrank from imposing his company upon their governess when it seemed clear she did not want it. Would she look upon a marriage proposal from him in the same light? Might she feel pressured to wed a man she did not love because he had damaged her reputation and because he might be willing to seek guardianship of the children she adored?

He would rather continue on as they had been than have her feel trapped in a marriage and gradually grow to resent him. He had failed too many people he cared about. He could not bear to fail her, too.

But what action should he take? During his naval career, Gideon had been accustomed to making swift, definite decisions, often under considerable pressure, with lives at stake. Whatever the outcome, he had been able to learn from it, live with it and move forward. Young Watson's death and the inquiry had changed that, making him second-guess his actions and bitterly regret his mistakes.

Staring out the great bow window of the Chinese drawing room, he contemplated the pristine beauty of the frozen lake and snow dusted trees. One day soon, the ice and snow would melt and new life would quicken according to an ageless plan. Perhaps the time had come to stop relying solely on his own all-too-fallible strength and judgment and instead seek divine guidance.

"Heavenly Father," he whispered, possessed by an unaccountable conviction that he was being heard. "Please help me do what is right for Marian and the children."

What would happen now, he wondered. Would the

Lord provide some sort of sign? Or would he suddenly know beyond doubt what he should do? Neither of those things happened. He was still as confused as ever about whether he ought to propose to Marian Murray. Both choices before him seemed likely to end in the one way he could not bear—with her hating him.

Had his prayer gone unanswered because he had not used the proper form? Must he kneel and bow his head as if he were in church?

Church. He had been so lost in regrets and indecision that he had scarcely noticed what day of the week it was. Now he realized tomorrow would be Sunday. Was that a random thought of his own or a divine nudge in the right direction? He might never know for certain, but Gideon chose to believe the latter.

The next morning he lingered in the entry hall, waiting for the girls and their governess to appear. He had not been there long when he heard the approach of footsteps and the chatter of familiar voices. A moment later, they descended the stairs.

"Cousin Gideon!" Dolly leapt down the last three steps and charged toward him. "Martha told us you'd come back. We begged and begged to see you, but Miss Marian said you were very tired from your journey and needed to rest."

Her rapturous welcome buoyed his spirits. Leaning forward, Gideon caught the child in his arms and lifted her into a fond embrace. Dolly returned it so vigorously, she nearly throttled him.

"That was very considerate of her." Gideon set the child back on her feet and turned his attention to her sister. Cissy might not express her emotions as emphatically as Dolly, but that did not mean she felt them any less. "But I am quite well rested now and looking forward to escorting my favorite ladies to church."

He cast a fleeting glance toward Marian, hoping she would understand that he included her among his "favorite ladies." Then he knelt in front of Cissy, who stared at him with unsettling intensity. "I didn't think you would come back," she whispered. "But you did."

When Gideon opened his arms, she surprised him by hurling herself into his embrace. Her parents had gone to a place from which they could never return. He understood how important it was to her that he had come back. He pressed a kiss to the crown of her head.

Until he'd seen and held them again, Gideon did not fully fathom how much he'd missed them and how deeply he had come to love them. He glanced up at Marian. Silently, he tried to tell her she had been right all along. He did need the girls, and it seemed they needed him. Perhaps when he told her he intended to seek guardianship, she might look more favorably upon him as a suitor.

As Dolly chattered away on the drive to church and Cissy gazed at him, her eyes shining with newfound trust, Gideon felt the awkwardness between him and Marian beginning to ease. It seemed she was willing to forgive and forget the inexcusable liberty he had taken, perhaps on the grounds of his distress over the inquiry. While he welcomed her forgiveness, he knew he would never be able to forget that wondrous moment of communion between them.

When they arrived at the church, the other parishioners offered Gideon a cordial welcome home. Perhaps

Marian had been right to reassure him that the local people would not hold the inquiry's decision against him.

During his sailing days, Gideon had often been moved by the distant majesty of the Almighty and the grandeur of His Creation. On a clear night in the middle of the ocean, he had gazed up into the limitless firmament crowded with blazing stars. He had watched the sun rise in all its rosy splendor, on the vast eastern horizon of the Pacific. But never in his life, before that morning, had he felt the presence of God so warmly wrapped around him.

By the time they returned home after the service, his mind was bubbling with plans for Knightley Park, for the girls—and perhaps with God's help—for him and Marian.

Mr. Culpepper met them in the entry hall when they arrived home. Before Gideon could get the door closed, the butler announced. "A guest has arrived while you were at church, Captain. The late Mrs. Radcliffe's sister, Lady Villiers."

Chapter Fifteen

Mr. Culpepper's announcement struck Marian like a bolt of lightning. For months she had dreaded this moment, worked and planned to avoid its consequences. Now just when she had hope God might answer her desperate prayers, it had come. Worse yet, the girls seemed to welcome it—Cissy certainly did.

"Aunt Lavinia!" The child seized her sister by the hand and pulled Dolly off in search of their aunt.

And Gideon...what about him? He cast a furtive glance at Marian, then followed the girls.

Breathing a quick prayer for strength, she hurried after him.

"Aunt Lavinia!" she heard Cissy's voice from the Chinese drawing room, more animated than in a very long time. "It's so good to see you. We were afraid you might never come."

When Marian and Gideon entered the drawing room, they found the girls being petted and embraced by their aunt. "Oh, my dearest darlings, how good it is to see you both again! I was quite prostrate with grief when I received the sad news about your poor, dear papa. I started for home just as soon as I was fit to travel, but I was in Naples, which is an excessively long way. And travel in the winter is such an ordeal. There were times I feared I might succumb to the elements!"

Her ladyship did not appear any the worse for her recent ordeal. At least not to Marian, who stood back quietly observing the scene. Lady Villiers's arrival had thrust her back into the role of servant after months of feeling like something more.

The girls' aunt was dressed and coiffed in the height of fashion. The rich peacock blue of her traveling gown set off her fine eyes and raven hair to perfection. She re-sembled her late sister in beauty, if little else, with fine features, luxurious eyelashes and a pert little mouth.

In contrast to such an elegant creature, Marian felt plainer and dowdier than ever. But that was nothing to the way her heart plunged when Lady Villiers paused in her gushing attentions to the girls and glanced up at Gideon. Her eyes fairly blazed with predatory interest, and her lips curved into a beguiling smile.

She rose gracefully and targeted Gideon with the full barrage of her considerable charm. "Bless me! Here I have been rattling on, so delighted to see you both again, that I am all sixes and sevens. Pray, my darlings, introduce me to this handsome gentleman."

"What handsome gentleman?" Dolly's nose wrinkled in a puzzled frown.

"She means Cousin Gideon, of course." Cissy shot the younger girl a glare of disdain. "Aunt Lavinia, this is Papa's cousin, Captain Radcliffe. He is the new mas-ter of Knightley Park. Cousin Gideon, this is Mama's sister, Lady Villiers."

The child delivered the introduction with impeccable

decorum, just the way her governess had taught her. But Marian could take no pride in the accomplishment of her young pupil at the moment. Instead, she stood transfixed as Lady Villiers swept Gideon a flirtatious curtsy.

"It is a pleasure to make your acquaintance at last, Captain Radcliffe. To think you are dear Daniel's cousin and I am Emma's sister. That almost makes us family... though not *too* closely connected."

Not too closely connected for what? Marian's lips drew into a tight, disapproving line. Though they had met once before, the girls' aunt did not even flick a glance in her direction. It was as if she had been rendered invisible.

Lady Villiers extended her hand toward Gideon. It was too high and in quite the wrong position to shake. Clearly she expected a more gallant greeting.

"Welcome to Knightley Park, your ladyship." The warmth of Gideon's greeting was tempered with a certain endearing awkwardness. He bowed low over Lady Villiers's hand but did not raise it to his lips. "I understand you have been traveling on the Continent. I trust you enjoyed your tour."

"Immensely!" Her ladyship sank onto the settee and pulled Cissy and Dolly up on either side of her, an arm draped around each child. "Seeing all the sights for myself at last was such an adventure."

"Cousin Gideon has had lots of adventures," Dolly boasted. "He has circum...circum...he's sailed around the world."

"Has he, indeed?" Her ladyship lavished the captain with an admiring smile. "How very fortunate I am to make the acquaintance of a bold adventurer! You must tell me about all the exotic places you have visited, Captain."

"Perhaps we can exchange accounts of our travels." Gideon started to take a seat, then recalled Marian's presence. "Come join us, Miss Murray."

Marian would rather have fled to the nursery to sort out her confused feelings and consider the consequences of Lady Villiers's arrival, but she was not at liberty to come and go as she pleased. She was hired to do her employers' bidding, and the master of Knightley Park had asked her to be seated.

At last Lady Villiers deigned to notice Marian, flicking a dismissive glance in her direction. "Oh, yes, the governess."

Edging around the perimeter of the room, Marian perched on the window seat. It was close enough to the others to satisfy the captain's invitation to join them while still being in keeping with her peripheral place in the household.

Once Marian had taken a seat, the captain sank onto his chair. "Miss Murray has been much more to your nieces than a governess in the past months. She has been mother, father, teacher and advocate. The girls were very fortunate to be in her care during this difficult time."

If Marian had needed anything to make her care for him more, his gallant tribute would have accomplished that. But she already cared for him far too much. The cruel stab of jealousy she felt watching Lady Villiers flirt with him warned Marian she must quash those dangerous feelings or risk worse misery than she had known since her school days.

"How commendable." Her ladyship sounded surprised that Marian could be capable of such conduct. "Emma and I had such horrible governesses when we were girls. I pleaded with Father to send us to school where we might have the advantage of many different teachers."

School. Marian barely stifled a whimper. Her worst fears about Lady Villiers had been right. The moment she took the girls from Knightley Park, their aunt would seek to place them in a school, all the while assuring herself it was in their best interests. And there was nothing Marian could do to prevent her. Any effort she made would seem like a selfish attempt to keep from losing her position.

"Did you enjoy your time at school, Captain?" Her ladyship seemed eager to turn the conversation back to him. "Which one did you attend, pray? You have the distinguished look of an Eton man to me."

"I received my education in the Royal Navy," Gideon replied. "If I'd had a choice, I would have preferred to remain at home with a governess or tutor."

Lady Villiers gave a trill of high-pitched laughter that pierced Marian like shards of glass under her skin. "I suppose we all hanker for whatever we have not had. Your naval training seems to have made a fine man of you."

Marian could not dispute that, though she resented Lady Villiers for being free to flatter him so blatantly when she had been obliged to guard every word.

Gideon did not acknowledge her ladyship's praise. "Surely you must admit your nieces do credit to Miss Murray's tutelage."

"They are perfectly adorable!" Her ladyship hugged Cissy and Dolly close, attention the girls appeared to welcome. "So like their dear mama. I am certain they would flourish under any circumstances. But come, Captain, you promised me stories of your travels."

Gideon obliged her with an account of his visit to New Zealand, a story he had shared with Marian and the girls some weeks before. To Marian's admittedly biased ears, he did not sound as relaxed and animated as he had then. Dolly interrupted him often in an effort to enliven the tale.

Marian itched to remind the child to mind her manners, but bit her tongue for fear it would only rouse the veiled antagonism she sensed from Lady Villiers. The last thing Cissy and Dolly needed was for their aunt to have any excuse to dismiss her. She would speak to Dolly later in the privacy of the nursery.

As the afternoon progressed, Marian sat watching from the fringes while Lady Villiers usurped the place she had so recently enjoyed in their little family. Her thoughts turned to Gideon's inquiry and his misery at the prospect of losing his command and reputation. She could not help feeling that her prayers might have contributed to the situation. At the very least, she had failed to keep her original promise to pray that he would get justice.

She must find some way to make things right for him. But how? If a man like him felt bullied, without influence or power, how could someone in her humble circumstances be of any assistance? She could appeal to God again, but would He pay any heed after she had changed her mind so often about what she wanted? It would be tantamount to taking the favor He'd granted her and throwing it back in His face. Gideon had been right—the Creator of the Universe was not a tailor to be bidden to make minute alterations to the garment of life.

It was up to her to help Gideon receive the justice he'd been denied. She could think of only one person who might possess the power to intervene on Gideon's behalf. Perhaps it would do no good, but she must try or she could never truly claim to care for him.

Lady Villiers did not appear to be in any hurry to leave Knightley Park. As the days began to lengthen and winter loosened its grip on the countryside, Gideon could not decide whether to be irritated or relieved. The latter, surely, for as long as her ladyship remained under his roof, Cissy and Dolly did, too. And so did Marian Murray.

Not that relations between him and the girls' governess had recovered since their kiss. It seemed to have transformed her back into the quiet, dour woman he recalled from the earliest days of their acquaintance. To see her now, no one would suspect Miss Murray was capable of chasing about with the children, laughing uproariously at a pantomime, or singing wistful Scottish love songs. No one would believe she could be such a sympathetic listener, such a dispenser of wise, compassionate advice. But he knew all those things and more. They made him yearn to have *that* woman back again.

He'd hoped by keeping his distance and treating her with temperate civility, he might coax her out again. But so far it had not worked. Miss Murray took every opportunity to remind him that she was an employee and not a member of the family, as she had once seemed. Was she trying to remind him that he had taken advantage of her position in his household to impose his unwanted attentions upon her? She need not have bothered, for he was well aware of how he had destroyed the fragile trust between them.

Much as he wished he could ask how to get it back, he feared any such overture would only make matters worse. Besides, when would he have an opportunity to broach the subject? She never visited the library in the evenings anymore. At least not during those rare occasions when he could escape Lady Villiers's company to seek refuge there, as he had this evening.

Or perhaps he had not escaped after all.

Without even the most cursory excuse for a knock, the library door opened—first a crack, then flung wide.

"There you are!" Lady Villiers invaded his sanctuary. "I declare, one would think we were playing hide-and-seek. Do you know, this is one room of the house where I've never been before."

She glanced around at the tall shelves of books, and her nose wrinkled in distaste. "Now I can see why. It is dreadfully gloomy. How do you abide it? And what is that odor?"

Stifling a sigh, Gideon rose from his chair. "I presume you mean the aroma of old books. It is more pleasant to me than any perfume."

Her ladyship gave an indulgent chuckle. "My dear Captain, you are delightfully droll! You need someone in your life to draw you out—someone to take care of you."

Gideon could not dispute that. He did need such a person, but he already had her in his life. Not only had Marian Murray drawn him out and taken care of him, she'd slipped into his private sanctum and enriched it with her presence. She had also helped him draw close to the girls…and closer to God. Was it selfish of him to want more than that from her?

Yet the way Lady Villiers spoke of it made him uneasy. Since coming to Knightley Park, she had gone out of her way to be attentive and agreeable, but Gideon had not warmed to her. Though she had not mentioned any desire to take the girls away, it seemed to hang in the air like an unspoken threat. Perhaps the time had come to stop this game of cat and mouse and bring the subject out in the open to find out where they stood.

"That is very perceptive of you, Lady Villiers." He motioned her to take a seat. "I have come to realize I also need someone of whom I can take care. During my time at sea, I did my best to look after my crew. Since coming to Knightley Park, I have taken great satisfaction in helping to care for your nieces."

"And a splendid job you have made of it, dear Captain." Her ladyship perched on the edge of her seat, leaning toward him. "The girls both seem so well and happy, considering what they have been through, losing their papa. I believe they have found a most admirable substitute for their father in you."

Her words touched Gideon. Perhaps he had misjudged the lady. "That is most kind of you to say. I have become fonder of the girls than I ever expected. Their welfare and happiness have become among my chief concerns."

Lady Villiers nodded. "As they have long been of mine, ever since Daniel and Emma asked Huntley and me to be the girls' godparents. To think I am the only one of the four left to take charge of those dear children."

She heaved a poignant sigh. "It comforts me to discover I am not entirely alone in my affection for them."

"You are not." Gideon assured her. "The girls also have me and Miss Murray."

"Their governess?" Her ladyship's handsome features twisted into a most unattractive sneer. "I will concede she is a considerable improvement over the gargoyles who made my girlhood so miserable, but it is her job to care for the children. That scarcely compares to your admirable concern, which is motivated solely by kindness and family feeling."

Gideon supposed he must make allowances for her ladyship's coolness toward Marian Murray, given her past experience, yet it never failed to grate on him. He must give Lady Villiers credit for beginning to acknowledge Marian's worth. In time, he had faith Marian would win her over entirely.

"My concern for the girls leads me to believe it would not be in their best interests to remove them from Knightley Park." There, he had said it. Now, before her ladyship could object, he rushed on to bolster his argument. "They have been deprived of both their parents at a young age. They need the stability and continuity of the only home they have ever known."

Gideon realized he was repeating the plea Marian had made to him when he first came to Knightley Park. He was grateful he had heeded it. Now, if only Lady Villiers would.

His heart leapt when she met his suggestion with a brilliant smile. "I declare, Captain, you and I are of one mind! After seeing their situation for myself, I had come to the very same conclusion. Only I did not know quite how to raise the matter."

A powerful wave of relief swept Gideon out of his chair to kneel before the lady, seize her hand and press it to his lips. "My dear Lady Villiers, words can scarcely convey my gratitude to you. I vow I will do everything within my power to see that your nieces are given the best possible upbringing. Of course, you will always be welcome to visit the girls at Knightley Park whenever you wish."

"Visit?" Her ladyship laughed in a way that made Gideon think of a chandelier tinkling as it crashed to the floor. "Oh, Captain, you are jesting again, aren't you?"

Her fingers gripped his with astonishing power for such a dainty creature. "Not only do the girls need to remain in familiar surroundings, they also need a new mother and father to replace those they lost. Since you are in possession of Knightley Park and I am the girls' godmother, is it not obvious we should marry and raise them together?"

Her ladyship's proposition struck Gideon dumb. Perhaps it should have been obvious what direction she'd been going all along. With his thoughts fixed on Marian and his worry that the girls might be taken from him, he had been blind to where it all might lead. He had taken no evasive action whatsoever. Instead he had sailed into an ambush.

"It is the perfect solution, don't you agree?" Lady Villiers took advantage of his stunned silence to rattle on. "We both adore the girls and it can be no secret what a great fancy I have taken to you. In spite of your diffidence, I believe you are not indifferent to me. Ours will be a match made in heaven!"

With that, the lady abruptly released his hands to seize him around the neck and pull his face toward hers, as her lips puckered for a kiss.

* * *

A match made in heaven? Hardly!

As Lady Villiers's declaration drifted through the half open library door, Marian stood frozen, staring into the room at Gideon on his knees in front of her ladyship. As she watched, they sealed their betrothal with a kiss. Her gorge rose and her heart plummeted.

Ever since Lady Villiers's arrival, Marian had been torn over whether to speak or keep silent. Now it was too late.

Concern for Cissy and Dolly had urged her to tell Gideon all the reasons her ladyship would not be a suitable guardian for the girls. Her lavish style of living and the debts that went with it. Her constant travel in search of a rich husband. Her unsavory set of friends known for gambling and loose living. Marian had overheard Mr. Radcliffe complain of those things when his sister-in-law had written to him for money. She'd been reluctant to reveal what she knew for fear Lady Villiers would learn of it and immediately remove the girls from her care.

At first, her ladyship's flirtatious manner toward Gideon had roused Marian's jealousy, yet she had assumed it was how the woman behaved around every new man she encountered. But as the days passed, Marian began to suspect Lady Villiers had set her cap for Gideon. But how could she put him on guard without appearing like a spiteful woman scorned, which perhaps she was.

Not that Gideon had scorned her, exactly. He was far too kind a gentleman for that. But the way he'd reacted to their kiss made it clear he regretted succumbing to an unfortunate impulse with a woman in her position.

He was too honorable to lay the blame on her, where it belonged. Instead, he chose to pretend it had never happened. Though her reasonable, cautious side agreed that might be for the best, another part of her wished he had acknowledged her feelings and gently explained why he could not return them.

Seeing him in an embrace with another woman set a cruel black beast to maul her heart.

Marian clapped a hand over her mouth to stifle a whimper of pain that might draw attention to her presence. Then she turned and fled back to the nursery. Her battered, aching heart wanted nothing more than for her to pack a bag and slip away from this house, never to return. Practicality and duty forbade it. She could not afford to leave without another position in place, and for that she would need a satisfactory reference from someone at Knightley Park. Besides, she asked herself as she slipped into the dark, quiet nursery, how could she think of leaving Cissy and Dolly after all the losses they'd experienced in their young lives?

As she changed into her nightclothes, Marian began to tremble, though not from the cold, to which she was accustomed. Once she was swathed in her nightgown and wrapper with a nightcap over her braided hair, she knelt by her bed, seeking comfort and strength in prayer.

"Heavenly Father, please…" What should she ask— that God intervene to prevent Gideon from marrying Lady Villiers? But what might the consequences be? What if her ladyship became so vexed, she took the girls away at once? "I want what is best for all of us, the girls especially. But I cannot be certain what that is. Only You can."

She'd convinced herself that Gideon's coming to Knightley Park might be part of God's plan. What if Lady Villiers had a role to play in that plan, too? Was it possible she had misjudged the woman, just as she'd initially misjudged Gideon Radcliffe? Perhaps being married to such a good man and serving as a mother to the girls might make her ladyship a better person, give purpose and meaning to her shallow, aimless life.

"I see now that I haven't always trusted You as I should, Father. There have been so many times when I thought You weren't responding to my prayers because You didn't give me exactly what I wanted. Please forgive me for that. I didn't understand."

She should have, though. Perhaps not when she was a child, but lately when she'd been responsible for the care of the Radcliffe girls. Much as she loved Dolly, she would never give the child everything she asked for. The result would be indigestion, ill-humor from being up too late, perhaps broken bones from sliding down the banisters. Nor could she always indulge Dolly at Cissy's expense—that would not be fair. A headstrong, young child like Dolly had no way of knowing what was best for her.

Compared to the eternal wisdom of the Lord, Marian realized she must seem even less than a child. How could she expect a loving God to give her everything she prayed for when those things might not be best for her and others? Once she acknowledged that, there was only one prayer she could lift to Heaven.

"Father, thank You for all the blessings You have given me. Wonderful friends and a good education to enable me to earn a living. A comfortable life at Knightley Park with a family who always treated me well."

And Gideon. She must not forget him. Even though they could not be as close as she would like, his presence in her life was a blessing she would always cherish.

It wasn't easy for her to surrender control after all those years at school fighting for what she and her friends needed to survive. Yet Marian sensed she must learn to trust in God's love and care for everyone involved...even her ladyship.

"Thank You, Lord, for bringing Gideon into my life. Even if nothing can ever come of my feelings for him, our acquaintance has enriched my life beyond measure. As for what will happen between him and Lady Villiers, I leave that in Your hands. All I ask is that You grant me the patience and strength to play my part. Amen."

With that she crawled into bed and tried to sleep. She would need her rest to face what tomorrow might bring.

Chapter Sixteen

"You wanted to see me, Captain?" When Marian Murray entered the dining room the following evening, her brow furrowed and her gaze moved restlessly.

Was she alarmed to find him alone there, without Lady Villiers or even any of the servants?

"I did." Gideon rose and gestured toward a chair he had pulled up near his end of the table. "Thank you for joining me, Miss Murray. I have a rather important decision to make, and there is no one whose counsel I value more than yours."

"Thank you, sir." She caught her lower lip between her teeth as she moved toward the table. "I hope you know I wish the very best for you, always."

Gideon nodded as she took her seat. Now that the time had come, he was not altogether certain how to begin. There was no use beating about the bush, he decided. Better to have out with it. "Lady Villiers and I have been discussing the girls' future."

A soft sigh escaped Marian's lips. "And what have you decided?"

"Nothing yet for certain." That was not altogether

true. He might not know precisely what he meant to do, but he knew what he would *not* do. He hoped the advice Marian offered him would give a clue to her feelings. Lady Villiers's disconcerting kiss had given him a hopeful insight. Now he needed to find further evidence to support the conclusion he yearned to believe.

"Her ladyship suggested she and I should marry so we could raise Cissy and Dolly together."

Marian showed no sign of surprise at his announcement. Her luminous brown eyes did not widen. Her dark brows did not rise. Her soft, generous lips did not fall open or tighten into a disapproving line. It was as if she had expected this all along.

Faced with her disappointing silence, Gideon was obliged to continue. "I know the girls' well-being has always been of the utmost importance to you."

"Indeed it has, Captain," she murmured.

It was a priority he had come to share, but surely there must be a limit to what they were willing to sacrifice for the children's sake.

"I would like your opinion of her ladyship's plan." As he watched her trying to decide his future, Gideon found himself picturing her glare of outrage when Dolly had barreled into him. Her uncertainty when they'd first encountered one another in the library and discovered their mutual love of books. Her sitting with him and the girls in church, head reverently bowed in prayer.

He did not want to lose her or be responsible for the girls losing her. That was why he must be quite certain of her feeling before he dared to reveal his.

Marian sat tall on her chair and squared her shoulders. Gideon could picture her as a child, gamely sticking up for her school friends. "I think it would be good for the girls to be raised by two loving parents, Captain."

Her answer took the breath out of him, like a hard blow deep in the belly. It was all he could do to keep from flinching. When he finally had command of his voice again, he ventured, "I am surprised to hear you say that. As I recall, you had grave reservations about her ladyship's suitability to bring up Cissy and Dolly."

"If you'll recall, sir, my objections were to her way of living. I believe marriage to you would have a steadying influence upon her ladyship. It would also mean the girls could stay at Knightley Park with you."

It sounded as if she'd already given the matter a great deal of thought. Had she foreseen Lady Villiers's intentions all along? Then why had she not warned him? Did she truly want to see him with another woman?

"There is only one thing I would ask of you, Captain." Marian's skittish gaze calmed and focused directly upon him, pleading for agreement.

"What is that, pray?"

"That you will not send the girls away to school." One of her hands came to rest upon the table reaching toward him. Before Gideon could take her hand, she pulled it back again. "That is what I have been trying to prevent ever since you came to Knightley Park. I swear I am not asking because I fear to lose my position."

"Of course not." Gideon wished she had permitted him to hold her hand, so he could give her fingers a reassuring squeeze. "I would never suspect it of you."

Apparently his words accomplished his aim. The tension that had gripped her features eased. "Thank you, Captain. I appreciate your faith in me. I know not all schools are as bad as the one I attended, yet I still do not believe any school would provide the girls with a better education than they can receive here at home."

She seemed ready with many more arguments. Much as he enjoyed listening to the sound of her voice, Gideon could not bear to keep her in suspense. "Let me assure you, I have no intention of sending the girls away from Knightley Park until they are ready and wish to go."

Marian let out a slow, shaky breath. "I am vastly relieved to hear it, sir. Will that be all, Captain?"

Preoccupied with his bitter disappointment that she had urged him to marry another woman, Gideon muttered, "I beg your pardon?"

"Was there anything else you wished to say to me, sir? If not, I should get back to the nursery."

Of course there was more he wanted to say to her, but did he dare? If he kept silent, they could go back to their previous arrangement, pretending to be a family. But that was no longer enough to satisfy him. Yet, if he spoke, it might frighten Marian away. He cared too much for Cissy and Dolly to want to be responsible for that.

Not trusting himself to speak, he replied with a brief nod.

Marian rose and turned to go, but at the last moment, she paused and looked back. "I wish you joy in your marriage, Captain."

Was it his imagination, or did her voice catch on the word *marriage?*

Torn by conflicting desires, Gideon raised a silent prayer. *Lord, please help me do what is right and true.*

True—what had made him add that? A verse from the Bible flitted through his mind. *"Know ye the truth and the truth shall set ye free."* He had concealed his feelings from the woman he cared for, giving himself all manner of noble excuses for his silence. But his true motive had been fear that she could not return his feelings. That fear had built a stout bastion to protect his heart. But lately it had become more like a prison.

Expecting Marian to set him free, by declaring her feelings without knowing his, was cowardly, and not at all fair to her.

By the time all that passed through his mind, she had gone through the door and was just closing it behind her.

"Wait!" Gideon forced the word out past the lump in his throat.

Marian peeped back in, her brows raised in a wordless question.

Trusting that the truth would set him free, he willed himself to continue. "There is one other thing I would like to discuss with you, if I may?"

Could he not let her get away before her composure deserted her entirely? Marian strove to stifle her impatience with Gideon. It was not fair to expect him to realize how difficult this was for her, when he had no idea how much she cared for him. Had she not just wished him joy in his marriage to another woman?

Determined not to embarrass herself with an emotional outburst, she inhaled a deep breath and headed back into the dining room. "What else did you want to talk about, sir?"

She closed the door behind her but refused to approach him any closer, for fear he might glimpse a suspicious trace of moisture in her eyes.

"To begin with, I wanted to thank you."

"For what, Captain?" For not creating any obstacles

to his marriage, perhaps, by threatening to tell Lady Villiers about the tender kiss they'd shared? Surely he could not believe her capable of such conduct?

"For helping me get to know Cissy and Dolly. They have brought joy and purpose to my life that I would never have discovered without your help. I have come to believe you may be right about God caring for me enough to give me what I truly need rather than what I thought I wanted."

A sense of bittersweet joy welled up in Marian to think she had helped Gideon find faith and love...even if it could not be with her. Her self-control was too fragile to permit her to speak. She acknowledged his thanks with a nod and a tremulous smile.

That seemed to be enough for Gideon. "There is almost nothing I would not do for the girls. But even for their sakes and in spite of your kind advice, I cannot wed a woman I do not love."

Gideon was not going to marry Lady Villiers after all? Marian clamped her lips together to contain a cheer. She was not certain how she could have watched the man she cared for wed to another woman—especially one she could not abide.

But that happy thought soon gave way to an alarming one. "But what about the girls? Lady Villiers will take them from you now! I fear she may put them in a school somewhere, then go live off their money."

Gideon took several steps toward her, then stopped abruptly a short distance away. "I was afraid of that, too, but you need not fret. I was able to persuade her ladyship to sign over guardianship of the girls to me."

Had she heard right or was this all a dream? "H-how did you manage that?"

Gideon gave a self-deprecating shrug. "It was not as difficult as you might think. I may not have a great deal of experience with women, but I have known enough grasping, unscrupulous people to recognize one. I offered Lady Villiers a very generous sum to appoint me as guardian to her nieces. We went into Newark today to have a solicitor draw up the papers."

It *was* true! From the nursery window, Marian had glimpsed them driving off toward town. She'd assumed they must be going to purchase a wedding ring.

Gideon gave a soft chuckle. "Her ladyship was all too eager to accept my money without having to endure marriage to a dry old stick like me."

"In that case, Lady Villiers is very foolish." Joy and relief loosened Marian's guard on her tongue. "No amount of money would be worth giving up the honor and pleasure of being married to such a wonderful man."

She bowed her head to avoid his gaze and clenched her lips tightly together to keep any more unwelcome revelations from slipping out. But that was rather like shutting the stable door after the horse had bolted.

Perhaps she need not worry, though. Gideon had shown himself willing to ignore worse lapses in propriety than that.

But not this time.

"Do you mean that?" he asked in an anxious tone. "Or were you only trying to spare my feelings?"

It would be prudent to seize upon the convenient excuse he'd offered her. But Marian could not bring herself to deny her feelings for him so blatantly.

"Of course I meant it," she snapped, half angry with him for making her admit it. "Now, if that is all, I will beg you excuse me."

"There is just one more thing."

What now? Marian wanted to make as dignified an exit as possible under the circumstances and try to forget her latest gaffe. She glanced up to find that Gideon had drawn closer to her. If she extended her hand, she could touch him.

"There is one point upon which I agree with her ladyship." Gideon's deep mellow voice seemed to penetrate to her heart and caress it. "I reckon it would be good for Cissy and Dolly to have two loving parents again. As excellent a governess as you have been to them, I believe you would make an even better mother."

Could Gideon possibly mean what her hopeful heart suspected? Surely not, cautious reason protested. For a penniless governess like her to secure a husband with wealth and property was like something out of a nursery tale.

She was too much accustomed to difficulties and disappointments to trust this unaccountable good fortune. "B-but you said that even for the girls' sake, you could not wed."

"I beg you quote me correctly." His strong, warm hand clasped her icy fingers. "What I said was that I could not marry a woman *I did not love.* I assure you, there will be no risk of that if you consent to be my wife."

Marian's mouth opened and closed, but she could not coax any words out. Her heart seemed to swell in her chest, so full of love and happiness that she feared it would burst. This was a blessing far beyond any she would have dared to pray for, yet here it was—hers for the taking. All her past hurts and deprivations made her treasure it that much more.

But Gideon could not tell all that was going on inside her. Instead, he saw only her hesitation to accept his proposal and perhaps the glint of a tear in her eye. "If I have mistaken your feelings and you cannot return mine, I beg you not to feel obliged to accept my proposal for the sake of the children. Whatever your answer, I would never think of parting you from them."

The look of bitter disappointment was etched so clearly upon his features that Marian could not doubt the sincerity of his offer.

When he tried to release her hand, she clung to his and refused to let go. Concern for his feelings shattered the doubts that had frozen her tongue. "Please, Gideon, you mistake me. I have no intention of refusing you. My feelings are quite the opposite of her ladyship's. I would be just as honored and happy to wed you if you had no fortune whatsoever."

"Are you quite certain?" He seemed to have as much difficulty believing her answer as she had his proposal. "I am no Galahad or Romeo."

"Perhaps not." Marian recalled the conversation they'd once had about marriage. "But in every respect, you are still the answer to *this* maiden's prayer."

Once she'd said that, what was there for him to do but kiss her?

Slowly he pulled her into his arms and bent to claim her lips. She sensed a slight hesitation in his approach, but now she knew it did not spring from reluctance or lack of feeling. Instead it mirrored her own sense of disbelief that such a deeply desired blessing had been bestowed on her. She could not quite escape the nagging fear that she did not deserve such happiness.

If that was how Gideon felt, she was determined to reassure him. Reaching up to caress his cheek, she surged onto her toes to close the last inch between her lips and his.

Her eyes closed instinctively, the better to savor the multitude of sensations and emotions this sweet intimacy provoked. The velvety warmth of Gideon's kiss told a wordless tale of slowly growing love that had put down roots deep in his heart. It whispered of steadfast devotion that would be hers for all time, asking nothing in return.

A month after his proposal, Gideon set out on horseback for the village church, where he would await the arrival of Marian and the girls. As he rode, he recalled the first time he'd accompanied them to worship. The countryside had been dull, barren and chilled by frost, not unlike his heart. Now, wherever he looked, fresh, vigorous new life was springing forth. His heart quickened in response.

A tiny voice in the back of his mind cautioned against drinking too deeply from the cup of happiness, for the dregs might be bitter indeed. Gideon dismissed such forebodings as wedding nerves, though he could not imagine why he should have those. He had no misgivings about wedding Marian…except perhaps whether he could make her happy. Even those had begun to fade during their brief engagement as he'd witnessed her transparent delight in their wedding preparations.

When he reached the church, he tethered his horse, then hurried inside where the vicar was waiting for him. Most of the guests were already assembled, and the rest soon arrived.

The bride did not keep them waiting. When the organist struck up the processional, Gideon turned to see Cissy and Dolly walking down the aisle strewing flower petals. Their radiant smiles were the crowning delight to his happiest of days. He and Marian had worried the girls might be upset by their aunt's abrupt departure. Cissy had been a little at first, but when she and Dolly learned that Gideon intended to marry their beloved governess and become their guardian, the girls could scarcely contain their elation. Dolly wore a purple dress with a bright yellow sash, while her sister wore a yellow dress with a purple sash. He wondered at the unusual choice of colors until he looked past the girls to catch his first glimpse of Marian carrying a nosegay of purple and yellow crocuses, those bright, hardy little heralds of springtime.

For her wedding march, she clung to the arm of Mr. Culpepper. The butler beamed with pride over being chosen for this honor.

Gideon could scarcely take his eyes off his lovely bride. Having only seen her wearing dark colors, he marveled at how well she looked in her creamy white wedding dress. It brightened her complexion and brought out the gold and copper highlights in her dark brown hair. But no dress could account for the luminous glow in her dark eyes or the sweet radiance of her wide smile. Those could only come from a source of joy within her heart. That sweet certainty banished Gideon's last lurking shadows of doubt. He savored the realization that their union brought her as much happiness as it brought him.

When Marian reached his side, he returned her loving gaze and lavished her with a doting smile.

"Dearly beloved…" The opening words of the marriage ceremony drew their attention to the vicar. "We are gathered together here in the sight of God and in the face of his congregation to join together this man and this woman in holy matrimony."

An instant of breathless tension gripped Gideon when the vicar asked if there were objections to the marriage. Some tiny part of him still feared Marian might change her mind at the last moment. But she responded to the vicar's charge with serene silence, and the service moved on.

So intense was Gideon's relief that he was only vaguely aware of the vicar addressing him. Then came a moment of expectant silence in which he realized he was supposed to reply.

Fortunately, Dolly came to his rescue. In a loud whisper she prompted him, "You're supposed to say, *'I will.'*"

Gideon's response was nearly drowned out by a soft ripple of laughter that ran through the congregation.

Fortunately, Marian did not seem to take his hesitation amiss. After the vicar asked her the same question about loving, honoring and keeping Gideon, she needed no help from the girls to reply with fond resolve, "I will."

Determined to make up for his earlier lapse, Gideon concentrated very hard on repeating his vows to Marian clearly and sincerely. "I, Gideon, take thee, Marian, to be my wedded wife, to have and to hold from this day forward, for better, for worse, for richer, for poorer, in sickness and in health, to love and to cherish, till death us do part."

Soon it was time to slip the gold ring onto his bride's finger and pledge himself and all he owned to her.

As the vicar prayed for God's blessing upon their marriage, and late winter sunshine filtered into the sanctuary, Gideon could feel the divine presence surrounding them and stirring within them. Deep in his heart there pulsed a prayer of thanksgiving for two of the most precious blessings in all of creation—family and love.

Epilogue

Nottinghamshire, England
1815

Would Gideon ever come home? That question ran through Marian's thoughts as she sat in the nursery reading a story to Cissy and Dolly.

The blissful happiness of her wedding day had quietly shattered a fortnight later when Gideon received word from the Admiralty that he had been absolved of any wrongdoing and was being returned to the command of HMS *Integrity*.

"I don't understand," she recalled him saying as he stared at the letter in bewilderment. "I was certain the board meant to make me their scapegoat."

"Do you suppose they changed their minds after Napoleon returned to power?" Marian suggested. "In time of war the Admiralty must know they need strong leadership, not men who are only concerned with advancing their careers."

Though her heart quailed at the thought of Gideon returning to sea, she could not be sorry he had gotten the justice he deserved at last. Besides the possible explanation she'd offered for his acquittal, Marian wondered if perhaps her friend Rebecca had persuaded Lord Benedict to look into the matter.

"You do realize what this means?" he asked, clearly torn between devotion to his family and duty to his crew and country.

"Of course." Much as she hated to see him go, Marian could not bear to add to his conflict. "You'll be able to return to your ship and protect your crew from those horrible bullies."

Though he hadn't spoken of it since the night he'd returned from London, Marian could tell that concern for his crew had weighed upon him.

Gideon gave a grim nod. "So I shall. But once this war is over, I intend to retire from the Royal Navy and return home to Knightley Park to stay."

Marian pretended to believe it would happen, though a streak of fatalism in her character insisted that any happiness she found in life would always be snatched away.

"This is something I must do," he murmured as he held her close and stroked her hair. "For my men and for my country. Before I returned to Knightley Park last autumn, my country was only a vague abstraction. Now it means so much more. It is you and the girls, our household, all the people of the parish, those school friends of yours whom I hope to meet someday. Everything I do as captain of the *Integrity* will be in your service."

The girls had reacted to his going in the way Marian expected. Dolly wanted desperately to go along and share his adventures at sea while Cissy seemed to feel abandoned by yet another parental figure. Gideon assured the girls he would write to them as often as possible and begged them to write him about all their doings. He promised when the fighting was over and he returned to Knightley Park to stay, he would bring them presents from London.

On the night before his departure, after tucking the girls in with a kiss, he confided in Marian. "Thank heaven we were able to secure guardianship of the children. If any harm should befall me, I shall have the comfort of knowing you will love and care for them always."

"Please do not speak of harm coming to you, my love." She clasped his arm tighter, wishing she never had to let go. "I cannot bear to think of that."

But it was not her only worry. She also feared what might happen when he was reunited with his first and greatest love—the sea. Could he give up a life of adventure and gallant service for the quiet existence of a country squire?

The morning he left for London, she sensed their parting was as difficult for Gideon as for her and the girls. For all their sakes, Marian strove to appear cheerfully resigned, pretending to believe her husband would soon return. It was only after his carriage disappeared from view down the elm-lined lane and the girls had gone to play in the garden that she indulged in a few tears.

As the days turned to weeks and weeks to months, life at Knightley Park returned to its old familiar rhythm, with a few important differences. Marian was now the lady of the house, a role in which she was not altogether comfortable. But, for the sake of Gideon, the girls and the tenants, she gradually rose to the challenge. Whenever she was inclined to feel sorry for herself, she tried to remember that she now had everything for which she'd once prayed…and so much more. With that thought in mind, she concentrated on treasuring her blessings rather than yearning for the one thing she no longer had.

Whenever the longing for Gideon overwhelmed her, she wrote him another letter or prayed for his safety and happiness. Somehow, that helped her feel close to him again.

Now, several weeks after Napoleon's defeat at Waterloo, Marian rejoiced that the war was over, but grieved that she had not received a letter from her husband in some time. Clearly, his other life had reclaimed him. Perhaps this was his way of indicating he would rather she did not pester him with mail.

Her voice caught on the words she was reading. She could not make out the next passage through the haze of tears that rose in her eyes.

"Is something the matter?" Cissy leaned closer to Marian and ran a hand down her arm in a comforting caress.

When Marian could not master her emotions to reply, Dolly heaved a great sigh. "You miss him, too, don't you?"

Swallowing her tears, Marian gave a shaky smile and nodded.

"Don't fret," advised Dolly as if their roles were suddenly reversed and she was now the adult. "He'll be home soon, you'll see, and he'll bring us presents from London."

The sound of rushing footsteps made all three of them look up as Martha burst in. "It's him, ma'am— Captain Radcliffe, driving up the lane!"

The book Marian had been reading to the girls slid from her fingers to land on the carpet with a soft thud. The moment she'd hoped for all these weeks had arrived at last…in answer to her fervent prayers.

"Are you certain it's him?" demanded Cissy, clearly reluctant to get her hopes up.

"Of course it's him." Dolly seized her sister by the hand and pulled her toward the door. "Didn't I tell you he'd be coming home soon?"

In a daze of happiness, Marian rose and followed the children. The tears of longing she'd suppressed welled up again from a deep spring of joy.

No long line of servants waited under the portico to greet the captain this time, only his family.

When the carriage came to a halt, he did not wait for the footman, but thrust the door open himself and sprang out.

Dolly and Cissy ran toward him, crying, "Welcome home!"

His face alight with happiness, Gideon caught the girls each in one arm and pulled them into a warm embrace.

He looked rather gaunt and weary, but Marian relished the opportunity to fuss over him, making sure he got plenty of food and rest.

Gideon pressed a kiss on each of the girls' foreheads. "That is the finest welcome I've ever received. But there is one other lady I have been longing to see."

When he looked up at Marian, his smile froze and his eyes widened. Striding toward his wife, he took her in his arms with restrained eagerness and kissed her tenderly.

"Why did you not tell me?" he whispered, lowering one hand to caress her swelling belly.

"I didn't want you coming back only for the sake of the child. I was afraid that once you returned to your ship, you would want to stay at sea."

"Never." Gideon shook his head vehemently. "In fact, there were times I got so homesick for you and the girls that I wanted to desert. Every evening in my cabin I read your letters and imagined myself back in the library at Knightley Park. Now that the war is over for good, and I have settled matters aboard the *Integrity,* I consider myself blessed to have such a fine family to come home to."

Feeling a familiar tug on his coat, which he had missed so keenly, Gideon glanced down at his darling Dolly.

"Did you bring us presents?" she demanded. "You promised you would when you went away, remember?"

"He came back." Sweet Cissy looked up at him with such love and faith that it made his throat tighten. "That's better than any present."

Gideon glanced at his beloved wife, whose eyes were shining with unshed tears of joy.

"It certainly is the best possible gift for me." He reached for Cissy's hand and gave it a warm squeeze. "But Dolly is right. A promise is a promise. I had great fun scouring the shops of London for things you might enjoy.

"Frederick," he called out to one of the footmen unloading his baggage. "Bring that small trunk into the Chinese drawing room."

A short while later, the whole family crowded together on the window seat as Gideon prepared to dispense the gifts he had bought. He could hardly wait to see Marian's face when he presented her with a gold locket in which he planned to put miniature portraits of the girls. Soon he would need to get her another one to hold the likeness of the child she was carrying.

"So tell me," he asked her as the girls opened the first of their presents, "when can we expect the newest member of our family to make an appearance?"

His question brought a gentle, brooding smile to her lips that made him catch his breath. "The midwife says the baby will likely arrive by mid-December."

As he recalled the Christmas that had made them a family and looked forward to many equally joyous in the years ahead, Gideon heaved a sigh of blessed happiness. "What better Christmas gift could we ask for?"

* * * * *

Dear Reader,

This story holds a special place in my heart. It came to me at a time when I was under contract to write another series. To keep the characters from taking too much of my attention away from those books, I wrote down a loose outline and bits of scenes, then stuck them away in a file.

By the time I was free to work on the story again, Love Inspired Books had launched its Historical line which I read and loved. I wondered if my governess story might be a good fit for the line. Taking out the old file, I began writing Gideon and Marian's story as an inspirational and found it worked so much better.

I had originally imagined the story taking place in the English countryside during the summer months, but when I checked the time frame of Napoleon's return to power after Elba, I realized that wouldn't work. Instead, the story would have to take place over the autumn and winter. Writing it as a Christmas story made all the pieces fall into place.

I hope you will enjoy this story of two lonely people, a pair of orphaned children and the Christmas that made them a family!

Wishing you the joy and peace of Christmas,
Deborah Hale

WE HOPE YOU ENJOYED THIS

LOVE INSPIRED®

BOOK.

If you were **inspired** by this

uplifting, **heartwarming** romance,

be sure to look for all six Love

Inspired® books every month.

www.LoveInspired.com

SPECIAL EXCERPT FROM

When a young Amish woman has amnesia during the holidays, will a handsome Amish farmer help her regain her memories?

Read on for a sneak preview of
Amish Christmas Memories *by Vannetta Chapman, available December 2018 from Love Inspired.*

"What's your name?"

The woman's eyes widened and her hand shook so that she could barely hold the mug of tea without spilling it. She set it carefully on the coffee table. "I don't—I don't know my name."

"How can you not know your own name?" Caleb asked. "Do you know where you live?"

"Nein."

"What were you doing out there?"

"Out where?"

"Where was your coat and your *kapp*?"

"Caleb, now's not the time to interrogate the poor girl." His *mamm* stood and moved beside her on the couch. She picked up the small book of poetry. "You were carrying this, when Caleb found you. Do you remember it?"

"I don't. This was mine?"

"Found it in the snow," Caleb said. "Right beside where you collapsed."

"So it must be mine."

Caleb noticed that the woman's hands trembled as she opened the cover and stared down at the first page. With one finger, she traced the handwriting there.

LIEXP1118

"Rachel. I think my name is Rachel."

Rachel let her fingers brush over the word again and again. Rachel. Yes, that was her name. She was sure of it. She remembered writing it in the front of the book—she'd used a pen that her *mamm* had given her. She could almost picture herself, somewhere else. She could almost see her mother.

"My *mamm* gave me the pen and the book…for my birthday, I think. I wrote my name—wrote it right here."

"Your *mamm*. So you remember her?"

"Praise be to *Gotte*," Caleb's *dat* said, a smile spreading across his face.

"Is there someone we can call? If you remember the name of your bishop…" Caleb had sat down in the rocker his mother had vacated and was staring at her intensely.

They all were.

She closed her eyes, hoping to feel the memory again. She tried to see the room or the house or the people, but the memory had receded as quickly as it had come, leaving her with a pulsing headache.

She struggled to keep the feelings of panic at bay. Her heart was hammering, and her hands were shaking, and she could barely make sense of the questions they were pelting at her.

Who were these people?

Where was she?

Who was she?

She needed to remember what had happened.

She needed to go home.

Don't miss
Amish Christmas Memories *by Vannetta Chapman,*
available December 2018 wherever
Love Inspired® books and ebooks are sold.

www.LoveInspired.com